THE IN-BETWEEN SERIES

THE RING

SAGAR CONSTANTIN

Copyright © Sagar Constantin 2021
Published by BUOY MEDIA LLC

All rights reserved.

No part of this book may be reproduced, scanned, or distributed in any printed or electronic form without permission from the author.

This is a work of fiction. Names, characters, places, and incidents are either products of the author's imagination or are used fictitiously. Any resemblance to actual events, locales, or persons, living or dead, is entirely coincidental. The content of this book is for entertainment purposes only and is not intended to diagnose, treat, cure, or prevent any condition or disease. You understand that this book is not intended as a substitute for consultation with a psychologist. Please consult with your own physician if you need help. The read of this book implies your acceptance of this disclaimer. The Author holds exclusive rights to this work. Unauthorized duplication is prohibited.

Cover design by Juan Villar Padron,
https://www.juanjpadron.com

Special thanks to my editor Janell Parque
http://janellparque.blogspot.com/

- facebook.com/SagarConstantinAuthor
- amazon.com/Sagar-Constantin/e/B093NXD4C2
- twitter.com/ConstantinSagar
- linkedin.com/in/sagarconstantin
- instagram.com/sagar.constantin.author
- bookbub.com/authors/sagar-constantin

1
BORN AGAIN

The skin on my cheek prickles slightly, and the pungent odor of onion makes my nose tingle. I lift my hand and run it carefully over the tips of the countless blades of grass that bend slightly at my touch.

All at once, the sky opens, a flash of light comes toward me, and it feels as if I am being lifted at breakneck speed. I can't feel my body. The grass disappears, and the sharp onion odor slips away. Just ahead, I can see a skinny woman running toward me. It is dark, and the street she is running on is narrow. The streetlight is poor and casts vague shadows on the ground. Her eyes are dilated, and she gasps for breath as she turns around in fits and starts. Behind her, I can make out a group of young men shouting and trying to catch up with her. She stops right in front of me and glances from side to side. Then, she turns left into an alleyway where the light is dimly reflected on the wet asphalt. She doesn't see me, but I feel her frenzied breath as clear as if she stood right next to me. The men charge toward me; they all wear light blue uniforms with red belts at their waists. She is running as fast as she can with her worn-out shoes and ragged clothes that stick to her body. When she reaches the end of the street, she stops, spins around so that her arms rise from her body and looks frantically around the alley. The walls of the buildings tower above her and disappear into the dark sky. She is trapped. Without hesitating, she rushes over to an old wooden door, where a weak light filters out from the gaps between the boards. With a clenched fist, she begins to pound urgently.

The door creaks when a short, older woman with slanted eyes opens it a crack. Holding a candle in her hand, she steps aside and lets the young woman past. The room is shadowy; only the candle in the older woman's hand and a candle on a table that is nearly burnt out interrupt the darkness. I want to step back, but my body doesn't react. Instead, I can see inside the house where the two women are standing silent opposite each other. A stale odor is prevalent. The older woman has a scar under her eye that looks like a permanent tear track. She looks at the younger woman and whispers, "Sit down," and pulls out a stool from under the old wooden table that looks like it has been sitting there for hundreds of years, keeping tales from an ancient time. "I don't know who you are, but I know that you need help. One can never know what a stranger brings." The older woman smiles, revealing the two teeth she has left in her mouth. Her voice is hoarse.

The image fades away, and the light disappears. It is as if I am falling through nothingness. Gradually, I can feel the wind clinging around my face again. A delicate tickle on my chin makes me open my eyes. I look straight up where the sun is suspended in the sky, insistent on being the center of heaven. The dampness from the cold earth slithers inside my clothes, and I move slightly. Slowly, I can begin to feel the pricking blades of grass and smell the sharp scent of onion. My legs start by themselves, and I have no say.

I don't understand it. What is happening to me?

There are no clouds in the sky, only the sun and the immense, icy shade of blue. No In-Between. I blink slowly and take a deep breath. My heart is pounding. It feels like I'm waking from a dream —one of those dreams where you are not sure if it was real or not and can still feel the intensity. The warmth from the sun awakens me within, and a sense of joy spreads throughout my body. But I am still unsure whether I understand the gravity of my mission or the fact that I am here. Right now, only Thomas, Gabriel, Shiva, and Yoge know about my journey, as well as the Master, of course. It has to stay that way; I have promised. I run my hands back and forth over my face. They are cold and a little rough. It doesn't matter; it only helps me to galvanize the gravity of my stay.

I have returned to the land of the living on a forty-two-day round-trip ticket to find the two missing persons who can complete the Ring. I pull my legs up under me, and a handful of butterflies are set free in my stomach at the thought of the insight that will be revealed, when, or rather, if I find the two missing ones.

A fresh, slightly tart scent from the grass cuts through my nose, making it itch. The wind blends the scent with the fragrance of wildflowers, and I inhale deeply, expanding my lungs. With a swift move, I manage to shake off the tingling sensation. Everything is so fresh, so new. It feels like forever since I have smelled nature at close quarters, but I remember it as if it were yesterday. I turn my wrist slightly and glance at my watch with its white crystal ring. The big hand moves a notch and is now pointing straight to the right, and the little hand has just moved past twelve.

I press my elbow into the earth and push myself up from the ground. A large meadow of wild grass comes into view. It continues as far as I can see, yellow and brown nuances meandering and disappearing into the horizon.

With a quick movement, I rise into a squat. The move makes me slightly dizzy, and I rest my hands on the earth, feeling like a teenager with growing pains shooting throughout my body.

Across from the meadow is a gravel road lined with many tall trees with showy tops. The road is filled with holes and untended on the edges. *I have landed in the middle of nowhere*, I mumble to myself. My heart is beating quickly, and I hold my breath. It feels like my perspective is drawn back, and I observe the world from a safe place inside, behind my facade. I can smell the fresh air and see nature, but it still doesn't seem like I am truly here.

I look at my feet. The black boots are needle-sharp at the toe. I move my toes a bit and notice that my legs are long, my waist thin, and my weight is probably just below average. My hand glides over my abdomen and continues over my breasts. They are firm. I let my hands continue up my neck, chin, and face, just to find that my nose is smaller than before. I let my arms down and sigh softly.

My right foot is about to take the first step carefully through the grass toward the gravel road. Though I have walked through grass many times before, my stomach is tingling with excitement. Colors and details are sharper than I have ever experienced them. There is more contrast, more green and yellow, and I am bathed with the life-giving energy of the sun. I rub my hands over my face. *How could I ever take that for granted?*

It's crunching under my feet as I begin walking on the gravel road. The small pebbles burrow into the thin soles of my boots, and the wind permeates my light blue, loose-knit shirt.

When I was alive as Eva, I sometimes dreamt of having a new identity, so I could disappear if it all got too much—like a secret agent with several passports and identities. This is probably the closest I will come to realizing it. Interesting that what I wished for has become my reality, just not how I had imagined.

My hand digs down inside my pants pocket, which doesn't seem to have been designed for that purpose. The Skycon is firmly nestled, and I take hold of it with my fingertips and ease it out. Slowly, in awe, I turn the slim black device between my fingers. There is a small square display and several small buttons on the side. I turn it on with an easy touch.

The Skycon is the only way to keep in contact with In-Between during the next forty-two days.

The thought sends an army of small rushes through my body. The little button on the side has a blinking red light that indicates it is searching, but there is no signal, and the screen is blank. A jolt runs through my body.

It must work.

"Enter code" starts to flash on the small display. I have plenty of time, and Thomas also said that the code should be entered precisely at one o'clock to work. I let the Skycon slide back into my pocket.

High above flies an eagle. It keeps circling continuously over my head. It lets out a scream that cuts through the air, sending a shiver down my back. It glides slowly above me without releasing me from its sight. I raise my hand to shield my eyes from the sunlight so I can see it better and take one step back. From here, its wingspan looks at least two meters wide.

"What do you want from me?" The words trip over my lips, and I clear my throat. My voice is a little thinner and not as firm as before. Thomas once told me that it is possible to communicate with animals. Not that I believed him at the time, and I don't now either, but there is no harm in trying. There is something about the way the eagle is circling above me that seems somehow familiar. The wind catches hold of a pile of leaves on the road and whirls them into the air. I hold out my other hand so that I don't get any in my face.

The eagle descends a couple of meters toward me. Its screech cuts into my skin, and I bite my lower lip. It is dark brown and on its tail is a triangle of white feathers that become brown again on the tips. Two white smudges break the golden-brown color on the wings. The feathers on the edge of the wings are long and thin, outlining an elegant fan. I stand still and direct my gaze toward it, and it regards me as it hovers above me. We observe each other watchfully.

All at once, it dives down and lands on the road about twenty meters in front of me. Quickly, I take several steps back. My heel is caught in one of the many holes in the road, and I twist my ankle. I fall to one side but manage to extend my arms and keep my balance while still gazing at the eagle. It spreads its wings out sideways and cocks its narrow head with the hooked beak. I say nothing, just stand completely still with my arms stretched out to keep my balance, staring at it.

In the distance is the sound of a car motor. I want to turn around, but I keep my gaze fixed on the eagle. "Is there something you want to tell me?" My voice is somewhat hesitant but a bit firmer this time. I cross my arms and squeeze my shirt.

Now, I know.

There was an eagle on my chair in the octagonal room where the Ring met in In-Between. That was where I first heard about the work of the Ring and the two missing members. I shut my eyes briefly and visualize the room. The suspended white walls, the ceiling formed like the top of a pyramid, and the empty chairs were placed in a circle. I can picture the eagle carved into the back of my chair. Its wings were very sharply incised with fine small curves underneath and the long narrow feathers at the tips of the wings. All members of the Ring had different animals engraved on the backs of the chairs. I never paid attention to those of the others and cannot envision them now. The room is empty, but the atmosphere is warm. I can't feel my body, only the heat from the room. The image shifts and is replaced by a picture of Luke running and laughing in a big field. My body contracts and my eyes snap open. I try to breathe calmly, but it is almost impossible. All I get are small gasps of air that only just reach into my lungs.

The sound of the approaching car is getting closer. It is coming from behind me, but I don't turn around. The eagle treads a couple of steps toward me with an elegant lightness. I do not stir. The motor's sound becomes more intense, and I am standing in the middle of the road with my gaze fixed on the eagle. We look at each other like two duelists. I sink before spinning on my heels in the direction of the motor noise. A cloud of dust is rushing toward me. The sound of tires crunching the small pebbles grows louder. I stand immobile on the road.

If only I knew what the eagle wants from me.

I turn my gaze back to the eagle. It is standing with its head tilted in a stately manner as if it owned the gravel road we are standing on. At once, the eagle pushes off and takes off right above my head. I duck to avoid being hit. It continues over the dust cloud, where a small blue car with round curves and a broken headlight comes into view. It is driving fast and heading straight for me. I stand completely still. The eagle is gone. I drop back my head to see if it is somewhere above me, but it is nowhere to be seen.

My hand squeezes into my pocket and grips the Skycon tightly. It is my lifeline right now. I can just make out a dark-haired woman talking on the phone behind the wheel. When she is almost in front of me, she snaps her phone shut and puts on the brakes. The dust cloud drifts past the car and disintegrates. In a quick movement, she rolls down the window.

"Hello there." Her eyes are hidden behind a pair of huge sunglasses with completely dark glass and white steel, making her skin look even darker, and her long, coal-black hair curls in all directions.

"Hi…" my voice is hesitant, and I clear my throat.

"You must have gone astray. What are you doing here?" She leans out the window, and the wind plays with the tiniest curls.

I keep a straight face and just look at her.

She smiles, pushes the sunglasses up on her forehead, and leans her face slightly so that the edge of the car roof shades her from the sunlight. "Are you all right or what?" Her deep brown eyes are almost black, and her eyebrows form a straight, sharp line. She shuts off the motor. I want to take a step back, but I am already on the edge of the road.

"No, I mean, yes. Nothing's wrong. Not at all." I struggle not to show any emotions. My face feels stiff.

"Well. If you don't want to walk any further, then I can drive you to town. It's about twenty-five kilometers from here. But you're welcome to stay here. Just don't expect that anyone else will pass by today." She drums on the outside of the car door.

I turn my head away from the car. I squeeze the Skycon tightly and clench my jaws. The road looks like it disappears into nowhere. I have no idea where I've been dumped, but at least we speak the same language I did the last time I was here. There's no water around and nothing to eat, so right now, it seems that the only sensible option is to go with her. I turn back and nod almost mechanically. "When can we get there? I have an appointment...."

She scratches the back of her neck and releases a hearty laugh. "You have an appointment. Were you counting on me to come by and pick you up? Do you think I'm an Uber looking for work?" She places her hands on the steering wheel and straightens up in the seat.

I stretch my arm and glance discreetly down at my watch. Thirty-five minutes until I should make contact with Thomas.

"It takes about forty minutes to drive to the city on a good day." She nods, indicating that I can get in. "If you want to come with, the time is now."

2
THE CONNECTION

"Eva! Angela!" Thomas is standing right next to the screen. His body is tense, and his hands are clasped. He is struggling not to let his uncertainty take over and looks down at the floor.

"She isn't connected yet." Yoge is standing right behind Thomas and speaks with a firm voice where you can sense no emotions. Thomas looks up, and Yoge steps closer. His square-shaped head is just as tense as his movement. Mechanically, he rocks his head from side to side. He is facing his most demanding assignment to date, establishing the new control room for the Ring. He must see that all technical aspects are functioning to make contact with Eva—something that has never before been attempted.

Thomas looks him in the eyes. Yoge blinks frenziedly, steps into the middle of the room, and begins to walk back and forth with his hands folded behind his back. A warm sensation settles softly on Thomas's back, and he turns around. Shiva pulls back her hand and gently pushes a chair toward him. The lines in her face are relaxed, and her dark eyes seem to have infinite depth. He can almost touch the calmness that surrounds her. As he takes a deep breath, he feels a sense of peace embrace him.

"There are three minutes left." The warm rusty, subdued voice belongs to Gabriel, who is standing on the other side of Shiva. His bald head is shining in the light from the large overhead windows. He is holding a round silver watch in his hand, with numbers that count both up and down. His body is bent over, and he rests on one leg. His gaze is concentrated. Deep wrinkles cut across his forehead, witnessing the severity of the task.

Thomas lets his fingers glide gently over the long narrow table with a dark red glow and fine grains that run from wall to wall lengthwise in front of the screens that hover slightly from the wall above. The surface is almost as soft as fabric. He looks at the screens that fill the entire end wall. They fill his entire field of vision.

"How can we know whether Angela has arrived safely?" There is no specific receiver to Thomas's question.

A furious clicking from a keyboard replaces his words, and he looks over at David, Yoge's right hand, who is the person who knows most about the technology at In-Between. He is sitting next to Gabriel and typing at top speed. His thin body nearly disappears in the chair, which is a simple semi-circle shape hanging above the floor.

"What's happening?" Thomas grabs the chair next to David. "Why isn't there a picture of Angela on the screen?" He can hear his voice tighten and tries to take a deep breath. Something pricks his chest lightly. He looks down at the small silver bear that hangs on the chain around his neck and rises and falls in time with his breath. He grabs hold of it and squeezes it tightly.

David's thin hair is wet through with sweat that runs down his temples. He dries his forehead with his hand and looks at Thomas with a despairing expression. "It could be that she hasn't entered the code yet...." He turns the chair from side to side while his fingers dance over the keyboard at high speed without missing a single keystroke.

"If anyone here knows the system, it's you." Thomas places a hand on David's arm.

"But if she doesn't enter the code at one o'clock on the dot, then…." David raises an eyebrow and looks back at the screen.

"Right now, we are attempting something that has never been tried before." Yoge comes to a halt in the middle of the floor and raises his voice. "Keep trying. Angela knows that it is crucial that she enters the code right on time." First, he looks over at David, who nods without looking at him, and then on to Thomas. Then he continues. "The frequency couplings that this mission requires are extremely complicated and…." His narrow face contracts into a severe expression.

"Do you doubt that it can be done?" Thomas rises and releases David's arm. He looks straight into Yoge's eyes. Yoge remains expressionless and does not speak. Then, he turns and continues to pace back and forth across the floor. He speaks speedily, and his words have a mechanical clang. "There is always a margin of error, and we cannot be certain that the force of the frequency that we placed in Eva's Skycon is adequate." He walks over to two egg-shaped, mint-green chairs that are placed across from the sofa. A bouquet of pink lilies and a red candle are on a table next to them. The furniture is situated opposite the wall of screens. "We have set the frequency so that it isn't possible for people on Earth to intercept it, but it is strong enough for us to pick it up." He bends forward, resting his hands on the back of a chair. "When I was on Earth last time, I was responsible for some of the most epoch-making mathematical calculations of the time. The problem now is that there are no limits as to what is possible. Our lack of talent only limits us." He falls silent and tightens his grip on the chair until his knuckles turn white. "It's all numbers," he says in a low voice and runs a hand over the back of the chair.

Thomas looks over at Shiva. She does not seem to allow herself to be affected by the conversation. With a slow, almost floating step, she walks over to Yoge and places a hand on his back. His shoulders sink, and then he straightens up and smiles at her. She has a very fine, almost transparent light around her. Her long black hair hangs loose and seems to pull back the lines of her face.

"Two minutes to one." Gabriel looks from the clock to the screens. They are still black. Only a blinking point of light indicates that they are turned on. A muscle next to his eye twitches. He falls silent.

Thomas looks from Gabriel to Yoge and Shiva. The atmosphere could be cut with a knife. The diffuse walls ensure that the sound does not have any reverberation. When light falls on them, they are almost luminous. Only the wall behind the screens is lit with a dark red color in glaring contrast to the black, paper-thin screens that are almost level with the wall like a painting.

Yoge begins to pace restlessly. His narrow black pants and snug shirt with a high collar make him look even slimmer. He runs his hands through his short, fine hair with wisps on both sides.

"There must be something we can do." Thomas's voice sounds firmer. He tries to clear his throat, but instead, his body gets tenser. "Shiva, I know that you have found your inner silence and prefer to let your energy speak for itself." He looks into Shiva's warm brown eyes. "But can you sense anything that you feel might enlighten us?"

She shuts her eyes and stands completely still with her hands resting on her chest. Then she opens her eyes again and looks at Thomas from a place with enormous depth. "I got a glimpse of a dark young woman with big, frizzy hair. She is carrying a great deal of fear from a previous life. It seems like she is trying to escape it by making herself tough." Shiva breathes slowly. "As I experience it, the woman is longing to understand more about life, but she doesn't dare to take in the knowledge. She does everything in her power to run away from her longing." Shiva's gaze drops. "I'm afraid that I cannot make sense of it right now."

Thomas places his arm around Shiva and stands composed. In the arm that embraces Shiva, he feels a calm trembling that circulates throughout his body. Remaining silent, he raises his eyes toward the skylight in the ceiling where a cloud glides in front of the sun, taking the light with it. The walls lose their shine, and the light from the lamps built into the walls increases automatically.

"One minute until the connection is shut off." Gabriel looks at the clock that counts down rhythmically, as it was set to do.

Yoge continues with brisk footsteps across the floor and sits next to David, who moves aside and raises his elbows sideways to mark his personal space.

"Is it possible for us to find her by using her ID number?" Yoge asks.

David shakes his head without looking at him. His fingers are still pounding on the keyboard, and his thin brown hair is stuck firmly to his head. He sips the high-frequency drink that is right by his side and stretches his face into an exaggerated grimace. "She doesn't have an authorized ID number yet. I've set one up for her, but it can't be activated until we make contact." He speaks quickly and drops the ending of his words. "So, until we make contact, we won't know what she looks like now or where in the world she has landed." He fidgets in the chair. Sweat drops onto the keyboard, and he wipes it away with the sleeve of his blue sweatshirt.

"Thirty seconds." Gabriel steps forward with his right leg, limping slightly. Thomas looks at him. Never before has he seen Gabriel so quiet and focused. They make eye contact.

Thomas stands perfectly still. He lets his lips slip apart and stammers a low, "But." He maintains eye contact with Gabriel.

"I know that we have never sent anyone back before once they have chosen to remain here." Thomas pauses, looks at Shiva, and breathes in her love. "But we must know where she is and what she looks like."

Gabriel breathes slowly, so his chest sinks a little every time he breathes out. "Unfortunately, not. That would make everything much easier, but it is simply not feasible." His calm tone leaves no room for doubt.

"But everything is possible here." Thomas struggles not to raise his voice, although he seeks a truth he has started to doubt.

Yoge gets up and looks at Thomas. "We had to manifest a new body for her. All the calculations show is a body that will last for forty-two days." He holds eye contact without blinking. "I wish that we had had more time. No one has ever left here with the knowledge that we exist, and that in itself is highly risky."

"Fifteen seconds." Gabriel lifts the clock a little so that the numbers are more distinct.

"David, is it in any way possible to extend the opening? If we don't make contact, Eva will be isolated from us." Thomas turns toward the screens where the white point is blinking unremittingly. He sits down again and moves right next to David, who draws in his elbows closer to his body. David shakes his head.

"Just connecting with an individual on Earth is insane."

"Come on, Eva, I mean Angela." Thomas looks earnestly at the little dot on the screen.

"Ten seconds." Gabriel's voice is washed out.

Thomas stares at the screen so intently that his eyes begin to sting. The speakers are humming with an insignificant, low whizzing sound. No one says anything. Everyone is watching the point of light that interrupts the black screen at regular intervals. Thomas notices someone stepping up behind him; it is Yoge who has stepped next to Shiva's side. His face is racked with doubt, and he is biting his teeth together so hard that it shows on his cheeks.

"Five, four, three…."

"Come on!" Thomas puts his hands on his chest and feels his heart pounding hard.

David squeezes his eyes together and taps frantically on the table with all ten fingers.

"Two, one…" Gabriel's lips tighten, and the words can hardly come out.

No one says anything, and no one moves. Only raindrops falling on the skylight interrupt the silence. Everyone's eyes are fixed on the black screen.

The point of light stops blinking.

3
POWERLESSNESS

The clock inside the car says seven minutes to one. There is plenty of time. The seconds tick steadily. Self-satisfied, I lean back in the seat that enfolds my back. The little blue car rumbles along quickly, and there is a bump before we finally start driving on the paved road.

"If you drop me off there, that would be great." I point at the sign that indicates a rest area further down the road. Jane nods and pulls over to the side. The car rattles when she reduces the speed and sounds like the engine has been kept alive a little too long.

There is a steep slope that descends from the road down to a little lake. The slope is covered with withered, yellowish grass.

Jane looks at me. "What are you doing out here, and why do you want to be dropped off at a rest area? Are you a criminal?"

I slide a little closer to the cold door and force out some dry laughter. *How can I find the right expression when I just want to appear innocent?* I raise my eyebrows and widen my eyes a little.

"A criminal? No, far from it."

"What then? You're acting really strange. Excuse me for being blunt." Her voice is sharp. She moves her foot over the brake and starts to signal as she pulls into the rest area. The sound of the blinking light ticks loudly and irregularly.

The rest area is empty except for two enormous trash cans strangled with fast food containers and cans. Just past them is a table that is bolted to the asphalt with a bench on each side. And further beyond is the steep slope, the lake, and a couple of big old trees with large serrated reddish-yellow leaves that provide shade. I can't see anything beyond that.

It's no use trying to explain what I'm doing here. That would just make it worse. Under no circumstances am I to reveal In-Between. I sit completely still as the thoughts sweep through my head.

"It's really very nice of you to give me a ride." I look down and put my hand on the door handle.

The car stops, and the motor sighs when she turns the key.

Jane grabs her purse from the back seat and rummages through it without looking at me. "Do you have any money, or…?" Her dark fizzy hair is gathered in a knot at the back of her neck, and a strand has torn loose. She must be in her late forties, but it is hard to determine. She could also be younger and have just driven herself too hard.

I look stiffly through the windshield, holding onto the Skycon in my pocket. According to the clock inside the car, I have four minutes to get away and make contact with Thomas.

"No, but I'll get by." I open the car door a bit, and it gives. "Thanks for the ride. That was very nice of you." We make eye contact for a split second, and then I turn away again.

"Well, not that it is any of my business, but honestly, what are you thinking? There isn't a soul out here."

Even though I have my back to Jane, I can feel her eyes looking at me insistently.

I pull my hand from my pocket and push the door, and I place one foot on the asphalt before turning back toward Jane. Her hands are resting gently on the steering wheel, and her head is tilted slightly. The sun is trying hard to get through the car's dirty windows, where many insects have lost their lives on the windshield.

"Here, take this." Jane pokes inside her little red purse with black racing stripes on the side and hands me a business card. "And this too." She takes a crumpled bill from the ashtray. I reach out my hand, and she places both things in it. My heart warms. *To think that she would help me for no reason, without getting answers to any of her questions.*

"Thank you. I have to go now." I look up and squeeze my lips together.

"Take care of yourself and call me if you need help." Jane places a hand on my shoulder and pats it a few times.

I nod guardedly and get out of the car. It can't be more than a couple of minutes at the most before I have to enter the four seven digits into the Skycon and make contact with Thomas and the rest of the Ring. Only a few minutes before my work begins in earnest.

The asphalt is worn thin in many spots, and there are many puddles. The slope is a couple of meters ahead. I put my feet on the ground and feel a sense of freedom. I turn back to smile at Jane, who is waiting to see what I'll do.

Does she think that I'm going to change my mind?

The slam of the car door marks our separation. Jane starts the motor, which seems to grumble over being on the move again. With a lunge, the little blue car sets off, casting a few pebbles off the tires. The window is rolled down, and Jane's slender hand waves outside the car as she turns onto the solitary main road. I raise my hand and wave back. The car becomes a blue point on the horizon.

I look around and march rapidly and purposefully toward the slope. Better get away from the road, so I can be sure that I won't be disturbed. My innermost response tells me that there isn't much time left, but I better wait until I down the slope to get out my Skycon from my pocket. I look up; there are still no clouds to be seen. The asphalt stops, and the withered yellow grass takes over.

My legs start to gain momentum as I go down the slope. A sensation of excitement bubbles quietly in my gut.

In a minute, I will hear Thomas's voice again.

At the foot of the slope is a lake. At its shore are three large trees desperately trying to hold onto their leaves while the wind shakes their branches. Past them, I can dimly see some untamed fields. Some hills further out on the horizon end my view of my surroundings. The lake is as clear as a mirror. The blue sky is reflected on the surface, giving it a metallic, luminous blue gleam.

My hand finds its way into my pocket. It is empty. My body starts in shock, and my eyes widen. Maybe I put the Skycon in the other pocket. Feverish, I pat my trousers with both hands at the same time. The other pocket is also totally flat.

This can't be.

I keep patting the front and back pockets with both hands. Then, I spin around on my heels so that they dig into the soil. My eyes scan the grass around me.

"Come on, Eva. Where can it be? Think," I say out loud as I squint my eyes and look back at the top of the slope that I just came from. Resolutely, I break into a run back up toward the road the same way up that I came down, but the Skycon is nowhere to be seen. *This can't be true. How could I be so careless, so impossible?* I clench my fists, pick up speed, and make it up the slope, back to the empty rest area where only the tire tracks on the asphalt indicate Jane's earlier presence. I lean against the empty table where many names are carved, marking the naive, innocent years of youth and raise my eyes to the sky.

"Where are you when I need you?" My lips are quivering, and tears are about to gush out.

The sound of a car is approaching.

"Angela…"

I look over to the road. It's Jane.

"This must be yours," she yells from the car, waving her hand out the window.

A tear finds its way down my cheek, and I take off running toward the driveway. She turns into the rest area and parks the car next to me.

"It was on the floor by the car seat and started to blink when I was a ways down the road. And since it isn't mine, I thought...." She smiles and leans out the window. I reach out for the Skycon.

A twinge of pain shoots through my chest, and I take a deep breath.

"Thank you..." Our eyes meet, and I feel a wave of gratitude rush through me.

Is that all I can say? She has saved me and the whole mission. The gratitude is replaced by an enormous sense of relief, but my heart is still pounding away. I don't know what to say. So, I don't say anything else. I hold on tight to the Skycon with my fingertips until Jane lets go.

"I really have to run." The clock inside the car says 12:59. I can't stand still. Briefly, I look into Jane's eyes. "I'm sorry." Then I race down the slope without looking back. My hands are shaking, and I try to get the image of the little keyboard up in front of me. My legs are circling automatically as I feverishly try to enter the series of sevens into the sender. It doesn't work.

I throw myself down on the ground and lean my back against a fallen tree next to the lake. My eyelids are blinking feverishly, and my hand is shaking as I try to adjust the Skycon so that I can enter the four sevens that will connect me to In-Between.

"Seven," I say aloud when I succeed in hitting the very small seven key the first time. The bark from the torn-up stump is cutting into my back, but I remain seated. "Come on seven—one more time." I look up at the sky. Thomas said that we only had one attempt and that it had to be precisely at one o'clock, but... My finger presses so hard on the seven key that it gives my arm a minor cramp. I shake my hand a couple of times and bring the Skycon even closer to my face. I place my index finger on the seven key and press one last time.

It works.

The Skycon starts to flash orange instead of red. Something happens, but I have no idea what. I look around in quick jerks. There is nobody else to be seen; I am all alone. The leaves are rustling in the trees, and out on the lake, several swans are floating with closed eyes.

I look at the little display on the Skycon. It says "Error." As I slam my palm against the bark, its edges cut into my hand. Raise my arm above my head and cast the hand holding the Skycon down toward the ground, but my fist stays closed.

It's too late.

One of the swans spreads its wings and gets ready to take off.

With one stroke, my entire body is petrified, and I stare vacantly into the air. So much for having a mission. Obviously, I wasn't the right one they sent off. I gave up my life to become a part of the Ring. I have given up Luke and chosen this mission instead of him. It feels like a sword is stabbing me through my chest, and I bend forward. Now, it won't come to pass anyhow, and I can't choose over again. The door to my life as Eva is closed. I can't go back and be his mother again.

All sound disappears, and I can only hear my breath. My whole body is smarting, and what I want to do most is stomp on the sender until it is crushed—and scream, scream as loudly as I can. But I can't scream. I have no words or sound inside me.

I look up at the sky, which seems enveloping. I try to breathe calmly, as I have learned at the meditations I attended in In-Between. It works reasonably, and I remember one thing I learned in In-Between. To remind me of what I know. I dry my face with my sleeves. The fabric scratches my skin, but that doesn't matter.

Unfortunately, I must admit that I know I entered the code too late. Maybe I should have driven off with Jane. Perhaps she was one of the ones I should find. No. That would be way too easy. It can't be that easy. I know....

THE RING

"Biiiizzzzzzz."
I jump off the ground.
My hand is shaking as I hold up the Skycon.
"Receiving," flashes the display.

4

THE HELP

"There." Several lines of numbers appear on the screen and start to flash. "Come on, Angela!" David slides forward in the chair, so it nearly slips away underneath him. He punches the thin screen, and the numbers disappear around his fingers. "This is too far out," David talks to the screen while moving his legs quickly up and down. "I have increased Angela's frequency by excluding all other frequencies in a radius of one thousand kilometers from here." He takes a sip of his tepid frequency drink in the shiny yellow and black can and pulls a face, making a new expression. "Thank you for entering the access code, Angela." He sighs and pops his finger joints one by one, emitting a hollow, dry cracking noise.

Thomas looks up at the screens, where the curve on one of the graphs gets bigger and bigger, and the crackle from the loudspeakers turns into a whisper from the wind.

He senses a hand on his shoulder and moves a bit to the side to make space for Yoge, who slides in between him and David.

"Well done, now the next challenge is to connect the two units. That will allow us to communicate with Angela." Yoge's expression is exhilarated and youthful, but when Thomas looks at him, he can sense the impression of an older man behind his expression. It is like the older man is feeding him knowledge. Yoge takes a folded piece of paper full of equations and long calculations out of his breast pocket. He looks at it and mumbles numbers and codes to himself.

Gabriel is standing behind Thomas, resting heavily on one leg, and even though his gaze is relaxed, his eyes are bloodshot. Shiva has decided to give the men space and is sitting in the mint-green chair by herself. She doesn't feel that she can contribute anything valuable right now and would rather save her energy. Her body is relaxed, and she is resting her hands in her lap. The white light around her follows her breathing like a soft dance.

Thomas turns back and leans toward the screens as he supports his elbow on the long narrow red table. "Angela... Angela, can you hear us?" He finds himself trying to straighten out the crease on his blue tunic with an ongoing movement. *Faith, have faith*; the word repeats itself in his head.

"Wait, she can't hear you yet. I'm not ready." David moves some boxes around on the screen, and a map of the world appears. The dot is imperceptibly small on the big map. With a slow, smooth move, it zooms all the way into the area where the red dot blinks. More details appear—landmarks, cities, and roads.

"She is back in her previous country." Gabriel looks over at Thomas, but his eyes are locked on the screen, and he doesn't sense anything else.

It is hard for David to sit still, and he keeps moving the chair from side to side. "If we can crack the code or maybe short-circuit the frequencies. No, maybe we can...." His eyes move from the screen to the keyboard and back, and his fingers are hammering frantically on the table, making an annoying sound. Yoge is in the middle of a complicated calculation. He crosses over and adds new numbers to his piece of paper until every tiny blank space is filled.

The screen display flickers, and the white noise is, in flashes, replaced with a picture of a lake.

"But how?" Thomas turns in his chair and looks straight into

Gabriel's eyes. At that moment, their eyes meet, and Thomas feels the doubt rising inside. He slowly moves his long dark-blond hair back away from his face. "We only had one chance."

"Now, the fun begins," exclaims David without paying attention to anyone else. He lifts one eyebrow, leaving the other one behind. "I have identified Angela's frequency, but we can't talk to her yet." He speaks out loudly, not caring who is listening.

Thomas turns toward David and says with a hesitating voice: "Angela needs to have the same code as us, and it can only be used once. How…"

David pops the finger joints he didn't get around to before. "Tell me something I'm not aware of." He makes the image of the lake smaller and pulls it to the corner of the screen, making space for other pictures of the same location but from different angles.

The signal is struggling to get through, but slowly and securely, the image of the lake wins over the white noise.

Thomas places his hand on his heart. A sinking feeling runs through him as a light breeze blows through the room. Shiva opens her eyes, and with light steps, she moves toward the others.

On the big screen appears an image of a woman with long dark hair with bleached stripes. She is sitting next to a lake, leaning her back against the stump of a fallen tree. Thomas reaches out for the screen and places his hand on it. It is soft and gives in like a piece of fabric as his hand gets closer. The room is dead quiet. Not even the sound of their breathing is to be heard. They are all staring at the screen.

"There is no time to waste. You have to find a way to give her a new code. We need to establish contact." There is a depth in Gabriel's rusty voice that reveals that he is talking from a place within himself where the silence cannot be disturbed. He places his hand on David's shoulder. David reaches out for the keyboard but holds back. The sweat is penetrating his blue shirt, leaving big dark splotches on his back. "Can someone get me a drink? I can't think straight." He runs his hand over his face several times.

The wall slides aside with a soft buzz as Shiva approaches, revealing a huge cupboard. It is full of bottles, cans, and machines that can make all kinds of hot and cold drinks. She reaches for one of the yellow and black cans. On the side, it says, *Gives strength to your concentration and overview*. She can't help but smile.

Thomas uses his foot to push against the floor, letting the chair glide over to the wall where there is a tray with glasses and a carafe of water. "Try to scratch a new code into the bark of the tree trunk that Angela is leaning against." He pours water into the glass and lets the ice-cold water fill his mouth. The ice-cold sensation brings a rush of clarity. Angela is sitting, still staring into the sky as if she were looking right at them. Her eyes are glassy and lifeless.

A cloud slides in front of the sun, and the light disappears. Thomas blinks a few times. The glow from the screen blinds him and makes everything look more black and white. Right now, he needs to be able to see all the details. Shiva hands Thomas the yellow and black can. It fizzes lightly when he opens it and splatters on the table. He places it right next to David, who takes a massive gulp without looking away from the screen. He keeps hitting the keyboard hard with his small fat fingers as if he were playing a song on a piano. The computer begins to generate a new code, and slowly it burns an eight deep into the bark right next to Angela, who is still staring at the sky. After the eight comes a one, a five, and at the end, another eight.

"Now, you just need to turn your head, Angela." David starts to tap on her image on the screen. "Come on, Baby..." he whispers and sits completely still without blinking.

Thomas swallows; it is oblivious that Angela is frustrated, her face is tense, and she is biting her lower lip repeatedly. If only he could talk to her and reassure her that they are here for her and she is not alone. He zooms in and sees a tear let go from her eye. It runs down her chin and hangs on before it falls on her shirt.

"What are we going to do? She isn't looking." David places the can on the table, so it is just about to fall over. He wipes his mouth with his shirt and tries to hold back a burp. His leg is still going up and down in a frantic movement.

Thomas looks from David toward Gabriel, who nods quietly. "Give her time. She knows that we are here...."

Clouds are beginning to fill the sky over Angela, and the rays of the sun disappear now and again. She moves a bit and pulls down the sleeve of her blue knitted sweater. Then she places her hands on the ground and gets on her feet slowly and tottering. The noise of wings and a rattle comes from the leaves on the big tree that leans over the lake. A huge eagle has landed in the crown of the tree. The swans swim to the other side of the shore. Angela shakes her head slightly, runs her hands firmly over her face, and wipes them off on her sweater.

"Use the eagle." Yoge places the pen on the table and pushes the paper aside. "You can use the eagle. According to my calculations, we can increase the frequency that we are transmitting on with three units. That means that Angela's Skycon will respond if it just gets the new access code."

David looks at him and wrinkles his nose. "If we can use the eagle, why can't we just punch her on the shoulder?" His hair is every which way.

"There are seven different animal frequencies we can connect to. The eagle is one of them. We can only communicate with humans through their intuition or clairvoyance, which requires them to listen to the frequency we are transmitting. Now, many people have opened to the skill to do that." Yoge talks with great zest.

"Cool," David pulls a face. "Where do I get that installed?"

Gabriel places a hand on David's shoulder and continues where Yoge stopped. "The older your soul is, the easier it is to get access to clear-sightedness. In time, it will open when you are ready for it and give you access to the information you need. But maybe not in this incarnation."

Thomas looks over at Gabriel; he is definitely an old soul. Very often, he sees things that no one else does. It was also him who realized that Eva belonged to the Ring and started to gather the members of the Ring from the very beginning.

The image zooms in and makes Thomas shift focus. Angela is standing with her Skycon in her hand. On the small display, it says, "Write code." Panic spreads over her face, and she presses feverishly the number eight four times. "Error." Her eyes are fixed on the small display. Four nines. "Error." She lets her arm down and looks around. The eagle spreads its wings and narrows its dark eyes with yellow circles around them. It lets out a loud scream that the wind carries away.

Yoge moves forward in the chair and lets the pen joggle between his fingers. "Remember, everything is numbers. All communication depends on frequencies and those we can control. But only the incoming frequencies. Clear-sightedness can also open to communication on other levels." He places the pen on the red table in front of him.

The image has stopped flickering. Angela slides her hand into her pocket and takes out a crumpled bill and a business card. She balances the business card between her thumb and forefinger, staring at it as if it were her only lifeline.

"Write the code on the back of the business card, quickly." Thomas points at the screen. Nobody else says a thing or moves.

David pulls around several small windows on the screen, types the code, and presses enter.

Angela puts the business card in her back pocket without even looking at it and walks toward the lake. Her shoes leave deep prints in the soft soil. The water in the lake is as clear as a mirror, and the brown muddy bottom sloping down toward the center of the lake is clearly visible. There is an area with high rushes on the right—a perfect hiding place for small birds that are trying hard to be invisible. The eagle has landed on a branch with a perfect view over the lake. Angela is standing at the water's edge, looking down.

"The eagle needs to be brought into play right now." Yoge

pushes David gently. He moves aside, leaving space for Yoge. He writes a long and complicated code and draws a line from the eagle to the stump. It lets out a loud scream and takes off.

5

SO CLOSE AND YET SO FAR

I pull my sleeve up a bit and kneel at the water's edge, close my eyes, and bend forward. The fresh air is filling my lungs, and my heart is beating fast. The sound of small birds has disappeared. All I can hear is the wind in the trees. I breathe slowly, gasping a bit for air. It feels like there is not enough oxygen that gets through to my lungs. *Come on, old chap. You have been to heaven and back; how hard can it be to find out what you look like?* I bite my lower lip, so it hurts, and run a hand through my long hair. *Now.* I lean forward and stare into the glassy water. My cheekbones are clear-cut, my lips pretty average, and my skin white. My nose is small, and my hair is dark with light highlights in it instead of gray. Carefully, I place a strand of hair behind my ear. My eyes, I lean a bit further forward; they are blue. At least some of me looks familiar.

Slowly, I reach for my reflection. It disappears as my hand touches the water. It startles me. The water is ice cold.

A scream from an eagle makes me pull my hand back and turn around.

"Are you still here?"

The eagle stares at me with its glowing yellow eyes.

It's getting a bit chilly, and the last rays of the sun have set fire to the sky.

I place my hands on the ground and let the weight of my body fall a bit forward. The soil is soft and gives in, leaving a slender hand mark.

The eagle lets out another scream.

I turn around and brush my hands off. As I walk toward the eagle, I raise my arms to the sides, trying to fend it off. It picks at the bark on the fallen tree and looks at me with intensity. Then, it takes off and flies away. Hesitant, I step toward the stump. It looks like some of the bark is missing right where the eagle was sitting. I take another step closer.

"Angela!"

It startles me, and I stop.

"Angela!"

Quickly, I turn and smile as best I can, not sure that I have gotten used to my new name yet.

It is Jane. She comes running toward me, waving her arms. Her face is one big smile as she gets closer.

"I'm sorry, but I had to come back. I just couldn't stand the thought of leaving you behind out here in the middle of nowhere." Jane is puffing, and her mouth hangs open.

I don't know what to say, so I don't say anything.

"If you need a place to stay overnight, you're welcome at my place. I'm sorry that I didn't invite you before." She supports her hands on her hips, and her frizzy dark hair is going in all directions.

The noise of wings comes right above us.

I look up. The eagle is back.

"Jane, I would like to come with you, but I just need five minutes by myself. Would it be alright if you wait for me by the car?" For a fleeting moment, our eyes meet. I can't stand still and look at my watch. It is nearly half-past one.

"Sure thing, no problem. I need to make a few calls anyway."

The eagle dives and passes right above my head; Jane ducks.

THE RING

"Watch out!"

I don't move.

She looks up, somewhat shaken, and adjusts her sunglasses in her hair. "They can be really dangerous, those ones, she points toward the eagle. "Whenever you're ready," she turns around, and at a fast pace, heads back toward the hill.

I pull the sleeves on my sweater down over my hands, holding my breath, and as soon as she is gone behind the hill, I gasp for air. The clouds have built up, covering the whole sky like a duvet with no more sunrays getting through. I start walking back toward the stump.

The eagle has definitely scratched some of the bark off. My feet pick up speed, and I start running and quickly turn to the hill just to make sure that Jane is gone. There is a small area where the bark is missing on the tree trunk, and the fresh light wood shines through. It looks like something is written there. I lean forward, stop, and carefully brush over the soft wood where the bark is missing.

A chuckle spreads from my stomach and makes the small birds in the rush take off. I pant for air. The numbers are tiny, but they *are* numbers. I blink and blink again and turn toward the clouds as I pull the Skycon from my pocket.

My gaze flicks from the tree trunk over to the Skycon and back again as I punch in a number eight, followed by the number two.

The lake is calm, and a pile of leaves in dark and golden colors is lying in a heap next to the tree. A row of ants is marching on the bark, heading for the area where the numbers are. They look like a period between the four numbers. I punch in the next number. Five. And then the last one, eight again. My feet are dancing on the ground, and my jaw hurts from smiling.

"Angela..." The sound is crystal clear. The voice belongs to Thomas.

"Yes..." A lump explodes in my throat and makes it nearly impossible to answer. I look at the small screen, and an image of

Thomas appears. His long dark blond curls fall softly around his face, and his blue eyes shine.

"Thomas!" I stutter.

He smiles, and his eyes light up the whole image.

I place the Skycon on my chin. It's cold.

"Angela, are you still there? I can't see you…."

"Sorry…" I remove the Skycon from my chin and wipe it clean with my sleeve before holding it in front of me. My body is shivering, and a sensation of happiness fills me.

"Angela." The image expends, and Gabriel steps forward. His voice is a bit rusty but calm, and his eyes are bloodshot. It is hard for me to tell if the images make him look worse than he is. "It is so nice finally to have contact. You look good, and I assume that the journey went well. Are you ready to continue?" The sound of his voice makes my body settle down.

I pull out a bigger picture from the Skycon, and it hovers in front of me. It is not solid; I can see the landscape through it, but the quality is amazing. Gabriel, Thomas, Yoge, and Shiva are all there smiling at me. I place the picture in front of me and kneel. My jaws are getting sore from smiling, but I just can't stop.

"We have gathered the information we believe can help you find the last two members of the Ring. It's our experiences and people that might be connected to the Ring."

The sound crackles a bit, and the image of Gabriel begins to fade out. He steps closer so that the wrinkles in his face get more distinctive.

"It is important that you listen to your intuition. You are the one who is closest to human beings. It's you and only you who can find the two missing members of the Ring. All we can do is support you."

I stare at the image floating in front of me. Gabriel's face fills the whole picture. A warm sensation rushes through my body. He looks just like he did last time I saw him, but why shouldn't he? We were just together a few hours ago. At this moment, it just feels like years.

"Gabriel," my voice is eager. The image begins to fade away, and more white lines take over. Gabriel's voice is drowned in a crackle. I hit the side of the Skycon. Nothing happens. A flash of light rushes over the small screen, and the light goes out. I look toward the sky in despair. It feels like the dark clouds are losing their grip on the sky and are falling toward me.

A cold sensation fills me and reaches my eyes. I shake the Skycon. Nothing happens. I keep shaking it till my arms sting with pain. Then, I stop. My breath is noisy, and there are no thoughts in my head and no action.

Time is standing still.

6
A GLIMPSE

"Are you coming or what?"

Jane's voice tears me out of my state of nothingness. Seconds have become minutes, and the Skycon is still lifeless. I force it into my pocket, turn, and start running toward Jane, who is standing on the top of the slope. My legs feel like jelly, and I try to flex my body to keep my balance.

The car door is heavy, and I tighten my grip on the handle and open the door just enough to get in and drop down on the passenger seat next to Jane, who is already sitting there. She is on the phone, looking like she is concentrating. Her cream-colored suit is tight and shows her female curves. She turns toward me in a swift move and places her finger in front of her mouth. I don't say anything and lean back in the seat quietly. On the little shelf above the glove box are yellow post-it notes full of phone numbers and a pile of plastic pens in different colors. Her handbag is on the back seat, which looks like it is only used for keeping her attaché case.

She turns off the small red cell and places it next to the ash tray.

"Is there anything else you need to do before we take off?" Her body seems a bit trapped in the custom-made suit.

THE RING

I shake my head no and lower my gaze.

"I don't live far from here," she continues in the same rather harsh tone that she used on her phone call. The car rattles a bit as she turns on the engine and lightly presses the gas pedal. In an instant, she takes out her hairband, and her wild frizzy hair sets off in all directions, a striking contrast to the more controlled expression on her face.

I take a deep breath and raise my gaze. Jane is a total stranger who has shown mercy and patience and picked me up. I have no idea where we are, who Jane is, or where she is taking me.

"Do you normally pick up strangers?" My voice is a bit shaky. I bite my teeth hard and tighten my jaw, not wanting to reveal that I feel lost right now. She turns her head to me and smiles.

"I have never picked up a stranger before, but there was something about you that made all my arguments not to fall to the ground." She shakes her head so that the frizzy hair rocks to the sides. "When I saw you standing there on the deserted dirt road, I suddenly heard my grandmother's voice in my head. I don't know who you are, but I know that you need help." She looks straight ahead and has a faraway look in her eyes. "When I was a child, my grandmother always said that I had to remember that it is impossible to know what a stranger brings." Jane pauses, sets the car in gear, and presses the gas pedal all the way down. "My grandmother utilized every occasion to remind me of it. It was her mantra, a mantra that she had taken over from her mother, my great-grandmother." She shrugs.

The car is up to speed and rumbling along the road. After half an hour, the traffic picks up, and we start to overtake other vehicles. Jane pushes the radio, and a speed-talking host makes the small loudspeakers shake. My body is beginning to get tenser, and I try to cut out the torrent of words that hit me.

The road is wide, and on both sides are rows of tall birch trees with white tree trunks and small jagged leaves. It doesn't seem that unfamiliar; my mother has birch trees in her garden. *I wonder how she is doing and if she has visited Luke and Andreas in their new house? The last time I checked in on her, she looked better; that was right before I left In-Between.*

More and more houses appear. I'm enjoying the view from my seat, where everything is at eye level. I roll down the window, and a cold breeze forces me to shut my eyes.

"Tell me more about yourself." Jane's voice pulls my attention back in the car. She turns the monotonous and rather aggressive music down slightly; it has taken over from the speed-talking host.

I turn toward Jane and smile. What can I say? I have to make up a story really fast since I can't tell her about my life as Eva.

"Well, ah, yeah, you know, my name is Angela." Great start, well done, I think to myself.

She smiles indulgently and raises her eyebrow, "Yes...?"

"Yes, well, I have been traveling to find some old friends. And my journey has brought me here." That sounded pretty convincing. I smile, self-satisfied. "And you...?" I hurry to say before she gets a chance to ask another question.

Jane laughs, a little controlled. "That was rather vague, eh?"

I don't move a muscle in my face, even though it is hard not to.

"Fine then," she smiles at me, and her voice has softened up a bit, now with a smooth edge. She has an elegant and careful way of pronouncing words.

"I'm a prosecutor."

Prosecutors are usually tough and cold-hearted, I think.

"I live by myself in a small house and have been there for years." The way she talks is like she is reading it from a teleprompter, and it's hard for me to keep focus. I can hear her words, but it is like an empty shell talking. A part of her sounds warm and caring, and another part of her seems more like a learned response.

We turn down a side road and get into a more residential area where high fences and gates hide the houses, so they can't be seen from the road. I can't sense the people who live here. There are no nameplates and no personal touches. Being an individual is irrelevant, and it seems like people are busy minding their own business.

I pull the sleeve on my blue sweater up a bit and try to look at my watch discreetly. It's already three o'clock; where did the time go? I have forty-two days counting today before I have to return to In-Between. *Hopefully, time won't continue to disappear this fast.*

"Is there anything you need to do?" Jane is pointing at my watch. "That's the fifth time you have checked the time."

I look up, a bit baffled. "No, well, I have to find my two friends." I pull my sleeve back down quickly.

"What are their names? Maybe I can help you. I know quite a lot of people around here." She throws the car around the corner so that the tires squeal.

"They are not from here," I try to sound convincing, but my voice is tense and makes me sound harder than planned. Jane reaches out for the pile of yellow notes and finds a nicotine gum packet buried beneath them.

"Do you want a piece?" She flicks the package open with one hand and offers it to me. I shake my head, no.

"I don't need that."

"I do, in a world where you cannot even decide for yourself what you put in your mouth and where." She throws the package back, and it disappears among the yellow notes. "Why don't you want any help? Are you used to dealing with everything by yourself?"

I look straight ahead and turn my shoulder a bit away from her. As I rock my head a bit to the side, I smile a bit strained. "No, are you?"

"We're here." She points toward a small driveway full of red roses that ooze of care. The house is set back from the street a bit. It's yellow with small, white-framed windows.

"Come on," she turns off the engine, grabs her bag and the briefcases from the backseat, and gets out of the car before I get to say anything. The smell of the roses is overwhelming and intense. I stop for a moment, just to smell them.

"Well, yes, those are roses…." She laughs as she walks in her very high heels toward the house, swaying her hips. Before I know it, she has gone through the front door and disappeared. I follow, even though I could use some more time just enjoying the amazing smell.

"Do you want coffee? Or perhaps you don't drink coffee?" Jane is standing in front of a monster of a machine in the kitchen. I only just made it to the hallway. She puts two small slim cups on the table and pushes one toward me. "Have a seat."

"Why do you think that I don't drink coffee?" My tone of voice is a bit irritated. I avoid looking at her and walk over to the bar table separating the kitchen's open space from the dining area. The kitchen is full of light from the huge windows that have replaced the smaller ones facing the garden. The ceiling is low, and it makes the space cozy. The garden looks like it minds its own business. Bushes are growing wild, spreading over what use to be a terrace.

"I inherited the house from my grandmother." Jane looks out the window; the atmosphere gets more relaxed.

I pull out a tall slim bar chair and sit opposite her. The coffee machine sizzles and puffs. On the shelves behind Jane is a selection of spices arranged in a dead straight row. If you wanted, you could place a ruler, and it wouldn't be any straighter. All the pictures hang perfectly horizontally. Jane looks at me and shrugs her shoulders apologetically. "The garden is my grandmother. I have only put my personal touch in here." She pours coffee and pushes a cup to me.

"Were you close?" I reach for the cup and blow some of the steam away. Janes waves her hand over the cup and takes a sip.

"Enough of that. Well, stranger, it's about time I got to know you a bit better!" She looks right into my eyes. A strong smell from the coffee reaches my nose and makes me cough. I don't drink coffee, but I'm not going to say anything.

"What do you want to know?" I struggle to maintain eye

contact, but an underlying feeling of unease builds up at the speed of light and forces me to look away. She wrinkles her nose and narrows her eyes.

"Who are you?"

I can't help but laugh a bit feigned. "That is some question. Do you know who you are?"

She moves closer and places her cup on the table. "Yes, it's not that difficult. I'm a woman and prosecutor at one of this country's leading law firms." Her tone of voice is superior.

I clear my throat and put a teaspoon of sugar in the coffee, so it nearly spills on the table. I would rather tell her how I feel—that I need some time by myself, some peace and quiet. If she is a prosecutor or a checkout assistant, I couldn't care less. It is just a title.

"I'm a Kindergarten teacher, and yes, as I mentioned, I'm out looking for some friends."

There is a scratching sound coming from the door.

"Coming…" Jane yells out.

I turn to see what is happening. When Janes opens the door, a huge sumptuous black cat comes marching in a majestic pose with its head held high.

"Hi there, Buzzer." Jane bends down to scratch it behind the ears. Buzzer walks straight toward me and jumps on my lap. I lean back and stare at it. Cats have never been my cup of tea.

"That is so strange. He usually keeps away from strangers." Jane crosses her arms and is watching us.

I'm not moving an inch. Buzzer has positioned himself, facing me, and is staring at me with no mercy. I try to move a bit when I feel something shake in my pocket. Buzzer repays me by probing his claws through my pants while purring loudly. I am sure that my pocket was vibrating, and perhaps I could also hear a vague hum. But if it was Buzzer's purr or the Skycon that is working again, I'm not sure. I look at Jane; did she notice it too?

"I need to make a call; is there anywhere I can sit?"

"Aren't you sitting?" She smiles at me with a glimpse in her eye.

"I mean alone…" and smile back.

"In here." She points toward the door where Buzzer came from. "I have a guest room where you can stay for the night."

Carefully, I lift one leg a bit up and down. Buzzer hisses at me and looks very indignant, so I stop.

"Hey, Buzzer, behave yourself. Angela is our guest. Here, let me take him." She reaches for Buzzer, who reluctantly lets go of my pants.

I step into the guestroom and close the door behind me.

There is a rectangular bright red couch with hard edges and a low wooden table struggling to keep upright under a huge pile of professional literature. Above the couch hangs a picture of a crying child. It stings in my heart as I remember all the times I have seen Luke sad on the screen and not been able to comfort him. I sit down on the couch. It is just as hard as it looks, probably some Italian design.

I take out the Skycon from my pocket. The display is still all black. Carefully, I press the buttons on the side and give it a little shake too. Nothing happens. Then, I lean back on the couch and rest my head on the back. It is cold in here. At the other end of the couch, there is a black quilt perfectly folded over the armrest. I reach for it and wrap myself up inside of it. A cold draft from the window right behind me keeps blowing on my neck, but I cannot be bothered moving. It's getting dark. Day one here on earth is coming to an end, and I haven't made any progress. I fold my hands around the Skycon. A cold sensation starts to spread in my body. I try to tense all my muscles to prevent it from taking over, but with no luck.

The only possibility to make contact with In-Between is gone. I'm all alone, or rather, the only one I have contact with is a cold and slightly cynical prosecutor. Behind her façade, I sense a softness, maybe a longing to be seen as the person she really is. That part doesn't get much space, but I was fortunate that she felt mercy for me. I guess I can thank her grandmother for that. My eyelids close softly, and it gets all dark. I try to breathe effortlessly with no luck. A stab in my chest makes me crumple. My mouth is dry. Sinking doesn't make it any better.

Suddenly, it feels like I get a knock on the head, I want to open my eyes, but the couch and the room are gone. Everything is looming white. I turn around a couple of times, but there is nothing to be seen. My body is gone, or rather I can't feel it. The room has disappeared too. *What is going on?* Have they pulled me back to In-Between? Is that possible? Have I failed already?

Suddenly, a tall man in his thirties is standing in front of me. His face is bright red, and his eyes are sunken and squinting. He is talking to a woman with wide hips and a beefy body. They can't see me. The woman is screaming so that small drops of saliva are flying out of her mouth. At once, she stops and freezes. A hand comes flying through the air, and it gives a snap as it hits her chin. Her head is torn to the side, and she falls to her knees.

I want to step forward and reach out for her, but I'm not really there, even though I can smell her fear and his acid smell of anger.

She lifts her head and looks him right in the eyes. Slowly, she gets up, reaches for her purse, and staggers toward the door. He is left behind, and a tear wrings loose from his eye and runs over his cheek, but he remains silent. She leaves the door open behind her. He remains standing, petrified, and watches her go. The material of his tight red shirt stretches as he braids his fingers behind his neck and bends over convulsively.

I try to look at myself, but there is still nothing to be seen. I have no body and no shape. Yet I'm still here, kind of. The room at Jane's house is gone, the stiff red couch and the chilly breeze from the window. Everything is white. Behind me is infinite light, and there is a jelly kind of reality in front of me that I can move around inside without being seen. It doesn't make any sense.

The woman from before is standing on the street. She is wearing a thick black sweater that is almost the same color as her skin and thick black hair. She places her hand on her chest and falls to the ground. People gather from everywhere. They are all dressed in long straight gray coats. A horse carriage is getting closer; the coach doesn't stop, and the driver looks straight ahead. The horse neighs and pulls at the harness as they pass.

At the same moment as I see the woman lying lifeless on the ground, I can also see inside the apartment where the man has walked to the window. He is looking down on the crowd that has surrounded the woman. As he realizes that the woman has fallen to the ground, he runs out of the apartment, down the stairs, and forces his way through the crowd. He kneels by her side and starts to shake her body. Every single tiny little muscle in his body is convulsing. He looks up into the sky. A white light rises from her body. She is standing in an almost see-through silhouette next to her own body, watching the man.

I want to tell him that she is still there, that she is going to a beautiful place. But I shouldn't intervene. This is his learning and not my task.

"I have lost her forever." His voice is filled with pain, "What have I done?"

A flashing light surrounds me, and now I see the same man walking on a deserted dirt road. He is carrying a small fabric bag over his shoulder and walks with heavy steps. It doesn't seem like he has any particular direction in life and no sense of belonging. His eyes are lifeless and are set even deeper in his head. His feet are dragging over the gravel on the road.

The image wipes away, and a cold sensation rushes through my body. I feel a hard pang in my heart and can open my eyes again. I run my hand over the couch and pat it gently. My eyes wander around the room. It's alright. I'm back again.

The sound of someone rummaging outside the door makes my heart beat faster. There is a key in the keyhole, and I quickly get on my feet but have to support myself on the corner of the couch to avoid falling over. I stumble to the door as I rest my hand against the wall. Quickly, I lock the door and collapse. I sit on the floor, staring out into the air. The sound disappears. My fingertips are pressed on the floor, helping me to keep my balance. I gasp for air and manage to get a bit into my lungs.

What is happening to me?

7

HAVE A LITTLE FAITH

"Are you ready?" Jane is knocking three times rapidly on my door that is partly open. I'm already up and dressed. All I need to do is make the bed, and then the room will be exactly as it was when I came, neat and tidy.

Jane lives in a suburb just outside a fairly large city, but what is far more interesting is that it is only 500 miles to the town where Andreas has moved with Luke and Longlegs. It is not that far away from where we used to live together.

The sun is up and blinding me as I stand in the room and run my hand through my shoulder-length hair. I try to see my reflection in the window facing the garden, but it is not possible. The experience from last night is still filling me. A glimpse appears for my inner vision of the old woman who gave the young woman a place to hide. She used the same saying as Jane, "You can never know what a stranger brings." My inner vision changes to the man who was walking in despair. I'm not sure what it all means or how to use it. I shake my head and grab my bag, feeling the excitement of what the day will bring.

Buzzer is sitting right in the middle of the hallway and purrs self-assuredly when he sees me. Jane is running from one end of the house to the other, collecting papers. Her tight suit looks like it has been sprayed on; today, it's blue.

My hand slides into my pocket just to make sure that I have the Skycon. If I'm lucky, it will come back to life. My mother would defiantly say, with the luck that I usually have, that it will. She used to call me Gladstone Gander when I was a child. I can't help smiling as I close the door behind me. Jane is ready, standing at the door with her coat on, hair pulled back tightly, and a frantic look in her eyes.

What if she is one of the two missing people I'm looking for. Somehow, it is too easy, like cheating in a board game where you take a shortcut no one else knew was there.

"Good morning."

Jane looks at her smartwatch and back at me. "Are you ready?"

"Yes." I didn't get any breakfast or tea, but it doesn't matter; I will grab some later. I'm not sure that I could cope with her for a longer period of time. *What if I made the same impression on other people when I was here last time?*

Jane hands me a cup to go. The smell of coffee rises in a fine steam. I take it. "Thanks, that is nice of you."

"Well, I was up at five, so I had my coffee long ago; this is my third cup." She opens the door, and I follow right behind her.

The wind lifts my hair when I step out of the front door and throws it in my face. I put my arms around my stomach and try to cover the loosely knitted sweater. Out on the horizon, I can see several groups of dark clouds heading straight for us.

Jane is walking two steps in front of me and speaks with a firm voice that is thrown back to me. "Well then, how are you going to find your friends?" She is heading straight for the car, and I try to find shelter from the wind behind her.

"First, I have to find a newsstand where I can buy a scratch card," I say as if it were the most natural thing in the world to do in the morning. I need to get some money to get by and buy a car.

Since no one uses money in In-Between, I didn't get a credit card, and I totally forgot to ask. But more importantly, I have to find out more about Jane. It is not certain that it was a coincidence that I met her.

She erupts into piercing laughter. "That is probably the stupidest thing I have heard in a long time." She turns to me as if I am from a foreign planet. "Come on. Nobody ever wins by scratching those gray squares. If you want to get more out of your money, buy stocks."

I stop in front of the car, but she shakes her head and points up the road. "We are walking. There is a newsstand next to my office. It's right over there." She looks across the road, where it seems like the house line grows taller and becomes more industrial.

Jane's house is the smallest on the street. The other houses are newer and more prominent. The lawns in front of them are cut to perfection, and even though they are close to each other, they look lonely. We walk on the pavement at Jane's exaggerated speed.

"It's all about faith." I gasp for air and try to slow down. Jane keeps walking at her speed.

"Believe in it?" Her voice is toned down with a sharp edge to all the words. "What else do you believe in? That there is a reason for everything?" She burst out laughing in a shrill and strained way.

I stare at the curbs partly covered in fallen leaves from the huge trees along the road. It begins to drizzle, and Jane increases her speed even more, if possible.

We turn a corner and join a bigger road. Ahead, I can see some tall office buildings with black glassy facades.

"I believe in life after death." Why did I say that? Why can't I just keep my big mouth shut? I clench my fists and hit them against my leg.

"Well, do you also believe that it is God who decides who wins the lottery?" Her voice has become a bit mechanical, and it seems like she is somewhere else in her mind.

The traffic is dense, and several cars are queuing up on the road next to us. The suburb is disappearing behind us, and the road gets wider. On the other side of the road is a massive sign with big letters advertising for a bank, a grocery shop, and different offices.

"Turn here." Jane pulls my arm, and we walk down some stairs that lead us through a tunnel and over to the other side of the road. The steps are narrow, and we edge past numerous suits that are heading in the other direction. They also look ahead, paying no attention to anyone else, just aiming for their destination. The light is dimmed, and the sound of cars resonates down here, making it hard to hear anything else.

"Do you still have my business card?" Jane shouts to make sure I hear her.

"Yes, I've got it." I look at her and notice that her hair has fallen down a bit, and the lines in her face are not as distinctive today.

"Remember to call if you need help." She looks straight ahead, and now it seems to be hard for her to offer her help. But something inside is forcing her to do it.

We are heading up the steps and are met with fresh petrol fumes. Ahead, a small shopping area appears, surrounded by gray similar office buildings and people crossing quickly.

"The newsstand is over there." She points to the left, where some signs advertise ice cream, the lottery, and newspapers. "Let's find out if it's your lucky day."

"It is," I smile confidently. "Are you coming?"

"Why not? You sound very convinced." She walks right behind me, letting out a burst of mocking laughter.

The newsstand is full of endless rows of magazines, sweets, and newspapers. A narrow corridor leads up to the counter.

"One scratch card, please." My tone of voice leaves no doubt about my conviction.

The man behind the counter has a gray beard covering his chin and deep folds under his eyes. He looks at me and reluctantly reaches for the drawer with scratch cards.

"Five." His voice is rough. It could be the first words he's said today.

I reach for my pocket, send Jane a glance, and hand him the fifty I got from her. She stands behind me with a complacent smile on her lips and her arms crossed.

"Let's go out where there's some air." I push Jane lightly as I pass her.

The light dazzles me as I step out. I have the scratch card in my hand and look up at the low-hanging clouds above us. *I hope you are there.* I saw how Ian played with the lottery winnings the day he showed me how to contact Luke. If he can do it, so can Thomas. My throat tightens, and my heart beats so fast that I have difficulty registering the intervals between beats.

Jane takes a stand right in front of me, crosses her arms, and looks at her watch. The time is only ten to eight.

"Are you in a hurry?" I hold the scratch card up in front of me and start scratching lightly on it with my index fingernail.

"No, I don't want to miss this." Her voice gloats; she looks at me and ignores all those who pass by while the tip of her shoe swings quickly up and down.

The first space is scraped free, nothing. My gaze runs across the nine spaces. To the right, it says that there is a chance to win a thousand, five thousand, ten thousand, fifty thousand, one hundred thousand, or one million. *How amazing it would be to be allowed to get the really big win, just this one time.* My nail whizzes across the next space, which is a purse with a thousand written on it.

Jane smiles. "Well, it doesn't seem to be today that the sensation occurs."

I keep my eyes fixed on the scratch card and scrape the next space, revealing another thousand. My nail almost scratches a hole in the paper. I have to have three of the same kind to win, but a thousand dollars will not get me far.

The amount of people around us is picking up. I start to stand a little restlessly. The cold creeps up through the thin soles of my slightly worn-out boots. Somehow, I just want to get it over with, but a part of me also wants to give Thomas a chance to make the combination on the card right. I don't know how long that takes. And I don't know if he is watching me. A wave of people comes by, and a young guy with oversized pants sets up near us and starts handing out free newspapers.

Finally, there is a money bag with a million. I just need two more of those; then I'm well off. I look up at Jane, slightly smiling as I try to look relaxed and scrape further across the remaining five squares without moving my gaze away from her.

Suddenly, she rips the scratch card out of my hand. "You've won." She stares at the scratch card. Then she steps close to me and narrows one eye. "You knew you were going to win. How did you know that?"

I shrug calmly. Relief spreads through my body, and a tear is about to writhe free from the corner of my eye, but I look up and blink a few times so that it gives up.

"Can I have a look?" I lean forward on my toes and look at the scratch card that Jane holds tightly in her hand. There are three sacks with 50,000 dollars. It gives a stab in my heart. It was not today I would get the million. I tense my face a bit. That would probably not make the task easier anyway. I smile and feel the gratitude deep in my heart. Now, I can move on.

"I better find a bank." I take my scratch card, and Jane reluctantly lets go of it. The guy with the newspapers looks at me as he hands out newspapers to the passers-by. It will take him years on the street with newspapers to earn the same amount I just won.

Jane's phone rings, but she ignores it. "It was nice meeting you. Take care of yourself." She extends her hand toward me.

"Thank you for your help," I step forward and put my arms around her. She's stiff as a plank. "Maybe we'll see each other again." I smile and warm my heart. "I'm very happy for your help."

The wind shakes her hair from side to side. "My grandmother always said that some people come by to help us move on; others stay so that we can develop with them." She smiles, "but that's just an old lady's words."

I reach out and take her hand. It's ice cold. We stand for a moment and look each other in the eyes. Then she steps back, turns around, and walks toward one of the many dark buildings, where one suit after another disappears through a large, ferocious gate.

8
THE REUNION

I turn into an empty parking lot next to a large, white villa adorned with colorful paper cuttings in the windows. Here, no one is to be seen; only the wheel tracks in the gravel testify to great periodic activity. The car I drive is an older model; it was the best value for money at the used car dealer near the airport. The car exudes a sour smell from old smoke, which fights against the perfumed scent of an air freshener dangling on a string around the rearview mirror.

I managed to get on a plane to the city where Andreas lives. It doesn't matter if I begin here or any other place. That is what I'm telling myself anyway. To be frank, I don't know where else to go. Again and again, I have repeatedly asked myself whether I came here for my own sake or the assignment. I'm not sure. That is the scary truth.

Before I boarded, I exchanged the scratch card for real money. I bought the car, a cell phone, a coat, and the best set of clothes I could find from a local store. Not my favorite choice, but it will do for now. I rub my hand against the window, and it makes a squeaky sound. There is still no one to be seen in the parking area. The scratched clock in the car says half-past two. The building next to me is Luke's new Kindergarten. Until now, I have only seen it from above.

My fingers are drumming on the steering wheel. It's so quiet here. I slide back in the seat. The springs dig into my back, and the windshield wipers moan as I turn them on. They are scraping over the windscreen, trying to improve my view a bit. In the rear-view mirror, I can see a constant flow of cars passing on the big road. Behind the road is a forest. I pull the Skycon from my pocket and place it in front of the speed indicator. It is still dead.

A green family car pulls into the parking area, and a woman gets out. She has short curly hair full of silver hair clips that tie it neatly to her head. She drops a small umbrella, picks it up, and disappears around the building.

I start to fiddle with the keys and gulp water from the bottle that lies on the passenger seat. The water is ice-cold, and my body shakes slightly as it sinks. Another car enters the parking area, this time a silver SUV with a massive radiator grille. It pulls up right next to me. I lean forward a bit to see who's driving. It's Longlegs, Andreas's new girlfriend. Quickly, I throw myself down. *How stupid is that?* I mumble to myself; *she couldn't recognize me.* Slowly, I rise back up and see her disappear through the big wooden gate that is almost hidden behind huge branches from a great chestnut tree.

I feel like I'm going to explode out of my body as it's overloaded with energy. My breath is rapid, and my lips vibrate as I breathe out. All I need is a glimpse of Luke; then I'll be off again. He is not going to see me, and I won't make contact. A glimpse, I'm entitled to that.

I get out of the car and walk toward the building. The gravel crunches under my feet as I walk toward the wooden gate. Time is dragging. I stop fifty feet from the gate and put my hands into the pockets of my newly bought jeans.

There, up ahead of me, Longlegs and Luke come out of the gate, holding hands. He is wearing a blue fleece shirt and pants with

THE RING

spiderman on the side. I can't hear what he is telling Longlegs, but she doesn't look that interested as her eyes wander. They walk toward me.

It feels like an electric shock hits me, and my heart breaks in two. I step forward away from my car, closer to Luke and Longlegs, but what I should be doing is turning around and going back to the car. The sound of a car braking catches my attention, but I don't move. I don't know what to say or do.

They are coming closer.

Luke nearly jumps ahead, pulling Longlegs' thin, skinny arm. She is wearing a beige coat that reaches down to her knees. Her narrow bony face is all pale, and it looks like her serious expression has gotten stuck.

Luke hasn't seen me.

It could have been me. The thought cuts through me.

Tears are building up behind my eyes, and pain is shooting through all my joints. I want to lean against something, but there is nothing within reach. I place my arms around my shoulders and embrace myself.

The sound of a honk rises like a wall behind me.

I turn and glare at the waiting van, lift my hand and wave as I step a bit back.

Luke and Longlegs are heading straight toward me. I want to turn around and leave, but I don't move at all. There are only 10 feet between us now.

"Is Daddy home?" Luke starts running toward the car parked right next to mine. It must belong to Longlegs; Andreas drives an old Toyota.

Now, Luke is right in front of me. He only sees the car. If I lift my arm and reach out, I could touch him, pull him close, and smell him. I could say all the things I never got around to saying while I had the chance.

"Luke," it's Longlegs' frilled voice, "you're in the back."

He is standing next to the front door and makes a pouty face and stamps his feet on the ground.

I start to walk toward my car; Longlegs catches up and passes me.

"Hi," she smiles, a bit strained, and avoids any eye contact.

"Hi," I manage to say with a husky voice.

"Luke, I don't want to argue with you." She gets in the car and slams the door.

I press my lips together, using all my willpower, and clench my fists. Then, I force myself to walk away. I can't stand it. It is pure torture. A voice inside my head shouts to rescue him and then drive off and never be found. But instead, I stand like a statue next to my car as if someone had a gun to my head and told me not to move. But I'm the one holding the gun.

"I miss my mum," Luke's little voice cuts through the window over to me, and I can't hold back the tears anymore. The door slams and his voice is gone. Longlegs reverses and leaves the parking space.

I'm standing there, all alone.

9

A NEW DIMENSION

The crowns of the trees are closing over me as I walk into the shade along a small pathway. The air is damp, and the smell of moss dominates. The huge trees are standing close to each other, and the path becomes narrower. The fallen leaves are crunching under my feet, and the light is swallowed by the shadows and loses its power. The forest is just on the other side of Luke's Kindergarten and surrounds the southern part of the city.

I sit on the ground, supporting my back against an old, winding, tall tree. It could be over a hundred years old. Roots are hanging from the branches all the way down the dark red trunk. My body is relaxed, and I breathe slowly.

"Angela."

It's Thomas's voice. I look around, but he is not anywhere to be seen. It's just me, the trees, and a ladybird that has just landed on my right knee.

"Angela," the voice is just as clear as if he were standing right next to me. I close my eyes and try to focus on the voice, but it's gone, and everything is dark. All I can hear is my own voice in my head, and I'm not saying anything worth listening to. Sometimes, I can wish for something so badly that I nearly start to believe it is real.

I sit up with a start. Thomas is standing right in front of me.

"There you are," he is laughing, so his straight white teeth become visible. The clouds are drifting by behind him. He is wearing his blue tunic with the thin golden thread running from the shoulder down. It is like watching a memory in front of me, only more real.

The air is getting chilly, and I feel like I'm being lifted up at high speed. Suddenly, the clouds are all around me. I step forward out of the cloud, and there is Thomas right in front of me. He looks relaxed and keeps smiling as he extends his arm toward me. I reach for it but can't feel his hand. When I look down, all I see is an outline of my body lying on the ground like an empty shell.

"Angela," Thomas looks at me, his gaze is relaxed, and his hair hangs loosely around his face. "I'm here if you need me."

Suddenly, I feel like I'm falling, and Thomas fades away. Something got a grip on me and lifted me back up. Somehow, I can still feel my body resting against the tree trunk, and then again, not.

"I need you," I whisper and press my lips together. "What is happening to me?"

Thomas steps closer; it's all white around us and a bit cold. The sun is hanging right above, and clouds are drifting in between us now and again.

"At this moment, we are communicating on a high spiritual level; none of us knew exactly what would happen when we sent you back to Earth." He pauses and swallows. His eyes become darker and seem even deeper. Slowly, his chest moves up and down as he breathes.

"When we can communicate on this level, it is because you have opened your spirituality and clear-sightedness." He breathes calmly. Some of the white cloud surrounds his body, making it look like he is wearing plumage. As far as I can see, there are clouds lying as a carpet full of holes above the sky.

"That means that you can always reach me if you are connected to that place inside yourself."

I don't say anything because I have no idea which part of me he is talking about or how I did it.

Thomas is still standing completely calm in front of me. He looks real, and then again, it could be my mind playing tricks. The wind plays with his long hair and makes his blue tunic cling close to his masculine body. "You will most likely experience more situations similar to this one. Each time is a gift, and they will all carry something important with them."

"But I don't understand it; I don't know how it works?" My voice is a bit reproachful.

Thomas doesn't move; he somehow just floats in front of me. "Maybe not now, just wait, it will come. When you're ready, it will come. You don't have to do anything." He keeps smiling with so much confidence in me that it is hard not to believe him.

"But..." I hold back. It doesn't make any sense.

Thomas starts to walk across the cloud, and I follow. I can still sense my body; it is as if I'm floating next to him; how, I don't know.

"The best way I can explain it to you is that your soul has found a way to move itself through time and space."

I can't help laughing; that is so far out.

"Can you do it too?"

He shakes his head no and waves some of the cloud away from his face. His movements are so elegant, and his fingers are long and slender. "I have never experienced it like this before. I have only heard of it from books I have read."

"And how can we know that it will keep on working?"

A larger cloud drifts in front of us, and for a moment, we are engulfed. When I see Thomas again, it feels like he is looking right through me. "You can't."

I stop. "How will I ever succeed when everything is so damn unpredictable?"

Thomas keeps walking; everything here is so quiet that a single word can seem noisy. "The best you can do is to be present in the moment; you cannot change the past or the future."

"But I can make an impact on the future." I take a few long steps, so I am next to him and won't let my voice reveal the insecurity eating me up from inside.

"That you can. You can take responsibility, evolve, and go with the flow." He smiles at me. "You can also try to control and reason everything you do and look for excuses and explanations. But if you are not listening to your heart, you will never find the two missing people from the Ring."

Is he implying something? Maybe he knows that I went to see Luke? Isn't that a mother's right? I clench my teeth so hard that my jaws hurt and try to keep my focus on Thomas's words and not my thoughts. We continue over the cloud. Nobody else is to be seen. We are all alone.

"Angela, it's only you who knows what the right thing is to do. We only get glimpses that might help you and lead you in the right direction. But you are the one closest to the two, and we can't know for sure if they are the right ones before they arrive at In-Between, and we can test them."

There is a clump of cloud in front of me, and I kick it hard, so it dissolves.

"Even though you came to terms with your situation and the assignment before you left, you will still be challenged in the choices you have to make. Do you remember the record?"

I nod. "The illustration of how we move in circles but have the opportunity to get closer to ourselves through personal development. And the closer we get to the center of the record, the easier it is and the more enlightened we are."

Thomas looks at me and pulls a smile so that the fine lines around his eyes become a bit more visible. "Exactly, and every time we get a chance to move a groove closer to the middle and our self, the challenge will increase to make sure that we have learned the lesson in the groove before we can let go of it. Sometimes, it feels

THE RING

like a storm is building up full of challenges that we have already dealt with. Only this time, they come on even stronger." He pauses and looks at me. "If we stand firm, then we will move one notch closer to our own center."

"So, it's not that strange that I went to see Luke?"

"What do you think?"

I keep silent. I have never succeeded in making Thomas take responsibility for me or just hand me the perfect solution.

"But what if I can't make contact with you again?"

"Security is an illusion." He looks at me without blinking.

The cloud we are walking on slopes gently up and down. There is no one and nothing else around us, only the white clouds and sky above. I can still feel my body, hear my voice, and see the outline of myself, and at the same time, I can smell the forest and hear the wind play with the leaves in the tree if I focus on my body on Earth.

"The heart doesn't need security as long as it is full of trust. It's our ego that needs security. I can't promise you anything. How could I?" Thomas raises his arms to the sides and turns toward me. He reaches for my shoulder, but his hand goes right through me.

"But," he lifts his hand, "when we start to develop, we involve ourselves in everything we are going through. You have a unique possibility to work on your personal development while you are searching for the two missing people. And maybe that is also a part of the search." He smiles so that his blue eyes sparkle. "You still have forty days left before you have to return to In-Between. A lot can happen."

10
DANIEL

"Hey, is this seat taken?" A young man in his late twenties is standing next to me. He is tall and looks like someone who has spent a lot of time in the gym. His hair is dark, nearly black; it looks casually windblown, but I guess there's nothing casual about it.

I'm sitting in an internet café close to the woods. After talking to Thomas, I needed to do something more down-to-earth and tangible.

It is busy here, and quite a lot of young people are here, absorbed in cyberspace. The windows are covered with posters, and the few plants look like naked skeletons. I'm torn out of my thoughts and lift my gaze.

"I guess it's free." I look at the empty chair with the worn-out orange cover that hangs in frays with the foam rubber sticking out in numerous places.

He smiles, revealing a deep dimple in his cheek, and places a sporty shoulder bag against the chair. It has an image of an eagle printed on the front. I squint to see the image properly and look at the guy. He sits down without paying any more attention to me and turns on the screen. Without saying anything, I turn back to my screen, write "eagle and communication," and press *search*. Thousands of search results come up. It seems totally confusing.

I lean back and take a sip of the bottle of water I brought with me. It is lukewarm and tastes a bit dull. But I prefer it over the cold high-energy drinks they keep in a fridge next to the counter.

Thomas told me that Yoge once had a vision of a sea of flames, and Gabriel saw a glimpse of many circles merged into each other in different sizes, some almost see-through. And Thomas had heard the same sentence over and over again: "Every illusion is a veil that covers something that you are not ready to see."

There are plenty of illusions. Sometimes, I think that this assignment is an illusion too. Why can't I just die like everybody else? Bang, over and out. Maybe death is an illusion as well. I laugh internally, and a warm sensation rushes through me. Of all the things I can do, I would most like to go and see Luke again. Is that my selfish longing? I look at the words on the screen but don't read them. Luke's smile, the way he walks. If only I had reached out for him or at least said something when he walked past me at the parking space. If only I could hold him tight one last time and tell him that everything is okay and I'm fine. It stings in my chest, and even though I try to convince myself that I have come to terms with my decision, it doesn't diminish the feeling of guilt. The guy opposite me rattles with a bag of wine gums and downs his cola in one swallow. He is pale, and it doesn't look like he sees the light of day a lot. I move forward on the chair and try to concentrate on my own business.

"Do you know how to get this to work?" The guy with dark hair next to me leans over and points at my screen. The way he pronounces the words is exquisite—like he lives abroad and is trying hard to speak correctly. He has a pointed nose and a scar right under his left eye that looks like a tear that has burned into the skin. I blink a few times; it seems so familiar.

I clear my throat and lift my head a bit, "I just clicked, and it started."

I look back at my screen and type, "how to find missing people." 1.100.000 results come up in 0.62 seconds. I have to narrow my search a bit, but right now, I can't concentrate and type, "Andreas Joseph Lancaster." A link to his Facebook profile appears at the top of the page, and I click on it. Nothing new there; he never posted anything personal.

It's getting dark outside, and the light that finds a way through the gaps in between the posters has a blue tinge. People are walking by the internet café in a confusing continuous mass. I'm getting tired and must admit that I'm no longer used to all the noise and people around me. It's like the surroundings are a valve where my energy leaks out. The time is almost five in the afternoon, and I better find a place where I can stay for the night.

"My name is Daniel..." the young guy with spiky black hair reaches his hand forward and smiles. He has a nice charisma without being a wimp.

"Ev... Angela," I smile a bit stiffly and let my hand slide into his warm, soft hand.

"Are you from around here?" He keeps looking at me and leans closer toward me.

I lean back in the chair, making it creak. My gaze rests on him, but my focus is behind him, where the traffic is like at a train station where young people come and go to and from the screens.

"I'm sorry. I should leave you be. It's just that I think you are beautiful."

I look at him and struggle not to react, but I fail and get annoyed with myself. My mouth gives in, and I smile as I sit up straight and try to pretend to be relaxed. Blood is rushing to my face, and I look at the keyboard.

"Have you eaten?" He leans self-confidently back in the chair. "Because I know a really great place just around the corner if you care to join me."

Is he hitting on me? If only he knew! Before I get to finish the thought, I surprise myself. "Well, why not?" Our eyes meet, and the temperature in my body rises a few degrees.

"Whenever you're ready, I'm ready too." Daniel zips up his white windbreaker, throws his bag on his shoulder so the eagle becomes visible, and pushes the chair under the table.

I guess I better get to know some people here. It might as well be Daniel as anyone else, I convincingly tell myself.

We leave the café, and, to my surprise, it is still light outside. Even though the streets are full of people, it is easier to breathe. The noise from the cars passing makes it impossible to have a conversation. That will give me time to figure out my next move, I think. Because we only need to walk three houses before he stops.

Daniel is standing in the doorway of a massive dark wooden door, holding it for me. As I pass him, a predominant wine-red color in the ceiling meets me. Several chandeliers with winding arms hang randomly and lighten up the room in a scattered sleazy way. The walls are dark brown and full of postcards from all around the world. A rug with a chaotic pattern in red, black, and golden colors is on the floor from wall to wall. I enter and can't help feeling like I'm walking into a hidden gem that you have to know exists to find and is not marked on a treasure map.

A small plump woman with a creased apron comes rushing to the door and greets us with open arms. She gets on her toes and reaches for Daniel, who politely bows and embraces her.

"And who is the beautiful woman you have brought here today, my darling?" She lets go of Daniel and pats him lovingly on the stomach.

He smiles at her and holds his hand toward me. "This is Angela."

"Angela." She puts her hands on my cheeks and shakes them with loving care. "You need some of Mama's good food. Come here and sit down."

There are only seven tables in the restaurant. She reaches for Daniel's hand, "Come, come." At the back of the room is a table where the wall is curved and makes a small oasis around the table. Two of the chairs have their backs toward the curved white wall, where you have a view of the whole restaurant. On the other side of the table are two chairs with their backs to the rest of the restaurant.

Daniel walks in front of me, and I follow. We are the only guest here, but most of the tables have a handwritten note saying *reserved* written on a folded cardboard sign sitting on a napkin. I look at my watch without anyone noticing it; it is only a quarter past five. The chairs are covered with velour in an awful olive-green color that doesn't match anything else in the décor. Daniel pulls out the chair for me with a firm grip, and I sit down with an acknowledging look.

I can't help aligning the cutlery a bit; it looks like someone just threw it on the table in a random way. At the same time, I have an eye on Daniel. He reaches for the water carafe and pours water in my glass. Music starts playing, and the woman begins to dance around the kitchen door, keeping an eye on us.

"Do you often invite women out for dinner?" I lean forward, resting my elbows on the table.

"Maybe..." he smiles. He is sitting opposite me with his back to the restaurant.

I can't help smiling and cast my hair to the side. It takes some time to get used to having this long hair. Why is he so mysterious? I'm fed up with men trying to make themself interesting by having secrets. Andreas was like that too.

"Why do you have an eagle on your bag?" I throw a glance at his bag that is sitting under the table.

He leans over the table, moves the candlestick a bit, and whispers, "I believe it is showing me the way."

Is he making fun of me? I lean back and reach for the water but don't get to drink before he continues.

"No, just kidding. I just like it." He keeps looking at me and pulls a smile.

I move a bit on the chair so that I can see the restaurant. Two women have just walked in and sat down at the first table. Then I look back at Daniel, determined to find out if I can trust him.

"So, you think that everything is coincidental?" Our eyes meet, and I fold the napkin a few times, just to keep my hands occupied.

"Did I say that?" He keeps on smiling at me. "No, sorry, I'll be nice." He bursts out laughing. "I don't know. What about you?"

I clear my throat and look at the ceiling. I have to be careful and, at the same time, try to find out more about Daniel. If only I had a manual telling me how to find the two missing persons in the Ring. I honestly don't know what I'm looking for, and this seems like the worst start of a date.

"I believe that there is a reason for everything." Did I really say that? I cringe in my boots. "Well, maybe there is also life after death." I smile a bit superciliously and lift my chin.

The mouthful of water he just drank is nearly choking him.

"I'm sorry," he dries his mouth carefully. "Life after death… that wasn't what I was thinking about." He winks at me and is struggling not to laugh. I maintain eye contact like a hunter who won't let go of his prey.

"Here you are." It's the woman from before. She is carrying two huge platters with the most delicate delicacies: fruit, greens, bread, fish, meat, and a small bowl of dressings in different colors. I am wide-eyed. The food doesn't align with the impression I got from the surroundings.

She begins to present the food and doesn't pause. It is hard for me to concentrate, and her words become sounds that don't make sense to me. Now and again, she pats me on the shoulder, and I reply with a smile.

"Eat now and let me know if there is anything else you need."

"Thank you; it looks delicious," I stammer.

Daniel gives her hand a squeeze and winks at her.

"An afterlife…" He looks at me with a sparkle in his nearly black eyes. "Why are you interested in that? Isn't it better to be here right now?" He raises his glass of water and awaits that I do the same.

There is a sensation of kindness around him as he sits there waiting for me while he looks at me.

I put down my knife and fork and reach for the glass.

"Cheers to the past, present, and future, whatever it may bring…." Daniel smiles at me and is not affected by my silence. We touch glasses.

Now, it's my opportunity to say something. But I have no idea where to start. I feel like I'm aiming at a target that I'm not sure where it is.

"Afterlife," I repeat, "It is just something that occupies my thoughts at the moment." I turn my head away and cough. I certainly did cut right to the chase. If someone had begun a date like this with me, I would have left already, thinking they were a lunatic.

"I find you very interesting," he says as if it were the most natural thing in the world to say. "There is something about you I have never seen in a woman before."

Quickly, I grab a strawberry and put it in my mouth. The taste of summer fills me. Right now, I feel trapped between two worlds. In one way, I'm here and so close to my own life that I can touch it, just in a different disguise. In another way, I need to find the two missing people in the Ring, which requires my focused attention to the task.

An older married couple enters the restaurant. The woman speaks with a loud voice so that the kitchen people have no doubt that she has arrived. They walk toward us and sit down at the table in the middle of the restaurant.

"We are having the usual," the woman is still standing with her overcoat and waves dismissively with her hand when the small lady tries to hand her the menu card.

"Would you care for a glass of wine?" Daniel is sitting relaxed, looking at me. He doesn't seem to be in a hurry. Maybe he has already achieved what he wanted in this life. But he is so young. I keep studying him as I eat another strawberry.

"Yes, please," I grab the bowl with strawberries and, in a jiffy, empty it onto my plate.

The small woman has escaped the married couple and is heading for us. A few brown curls are hanging loose under her scarf. She has a big smile and pats Daniel on the shoulder. "Well, it looks like your girlfriend likes my cooking." She looks at me, and I look a bit embarrassed at my plate, which is empty.

"It is impossible to go wrong with your cooking." Daniel reaches for the empty bowl. "We better get a refill."

I shake my head and hold my hands dismissively in front of me. "Not for me...."

A smaller group enters the restaurant, and the little woman disappears with the empty bowl.

"Can you recommend a nice hotel close by?" On the one hand, I would like to get to know Daniel better, but on the other hand, I'm not sure I'm ready and prepared for my assignment yet.

"Yes, I know a lot of places. But the very best place to sleep is at my castle."

"I just need a hotel." I put the last strawberry in my mouth and pretend not to have heard his comment. "I need to move on tomorrow."

"Always on the move; is there something you need to do?"

"Well, yes... I have an appointment with some other people." I look around the restaurant. The woman from before has finally settled down and has mixed all the small dishes on her plate into one big pile. She shovels the food in her mouth without looking at it.

"Here, take this; have you tasted it?" Daniel passes a teaspoon toward me with something bright red on it; it looks like grains with a sticky jelly on top.

I furrow my brow and pull my face into an evasive expression.

He holds the teaspoon right in front of me and just waits for me to gather the courage to taste it. He doesn't say anything and leaves it up to me.

Is there a reason that it's Daniel I bumped into and not someone else? Is it really like Thomas once told me that when I evolve, I will automatically attract a different kind of person than I used to? People who will challenge me in a new and different way.

I let my lips slide apart, and a fresh taste spreads in my mouth, followed by a sweet scent with a bit of a hot aftertaste. Daniel is still sitting relaxed. It is nice that he doesn't need to talk all the time—that he can enjoy the silence too.

I have always been fascinated by his type, he is actually really nice, and I must confess that I am skeptical. His kind has never even noticed me before. Somehow, I told myself his type was out of my league.

"What is it?" I lick my mouth.

Daniel raises his eyebrows up and down a few times. "It is a secret of the house."

The hand on my watch catches my attention. It is almost seven o'clock. I have to decide. Do I stay and get to know Daniel a bit better, or do I leave? I place my knife and fork side by side on the plate to indicate that I'm done. A yawn is pressing from inside, but I manage to swallow it.

"Shall we leave?" Daniel reaches for my hand. "As I said, you are most welcome to spend the night at my castle. And if you insist, you can even sleep next to me...." He sends me a sly smile.

I can't figure out if he is pulling my leg, and I try to laugh a bit awkwardly just to stay in the conversation. "Well, yes, I guess...." I run my hand up and down my leg so that it gets all warm. My time in In-Between has dimmed my sharp-edged mind. Daniel is looking at me, just waiting for me to make up my mind. The pause feels so long that I feel like I'm having an internal time-out.

"Come on," Daniel gets up, walks behind me, pulls out my chair, and hands me my jacket. On the way out, he goes to see the small plump lady and exchanges a few words. She smiles and gives him a big hug. I can't hear what they are saying even though I try.

The restaurant is completely full now, and during the evening, people have been turned away at the door. A young couple is waiting in the doorway, hoping to get our table when we leave.

Daniel comes back over, "So, what have you decided?" He reaches for his sporty windbreaker.

"I haven't decided yet." Am I wasting my chance here? Maybe I should just go with him? If I want to find out more about Daniel, I better get back in the saddle. I look over at the small lady and smile, "Thank you for the delicious food."

"You are always welcome," she smiles back and squeezes my arm.

Outside, the rain is pouring down, and the sound from tires against the wet road surface nearly drowns out my thoughts.

There is a pull on my arm. "Come on before you get completely soaked."

"But…" Maybe I should just try to go with the flow—not decide everything up front and just take things as they come. "I have a car…."

"So do I." Daniel puts his arm around my shoulders. My whole body is tense.

"But…" I try to slow down, but Daniel keeps going at his steady pace and pulls me with him.

"EVA!"

I stop and turn around. On the other side of the street stands a woman waving her arm. I don't know her, or do I?

"Eva, I thought your name was Angela?" Daniel turns his head toward me and pulls a face.

"Yes, yes, it is. I was just a bit surprised." I try to smile, but it comes out all fake.

Daniel lets go of me. I step out on the street and walk over toward the woman through a wall of rain. It's dark, and I can only see her vaguely in the ray of light. She takes her arm down and waves dismissively to me. She is fit, her mid-length wet hair is plastered to her head, and her eyes are blank.

"I'm so sorry. I thought you were someone else. You remind me of someone I used to know. The way you walk...." She shrugs and steps back and is about to turn around.

The raindrops make a constant stream of water running down my face. I blink a few times to see a bit better. My sleeve scratches against my cheek when I try to dry my face. In front of me on the pavement, totally soaked and not changed at all, *it is Lucy!*

I stop and stare at her. My coat clings to my body, and hair encases my face. My old friend Lucy, who I saw last time in In-between. Back then, the meeting was just as surprising.

She turns around and walks away from me.

"Excuse me," I call while running after her. My boot lands in a puddle, and the intensely cold water seeps through the sole. I guess I calculated the distance with my old stride length. "Excuse me...." My voice drowns in the rain.

She slows down and turns around. We are standing in front of each other. She looks serious and holds her hand over her mouth as she looks at me.

"I'm so sorry, the person I got you mixed up with is dead. I really don't know what I was thinking." She backs away from me and starts to fumble with her red and white dotted umbrella while the raindrops pour down her face, making her eyes look even more blank. I look at her with an urge.

The sound of footsteps behind me gets louder, and I can see Daniel from the corner of my eye. He is coming toward us. My gaze is fixed. "How are you?"

She laughs and furrows her forehead. "Do we know each other after all?"

"Hey, I'm Daniel, and this is Angela, right?" He steps up by my side and wipes his hand on his trousers before offering it to Lucy.

Cars are passing behind us, splashing rainwater onto the sidewalk. I stand completely still, not caring about the rain.

Then I nod and smile at Daniel. "You're right; my name is Angela."

Lucy looks me straight in the eyes. "You really do seem familiar.

I don't know, it's crazy, but there is something about you...." She shakes her head in wonder.

I don't say anything, and my lips are sealed. The words are queueing up, ready to get out, but the exit is closed, which is how it should be.

"Shall we move on?" Daniel looks at me, "Or is there anything else you need to do?"

"Well, I'm cold," Lucy smiles and shakes her shoulders a bit. She has such mild positive energy around her. I always get in a good mood when I'm with her.

"Do you live around here?" I whisper, and the words are nearly wiped out by the rain. But Lucy catches the question and nods slowly.

"Yes, I live here." Then, she turns around and disappears in the rain.

11
THE MESSAGE

My legs start to shake, and I tighten the grip on my toothbrush. The right leg takes the lead, and I try to control the other. I fail. I'm in a bathroom at Daniel's place. It is small. There is only space for a sink and a toilet. The old mirror in front of me reveals bags under my bloodshot eyes. The walls are decorated with small brown rough stones. It looks expensive. I can hear the sound of a toilet flushing upstairs. Daniel convinced me to come with him, and since I had no hotel and my clothes were all wet, it seemed like the best option at the moment. We drove for half an hour out of the city and into a more country-like area with no streetlights or houses to be seen. I left my car in the city and will deal with that later. My eyes close, and I bend my knees a bit to make them relax. This is most likely a reaction to the transition from In-Between to Earth.

A sting of pain starts to drill into both my wrists. My hand gives in, and the toothbrush falls to the floor. Slowly, my arms begin to lift to the side, and I sense the smell of dust and heat. It doesn't make any sense. I try to open my eyes, but nothing happens. It is like I'm beginning to see even though my eyes are still shut. I'm standing on a hill and in front of me is a small village. Something tightens around my ankles, and I look down. They are tied with a thick rope. I'm no longer inside my own body but in a man's body that is nearly naked. Men, women, and children are passing by at the base of the hill. Some stop and look at me, and others don't even notice that I'm there. The houses in the small village are made of clay, and they form a defined circle. Around the village are scorched fields.

The pain in my hands is increasing, and I look to the right. Thick nails are drilled through my wrists, and blood is dripping off them. The sun hangs, burning red on the horizon; the air is humid, and sweat runs from my eyebrows into my eyes. It stings and distracts my attention away from the pain in my wrists.

I turn my head to the left. A bit up the hill next to me is a wooden cross. A man in his mid-thirties hangs on the cross. And behind him is another man. I squint; the man closest to me is unconscious.

Michael, your name is Michael. The voice is resounding clear in my head.

Nonsense, Michael who? What am I doing on a cross?

Michael, your name is Michael.

That is enough; go away voice, I shout inside myself, but it doesn't help at all. Up until now, I have been the observer to my visions. Now, I am the main character. Powerlessness fills me. My legs shake, and the pain stings even more from the wrists through the whole body. I'm conscious but have lost control over my body. I can't sense the bathroom anymore. I'm here on the hill hanging on a huge wooden cross. I look over at the man by my side. His head hangs loose on his shoulder, and his long golden-brown hair is held back by a piece of fabric tied around his head. There is a divine light around him, and he looks so innocent as he hangs on the cross. He is only wearing a light cloth around his hips; the rest of his muscular body is naked.

The crowd slowly thins out in front of us. A dog lumbers by, and goats are bleating. They walk freely. Kids are running around playing, but they ignore us. Somehow, I feel calm. I know I'm leaving, but I also know I have a strong connection to the man beside me. We have talked about this moment many times in the past, knowing that it was a question of time before the people who felt threatened by us wanted to punish us. We have divided our assignments.

Where does the inner calmness come from? What is it I need to do?

I look at the man again. His body is weak and is only held by the ropes around his neck, hands, and feet. The blood has stopped dripping from his wrists.

The sun sets in a gradual transition, and darkness takes over. The village people disappear into their clay cottages, and the space in front of us is empty. We are alone on our crosses. The air is still warm, intense, and full of the smell of spices. I can hear voices in the dark but see no one.

A glow of light from a torch appears behind one of the cottages. Slowly, a small group of women gathers at the base of the hill. They start to crawl toward us without saying anything. When they reach us, they split up between us and begin to loosen the ropes on our ankles, hands, and necks. I look at the man by my side; he is still unconscious.

Slowly, I fall into the arms of the women. There are four of them. I fight to keep my eyes open, but my body feels numb. They carry me on their shoulders to a small cabin hidden a bit behind a big tree. Inside the cabin is a vague sparkle from the flames in the fireplace. The space is warm and tiny. They place me on my back on a bunk, and I close my eyes.

"The time is now," a voice in my head says. "You know what to do."

The woman puts warm rags on my wounds and washes my face. I breathe calmly. Everything is as it should be.

A shiver runs through my body, and I hit the cold stone floor. My eyes are still closed, and I crouch into a fetal position. It is nearly impossible to move, and I have no sense of time. I'm back in the bathroom at Daniel's place—back in my own body. The heat is gone, and so is the dust, the women, and the stinging pain. I rub my wrists and wheeze while I clasp my hands on my chest, trying to get rid of the feeling of dust in my lungs. I have to do something. I can't just lie here. I have to pull myself together and get on my feet. But I don't move an inch. There is nothing in my body that responds to my commands right now.

"Angela!" There is a soft knock on the door.

"Yeah…" the words only just make it out of my mouth. "Come on in," I answer, but no sound comes out. Another knock.

"Are you alright, Angela?" It is Daniel's voice.

The door creaks a bit, and I feel Daniel's hand on my hip.

"What happened? Come, let me help you up." He wipes his hand over my sweaty hair and takes a firm grip around my shoulders. I try to open my eyes, but they are as heavy as lead. My whole body is limp.

"We better get you into bed. Can you stand?" Daniel lifts me. My legs are hanging loose from my body. I can't feel or control them. I have no energy and only get glimpses of where we are going —down a long corridor with hardly any furniture. On the walls are massive paintings with dramatic illustrations. Sweat keeps running from my face, and my whole body is sore.

We enter a large room. Even though the ceiling is high, it feels constraining. I gasp for air. "Can you open a window, please?" I whisper and manage to lift my eyelids and make eye contact with Daniel.

There is a large bed with a view over the city in the distance. I collapse. Daniel grabs a remote control and presses it softly. A window opens a bit, and fresh air hits my face. I pant and lie down with his hands supporting me.

He sits down next to me and pulls a soft brown blanket around me like a pupa. "Who are you, Angela?"

12
THE TEMPTATION

"What time is it?" I sit up and look around. The room is almost dark, and there is not much to see. Daniel is lying on a thin mattress on the floor. He is still dressed and fast asleep. It is night, and the lights from the city lay like a blanket on the horizon. The big windows are facing a terrace, and there are no other houses to be seen.

I pull my legs up under me and rub my eyes. The blanket rests heavily on my body. My thoughts begin to wander around Thomas. The other day when I saw him, he was here and then gone again. Was it something I said or did? If only I knew how to contact him again.

I reach for the Skycon in my pocket. There is no reason to think that it can't come back to life. Slowly, I turn it between my fingers while observing it. Daniel moves a bit, and quickly I return it to my pocket. He turns on his back, his mouth is slightly open, and his breathing is heavy. The bed is placed opposite the windows. The decor is very sparse, and the furniture nearly shouts at each other over the polished wooden floor. On the right, I can just make out a door, partially open to what could be a bathroom.

THE RING

My head spins a bit, and I push the blanket aside and let my legs tumble over the side of the bed. A massive swelling on my leg appears and reminds me of the turbulent time in the bathroom last night. Something is conflicting about this place. In a way, everything looks new, but the sensation here is old, very old.

The floor gives way and creaks a bit as I get up. Daniel doesn't move. Slowly, I walk toward the large glass section, put my hand on it, and gently push the door open. The air is perfectly fresh, as if all the old has been wiped away by the rain and darkness of the night. It's chilly. I reach for Daniel's sweater on the chair by the door and step into my boots without zipping them. Then I grab my trousers from the floor. I disappear in the sweater, and it covers my hips and hides my hands.

The terrace is large, and on the right, an oval swimming pool is surrounded by palm trees and garden furniture looking a bit Zen-like. The light is on, and it looks inviting. There are clay pots with tall, thin trees all around. I step onto the terrace and walk toward a fence that runs all around the premises. In front of me, further down the hill, is the city. There are still no other houses around here to be seen, only trees and bushes. The trees are filled with small, yellow flowers.

Silently, I step closer to the fence. It is made of iron, and the rods twist in an elegant pattern like a flower stalk. I rest my hand on the railing. The experience from last night comes back in brief glimpses, but I cannot sense the place as I could yesterday. It was so real. If only I understood a little more. *Michael*, I do not know who *Michael* is. And I have not heard of anyone in the Bible with that name.

The only thing I can relate the experience to is the dream I had in In-Between, where I first experienced the Ring. It was also so real and yet incomprehensible, well, right up until it all made sense when I sat with Thomas, Gabriel, Shiva, and Yoge in the octagonal room. Maybe this will make sense one day too.

I rest my chin in my hands and lean a little forward. It's so quiet here. The city sleeps, but the universe does not.

Maybe there's a meaning to me being here with Daniel. I push away from the railing and walk along the curvature toward the swimming pool, where fine beach sand has been spread out in an even layer. On the opposite side, several large palm trees sway; below them are deck chairs and a table.

I've been back on Earth for two days. There are forty days left. A voice in my head tries to convince me to pull myself together and move on—be a little more efficient, but I do not bother to listen to it. I shake my head and think of Lucy. It has not quite dawned on me that I have met her again. What made her recognize me? Could it be something about my appearance? Or maybe it is true that the eyes are a mirror of the soul, and it doesn't matter whether I am Eva or Angela? I take a deep breath and hide my face in my hands, thinking about the moments we have had together—all the times we have doubled up with laughter at something that no one else could see the fun in. And Luke, if only I could be present with him. There are far too many times where I have been absent or have prioritized work before him. If only I could fall into my old life, just for a short while.

"How are you feeling?" It's Daniel's voice. I let my hands slide down from my face and straighten up a bit before turning around, trying to look relaxed.

"Fine."

He comes right up to me and gently puts his hands around my shoulders. He is wearing jeans, worn in the right places, and a pink, body-hugging knitted sweater.

"Nice view, right?" I nod, nothing blocks the view as far as I can see, and it gives me the feeling of being a part of it all.

"It must be expensive to live here." I turn a little, so I'm facing him. He looks tired, and his body is not as muscular as I remember it. "What do you do workwise?" Now, I better get a head start and get some information out of him.

"Nothing," he says.

Great start. I kick lightly at a rock on the ground. If I keep quiet, maybe he will say a bit more.

He smiles and nods slowly. His voice is slightly rusty, and he clears his throat. "Sorry, I'm not fully awake yet." He's signaling for us to walk. "I've worked a lot before, but I got sick and had to stop. It dawned on me that there is another way to live your life."

We walk through a gate into the swimming pool area. As we enter, the light in the pool and under the big palm trees fades up. His body is relaxed, and he speaks more openly and honestly than last night. It is as if the words no longer have to go through a filter.

"I was identified with my work and was good at it. It was my one and only, a kick twenty-four hours a day where I was available."

I grit my teeth. He might as well be talking about me when I was alive.

We walk in the fine sand along the pool edge toward two sun loungers.

"But one day, when I was on my way home from a business dinner, I stopped on the street. I had only had water to drink because I had to go home and continue work. Suddenly, I started throwing up on the sidewalk. At that moment, for the first time in a long time, I felt my body. It rebelled against my lifestyle." He stops and reaches out for my hand. "I was lucky… if I had not understood the lesson then, it is not certain that I would be here today." He takes my hand and squeezes it. I step a bit to the side, let go of his hand, and hold my breath. Has he seen through me?

Daniel walks on as he speaks. I stand as if frozen solid.

"I had a choice," his voice dies down a bit, "I could continue my lifestyle and ignore my body or stop and take responsibility." He shrugs. "The choice was not difficult to make, but hard to implement."

I force myself to move and get up by his side again. Imagine if I had stopped in time and had listened to myself. Maybe I would not be here now as Angela. I had goals, ambitions, and I thought I was indispensable. Would I ever have woken up if I had not been in the plane crash?

There is a wooden chest next to the deck chairs. Daniel opens it and picks up two thick white cushions. "Here, Princess, would you like to sit down?"

The water in the pool is smooth as a mirror. A fallen leaf breaks the surface, and several small insects whiz from side to side. Daniel sits down and stretches his legs comfortably forward.

"I knew there had to be a bigger shift, and it was not enough to work fewer hours or take some time off. It would only be a matter of time before I would be back in my old pattern." He leans back and braids his hands behind his neck. The spotlight pointing up at the large palm leaves touches one side of his face, leaving the other dark. "It was tempting just to keep going; I got a lot of recognition." He looks at me and sighs. "I stopped working. It's the best thing I've ever done."

"But not everyone has that opportunity." My voice is sharp and a bit judgmental. I move my deck chair a little away from Daniel, so there is more distance between us, and sit down with my back quite straight. I have a burning sensation in my stomach but try to drown it out with my words.

Daniel raises his hands repulsively, "It was not an attack on you." He leans forward toward me. I lean back correspondingly.

Only now do I see that it actually is a castle that Daniel lives in. I just thought he was trying to be jaunty. It is built of light bricks, which are broken in several places. There are three floors; the windows on the first floor are white-rimmed with small bars, and there are small statues above the door. On both sides, there is a little wing that goes up into a tower. The whole castle is lit up very gently so that it appears elegant.

Daniel looks at me hesitantly, and when I say nothing, he continues: "Now, I can see that I tried to live up to my parents' expectations through my work. It was not my longing; it was theirs I had taken over, and I longed for their acceptance."

His otherwise calm facial expression crackles and a vulnerability begins to shine through.

"But…" I frown a little. "Why were you at the internet café? You do not exactly look like you are missing out on anything."

"Well, sometimes, I would like to be able to check emails at home, but I have chosen not to have an internet connection." He laughs heartily, but the seriousness quickly chases his laughter away. "Sorry, there is still a lot I am missing, but if you're thinking about money, I have earned my share." He closes off a bit with his tone of voice, and the fine vulnerability is packed away again. In a quick move, he comes over to my deck chair and sits right next to me. Before I have time to react, I feel his soft hand against my cheek. "Why don't we go back to bed?"

The sound of a phone ringing breaks in and saves me.

"Sorry, I have to take it." Daniel pulls his hand away and disappears through the gate heading for the bedroom.

I'm alone again. My body is tired, and my heart is beating slowly. I sink even deeper into Daniel's sweater and wrap it firmly around me. He makes me feel alive again, even though I know it's on borrowed time.

His sweater exudes man. I inhale the smell, smile, and feel like a teenager stealing a bit of the forbidden scent. Right now, I wish I could take a timeout and just enjoy the moment with Daniel without thinking about the task or that I must be back in forty days. A rush of heat travels through my body. I look over my shoulder. Daniel is completely absorbed in the phone call and stands with his back to me.

I walk to the swimming pool, kneel in the sand, and draw a cross with my index finger. From the intersection, I draw a line and write Michael. I was part of the experience on the cross, whereas I was a spectator to the young woman being rescued by the older woman and to the couple where the woman died. I rest my hand on my knee. The words come back to me. *I do not know who you are, but I know you need help.* Those are Jane's words, but exactly the same words, the older woman with crooked eyes said as well. I look up. My heart beats fast. Daniel's scars are eerily reminiscent of the older woman's scars. I write D in the sand, draw a line, and write J.

"What are you doing? It looks exciting…."

It makes me twitch. I run my hand hectically across the sand and blur out the words and lines.

"Nothing, absolutely nothing." I try to laugh a little superciliously. Daniel is standing right behind me.

He frowns and smiles as he leans forward. "What was it you drew?"

"Nothing!" I get up and want to step back but fall over the deck chair and sit down with a bump.

"Okay. But then tell me what's going on?" Daniel reaches out for my arm, teasing me a bit.

I look up at the castle and realize that I do not even know how to get out of here.

"I cannot." I put my hand in my pocket and clasp it around the Skycon. "I have to go now." I push him lightly as I get up and try to get past.

"Do you always go when things are slipping out of your control?" Daniel politely steps to the side with a slight bow.

"I have to pick up my car."

Daniel shakes his head.

"You do not get to decide what I do." My voice is about to crack, but I manage to control it and step back toward the gate away from the pool area.

"It is not necessary." Daniel follows me and lifts his clenched fist toward me. Glimpses of the couple who were arguing break into my sight. I walk quickly through the gate and toward the door into the bedroom. Have I been wrong about him? Is he not as nice as he indicated?

He reaches out for me, "Angela."

I can feel his other hand around my arm. I stare at his fist. The seconds feels like minutes. Slowly, he turns his hand and opens it. I stare at it, and my shoulders sink. He holds my car key in his hand.

"I permitted myself to have your car picked up, and it is parked right outside. You can go whenever you want." He holds his hand open, smiles, and awaits my decision. "You can also stay and go in the morning when the sun comes up."

I bite my teeth together and swallow once, looking up to the black sky where stars are shining. I must not lose myself. Daniel stands quietly by my side.

"As I see it, it is either a cold car or a warm bed." He blinks at me. "I have chosen." Then he lets go of my arm, puts the car keys in my hand, and goes into the bedroom. I turn the keys in my hand and look for Daniel. He has disappeared into the darkness.

I crawl out of Daniel's sweater, pull my pants off, and I hurry down under the duvet to Daniel. His body is warm, and I slide into his strong arms.

13

A DAY MORE OR LESS

It's been so long since I've had eggs and bacon. The slightly salty taste fills my mouth, and I run the tip of my tongue over my lips. Ketchup, it's always great. I reach out and shake the bottle before pouring it out on the plate. Daniel sits across from me in his workout clothes. If I had just been alive, I would have run away with him. Why do I have to meet him now that I'm half dead? Does it have something to do with me being in better touch with my feminine side, which Annabel helped me open up to?

"Would you like some more?" Daniel hands the basket of freshly baked bread over to me, interrupting my flow of thoughts.

I grab a piece. The bread is still warm, and the butter melts as I run the knife over it. The smell takes me to my great-grandmother's kitchen in her large, old house, which exuded security and presence. The space is bright and open with large windows from floor to ceiling, and all the furniture is made of wood. A large island is in the center of the kitchen with three white origami lamps hanging down from the ceiling above it. The floor is tiled in large black and white squares. It's not my style, but it's definitely expensive. In the distance, I can faintly hear the sound of a vacuum cleaner coming from upstairs.

"It's my maid…." Daniel smiles at me and nods in the direction of the sound.

"Not bad." I cannot hide a smile. My gaze wanders around the kitchen. It is clean and tidy; there is nothing to put your finger on.

"She is here every day to cook and clean."

I take a sip of the freshly squeezed vegetable juice and cough a bit. "What is it made of?"

Daniel laughs, "It's my favorite, but it can be a little harsh if you're not used to that kind of juice."

I cannot pretend that I am.

"It's beetroot, white cabbage, apple, carrots, orange, and some ginger." He takes a big sip from his glass. "It prolongs life expectancy by many years."

Most of all, I want to throw myself back in the chair and just enjoy the moment. Instead, I straighten up. "I'd better get going." My chair gives off a slight squeal as I eagerly push it back.

"You are welcome to stay. I don't have any plans today." Daniel reaches for the freshly baked bread. His dark hair has settled down, and the dimple in his chin is covered with stubble.

"I better not, but thanks; I have to move on." I fold the blue napkin and place it on the table.

"What is so important?" He gets up and comes toward me.

Was it not me who was to interrogate him? I try to laugh defiantly. "Don't get me wrong. I think you're really nice."

"Yes…" He raises his eyebrows and sends me a cunning smile.

"I'm just moving on."

"Come now, stay…." He puts his arms around me, and I do not resist. "For my sake," he whispers in my ear.

I am done doing things for the sake of others; that much I have learned in In-Between. I reluctantly shake my head. "Sorry, I have to move on."

I press my hand into my pocket and squeeze the Skycon. If I do not go now, I will blame myself for the rest of my life.

"I have an appointment in the city." I place my hands on his chest and avoid looking him in the eyes. His arms fall along his body. My toes are curled together in my boots, and inside me, I'm trying to control a fight between sense and emotions. Why is it so hard to leave, and why is it necessary to lie?

"It's your choice, Princess," he moves a strand of hair behind my ear and strokes my cheek. My stomach sinks.

I look down. What if Daniel is one of those in the Ring, and I just have not seen the whole picture yet? Is there not meaning to everything? This cannot be an exception. I start walking toward the hallway, which is an extension of the living room.

"Will I see you again?"

I stop abruptly and look at Daniel.

He bursts out laughing when he sees my facial expression. "Sorry, I didn't mean to put any pressure on you."

I try to get my face back into a natural expression, whatever that is. "I do not know exactly where I'll be for the next couple of weeks." If only I had a bag I could rummage through or a calendar that looked important. All I have is myself, and I feel a little awkward in my jeans and light blue knitted sweater. I would like to see him again. So, why am I not just saying that?

I step out into the hall. The ceiling is high, and the walls are white. To the right of the double door hangs a huge silver mirror with a complicated pattern in the silver frame. I can see that my body is tense, and the sound that resonates as I step on the stone floor makes me tighten up even more.

"You know where I live, and if you are in the neighborhood...." Daniel walks over to a small table where there is a pad of paper and a ballpoint pen. He writes down a number and hands it to me.

My heart is pounding.

"Thank you. I enjoyed it too." I reach for the pen, write my number on a piece of paper, and place it on the table without looking at him.

The fresh morning air hits me as we step out the front door. The courtyard is round, and in the middle, there are shrubs adorned with large pink flowers. Just as Daniel said, my car is parked on the right. It does not quite fit here. The scratches line up on the side, and the paint has peeled off in several places. We go down the stairs, side by side. I have no luggage and just need to get in the car, drive away, and get on with my task. The stones move and crackle as we walk toward my car. If I'm not mistaken, the car has been washed. We stop when we reach it. I extend my hand; he ignores it and kisses me on the cheek. Then I get in the car, slam the door, and roll down the window.

"Angela."

I look into Daniel's black eyes.

"If you're done with your appointment after lunch, I'd like to invite you out." He smiles at me, and small fine wrinkles appear around his eyes.

"Thank you. It's nice of you." I turn the key. "I'll call if I'm nearby."

The sound of the engine silences my voice.

"Thanks for now." He takes a step back and looks like a lone knight as he stands there in the courtyard in front of his castle.

I put the car in gear, and the wheels peel off the small stones as it starts. Now, I just need to get away, move on. Where to? I do not know. But one thing I do know is that Daniel can make me forget why I'm here.

14

A STICKLER FOR THE RULES

I have parked my car a bit away from the main road, on a small side road that leads further into the woods. *The forest path*, it said on a crooked sign on the main road. From here, I still have a view of the city. The fence next to the road is broken in several places, and random bits of rubbish are dumped along it. On the slope behind me are several conifers; most of their lower branches have withered in the sun.

I push the seat all the way back in the car and stretch my legs the best I can. If only I understood a little more; if only I were better prepared for the task. Right now, it would be great to talk to Thomas. I close my eyes. Nothing happens, then I straighten up and fold my hands in front of my chest—still nothing. I open my eyes again. Outside, an old plastic bag blows up in front of the car window and continues beyond the slope. I pull the Skycon out of my pocket, where it always lies and reminds me of my task. It balances between my thumb and forefinger while I stare at it. My body is still sore after the trip to Daniel's bathroom floor. I try to shake my shoulders a little, but it just provokes a spasm of pain in my neck.

"Just because you've been close to heaven doesn't prevent you from new challenges."

The Skycon falls between my legs, and I quickly look to the sides. The slope, the trees, and the car—it's all still here.

There, right in front of me, Thomas sits in a lotus position on a cloud. It is light around him, and no one else is to be seen. I can see him, but not with my normal vision because I can simultaneously see the car and my own body. The image of Thomas hovers in front of me like a hologram, and I see him from the point of view that somehow appears from another place.

I reach out my hand to touch him. Instead, it hits the steering wheel, and my fingers crack backward. The picture of Thomas disappears; now, I can only look out the windshield.

"Thomas," I whisper softly. "Are you there?" The heat flows from the center of my chest, and it feels like a hard shell that cracks open and lets a hot thick liquid seep out and spread in my body.

"Angela, I'm here."

It hurts painfully in my head and at the point between my eyebrows. I cannot see Thomas, only hear his voice. I fall back into the seat. My stomach is tensing, so I can barely breathe, and the material on the seat itches.

"What do you need?"

It's been a long time since anyone asked me that. I don't say anything; my mind is hunting for an answer, but nothing shows up. The scorched trees next to the car get blurry, and I try to blink.

"I do not understand what is happening, how I get in touch with you; what is it I have to do?"

Suddenly, the image of Thomas comes back, and the pain in my head subsides.

He gets up and starts walking across the clouds. The image hovers in front of me, and I reach out but cannot touch it.

"I don't know." His gait is light, and his face gentle. "But I know you're the only one who can figure it out." He smiles, and it starts buzzing in my body. "You have the opportunity to become your own expert. Explore it, play with it, see what happens. Only you can do it." The wind lifts his half-length hair and drops it in front of his face. He turns around and walks back into a cloud. "Maybe what you experience is possible for everyone. You are just the only one who has found out." He reappears, smiles, and says no more.

I reach out, turn on the engine, and turn the heat to maximum. One chill after another travels through my body.

"People live in anxiety and yearn for evidence. They play it safe in their comfort zones, and no one dares to stand out. Imagine if you had found a new path which no one else dared to see and recognize."

I sit completely still. My body starts to shiver, and I freeze even though I have put on my jacket. The heat from the car blows right into my face and down on my feet, but it doesn't help a bit. Thomas's words are so grand that I have a hard time taking them in. I try to keep them at a distance, not feeling the meaning of what he says.

"I think it's because I'm half dead that I can get in touch with you. It was not possible when I was alive." My voice is determined and leaves no doubt about my attitude.

Thomas keeps silent. He strolls across the cloud, which changes color depending on how much sunlight breaks through it.

"Don't you think?" I cross my arms and look out the side window. The wind shakes the treetops and sends several loose spruce needles toward the ground.

Thomas lets out a loud laugh, which resounds inside the car. I grit my teeth and try not to look at him.

"Beautiful soul, you judge yourself harshly."

Am I judging myself? I don't think so. That's just the way it is. I sit and stare a little blankly into the air.

"Remember how we talked about the part of us that always has an opinion about what is right or wrong? The part of your personality that always knows best and is ready to hit you in the head if you don't do as it wants?"

"Yes, thank you, I remember that." My tone of voice is a little annoyed, and I pull my legs up under me.

"We can name it," Thomas raises his head and speaks slowly and thoughtfully. "Then it's easier to get to know it."

I nod. "Be my guest; you can find a name...."

Thomas says nothing.

"Okay, so let's call it the stickler," I say reluctantly.

Thomas smiles, "The stickler is not easy to get rid of. Many people are identified with it and cannot separate from it. Remember that the stickler is like your mother's and father's voice from the past, a kind of sound recording. It never develops, and it always says the same thing, in the same way."

"Okay, sure." Now, it's getting interesting. I let go of the grip around my legs and lean forward so I can hear Thomas better.

"It is employed to help us survive, but it keeps us from living."

I skid around the seat to find a comfortable position but only succeed for a short time. The wind moves a ragged cardboard box up onto the radiator, and the clouds drift across the sky at a rapid pace. There is a storm building up around me as well as inside me.

Thomas walks along the edge of the cloud. The changing light from the sky makes his eyes even bluer. Now and again, the wind gets a hold of his tunic and lifts it up a bit. "Judging oneself and others is the greatest source of inner suffering and dissatisfaction. The stickler prevents you from living in the present." He takes a step to the side where the clouds are parked in the sky. "The stickler can make us feel wrong, less worthy, ungifted, doubt ourselves, yes, on the whole, it speaks down to us and rebukes us. It breaks us down slowly." He puts on his black coat and buttons it up. It looks cold up there.

"But what does it have to do with me?" I start to sit a little uneasily on the seat.

"A fair bit. Be aware that as long as it has control over you, it can make us do things that we, deep down, do not want to do. Or, for that matter, make us compromise with our longing and insight."

"But…" I try to interrupt, but Thomas lowers his hand and signals that I should wait. I hold back.

"The stickler can appear in many disguises, but his mission is always the same: to prevent us from evolving. Development is the silent death of the ego, and the stickler is a part of the ego." He falls still and looks at me. Then he turns around and continues over the cloud at a leisurely pace. "The ego rules over your personality, which consists of many smaller personalities, each of whom wants your attention." He stops, and the cloud disappears under his feet, but he walks quietly on. "If you get to know the personalities, begin to accept them and learn from them, then they will loosen their grip on you. If you try to ignore them and pretend they are not there, they will take control over you, unconsciously, of course." He looks directly at me. "They each have something they want to teach you; they are associated with pain from the past. As long as our personality is dominant, we cannot enter into our core, into our essence, and we are not free."

"But…" I try again and move forward in the seat.

Thomas smiles. "One moment, Angela." The wind keeps blowing in his face, but it doesn't seem to bother him. "The personality feels safe to all of us; that's what we know," Thomas continues. "And since the ego is afraid of losing ground, it will do anything to keep all your sub-personalities alive." He pauses. This time, I say nothing, just sit still and listen. "All development means less power to our ego and thereby to the stickler and all the other sub-personalities, the voices that speak to us inside our head."

I press my hand over my forehead. "It sounds logical, but also illogical." I sit back in the seat and start to fiddle with the buttons on the dashboard. "Now the voice in my head says it's nonsense," I bite my lower lip, and Thomas smiles at me. I know the voice is not right. "Thomas, now it says I'm pretty stupid if I believe that kind of nonsense." I blow up my cheeks and let go of the air again.

"It's got a hold on you." Thomas smiles so that his blue eyes sparkle. He reaches out and plays with a small cloud hanging next to him. I roll down the window, and a gust of fresh air hits my face.

"You said the stickler's words come from my father or mother, but what about society?" I open the car door with a quick jerk and try to avoid stepping on an old beer can as I get out. The vision of Thomas slides in front, and I cannot help but smile. I can see my reality and Thomas at the same time; that's clever.

"You are right. Society also has something to say, and religion too, very much so. There is a lot to deal with if you want to be free of your ego. The majority of people live so far from their essence—the pure place inside them where they just are. In that place, there are no games, only peace and love. But most people cannot even feel that they are not connected to their essence." Thomas turns around and stands right in front of me.

"Are you saying that our inner sub-personalities govern war, religion, and hatred?" I tilt my head sideways.

"It is not only the so-called negative emotions and actions that they control. They have control over all our emotions. No matter how we try to cover up pain or a failure, our defense mechanisms are controlled by the sub-personalities, and they help us survive." He stops and puts his hands on his chest. "When we cannot feel our longing, we leave the responsibility to others and listen to our sub-personalities. They live by our anxiety and repressed pain. We employ the sub-personalities to make sure that others do not galvanize our wounds. If we have experienced failure in childhood, we will either find a partner who confirms the failure by failing us or choose to live alone, making sure not to be let down again. We can also find a partner who we know will not let us down. But whatever we choose, we do it to cover up an old wound. We cannot choose freely."

I take a deep breath. No doubt, I chose Andreas because I felt comfortable with him, and I knew he would not leave me. And he let me be; he did not prick my wounds. But in the long run, it also got boring.

Thomas steps closer; the picture of him is hovering in the air right in front of me. Even though the wind is blowing hard, the image hangs completely still.

"A sub-personality can also be the one who always has a funny remark, is superior, or plays the victim. As long as we believe we are one with our thoughts and feelings, then we are identified with our personality." The small muscles around his eyes tighten. "Why do you think there are so many wars in the world, so much hatred and violence?" He keeps looking at me. "People have shares in emotions, religion, and things, solely to avoid taking responsibility and listening to themselves. We live out of fear and not love. We act on symptoms and never come close to the cause of the pain that we have hidden away."

The sound of a lone bird and the whistling of the wind in the trees break into Thomas's voice. I'm walking toward the edge, looking out over the city.

"If you're identified with a religion, an emotion, or another person, you'll feel hurt if others say something bad about them. But if you're not identified, you know it's not about you, and it is easier to let it go. To find out who we really are and what qualities we possess, we need the courage and the will to find the truth." He turns around and starts walking away from me, the sky framing him like the most beautiful painting I have ever seen.

"Let me get this straight." I raise my voice a bit. "The truth? Is there just one truth?" I kick the overturned fence posts and let my gaze wander off into the horizon.

Thomas says nothing. He turns around and just looks at me.

There's a knot in the pit of my stomach. "Come on…" I spread my arms and look up. "It's too far out, and I was just about to change my mind because you didn't say anything. Just to make it 'right.'"

Thomas nods. "We need to be alert at all times; it is like a virus, fast, and it often catches you off guard. Most of the time, we don't manage to register that our emotions control us." The wind picks up, and he narrows his eyes.

I stand completely still. My inner eye sees a row of falling domino pieces—one experience takes the next. When I was a child, I found that my father often had to show that he was better than me. Now, I can see that this is why I have felt less worthy and thought that others always knew better. It's my father's voice that one of my sub-personalities has embraced. Another often tells me that women are weak and less valuable than men. That was what my mother showed me by always giving in to my father. When I have stayed in relationships that didn't make me happy, it is because I have learned that pain equals love.

"You will probably see many links from your life experience to the way you act out, feel, and what you tell yourself, now that you are aware of them. But remember, there is only one way to get the stickler off the hook. Do not negotiate with it, do not listen to it, and do not justify what it says." Thomas smiles at me with infinite love. "But get to know it and accept it because it is also a part of you."

"But..." My voice falters a bit as I walk along a small path that leads away from the car. Here is an acrid and harsh smell. On my right, water runs down the slope, forming a small stream. I run my hand through it and feel the icy cold sensation bringing a rush of energy.

Thomas speaks calmly on, "Every time you are provoked by something, you have an opportunity to learn about yourself." He stops to make sure I follow. I sit down on a rock next to the stream.

"Let's say you are doubting whether you can find the two missing people in the Ring. First, you check if you can acknowledge the doubt. If you can, look back in your life and feel when the doubt arose." He walks through several thin clouds as he continues to speak. "When did you have to pretend you were in control, and what did you do? How did you survive?"

Thomas has reached the oasis in In-Between—the place I went with Annabel and kissed a woman for the first time in my life. After that, my stickler was totally stressed out. But with her, I experienced the essence of the female qualities. It was the first time I really took the feminine quality in and felt the strength of being a woman. I feel a stab in my chest. Back then, I doubted Annabel's intentions; now, I can see it was the stickler that carried the doubt.

The picture of Thomas slides easily to the side, and there, right in front of me, sits Annabel. She does not say anything, just sits and looks into nothingness, as if she is waiting for something. Her green eyes light up, and her subtle, feminine energy floats effortlessly around her. I reach out my hand.

"Are you listening, Angela?" Thomas looks right at me, and I nod.

"When you acknowledge all aspects of yourself, you become free. The first step is to see how old survival mechanisms govern your life."

"It's a big mouthful...." I blink a few times, and the picture of Annabel fades away, and I fight to keep the tears that are building up in the back of my eyes in place.

Thomas walks down the path through the bushes arranged like a maze toward the center of the oasis. "It's like learning to walk again, a muscle you've never learned to use; it needs to be exercised. It is the way to inner freedom." Thomas stops at the wooden table. "You can also say that you bring light into the darkness."

I know he is right. Somehow, it seems so logical but also confusing.

"The trick is to have time to observe your inner reaction before you speak or act. In that way, you have a choice. Right now, you have no choice. You are a slave to your thoughts and feelings. Only when you can choose will you be free. The key to freedom lies within yourself." He sits down on the bench next to the table, surrounded by the most beautiful tulips in bright, deep purple colors.

"Thomas…"

Two large Harley Davidson motorcycles are turning my way.

The noise from their engines nearly drowns out my voice. I get up and try to hide behind the withered branches of a tree next to me. They stop, and two muscular guys get off their motorcycles. One has a tousled mustache, and his hand is covered in tattoos. The other is wearing a leather jacket with a big flipped finger on the sleeve. His thin hair is gathered in a ponytail. They talk as they walk over to a tree and urinate.

I lower my voice and try to pull myself a little farther away without attracting attention. I can just make out an abandoned hut in between the spruces, and it looks just as lonely as I feel right now.

"There are so many things I wanted to ask you, Thomas." I stop. Is the timing right? The doubt hits me from behind like a rock. I observe the doubt and continue. "Do you think there is a reason why I meet the people I do here?"

I kneel behind the scorched tree trunk and move a few branches that stick in my face.

"What do you think?" Thomas leans back on the bench and smiles slyly at me.

I sink. Maybe I shouldn't have asked. But on the other hand, I went up against my inner voice, and it felt good. I cannot win every time, and in the end, I get to decide whether it is a defeat or not.

"Hey, let's just check out the old banger that is parked over there." The guy with the ponytail walks toward me.

I press my body against the sweaty trunk.

"There's a chick here." He comes closer. I get up and turn toward him. Now, I am definitely not in control.

"Aloha, what do we have here?" He has a scar running down his cheek, and his voice is rough. I'm feeling pretty small right now and don't say anything. I stand completely still.

"Who are you talking to?" Thomas asks.

The wind blows in my direction, and the air exudes alcohol and a sweet smell of hashish. The guy with the tattoo is still standing by the motorcycles, "Come on, Mikey; we're in a hurry." He turns the gas handle.

"Aren't you a little far from home, sweetheart?" Now, he is only a few feet from me.

I stand with my back pressed up against the scorched tree trunk, and my face is locked in a vacant expression, trying desperately to silence my inner stickler.

"Mike, drop it," the other guy shouts, annoyed. "We have more important things to do."

The guy with the ponytail sends a gob of saliva to the ground, which lands right next to my boot. "It's your lucky day, sweetheart. Or maybe it's not." He laughs contemptuously, turns around, drills his foot into an empty can lying on the ground, and walks back toward his motorcycle.

I stand tensely and follow him with my gaze without moving.

"Isn't it allowed to have some fun anymore?" He looks scornfully at his friend, gets on his motorcycle, turns the key, makes an excessive wheelspin, and disappears.

I wait until they have turned out onto the main road and close my eyes briefly. When I open them again, Thomas is back.

"Are you all right?" Thomas is very far away right now. I step forward to get closer to him, but the image dissolves around me.

"Yes, I just think it's a little difficult. In a way, I found it easier the last time I was here." My voice is low and trembles a little. I look away and press my tongue against the inside of my teeth.

"When we open our hearts, we also become more vulnerable. There is a very fine balance to function in the 'normal' society and at the same time have an open heart with a spiritual connection." He leans forward and supports his chin on his hands. "So far, very few have succeeded." He looks down. "Some cannot cope with life on Earth and leave before their time; others choose to stay and create the light that is possible." He speaks quietly, "The energy of love does not have any ambition or direction. Therefore, it does not spread as fast as the negative energy."

I start walking back toward the car.

"Many people experience that their lives are not as they

expected—that they are not satisfied. They blame their work, girlfriend, or children, everyone but themselves." The cloud glides along as he sits still and speaks in a warm voice. "There is a longing for life to be different, an eternal hope, but a sea of excuses keeps them from changing anything."

A seagull lands on the table in front of Thomas; it walks proudly back and forth. He reaches out and scratches its head.

"People dream of another life. Some take courses, others read books or go to lectures and sense their longing. But they dare not let go of what they have and live out their longing. Most people do not even know what they're longing for." Thomas extends his hand, and the seagull nibbles lightly on his finger. "They wait until they have an accident, get sick, or someone in their family dies, then they are forced to take their lives seriously." The seagull spreads its wings and sets course against the wind. "It sounds so simple, but for most people, it is impossible to let go and live the life they long for. Their life is an illusion. They fall back into the herd and cover up the pain."

I have reached my car and lean against it. "Why is it so difficult?"

"Because it's dangerous. It requires you to review your life, needs, values, and ideas. You have to let go of compromises and drop all excuses. Just take a look at yourself; you needed to be in a plane crash to wake up."

I bend forward, touché.

Thomas sits back, and several small thin clouds drift in front of him. "It takes courage. Most people are weekend-seekers or convince themselves that they have a good life. They stay busy not to feel the pain or frustration: work more, drink, eat, exercise, or smoke. It all helps keep the pain at bay." He looks at me, and I look at him. I stand completely still and listen.

"They become beggars who need others to shut off the pain that arises when they lose touch with their core, their inner child. They are not happy, and they will never be if they do not start accepting that they aren't daring to let go of all the excuses." Thomas looks serious. "To live the life you long for, you have to take responsibility and realize that only you can make yourself happy."

My smile stiffens. "I'm not sure I was happy when I was alive."

The wind is rising, and a big, black cloud comes quickly toward me. The lights are turned on in the city that lies ahead.

"To find the last two in the Ring, you have to be aware of how you will subconsciously lead yourself astray."

"It sounds far out. Why would I do that?" I walk toward the slope.

"What we do not acknowledge will govern us. The part of yourself that you are unconscious about has the power inside you."

"But I think I know myself pretty well by now." I smile contentedly.

"There is more, Angela. The universe will guide you on your way. When you know that everything that happens is to teach you something, you are well on your way, and if you succeed in finding the last two members of the Ring, you can look forward to showing other people the way."

"What?" I pull a smile and lean against the fence that prevents me from falling down the steep slope.

Thomas smiles. "Right now, it's important to focus on finding the last two. Then you will know more when you return to In-Between."

The sky turns on the waterworks, and I hurry back to the car, crawl into the front seat, and close the door behind me. "You have to tell me more."

"Not now; we will have time when you return."

How I wish I were sitting next to him right now.

15
WHEN THE PAST SNEAKS UP ON YOU

"I know who you are and why you are here."
I am startled. I know that voice.

It's rush hour, and it feels like everybody has chosen to go grocery shopping right now. I stand by the vegetables in the local supermarket, concentrating on my shopping list that only has all the basic things on it, trying to figure out what I feel like having for dinner without my stickler interfering when the voice whispers in my ear. I turn around with a jolt.

The fluorescent tubes hang naked down from the ceiling, spreading a bright cold light. Right in front of me stands... I blink a few times. My heart beats as if it were a matter of life or death. It cannot be true. If I really see the person I think is standing right in front of me with a sneaky smile on his face, something is completely wrong.

"Hi, Eva, or is it Angela now?" His voice is filled with false sweetness.

I stand completely rigid, and my gaze drills analytically into his. My legs are locked, my mouth closed, and my eyes are drying out because I am not blinking.

"It's great to see you again. How are you?" He grabs my shoulder and shakes it lightly.

My tongue presses hard against my clenched teeth. I squint and try to move, but my body does not obey.

"Remember today's special offer, half a kilo of pork loin; you will find it in our refrigerated display counter." The sound from the speaker cuts through the crowd like a wave leading people from the vegetable department and on to the refrigerated display counter. We are left alone with the organic apples and oranges.

"Frank." The word comes silently out of my mouth against my will. It trickles cold down my spine. I will never forget when I met Frank together with Lucy in In-Between. It was out on the ledge. He stood just as self-important, recounting how he had cracked the return code. Now, he stands right in front of me again with the same slightly superior attitude. He steps forward and hugs me.

"It's great to see you again; what a fluke to bump into each other here!" His shiny bald head reflects the light from the ceiling, and his withdrawn eyes look self-satisfied at me.

This is not a coincidence; it cannot be. A hysterical alarm bell rings inside me, and I'm ready to pursue this until he gives me a really good explanation.

I take a small step back and lean on the fruit stacked in piles in a long row. A shiny red apple is pushed free and falls to the floor, and I do not respond.

"How do you know what I look like and who I am?" I stare at Frank with a frosty gaze.

Frank bursts out in a loud laugh. "Oh, Eva, sorry, I mean Angela, you're so straightforward." He reaches for two oranges and juggles them in the air. "It was not hard to work out where to find you. Your son lives nearby." He catches the oranges and puts them back on the shelf.

"But..." I have to stay and find an explanation. My brain can't keep up at all; I don't know what to say or do. Maybe I should be honest and tell him I'm confused and a little insecure knowing he's here, but that will make me vulnerable. I have to be tactical instead.

I put my shopping basket down. "You are right, but how could you know that I am me? I look different now." My voice is determined and has a tinge of mistrust in it that I'm trying to cover up with a smile.

An elderly lady pushes toward me in an attempt to reach a bag of apples.

"Here, let me help you." I reach out for the apples and give her the finest I can see. She smiles at me and moves on to the potatoes. A young man is restocking the goods; he's keeping an eye on us.

"Eva, no, so sorry, Angela, I tried to contact you this morning before I came here, but you did not answer. Don't you have your Skycon with you?"

I gasp for breath and try to find a natural place to look. My Skycon is in my pocket.

Frank reaches out for me. "Would you like to go for a cup of tea? I know a place just around the corner." He smiles, and his slightly yellow crooked teeth appear and stand in contrast to his effectively manipulative nature and expensive taste in clothes.

"Yes, why not?" I try to find a suitable grimace and smile a little artificially at Frank. Now, I have to keep focus and be persistent. Even though Frank makes my stomach turn, I have to figure out what he's doing here.

He smiles self-assuredly, reaches out, and lets his hand slide down over my back. "Let me carry your shopping basket; it looks very heavy."

"No, thanks, it's all right; I can carry it myself." I bend down and grab the handle. The guy restocking the goods is finished and leaves with an empty cart squealing as if its last hour had come.

The queue at the checkout disappears as we approach, and we go right through. My basket is filled with vegetables, fruits, and some lean meat—enough to fill up the fridge in the small kitchenette in my hotel room.

"It looks really healthy and delicious." Franks grabs the apples from the conveyor belt and puts them in the bag, "and it's all organic. One would think you were trying to prolong your life, Eva."

I send Frank a frosty stare; there is nothing worse than people who comment on what I buy.

"Here, let me help you now." Frank reaches for the bag; it's heavy, and I smile, loaded with glee.

We walk out of the supermarket side by side; the air between us is icy cold. The short walk to my car allows me to sort out my thoughts and try to think clearly.

"I'm parked over there," I nod in the direction of my car and open the trunk.

"What a lovely car you have, Angela."

There is no one like Frank who can make my skin crawl.

"The café is right there," he points to the street corner at the end of the parking lot, but I can't see it. I close the trunk. Frank is clinging to me, standing way too close for my liking.

We edge past the billboards in front of the supermarket and turn the corner. A café with small dark windows appears. Next to the door is a flowerpot with some cemetery plants and an overflowing ashtray.

"Do you live nearby?" I walk right behind Frank, who pushes the café door open.

He nods and holds the door for me. The café is dark and dingy, and I pause in the doorway to allow my eyes to adjust.

"Do you want to go somewhere else?" Frank turns toward me and puts his hand on my shoulder. Had it been anyone but him, it would have been nice and caring, but not Frank.

"No, it's fine." I smile, slightly strained.

Frank walks up to the bar, and I let myself drop onto a wooden bench at a vacant table next to the wall. It is angular and hard with no cushions. The café is half-full of people who seem to feel at home. A bit of light finds its way through the stained windows.

On the walls hang several pictures of spectacular sunsets. One where the sun is going down between two mountain peaks, "The Roof of the World" is written in big letters on it, another where the sun hangs like an orange fireball behind the pyramids, and finally a picture where the sun lights up the sky and clouds. All the images have a slightly yellowish tinge, but their power shines through.

"Here comes the tea. It hasn't been that long since we had tea together last time." Frank smiles and seems carefree in his attitude. He sits across from me with his back to the other guests.

"You never told me how you were able to recognize me." I lean forward and keep my gaze locked on Frank. He pours the tea, and the steam rises like a veil between us.

"The best tea is made from water that is eighty degrees and brews for six minutes. Did you know that?" He keeps smiling at me, and if I didn't know better, I would believe that he was just being nice.

I don't respond. It's warm in here, but I keep my jacket on. Frank pushes a cup of tea closer to me and leans over the table.

The sound of laughter and low-pitched chatting fills the room mixed with rock music from the seventies. Several people hang out at the bar; others sit and have lunch at the small, square tables randomly placed in the room.

"There was a rumor up in In-Between that you had returned to Earth, and since I was coming back here myself, I decided to take a look at your file. It wasn't easy to hack the file, but a little challenge is always nice. And I must admit, it didn't take me that long after all." He maintains eye contact, like a hyena circling its prey. "Your file was updated with a lovely picture of you and your new name." He smiles smugly and drums complacently on the table.

"But how did you know I had a file?"

He turns his head haughtily from side to side. "It's just a matter of knowing the right people."

I try to shut out the noise from the room and concentrate only on Frank. Who helped him get back here, and who gave him the insight into the secret files? And why?

The music is turned up, and a fast, monotonous rhythm spills out of the speakers.

"Well done, Frank; what else do you know?" My voice cuts its way to Frank, who is blowing on his cup of tea.

"Nothing else." His words hang in the air, and he takes a sip of the warm tea.

I am shaking my head. "Do you really want me to believe that?" I have a sense of unease, a feeling that something is completely wrong. I try to smile but fail.

"Do you like the tea? It comes from India, and I thought it might be to your liking."

More people enter the café, mainly younger people in groups. The stuffy feeling eases a bit when the door is opened. I breathe and enjoy the fresh breeze while it lasts.

Frank puts his cup down and places one arm over the backrest of his chair. "Eva, tell me why you're here as Angela and not Eva. What's going on?"

I keep shaking my head and look at him with a fixed smile. Could it be that he doesn't know the truth, and he is fishing? I squint a little. "It's a long and boring story, Frank." I want to move a bit further away from him, but the bench is pinned to the floor and pressed up against the wall behind me.

"But why don't you tell me why you're back?" I send him a cunning smile.

"I chose to say no to becoming an apprentice. I would rather enjoy earthly pleasures than try to save others. And Lucy is also in town, have you seen her?" His gaze flickers. I keep staring at him, wishing that I could pull the truth out of him. He begins to sit restlessly on the chair.

"I'm hungry. Do you want anything?" Frank reaches for the menu card and starts flipping through it. I don't want to be here any longer than needed, but I have to suppress my desire to get away from Frank and stay for the mission's sake.

"Yeah, let me see; I would love a salad, and you?"

The small scars on his face appear deeper; he looks worn out. I will have the same as you, Eva."

"I'll get it." I edge myself off the bench and walk with quick steps toward the bar. I exhale, relieved, and try to gather my thoughts.

"How can I help you?" A young girl with ultra-short, blonde hair that clings around her face smiles kindly at me. The bar looks way too big for her, and I lean forward so she can hear me better.

"Two Diet Cokes, please." I can't cope with all the options on the menu right now, and the pace here is somewhat faster than I have been used to in recent weeks. I grab my purse from my coat pocket and put it on the counter in front of me. A younger woman pushes herself in front of me, and I step a little to the side. She doesn't look at me and starts to wave her hand at a young man behind the counter.

"Where are you sitting?" Her smile is stuck, her eyes have lost their spark, and even though I'm talking to her, it seems like she's somewhere else.

I turn and point to Frank, who has turned around and is facing me. "Over there." Frank waves back.

"And I'll have a green salad too."

"One or two?" She asks without looking at me as she writes the order on an iPad. At the same time, she finds two glasses and starts filling them with Diet Coke.

"Two please." I raise my voice and cast a sidelong glance at the iPad to make sure she got the two salads right. Under no circumstances will I share a salad with Frank. My tone of voice has changed, and I notice that I speak faster.

The girl hands me the bill and makes eye contact with the next customer. I give her a note and tell her to keep the change. Then I turn to Frank and signal that I just have to go to the bathroom. It will give me a chance to think through my next move.

There are two doors inside the bathroom, a small open window, and a sink with a small, cracked mirror above it. I push open the door to the first vacant stall. There is someone in the other toilet, and I quickly secure the lock.

It would be easier if I could just push a button to connect to Thomas. I close the toilet lid and sit down. It's cold in here but fortunately not as stuffy as inside the café. The sound of a toilet flushing echoes through the thin wall, and I sit completely still. There is a gap between the door and the floor, and I see a pair of feet leaving. The walls are light gray, and messages have been written all over. "Kim, I love you" and a heart. A penis with a bow on it and a needle. I pull my legs up in front of me, support my heels on the toilet seat, and press my knees against my chest. Right now, it would be nice to have a small handbook for searching souls who have returned to earthly life.

Thomas has repeatedly said that there is a reason for everything. When I saw Frank, he reminded me of someone or something I cannot quite put my finger on. The feeling vanished, and now I can't recall it.

The door slams shut, and I can see a pair of big black boots walking by. The door to the toilet next door is slammed and locked.

If only I knew how to get in touch with Thomas. Everything seems so annoyingly random. My head drops forward, and I press my brows against my knees. Thomas, I want to talk to you. I take one deep breath and another one.

NOW.

Nothing happens. I sit completely still, trying to close my eyes and breathe calmly.

Still nothing.

16

A GAME

I jump up in the air at the sound of someone knocking firmly on the toilet door.

"Are you stuck in there? Others are also in need." I can see the toe of a red boot tapping hectically up and down right outside the door.

I open my eyes and straighten up.

"Hello, your time is up." The door shakes as she knocks on it again.

I flush the toilet, get up, and unlock the door. Outside, I am greeted by several women with angry looks. If only they knew that I'm on a mission here. One seems more upset than the others. I put my hand on my stomach, but there is no need to try to look pressured because I am.

The salad is already on the table, and Frank has nearly finished his.

"I'm sorry it took so long. I have stomach pains." I slide back onto the bench, facing Frank again.

"If you have stomach pain, just drink this tea, and it will pass." Frank points at the tea section on the menu.

I take the cup of tea that is already on the table, and it spills a bit as I lift it and try to smile at him.

"Eva, I have a lot of experience with sickness."

I control myself to stop from rolling my eyes. "That's great, Frank. I'm okay now." Taking deep breaths usually helps me under pressure, but not now. I have to find out why Frank is here and what he knows. My cup hits the table with a little bang as I put it down.

"Once upon a time," Frank takes a mouthful of salad and takes time to finish chewing before continuing, "I had a stomach pain so bad that I had to be picked up by an ambulance. And my cousin has had several stomach ulcers."

His words turn into an empty sound that goes in one ear and out the other. I look down at my salad. There is cucumber, feta cheese, lettuce leaves, olives, and an orange dressing all over.

"I'm sorry?" I look up from the salad.

"I said, I know more than most people about this issue." Frank puts down his cutlery and tilts back on the chair.

"Thank you, Frank; it's nice of you. I'm fine." I look up and nibble on a piece of feta cheese I've picked up with my fingers. "I'll keep that in mind if it comes back." I don't have to be like him. Thomas once told me that if we go to war with others and play their games, we will be like them. Even though we eventually feel like winners, we have lost because we became like our opponent and gave in on our values to win. I try to stay on my half of the court without fighting him or playing his game.

"Frank, did you tell Lucy I'm here?" I lean forward and look around the room to make sure no one is listening to our conversation.

"What do you think?" He takes an olive and throws it in his mouth.

"I don't know." It is so hard not to play his game, and I really have to concentrate. If I just stick to what I know, then maybe he will answer me.

"Okay then, if you guess right, I will tell you." He leans forward again.

"Excuse me for a moment," I get up. There's not much space between the tables, but enough for me to step away.

"Do you want to guess or what?" Frank raises his voice.

I stand with my back toward him and do not turn around. If I say yes, I'm playing his game. If I say no, I risk not being told anything. I'm caught between a rock and a hard place. My thoughts are about to short circuit. Trust, it's all about trust, I whisper to myself.

"What is it going to be, Eva?" Frank starts to drum against the table.

I cannot see Frank, but I know he is looking at me. I empty my lungs, turn around, and sit down in front of him again.

"It would be great if you would tell me." I look right into his cold withdrawn eyes.

If possible, the room is even stuffier, and it is filled to the brim with people. It is hard to breathe and get any air in here.

Frank waits and hits his index finger several times on his lips. "Maybe another time." He pushes his plate to the middle of the table. "Now, unfortunately, I have to move on; time goes fast in good company, but maybe we can see each other again?"

"Yes, if you give me your phone number, I'll call." My heart starts beating fast, and cold sweat runs from my armpits.

He smiles his superficial smile, "I'll find you, Eva; don't worry." Frank turns, and in his exaggerated way, asks some people behind him to move. "I'm sorry I do not have more time, but if I had known I was going to run into you, I would not have made any plans for today."

I get up and face Frank. The small scars on his face seem more distinct. If I were to rate myself for this conversation, I would have failed. Frank stretches out his arms and hugs me. His slightly rotten smell reminds me of the day we sat in the café in In-Between, where he told Lucy and me about the repatriation. He said it was his duty to give others the opportunity to return to their lives on Earth before the forty-two days had passed. The way he said it was with an exaggerated sweetness as if he were God's emissary.

Frank takes a step back and looks me in the eyes as he smiles another of his assumed sweet smiles. "See you, Eva."

I use all my self-control to keep my mouth shut. Why is he back? I stomp on the floor with my heel in annoyance. Frank disappears into the crowd along with the answers I wanted.

17
ALL ALONE

Thomas looks at the images of Angela on the screen in front of him. She is sitting in a stuffy cafe, all alone. The frustration radiates from her. A wave of compassion washes through him, and he strokes his finger gently over the skin under his eye. Gabriel is sitting next to Thomas.

His face is serious, and his eyes a little shiny.

"What do we do now?" Thomas breaks the silence and sits back in the floating chair. He looks at Gabriel, and neither of them says anything. Waiting. They are by themselves in the control room created especially for the members of the Ring. Shiva and Yoge are out working on their personal processes.

The air is cool, and it brings a freshness with it and starts a quiet shiver in Thomas's body. Angela's image evokes powerlessness in him, a feeling he has not been in contact with since he left his life on Earth. He has done everything he could to keep the feeling locked away for years, but now it's back.

Slowly, Gabriel raises his hand. "I'm sure it was Frank she was talking to. I received him when he came to In-Between." He starts coughing and reaches for a glass of water on the table.

Thomas leans forward. "Angela looks resigned." He knows her pretty well by now—well enough to see when she is under pressure, like now. He looks over at Gabriel. "The Master has mentioned that someone tried to crack the return-code, but I don't think he is aware that they succeeded." He folds the sleeve on his tunic up very precisely, and tiny goosebumps become visible. Gabriel sits completely still; he has a distracted expression on his face. Deep wrinkles cut through his forehead, and his eyes are bloodshot.

"When are we going to give Angela the rest of the information we gathered yesterday?" Thomas pushes the chair back in a sliding motion and gets up to turn down the speaker. The sound from the café fades away.

Gabriel takes his time and breathes calmly. "We have to give her time to get on track; that way, she can hopefully get more value from the fragments we have. Right now, they will confuse her more than they will benefit."

"If only I could help her." Thomas places a hand on the screen. It's soft and gives way, encompassing his hand. A low hiss makes him turn toward the door, and it slides open, and a light, bright figure enters. With slow steps, he walks closer. Thomas steps forward and folds his hands lightly in front of his chest. The heat in his body is replaced by lightness. He gets a sinking feeling.

The light of the sun breaks through the clouds and makes the little swan on the chest of the Master's robe shine. The robe is long, white, and with pearls in the opening around the neck. Thomas bows slightly while looking at the Master.

"You have sent for me. I have received your briefing." The voice is deep, and the words come one by one so that each of them could almost form a sentence. His eyes are infinitely calm, and his slender body makes the Master seem fragile, even though he radiates an enormous strength.

Thomas feels a grip on his arm; it is Gabriel who pulls himself from the chair. "We need your advice." His voice is firm.

The Master looks at Gabriel and then right into the eyes of

Thomas. A blow from his gaze flashes against Thomas, forcing him to sway his upper body back. The Master nods slowly. Behind him stand two women dressed in long white dresses that fall lightly around their elegant bodies and make them look like angels. Thomas has seen them a few times before when the Master has been outside his territory, but he has never spoken to them. He experiences an extraordinary affection for them. They seem as if they do not belong here. Like they are already on the ongoing journey of their soul.

Thomas looks at the Master. His luminous figure stands right in front of him. The Master closes his eyes and remains silent. Both Gabriel and Thomas stand still. Waiting. Then he opens his eyes again and looks directly at Thomas. "You must shut down all connections to Angela and all other means of communication from here. Have faith that she will solve the task she has accepted." He doesn't pull a muscle in his face. "In the meantime, you must check our security systems. We don't know how much Frank knows, and we can't risk any communication or interference from Earth." He folds his hands in front of his chest and bends slightly forward.

Thomas can sense Gabriel's gaze resting on him, but he only looks at the Master. His light fills Thomas with clarity.

"What about the information we have about the two missing people she is looking for?" Gabriel speaks with great calm, and Thomas senses that he chooses the words carefully. He feels Gabriel's hand tighten the grip on his arm.

"From now on, Angela will have to fend for herself."

The Master turns around and disappears silently out of the room. The intensity of the light decreases as the door shuts behind him. If Thomas felt powerless before, it is nothing compared to what he feels right now. So many times in his life, he has felt trapped. He doesn't want to open up to the memories right now; it is not the time. He has to stay focused on Angela and the task. Gabriel starts to stand restlessly, and they walk toward the mint green chairs.

"Are you all right?" Thomas looks at Gabriel. His body has collapsed even more, and his eyes have lost their sparkle.

"Yes." He drags his left leg over the floor.

Thomas glances back at the screens. Angela is standing on the sidewalk and looks around in despair. He helps Gabriel sit down in the chair and walks to the wall with hidden cupboards. He presses the green button that opens the cabinet of drinks and fills two glasses with water. The cupboard is full of bottles in all the colors of the rainbow. Thomas reaches for a small blue bottle and drips three drops into the water, which gives it a slight bluish tinge until the drops dissolve.

The sound of the door opening gets Thomas's attention. A sigh of relief runs silently through his body as he sees Shiva. Right now, he needs all the help he can get.

"Shiva, it is great to see you; please, come and sit down," Thomas points to one of the green chairs and turns to take one more glass from the cupboard. The sound of a bump makes him turn back in an instant. He resolutely places the glasses on the table.

"GABRIEL."

Gabriel lies on one side with his face pressed against the floor. His mouth is slightly open, and his eyes are closed. There are no signs of life.

18
LET IT GO

I look at my watch. The ring with crystals shines in the ray of the sun. It's a few minutes past three. The wind lifts a pile of leaves into the air and sends them out into the street in front of a car passing by at high speed. I start walking down the road where shops lie side by side on one side; on the other side of the street is a park. My hands slide as deep as possible into my jeans' pockets, and my shoulders are pulled up to my ears. The light turns red. I'm going anyway.

"Hey, watch out, idiot!"

A man holding a little girl's hand grabs my arm, and the driver sends me an angry look before tapping the gas and taking off.

"Thank you. I was lost in thought." The light turns green, and I cross the street.

There is a tall, dense hedge around the park with a curved opening in the middle. The sounds change as soon as I step through the gate, the traffic noise fades away, and the chirping of birds takes over. A chipmunk comes jumping toward me and stops at my feet, looking at me with hungry eyes.

A little further ahead is a bench overlooking a small lake where several ducks frolic.

I sit down. A lady with long hair in a tight outfit passes by with her very close-cropped poodle, and she does not see me. Several areas have small orange-red flowers, shrubs that form shapes, and willow trees with long branches that hang loosely with green and yellow leaves. Two younger men with very tight sportswear make their way past at high speed on roller skates. I get tired just by looking at them and sit back. My thoughts will not let go of Frank; they revolve around him all the time. I stare into the air without seeing anything.

"Is anyone sitting here?" An elderly man hits the bench with his cane.

"Yes." I shake my head. "Sorry, no, it's just me." I wave apologetically with my hands.

"It's a lovely day.' The older man leans on the cane and sits down stiffly. His hands shake as he straightens the little gray hat on his head.

I slide down, supporting my neck against the backrest of the bench. All I can see is the blue sky above. Then I close my eyes, embracing the darkness inside me. All the thinking makes my body tired; I hadn't noticed till now. Even though I try to relax, it doesn't make a difference.

"Have a good day."

I open my eyes a bit; the older man struggles to get back on his feet. I nod to him and close my eyes again. The darkness is back.

"Just let go," a deep voice resonates inside me.

I lean slightly to the side and support my elbow against the armrest of the bench.

"Just let go." The voice speaks louder, nearly drowning my thoughts.

"Who are you? What do you want?" I ask inside myself, sensing a light out in the distance. It's coming closer. Inside the light is a black dot with diffused light around it, which gets bigger.

THE RING

"I do not want anything from you. You came to me," the voice says.

"Came to you? I didn't, I mean…." I try to straighten up, but nothing happens. I can no longer hear the chirping of birds, but I can feel my body resting on the bench. Heat spreads from the center of my chest and into the rest of my body.

"I could use a little help," I whisper almost apologetically inside myself.

It gets completely quiet inside me. The light disappears, and the voice is gone. *Coward*, I think to myself. I know your type; as soon as others express their needs, you slip away.

I sit still and wait. It's completely dark here in my universe.

"You can get all the help you need. All you need to do is ask."

The white light comes back and is moving fast toward me. I get dazzled. Out of the light floats a butterfly in crystal clear blue and violet colors, and it hovers with great precision in front of me.

Loud, piercing laughter echoes all around me. But it's not my laugh.

"Come on, who are you?" My voice is firm and confronting. The sounds from the park and the smell of the flowers are still gone. To the best of my knowledge, I might as well be sitting on the moon.

"I am your lifeline to the universe. You have dialed yourself."

I have not dialed anyone or asked to be so heavy in the body. The light changes, it turns pink, and the butterfly sits on a ring—a large luminous gold ring. Several smaller rings appear inside the large ring, all connected.

I sense a faint throbbing from my heart, and a cold wind gently moves my hair a bit. I try to open my eyes, but they're stuck.

"Can you help me?"

It's quiet again. I do not move and hold my breath.

The butterfly opens and closes its wings while looking at me. The pattern on its wings is so simple and profound. The black lines that form large and small squares and dots are placed with precisely equal intervals.

"I can help you help yourself. It is very simple; all the answers are already inside you. Your soul knows the way." The voice is everywhere, around me and inside my head.

"All you need to do is listen and be present. And then it always helps to ask for specific help. It's a little easier to understand than just *help*."

I cannot make heads or tails of it. But I know I have a choice. I can either fight against the voice or surrender and play along. I choose the latter option.

"Okay then, should I write an application with elaborate reasoning, get down on my knees, or address you in a certain way?"

"I am what you want me to be. What you call me does not matter, but to get my help, you have to ask for it and watch out for the signs. And remember, if you judge the help that arises, you will miss it."

The butterfly takes off and disappears into the light and resolve.

Now, there is only white light left. It surrounds me, and I'm showering in it.

"When can I ask for help?"

"It's up to you. There is always an answer. The question is whether you listen."

The figure seems far away; I want to lean forward to see it clearly, but my body does not react.

"I would like help finding the first of the two people I need to bring back to In-Between. And then I need help figuring out what Frank is up to...." I pause. Is that too much to ask?

The figure comes closer, and I sense the outline of a person.

"What is most important right now, and what is the easy step to take?" The voice does not change tone; it speaks monotonously and mysteriously.

"Frank. The question concerning Frank is building up tension inside me. But I don't know if he is most important."

"Once you have found out, you can ask for help. And remember that help does not always come as you expect or want it, or as quickly as you want it."

The figure vanishes, and in the same moment, the weight in my body lightens. I open my eyelids a bit. A pair of women's shoes pass me, and a little later, a couple of smaller feet follow.

"Look, Mum, do you think that lady is sleeping?" The small feet step closer.

"Laura, no, let the lady be." She gives a jerk to the girl's arm, and she flies in the other direction.

I stay seated with my eyes half-closed. The sound of chirping birds comes back, and calmness fills my body. Deep inside, I know that I'm on the right track. Everything will somehow work out. I have no doubt, at least not now in this very moment. I look up and squint a bit. On the other side of the path is a large, old tree. It must be several hundred years old; the bark is knobby, and names have been scratched into it. I grab the armrest on the bench and pull myself up. My gaze is locked on the tree.

"Watch out, lady!" A cyclist rings her bell persistently.

I step over a low fence and onto a freshly cut lawn, which is not supposed to be walked on. The tree with its vast crown is right ahead of me.

"Can't she read the sign?" says a stranger's voice from a distance, but I ignore it.

The tree is enormous. I stretch my arms as far as I can around it, pressing my body against the trunk. A leaf drops and settles on my head. If only it could talk, what would it tell me? That I should not worry? That everything will be okay? I start to shake inside.

I lose track of time, and suddenly it does not seem so important.

19

THE JOURNEY OF YOUR SOUL

"Let me show you a little more."

The voice is back, and the light has returned—from where and how, I'm not sure. I only just managed to get into my car when the light started to burn through the windshield and blind me.

Out of the light emerges a small figure. I can only see a fine outline. The person is chubby, and it looks like braids are hanging down on each side of the face. I cannot see the face clearly but sense some old features. I close my eyes, but it makes no difference.

"To understand life, you must know the journey of your soul. You have traveled this Earth many times." The light blinds even more if possible. I want to raise my hand to shield it, but it does not respond.

"Why are you talking to me?" I try not to sound too suspicious.

The voice continues in the same slightly monotonous tone of voice. "You are ready."

It goes all quiet. I cannot hear the traffic, my breath, or the voice anymore. "Ready?" I ask. The light increases and changes color. In front of me emerges a woman in tattered clothes. She walks barefoot in half a meter of snow. In her arms, she carries two infants wrapped in skins with spots of clotted blood. Her face is pale and tormented and behind her lie high mountain peaks. She walks down the mountain alone.

"Do you recognize anything?"

A shiver of energy pervades my body. *Is there anything I need to recognize here?*

"Well, not really...." I manage to answer.

"Look carefully and hear what your soul tells you."

I look at the woman; she's not that tall, but her willpower is strong. She rests her gaze on her children, a boy and a girl; they both have their eyes closed. Their facial features are fine, the skin has a dark glow, and the noses are broad.

"Is it me?" I ask hesitantly and let the words erase themselves. It goes quiet.

The picture changes. In front of me sits a chief with an elaborate feather crown on his head. He sits alone on a rock ledge with a large bearskin over his shoulders. His eyes are closed, and he wears a long necklace made of bones from animals. The sun is setting in the distance. His back is straight, and behind him, flames rise from a bonfire up to the sky.

"If I'm not mistaken...." I halt. It can't be.

"You recognize him. Let me show you a little more."

Loud screams suddenly break the silence. They creep under my skin and tear my heart. I can hear the sound of horses galloping. The screams get louder, and the smell of smoke makes me cough. Through the smoke, a small village comes into view. Women and children run in all directions and try to save each other. Men with black and white painted faces riding on horses, swing torches, and set fire to the huts. They throw their tomahawks, and both young and older men are slain and fall to the ground. Several of the women are screaming as they are thrown onto the backs of the warriors' horses. A woman with long black hair runs toward me. She carries a small child in her arms and stares at me while she runs for her life. Behind her comes a rider, and I can see a tomahawk being swung. She screams and falls to the ground. The horse lurches and screeches loudly.

It is me. I am the woman.

It becomes completely quiet inside me. Before I have time to think, the picture changes again. The chief from before rides into the charred remains of the village. He dismounts from his black horse with the white blaze. Tears are running from his eyes over his face with deep lines. Slowly, he walks over to the woman lying on the ground with her baby in her arms. She is right in front of me. He kneels by her side, lifts her, and hugs her tightly as if he could bring her back to life. His eyes are bright blue and in stark contrast to his dark hair.

"Do you recognize him now?"

I don't say anything. I do not know what to say or if I want to know what is going on.

"We all come down to Earth in different disguises to learn something. If we do not learn what our souls have set out to learn in this life, we will face the same challenges again in the next life, just in a different time."

The picture splits in two, and now I can see both the woman walking in the snow with her two small children and the chief.

"Take a good look at them—not at their disguise. Look with your heart."

I look at the woman carrying the two small children in her arms. She turns her head and looks straight at me, and I get the feeling she can actually see me.

"Is it...?"

The chief straightens up and begins to make some ritual with his hands over the woman's face.

"It's..." The words are stuck in my mouth.

The woman in the tattered clothes stops on a piece of ground where the snow has melted, and several small blades of grass have broken through. She lays the little boy and girl on the ground. Their

THE RING

eyes are closed. With her bare hands, she begins to dig a hole in the ground.

"It's Thomas..." my voice trembles, "the woman in the tattered clothes is Thomas, and so is the chief. In two different lives."

The voice says nothing.

The woman digs on, and her hands begin to bleed. The chief stretches his arms toward the sky, and his eyes are mirror bright.

"The dead woman in the chief's arms is me, and so is the little girl on the ground." I don't know where the words come from, but they come to me with indisputable certainty.

"The little boy lying next to me. Is he a man or a woman now?"

"He is an old soul." The voice speaks with great calmness. The light begins to burn the images away, and it feels like I'm sitting in the middle of a bonfire. Now, everything is completely bright. My brain is working overtime, trying to come up with a logical explanation. The light changes, and the heat rises.

"Do you want to see more?" resounds the voice; it is all around me now.

The temperature in my body rises, and my skin begins to burn. The light is all around me, and I feel like I can walk into it.

"I don't understand it."

"People often look for a logical explanation, and they tend to make things complicated. The path of the soul is simple, but it cannot be understood or explained. To benefit from it, you must recognize it."

"But how...?" I want to move in the seat of the car, but my body doesn't respond.

A new image breaks through the bright white light. This time, it's easy to see that it's Thomas. He looks exactly as he does now. He is walking on a busy street full of people.

"Souls who have traveled for many lives get a white circle around their pupils. It grows stronger and stronger with their lives. As the insight grows, their eyes also get depth like an ocean."

I try to get a look at Thomas's eyes, but the picture is too wide, and he's too far away. He is wearing a long black coat and tall boots. As he walks there, he looks like a stranger visiting a world where he doesn't belong.

"To the wise soul, it can be a great challenge to engage in today's superficial and harsh world, which is created by fearful young souls."

Thomas enters a stairway and jumps up the stairs to the first floor, where he unlocks a door.

"The young souls who rule the world today are greedy. They have based the values of life on money, power, and desire. On fear. They are self-centered and do not care about others."

The voice pauses, and the white light burns away the image of Thomas.

"They are young souls who long for the only valuable thing in life, love. But they don't listen to their heart or the universe. They are too occupied running away from themselves."

The image of Thomas is slowly coming back. He is staring into the air, and there is no sparkle in his eyes. The apartment is tidy, and everything is perfectly placed. It is like looking at a black and white photo, where all life has disappeared.

"Most people construct an identity based on other people's opinions or on how they believe they should be. That is why they long for someone who can show them the way. However, the people who are in charge are unfortunately out of balance themselves." The voice speaks calmly and precisely. "No one who is in contact with their soul would go to war or harm another soul consciously. We are all souls visiting the Earth in a brief glimpse, each of us wrapped in bodies, and each of us with our lessons to learn."

I feel like I'm being pushed back into the seat, but I still can't feel the seat. If possible, it gets even warmer around me.

"We choose all our challenges ourselves before we enter a new life, and the experiences we have made in previous lives, we take with us. Some people call it talent; they are ignorant. We need to connect to the wisdom within ourselves to recognize it in others.

Until then, everything will be intellectual and learned knowledge, a poor and hollow knowledge."

Now, a big river is running in front of me, the current is strong, and the water looks cold. The picture widens, and a big, fiery red bridge appears in front of me. Thomas is walking on the bridge. His steps are easy, and he looks straight ahead.

"When we connect to our soul, we also find a sense of inner peace and certainty about our actions. We experience the whole and know that we are just a piece in a larger puzzle, and all pieces are equally important to create a whole."

Thomas leans against the railing, looking out over the river. A strong wind is tearing his half-length hair back from his face. Behind him pass several tourists with their cameras; they try to capture the moment. He just stands there like he is waiting for an answer.

"We have a choice in every single moment. We can choose the path of the soul or the path of the ego. One brings us closer to ourselves, the other farther away from ourselves. If you choose the path of the ego, you will find that all your decisions are based on fear. If you choose the path of the soul, they will be based on love and trust."

It has turned dark, and the bridge is floodlit. The light makes the red color of the bridge stand out. The tourists are gone. Thomas is still standing there, looking out over the river. He takes a step back. With a single jump, he is up on the railing and over onto the narrow ledge on the other side.

A feeling of unease fills me. *Thomas*, I shout, but there is no sound to be heard. He doesn't know that I'm here watching him.

He holds a railing post with one hand and stands with his feet together. Then, he bends down, ready to jump off.

"STOP!" I shout; this time, my voice is heard. He halts. The picture zooms out. A young woman is reaching her hand through the railing. She continues talking to him, trying to convince him to step back. It was her voice, not mine. He turns. His eyes are swollen, and tears are running in a steady stream over his marked cheekbones.

"Nothing is coincidental. No soul is the chosen one, and each soul has its challenge. And we all need help sometimes. Some souls are older than others; they have to take the lead, even though it's not always easy."

20

A DOOR TO THE OLD LIFE

I tighten my grip on the steering wheel; it feels real. Then I pat my legs and let my hands slide up over my belly. I am back. My body shakes a bit, but not in an uncomfortable way. The rearview mirror allows me to see myself. I grab it and move up close. There, right inside my pupil, is a bright, slightly frayed light circle. I'll be damned. The voice is right; I've never noticed it before. Ice cold energy rises from my loins and up my back. I sit completely still and watch the ring. A sense of calmness washes over me. I've lived before; it's there in my eyes. I would never have believed that a few months ago. I can't help but smile and cast a glance up at the sky.

The car is parked next to the supermarket and the café where I met Frank. The park is just across the street. I can see the large treetops from here. The clock changes and reminds me that time goes by, and I stare in anticipation at the display. In a minute, it will change again, leaving me less time to succeed. I am constantly being distracted. Every time I set a goal, something pops up, pulling me in a different direction. I can't let go of Frank; he keeps invading my thoughts. But I have to push him aside and have faith that they are taking care of him from In-Between. I already have a task to complete and don't need another one.

I jump in the seat when someone knocks on the car window. I roll it down, and a woman bends toward me.

"Excuse me; I just want to know if you're on your way out because if you are, I would love to have your parking space."

"Lucy!" I exclaim without having time to think first.

"Oh, my God, do we know each other?"

No, no, no, I'm a big fool. Why can't I hold my tongue? "I'm leaving," I reply quickly and let the words seep out between my lips and pretend that I don't know her. Lucy looks at me and starts laughing. She is wearing a polo shirt and black pants, looking a bit formal. The parking lot is filled to the limit and a bit more. Several cars have parked outside the lines; more are on the lookout for an empty space.

"Hi, it was you that I got mixed up with an old friend last night, wasn't it?" She pauses, and her smile fades. "How do you know my name?"

I look her in the eye without blinking and clear my throat. "You're wearing a name tag." *Saved by the bell*, I think to myself and feel very smug.

She pulls on her polo shirt and shakes the name tag slightly. "Oh, no, I'm so sorry. I'm a little touchy. I just started a new job at the supermarket over there and had a long day at the checkout. There are just so many weird people, you know?" She lets out a loud, hearty laugh. "Just had to run some errands on my lunch break."

A lady with a shopping cart filled to the brim and a screaming child bumps Lucy as she walks by.

I want to ask her how she is and if she's pregnant, but I can't reveal the knowledge I have from In-Between. There is no way I can let her know that we go way back.

"My break is almost over, so I'm in a hurry to find a spot for my car. So, if you don't mind...." She apologizes with her arms and smiles.

"Are you pregnant?" The words fly's out of my mouth even though I had just decided not to say anything. I bite my lip hard and turn the key.

"Noooo way, can you really tell? No one else has noticed, or maybe people are afraid to ask, in case I just got fat." Lucy laughs out loud so that her crooked teeth come into view. Then she straightens up and pushes her stomach forward while sliding her hand gently over it.

"Congratulations." I smile and make signs that I am reversing.

She puts her hand on the window and has a smile all over her face. "You know, there is something about you that I really like. It's so strange. I actually feel like I know you, but I know I don't." Her laughter is so contagious that I can't help but laugh too. It's like in the good old days. Lucy and I always had so much fun together, and we could laugh at the most ridiculous things that no one else thought was funny.

"I'd better get going...." I lift my foot off the clutch too fast; the car jumps, and the engine shuts off. We make eye contact, and it strikes me that Lucy also has a white circle around her pupil, not as powerful as mine, but it's there.

Lucy straightens up. "I'll get out of your way, but you know what? I have a 'women's night' once in a while. Would you like to come? The next one is tonight." Her golden-brown hair falls into her eyes, and the location of her mascara reveals the bustle of the day.

A man in his forties has lost patience and leans on the horn. Lucy turns and waves happily to him, and the sound fades.

"It's always nice when new women come along." She straightens up and clicks the car key off a black string she wears around her neck. "I'd better run," she pulls a face, glancing at the grumpy man, "not everyone has great patience."

Lucy is so nicely straightforward; there are no hidden agendas with her. I can't help but laugh and feel the warmth flowing up my cheeks.

"God, no, you need my address," she rummages in her pockets and finds a receipt, writes on the back, and hands it to me. "It's not that far from here."

I take the receipt and look at the address. "I'll find it; what time?"

Lucy clasps her hands together in front of her. "Oh, my God," she laughs again, "I nearly forgot—we meet at eight o'clock."

"See you at eight o'clock. Do I need to bring anything?"

Lucy shakes her head. "Just come as you are; I've got it all covered."

I smile and wave as I reverse. As I drive away, I watch Lucy in the rear-view mirror drive into my parking spot. Was that the help I asked for? It begins to tickle in my stomach.

It's only ten o'clock. I have all day.

Luke's Kindergarten is five minutes away from here. Even though it makes no other sense than a mother's urge to be with her child, I still feel that something else is pulling me. He is all I can think of right now, and I don't know where else to go. No matter how much the voice in my head tries to make me feel guilty and convince me that I have chosen to continue without him, it still feels right to go and see him.

The large, white villa with the decorated windows appears before me as I turn into the parking lot. Nobody is here, and it looks closed, but it's only half-past two.

I turn the handle on the tall wooden gate. It has seen better days and opens reluctantly as I push it. There are pavement slabs all around the building, and several large tree stumps lie on the ground.

"Hello, can I help you?" A young girl with bright pigtails smiles at me. She is only a head taller than Luke and has a black cap on her head.

I bite my lower lip and smile as if everything is in perfect order. "I once had a son who went here and just came by; I thought it would be fun to take a trip down memory lane."

"Sure, I'm new here, but you're welcome to look around. Tell me if you have any questions." She walks over to the sandbox and starts collecting shovels and buckets.

The garden is not that big. At the back is a swing and a climbing frame, where the paint is worn off. It feels like walking back into my old life; the surroundings are similar to the old Kindergarten Luke went to, but I'm no longer a part of the daily routine. I stop.

This is no good.

I feel a hand on my shoulder, and it dawns on me that I'm blocking the entrance to the blue section. Quickly, I step aside and turn to say sorry, but the words are glued to my lips. Andreas is standing in front of me with his day-old stubble and slender body. He smiles and walks past me with long strides. I stand completely frozen and look at him without moving a muscle. For the past seven weeks, I have been watching him for hours on a lifeless screen from In-Between. I have scolded and commented on everything he has done. And now, now, I can tell him everything that I didn't get to say to his face. He disappears through the glass door and around the corner farther ahead. I follow, and the door slams behind me.

"Daddddyyyy," it is Luke's voice. A tear runs down my cheek. I have to get out of here, now—before he sees me. I can't show my feelings here. But it's too late. I've walked through the door to my old life, and I can't hide.

"Come on, Dad; we're going home. Come now." Luke comes running at full speed around the corner and runs straight into me, so he's about to fall. I take a step back and laugh uncertainly.

He looks up at me. "Why are you crying?"

Andreas has not yet appeared. Luke is getting his footing and looks at me. There's something about his eyes. I've always thought they were special, but now I can see something else. In a way, he reminds me of Thomas, just in a younger version. I'm not sure. I wipe the tear away from my cheek and smile. "I was just thinking of someone I miss."

Andreas has still not appeared.

"Who is it?" Luke stands in front of me, looking me right in the eyes. I kneel, so we are at eye level.

"I once had a son like you, and I miss him." I gasp for breath and press my teeth so hard together that it hurts.

"Where is he?" He puts his hand in his pocket and pulls out a stone. "You can have this one. It was actually for my mother, but she's in heaven now." He points up and leans forward as he whispers, "I have held on to it, just in case she would come and pick me up one day."

His little hand reaches out and grabs mine. "But I don't think she will come." His tiny fingers are so soft and warm. I open my hand, and he places a small red stone in my hand.

"You smell like my mother," he smiles all over his face.

I lift my hand slowly and stroke his hair gently. A sinking feeling blasts through my body, like a stream of heat exploding.

"Luke…" Andreas calls. Before I have time to get up, he turns the corner. "There you are." Andreas smiles politely. "Hello." He has a yellow tote bag in his hand and a blue jacket with a white horse on the sleeve over his arm.

Luke gets up and runs to Andreas. I support my hand against the floor and try to pull myself together. In an instant, everything goes black, and I lose my direction. I feel a hard squeeze on my arm.

"Are you all right?" I look up and straight into Andreas's eyes. The wrinkles on his face are marked, and he looks worn out.

"Thank you, yes, I just got a little dizzy, sorry."

"No problem," he lets go of my arm. He's wearing a checkered shirt that hangs loosely over his pants and a pair of sneakers that I gave him as a birthday present just before we split up.

THE RING

THE RING

"Come on, Luke; we'd better get home." Andreas takes Luke's hand and walks toward the exit.

Luke turns to me and waves. "See you."

21

A SOUL MEETING

I walk up the narrow staircase, which creaks every time I take a step. The light from the ceiling cannot illuminate the stairs and leaves a dim atmosphere. The sound of conversations behind the doors changes every time I reach another floor. On the fourth floor, I breathe and stop.

If I were my old self, I would have prepared a cover story and solid answers just in case anyone asks me anything. But I didn't. If I have anything that can be called a plan, it must be seizing the opportunities that emerge. Normally, I would have spent hours preparing, thinking about the other guests and what kind of clothes I should wear. But not tonight. I empty my lungs; it's a relief.

Even though I'm tired and would rather lie down on the hotel bed with my feet up and watch TV while enjoying some delicious chocolate and a cup of tea, I have to do what I can to dive into the opportunities that arrive. Maybe it's a chance to track down the two people who I have to convince to come back to In-Between with me. It's probably a really good idea to get a bit distracted from my meeting with Luke earlier today.

Behind the door are the sounds of different voices. Lucy's

laughter drowns them all from time to time. I pull down my jacket and shake my hair a little. The bell buzzes as I put my finger on it.

The sound of quick footsteps on the other side comes closer, and the door is ripped open.

"Hi, Angela. Great to see you; come on in." Lucy has put on a tight-fitting black dress, which shows a slight bulge on her stomach.

I smile and hand her a bouquet of mixed tulips, which I just managed to buy on the way here.

"Thank you, how sweet of you." She glows and takes a step to the side so I can get in.

The hallway is small, and a light bulb hangs freely from the ceiling on a white cord. The coat rack on the wall is filled to the breaking point with jackets. Shoes, bags, and some brown cardboard boxes fill up the space and do not leave much room to pass.

Lucy is already on her way to the kitchen, which is right next to the hallway. I hang my jacket on top of one of the other jackets and follow her because I do not know where else to go.

"It's so cool that you wanted to come; it's always nice with new faces." She steps up onto a small stool and stretches toward the top shelf of a cupboard. It's filled with vases of all sizes. The water on the stove starts to boil; she grabs the nearest vase and steps down.

I stand completely still and try to breathe casually, but chaos inside ravages me. If only Lucy knew that it is only the face that is new, that she knows the person behind it very well.

"It's funny; I've been thinking about you all day. Are you sure we don't know each other from somewhere?" She turns her head and pours more water into the teapot.

"I don't think so," I say without hesitation. "Is there anything I can do to help?"

I look around the kitchen while keeping one eye on Lucy. The fridge door is covered in small magnets that keep track of memos. One says, "To dare is to lose oneself for a while; not to dare is to lose oneself." It's written on a small yellow post-it note.

"No, I've got it under control." She takes out a tray and places cups and plates on it. "Are you from around here? What school did you attend? There's got to be something…." She stops and looks at me with her deep brown eyes.

I shrug, fiddle a bit with the note, and turn toward her. "Do you live alone?" My voice gets a little harsh; that was not the intention. Before she answers, I can't help but let my eyes wander quickly around the kitchen once more. The light blue paint on the walls is worn, and there are several holes in the wall, not what I would associate with Lucy. The windowsill is filled with small, round lit candles; it seems more like her style.

Lucy steps toward me, shaking her head as she smiles. "No, I do not live alone," she points to her stomach, "but he is not home tonight."

I laugh warm-heartedly and pretend I don't know she lives with Tim.

I reach for a pen attached to a small block on the side of the refrigerator and write, *any illusion is a veil that covers something you do not want to see*. I pass it to Lucy. "This is one of my favorites."

She takes it eagerly and reads it.

"My God, it's beautiful." She moves some of the other post-it notes around, and a postcard comes into sight with a magnificent Native American chief. I freeze completely. That cannot be a message meant for me. Lucy has already been in In-Between. They would have known if she was one of the two I'm looking for. Or maybe they missed her; they can't be perfect all the time.

"I have always been so busy with what others thought of me, but recently it dawned on me that it was all something that was going on inside myself. Maybe that is my illusion." She places the note I gave her in the middle of the refrigerator. "Well, you can always hear about that another time; now, let's go and see the others."

I nod.

"Here," she hands me the tray with cups, which are decorated with blue flower vines and have a curved handle. There is also a bowl with biscuits. "Oh, sorry, I just have to put the flowers in water.

Just go in; the others are in the living room. It's further down the hallway, and I'm coming."

I enter the hallway and continue toward the living room. There are pictures of Lucy and Tim hanging everywhere in old silver frames in different sizes and all sorts of situations. The sound of female voices gets louder. A picture of Lucy and Tim bathing in a lake, one where they are riding on an elephant, and... There is a picture of Lucy from the time she was in a coma. Tim sits by her side, looking devastated. I stop. My heart begins to gallop. I stare at the picture and balance the tray in one hand while letting the other slide gently over the glass.

"It's from the time I was in a coma." Lucy suddenly stands next to me, and I startle, making the cups rattle.

"I'm so sorry; I didn't mean to scare you," Lucy laughs out loud.

"It's all right; I scare easily," I laugh a little stiffly.

At the end of the hallway, a living room appears. Lucy leads the way, and I follow.

"Hi, everybody, meet Angela." She says out loud and turns toward me. I step into the living room and stand next to Lucy, and seven women turn their heads simultaneously and look at me.

By the window sits a chubby girl with ultra-short hair, which is clearly bleached. Next to her sits a slightly older woman in a beanbag chair; she has freckles across her nose and is so thin that you can almost see through her. They sit on everything that can be sat on, and they sit close to each other. I fidget a bit and let my gaze wander around without really looking at the rest of them while I mumble hello and smile.

"If you just squeeze together, you can make room for Angela." Lucy gazes at three women on the couch who look like they own it and definitely got here first.

I take a step forward, but my foot gets caught by a strap on a bag. I lose my balance. My arms jerk to the side, and the tray slides out of my hands. Time stands still inside me as I see all the cups in free fall against the wooden floor. At the same moment, I make eye contact with a woman on the couch. It's Longlegs. The cups hit the floor and splinter to all sides. The sound cuts through the living room, and a wave of uncertainty rushes through me.

"Hey, don't worry about that." Lucy turns around and disappears into the hallway.

I stand completely numb. Now, they all know for sure that I have arrived. The light is dimmed in the living room, and there are lots of candles burning on the windowsill and the dresser to the right. I squat down and start picking up the biggest shards. All the cups are broken, and the biscuits are spread out over a large area.

"If you just jump on the couch, I'll take care of this in a snap." Lucy is standing behind me with a broom and a vacuum cleaner. Longlegs sits as a spectator on the couch with two other women next to her. They reluctantly move closer together to make room for me. One of the women appears to be in her forties; she is stocky with very short, black hair. The other is plain of build and dressed in some very variegated homemade clothes. She is in her early twenties and looks like a gypsy.

"Hello," I say in a low voice. I would like to face them but cannot. "Please, let me help you, Lucy." I'm frantically looking for another place to sit, but there are no other vacancies.

"No, just sit down; I can easily manage." Lucy is busy removing the remnants of the biscuits. The sofa looks more like a three-seater sofa than a four-seater. Fortunately, it is the end seat that becomes available. I squeeze down next to the girl with the variegated clothes. Longlegs sits at the other end.

"Hello, my name is Emma." Longlegs leans toward me and reaches out her skinny hand. She looks directly at me, and I send her a fixed smile. Our hands meet, and her skin is hard and ice cold.

"I didn't get your name?" She keeps staring at me.

"Angela," I say with forced confidence in my voice.

"Wonderful, we are all here now." Lucy places a tray on the table with new cups and some new biscuits sprinkled with sugar. "Since there are several new people here tonight, I just want to tell you that we usually take turns bringing up a theme, and then we each come with input to that theme." She smiles from ear to ear and squeezes her bum down next to the woman on the beanbag chair.

I look around at the others. They sit well-behaved and listen. A beautiful woman with long, gray hair cut like Cleopatra and dark blue eyes catches my attention. She is sitting in a black armchair next to the window. The others seem pretty ordinary.

It has turned dark outside, and the gleam of the streetlights is hitting the bare walls. Several pictures are still sitting on the floor. I'm not sure how long Lucy has lived here or if she is about to move out. It could also be Tim's apartment she has moved into.

"Angela, would you like to choose a theme? You are new; it's always exciting to get new participants' ideas to a theme that we can address. We always talk about the same things—men, sex, and children." She laughs, and the women on the couch follow like an echo.

"Sure." My eyes wander around the room. They all look at me again and await my proposal. Not exactly what I had hoped for.

"You choose whatever you feel like, and there is nothing that is forbidden to talk about." There are two slightly stiff women sitting next to each other by the door, and they start giggling. Lucy ignores them, reaches for her tea, and smells the scent.

I smile and tilt my head slightly to the side. "Well, then, I think we should talk about past lives."

The room becomes dead quiet. Longlegs' mouth tightens, and several of the others look at each other a little indulgently.

No one says anything. One pours tea, another checks her cell for messages, and a third gets up and goes to the bathroom. I look around without moving my head. It looks like the woman with the long gray hair wants to say something, but she looks down when I look at her.

"Come on, honestly. Don't be cowards. That's a cool topic." Lucy puts her cup down on the windowsill. "I'll start since I have actually been almost dead."

I move back on the couch, sit up straight, and try not to touch the woman next to me. The woman with long gray hair looks up, and our eyes meet; she quickly moves her gaze over to Lucy. She has a brown leather cord around her neck; it holds a pendant of a narrow, oval silver piece of jewelry.

"Well, as most of you already know, I was in a coma for six weeks." Lucy nearly falls back when the woman with whom she shares the beanbag chair moves. She just manages to grab the chair next to her and stay seated. "After I woke up, there were some days where I had a strong sense of a dimension other than life. I'm sure there is more between Heaven and Earth than we know of." She looks around and shrugs her shoulders. "But now the sensation has gone. The most important thing is Tim and…" she smiles a little shyly and caresses her stomach.

I breathe a sigh and reach for my tea. The cup is still hot, and I wrap a napkin around it and take a cautious sip.

"I don't believe in any of that nonsense at all." Longlegs crosses her legs, and her mouth constricts even more. "It's only people who have nothing else to devote themselves to who are interested in whimsical subjects like that."

I choke on the tea. Andreas has met his match there. At least he is a bit spiritual.

Longlegs looks around to see if she can convince everyone that she's right. "My husband's ex-girlfriend was also in a coma. She's dead now, but is she supposed to come back and be born again?" She raises a loud, shrill laugh, and several of the others follow. "No way, I hope not. Let's have some coffee. I hope it's strong, Lucy." Longlegs reaches out for a cup and fills it while she sends Lucy a merciful smile.

My body starts to boil, and my face becomes dark red. I tighten the grip on my cup. I better not say anything right now. It is impossible to come up with anything nice, and I'm afraid of revealing myself. That would be a disaster. Please, someone, say something before I explode. I press my teeth firmly together so that no words slip out and allow my left foot to tilt up and down.

THE RING

The woman with the long gray hair looks at Longlegs, then over at Lucy, and finally at me. With the finest silky voice, she takes charge. "I believe in past lives." Her tone is gentle and trustworthy. "Because I've experienced it."

The living room becomes completely quiet. Longlegs puts her coffee on the table with a slap and leans back with crossed arms and her chin high. The sound of a car horn from the street breaks the silence. Quietly, a very fragile energy starts to take over my body; suddenly, there is space inside me. Anger becomes joy, and gratitude flows through me. Everyone is sitting, waiting for her to continue. But she's not in a hurry.

"My past lives come to mind as fragments of a story." She sits perfectly still, resting her hands in her lap as she speaks. "I never know when. But in a way, they always make sense."

My jaw drops down, and I'm completely absorbed in her words. My throat swallows, her words touch me. It's not only what she says, but it's also the way she says it. Her voice is like a melody, like a tone that is sung and creates resonance inside me.

"The images I see are so real. I can smell the places, taste the ambiance, and feel the atmosphere." Her long gray hair falls easily around her face, and she wraps a strand around her fingers.

Something happens to Lucy as she speaks. She begins to look distanced, and a white light appears around her. I've never seen anything like it before. It looks surreal, almost incredible. I rub my eyes and look again, and it's still there. I have never heard others talk about past lives like that. What she describes is exactly the same as what I have experienced.

"It sounds really exciting," Longlegs interrupts. "Does anyone want a biscuit?" She laughs haughtily and looks over at Lucy as she turns to the woman next to her and whispers loud enough for me to hear, "Maybe she also had a psycho boyfriend in her past lives." They both laugh knowingly.

The girl with the variegated clothes holds out her plate. "I would like a biscuit, please." Her voice is hesitant.

Lucy still has a far-away look in her eyes, but there is a different calmness around her now. She turns her head and looks me straight in the eye. My stomach sinks, and I grab my tea and finish it.

One of the women gets up and leaves the room. Several of the others start chatting; they obviously know each other well. I get up and try to make my way over to the woman with the long gray hair.

"Angela…" Lucy is calling. I turn around, and she is standing with the woman in the variegated clothes. Longlegs has ganged up with two of the others, and they are standing by the door whispering.

"One moment, Lucy." It dawns on me that the woman with the long gray hair has disappeared from the living room. I edge past Longlegs' group, who stop talking as I pass them. They all stare mercilessly at me. The woman with gray hair is nowhere to be seen. Not in the living room or the kitchen. The hallway is dark and long. I grope my way forward and hit a few of the pictures on the wall. The sound of a door slamming ahead of me makes me pick up speed. I grab the front door and open it with a brisk pull. There is no one out in the stairway.

"Excuse me; can I get past?" The voice behind me belongs to the woman with long gray hair.

I turn around, and there she is. My body sinks in relief, and I smile. "Sure, yes, but I actually didn't get your name before?" We are facing each other. She is wearing the most beautiful earrings with gold and turquoise that alternate with each other. They look Egyptian.

"Meera," she says in her fragile voice, standing relaxed in front of me with her coat over her arm. She's not as tall as I am. The moment feels infinite yet like a split second; we stand there in the hallway facing each other without saying anything.

"My name is Angela." I reach out my hand a little hesitantly.

"I've met you before." She doesn't move a muscle in her face.

It gives me a start. What is she referring to? Now, I better make sure to get her phone number or find another way to contact her.

She starts putting on her coat. "I have to go now; tomorrow, I am traveling to the Himalayas." Meera's voice is so delicate, and just the sound of it makes me fall into a trance-like state.

"Wow, I must say. That sounds interesting." I step on my own feet; now I have to do something. "Do you want to meet again? I think what you said in there was very interesting." I feel like a five-year-old little girl knocking on a big door to hear if Meera wants to come out and play.

She takes my hand. "It is always exciting to reconnect with old acquaintances. But then you would have to come with me to the Himalayas."

22

THE HIMALAYAS

The view is frighteningly large. The mountains undulate endlessly, and their peaks try to reach the sky, while the snow lies untouched like sprinkled sugar. I'm used to great views, but this is different. We have walked for four intense days, and here, my boots won't keep me from falling. Most of the time, we've been walking in line, and at night, I've been so tired that we have hardly spoken to each other. Meera walks right in front of me, and in front of her is a local guide. We are at an altitude of 3100 meters, and I can feel that it has been a while since I have been in thin air. I gasp a little, and a headache comes and goes.

After saying goodbye to Meera at Lucy's apartment, I was ready to take off with her. But the next day, the doubt came rushing in. I spent a week suppressing my doubts so I could act on my first instinct. Before Meera left, she told me where she was going and where and when to meet if I wanted to come. I met her in the village at the foot of the mountain we are climbing.

At times, the path we walk on is non-existent. If our local guide weren't leading the way, we would definitely get lost. The sun is hanging above us and is generously heating the cold ground, leaving piles of snow under the bushes. We cross over small streams with water so fresh that you can drink it. And we climb up stairs made of rocks that seem to have been laid in another age. I get the feeling that with every step we take, we go deeper into the soul of the country.

I have tried to get in touch with Thomas, but I can't get through to him no matter how I sit or what I think about. Before I left the city, there were a few days where I felt utterly lost. All I could think about was finding two random people to take back to In-Between. Just to get it over and done with. Of course, I didn't, and now, I have found peace within again. The contact to Thomas comes if it comes. It's out of my hands. Twenty-seven days, that's how long I have left to find the missing two.

My conversation with Meera kept haunting me, the things she said, the way they resonated inside me. It was as if she were speaking to a deeper place inside me where words are not needed. I have never experienced that with a person on Earth before. And even though I've had long conversations with myself, I could not find any justifiable reason not to throw myself into this journey and join her.

So, here I am with big hiking boots, thick socks, and a backpack with a water bottle and some extra clothes. The rest of my stuff is carried by some of the locals who are already far ahead of us. They carry thirty-five kilos each, impressive because I think it's hard enough with the few kilos I have to carry up the mountain. Five porters, a chef, and a guide just for the two of us.

The air is thin and pure, and it tickles a bit with every breath I take. High above us, several large birds are circling. I kick a rock on the path, and it flies over the edge. One wrong step, and I'll be heading the same way. Meera is walking a short distance in front of me, and she is talking to the guide. Right now, the path is wide enough to walk next to each other, but farther ahead, it narrows again. I can't hear what they are saying, but the guide gestures heavily.

It would be nice to find the first of the two missing people in the Ring. It would give me some peace of mind and the certainty that I have plenty of time to find the second one. If I don't manage to find both of them, I could at least say that I found one. I push the thought aside. It's not true. If I don't find them both, it's all been in vain. It's one of my sub-personalities trying to invent a new reality in order to fool myself into not grasping the seriousness of the task.

My lungs begin to sting every time I breathe. I slow down and support my hand on the rough, nearly vertical cliff next to me. To my left, the mountain just drops down into a dark abyss. Meera has stopped for a drink and is a little farther along the path. What if she is one of them? How do I convince her to come to In-Between? Maybe I could push her over the edge; then it would be done. And no questions asked.

Meera looks back. "Did you say something?"

A shiver runs through my body. "No." I shake my head eagerly.

She is well wrapped in a green windbreaker and black trousers. Her long gray hair sticks out from under a black hat, and her feminine hip sway shows as she walks.

I pull out one of the lonely, green twigs that grow on the bare mountainside. It has struggled its way through a crack and now has to let go of life just because I am frustrated. Far below, I can glimpse a village, and up on the side of the mountain, farther ahead, is the ledge we are aiming for.

We continue to walk for the next five hours, only stopping for a short lunch break. Meera is still talking to the guide or walking by herself. It suits me fine. I enjoy the time by myself and fall into a space of meditation—reconnecting to the place inside I discovered in In-Between after days and weeks of practice. It is a place where there are no thoughts and just peace. I can connect for longer now and just be at one with my breathing, walking, and nature. If anyone had told me that this was possible three months ago, I would have thought they were crazy. I look around. We have moved above the tree line, and now the surroundings are harsher. The ground is covered with small purple flowers and bushes. Now and again, we meet a local who seems to have been here for their whole life. To my surprise, they live in the most incredible places with no water or electricity. This is another world, so simple and pure.

The sun is disappearing on the horizon really fast. It's only five o'clock, and we have reached the camp at 3500 meters altitude. There is a ledge where small rocks are placed in a circle, and inside is a campfire. Next to it is a bare patch where we can put up our tent. The air is freezing cold. The heat from the sun is completely gone now, and the glow of the moon is taking over. Meera is arranging her sleeping bag; I decide to wait outside the tent and jump up and down to keep warm.

The porters, the guide, and the chef have put up their tents on the other side of the camp. They are preparing dinner. There is a constant flow of words, but I don't understand what they are saying. Meera doesn't say much either. I have begun to appreciate silence more, the silence that had been so frightening to me before.

The mountains lie in silhouette in front of us, with a fine outline against the dark sky. We have collected wood for a bonfire, and I walk a bit away from the camp and stand on a small ledge. The depth is right in front of me even though I can't see it. A white flash makes me bend forward. I close my eyes and support my hands against the ground. My head is buzzing, and I'm losing my balance. A place similar to the place where I first met the Ring appears in front of me.

I get up and step forward a bit. There I am, and Thomas, Gabriel, Yoge, and Shiva are there too. To the right of Shiva is a person with her back facing this way. I try to see if I can catch a glimpse of the person, but the image begins to flicker and disappear. I reach out, but it's gone.

"What do you see?" Meera is standing right behind me, and I quickly take down my arm.

"I just saw a place I've seen before." Should I tell her what it is and see if she recognizes the place? Right now, I haven't got a clue how much she actually knows of previous lives. What is her experience, and in what way? And could there be a connection between her flashbacks and the Ring? I'm up against time, but I have to build up trust and not push too hard.

She looks at me, and her expression gives nothing away.

We walk back to the bonfire without exchanging words. The flames from the fire rise high up into the sky. The heat penetrates my clothes and caresses my skin. I sit down on a tree stump, and Meera joins me.

"You seemed very confident when you shared your experiences with past lives at Lucy's place." I move a little closer to the bonfire and stretch my legs toward it.

"It's something that has always been a part of my life." She rubs her hands together and holds them up against the flames. The fire lights up her face. "For many years, I have ignored it. I was too busy with my career and friends." She shrugs and moves a strand of hair that has fallen in front of her eyes.

Our guide comes over with a sleep mat. I fold it once and sit on it so the cold doesn't break through. He is not that tall and very skinny. It is hard to tell his age because of his windswept face and rough hands, but his knowledge of nature testifies to many years in the mountains.

"I've always dealt with a lot of things myself." Meera's gray hair gets a luminous touch from the flames, and her cheeks flush.

I sit still and look into the fire while the calmness fills me—no thoughts, no words—as long as it lasts.

"I have also always dealt with everything myself." I look at Meera. "When I was younger, I sometimes felt like I was a slave to my emotions." I push a piece of firewood with my foot. The fire is increasing. "I could go for days with a burning sensation of something I wanted to say and know exactly how I wanted to say it, but I could not get it out of my mouth. It was like my mind was a prison, not letting the words out."

Meera does not respond; she looks present, but I cannot figure out what is happening inside her. Every little muscle in her face is relaxed.

"I was really scared of other people's reactions. Weren't you when you shared about your experiences at Lucy's?"

She slowly shakes her head and moves a little closer to the fire. "I have held back and compromised for many years." She blinks a few times, and the glow of the flames dances on her cheek. "I have been dependent on other people's recognition and have gained it through my work. But it's like watering a desert."

I was also a slave to recognition when I worked as a journalist. The recognition was better than medicine, alcohol, or sweets, all combined. I look at Meera and take a deep breath.

She places one of the long gray strands of hair behind her ear and speaks softly with her gentle, silky voice. "I don't want to depend on others anymore. It is a decision I have made. Now, I challenge myself on every given occasion. The night we met was one of them." A laugh comes from deep down in her stomach and resounds in the silence.

I smile and feel a quiet joy bubbling in my heart. Sitting here with Meera is like being on a journey with an old school friend you haven't seen for years.

The moon hangs high in the sky in bright contrast to the black sky, and the clouds flow quietly by. The flames break the darkness and create a secure space for us in the dark.

"In fact, I've been quite sick in my life." The laughter stops immediately, and she looks at me seriously.

I pull down my jacket and fold my hands. My smile fades away.

A small light appears by the kitchen tent. It is the chef who comes out and shouts at one of the porters; then, he disappears into the kitchen tent again.

"When I was a child, I experienced that when I was sick, I got attention, and I got it mixed up with love."

I listen and feel honored that she trusts me with her experience of life.

"So, unconsciously, I have made myself sick throughout my life to get attention and thereby love."

She is one of the few people who does not wear a mask to hide her true feelings. I can feel her speaking from her heart without prejudice or reproach. She seems so brutally honest. I swallow and press my tongue against the inside of my teeth.

"Someone once said to me, 'Never love sick people; look after them and care for them, but do not give them love.'" Meera's voice echoes in the darkness.

She sits completely still, and a tear runs from the corner of her eye. "There are two kinds of sick people—those who benefit from it and those who don't. Sick people must experience that it is more fun to be healthy. That they are loved and rewarded when they take responsibility to get well instead of turning into a victim and being dependent on others' support and attention." She pauses, "It goes without saying that if a person is deathly sick, then you love them all you can and more."

Several of the flames have turned into embers, and the heat disappears. I put a piece of wood on the fire and some dry leaves. The flames flare again, and thick smoke blows over us.

Meera waves her hand lightly. "It was not until I found a therapist who worked with the body and not only the mind that it dawned on me how much pain I was carrying." She turns her head and looks me straight in the eye. Her dark blue eyes are blank. "It was shocking to find out how much I had shut off my body. I could not feel it at all." She presses her lips together and wipes the tears away. "I have shouted, hit pillows, kicked, and danced my way through the pain. It helped to release it and get in touch with my body again. Today, I am very sensitive, and my body is my most important tool."

Our guide steps out of the darkness with two steaming bowls. Inside is a hot, all-red soup. He places it in front of us, smiles, and disappears again.

I grab a spoon and bring the hot soup to my mouth. The scent spreads up to my nose, and I blow on it carefully.

"How can you tell the difference? I mean, what comes from the mind and from the body?" The taste of the soup spreads in my mouth. It is spicy without being too hot.

Meera sits still; maybe she's waiting for the soup to cool, or perhaps she's just waiting.

"I experienced the big difference when I no longer asked why."

"No longer asked why," I mumble into the soup.

Meera blinks slowly and smiles at me. "When you ask why, you shift focus from what is to your mind." She pauses. "And in your mind, you will find no useful answers to those questions." She dips the spoon into the soup and fills it in a sliding motion.

I nod and try to look as if I understand.

One of the porters comes out of the darkness with bowls of rice, potatoes, and mixed vegetables.

"More soup?" He points at my half-empty bowl.

"No, thank you. It was delicious."

Meera takes one more spoonful of soup, then she continues with her gentle, silky voice, "Instead of asking why you have a headache, you can feel the pain, describe, and contain it. You can ask the headache what it wants to tell you or show you."

I can't help laughing but quickly bite it back and peck a little embarrassedly at a potato. "When I have a headache, all I care about is getting rid of it, and the best way I know is a pill," I say, knowing that I just revealed my ego's ignorance.

Meera tastes each spoonful of the soup as if they were different.

"If you just take a pill, you remove the symptom and do not transform the cause. There is a reason why you get a headache." She keeps a straight face and must be used to their hot spices. "Your body will tell you that something is wrong, and by removing the message, the headache, you will never find the cause." She stops and puts down the spoon. "And the signals will only get louder and louder. If we do not listen, illness is the only way our bodies can get our attention."

I stop chewing and breathe deeply.

"What was the matter with you?"

The fire sputters, and several sparks fly in the air.

"I had diabetes."

"Had?" I raise my eyebrows.

Meera looks at me in a loving way. "A lot of things happened when I started going into the disease and looked at it as a lesson. I had to go through many layers of anger, sadness, guilt, abandonment, and not least jealousy toward my little sister, who, throughout my childhood, got my parents' attention." She speaks calmly and chooses the words with great precision. "Over time, my body changed."

I put down my fork and look at her vacantly.

She pauses and reaches for the vegetables, carefully picking out four pieces and moving them onto her plate. "The hardest thing was to admit to myself that I had wanted to get sick and was really afraid of what I would be without my illness." Slowly, she puts the bowl of vegetables away.

I don't say anything. I'm just looking at Meera, her beautiful facial features, her natural, warm radiance. Her honesty is striking.

"Did you know that all the organs in our body restore themselves? That is, after a certain number of days, we have all new organs?" Meera emphasizes every single word. "When I studied to become a doctor, I came across so much interesting research that isn't known to the public."

I frown and put down my fork as I reach for my tea.

"For example, the kidneys, they restore themselves at intervals of seven days."

"If they do, then why is there anyone who needs a new kidney?"

She looks at me; love flows from her gaze, which seems infinite. "Our body remembers everything we experience, even though we forget or repress. It also passes on information, and if our kidney is carrying an emotional imbalance such as anxiety, then that feeling will be passed on to the new kidney unless we work on our anxiety and release it."

I keep quiet, grab a stick, and shake up the embers. The flames send small sparks into the air, which quickly die. Her words make sense in an inexplicable way and resonate in my heart. But my mind is working overtime, finding arguments of the opposite.

"I have always felt very lonely." Meera stops eating and looks at me. "I did not feel that others understood me and hoped that one day, I would meet someone who would save me and see me as I am." She looks into the fire as if it is helping her stay in her heart. "Even though I have been busy with friends and work, I have basically been lonely. Others have always seen me as popular, but inside I felt alone, and I was always trying to run away from it."

It tears at my heart. "I have also been lonely in my life." I look at Meera through the flames. I've never admitted that to anyone before.

We sit still in silence, holding each other's vulnerability and truth. The fire dies down but is still generously sharing its last heat. All I can hear is the crackles of the flames.

"No matter if I'm lonely or ill, I have concluded that there is only one person who can save me." She grabs her thighs and pulls her legs toward her.

The moon hangs in the sky just above us, surrounded by countless stars. I move a little closer to the fire, which is about to die out. "Who doesn't want to be saved, just a little bit?" I look intently at Meera.

"Well, I have tried to save other people all my life, both in my private life and professionally." She looks up straight ahead. "I was in a relationship with this charming, caring, and funny guy. He was so nice and gave me so much attention. He lifted me up. We had fun together and great sex." She can't help but smile a little. "Then, after two years, he changed. Suddenly, he pulled away from me. He began to manipulate me, and slowly, I lost my self-confidence. I didn't see many of my friends and thought it was me who did something wrong." She shrugs. "I didn't think anything like that could happen to me. I'm well educated, smart, and had a lot of success. But that is what they are attracted to, the psychopaths. And he hid his darkness so well. It wasn't until I wanted a divorce that he became violent."

I sit still and listen, giving her the time and space to dive into her story. It feels like she is transforming the old pain as she speaks. Her long gray hair is glowing in the dark, and the reflection from the flames lights up her dark eyes.

"He didn't hit me physically, only with his anger and extremely manipulative behavior. Those bruises are so hard to prove. He would go away for the weekend and leave old food in the fridge. If I threw it out, he would accuse me of interfering with his things. He moved out of the bedroom but kept his clothes in there. Each morning, when he came to get his clothes, he would turn on the light and open the closet. He'd take out some suits and put them back. And in the end, he would leave with a pair of socks. The rest he had already." She pauses. She sits for five minutes without saying anything and then looks at me. "I cannot save others, only myself. But that is also a big task." She smiles, the flames die down, and the light on her face disappears. "Maybe I will never succeed. New challenges always arise." Her eyes get a little distant.

"You can say that again," the words spill out of my mouth. A yawn penetrates. I get up and shake my legs. "I need to get some sleep."

Meera nods at me and reaches out her hands toward the last embers.

She fascinates me, but not in the same way as Annabel. She had a female energy that nurtured me. Meera has something else, an insight, or perhaps rather a life experience. I smile up at the dark sky where a cloud slides in front of the moon. I swallow a lump in my throat, and a subtle trickle runs down my spine. If only she's the one I need to bring back.

23

HAVE FAITH IN YOURSELF

The sky is deep red, and the sun is making its entrance in the distance. The clouds are drawn like racing stripes and create a lively pattern. I sit on a rock and tie the laces on my boots. The Skycon is in my pocket. There is still no signal, no help from above, not even through the contact I created. But somehow, I have come to terms with it. Whether it's because I'm shutting down or because I feel confident that I'm on track, I do not know.

My conversation with Meera last night has made an impact on me. I have to find a way to figure out whether Meera is one of the two I have to bring with me. It will take two more days before we reach our destination—a mountain top at 4500 meters altitude. There is still time.

Meera is sitting on the edge of the slope. She has been sitting there for the last half-hour without moving. I'm not that efficient in the morning, and it suits me fine to get ready at my own pace while she fixes her inner self. I can glimpse a river winding through the landscape further down the valley; it glimmers in the sunlight. The terraces with the almost luminescent green grass unfold along the mountainside. The place has a divine calmness to it, so unspoiled and pure. My backpack is stuffed to the brim. I had to use my fist to press the top down to get it closed. I didn't bring that much with me, but unfortunately, dirty clothes take up more space than clean ones. I bend my knees and get the backpack lifted into place. My legs give way, and I sway in the cool breeze. A morning like this makes me feel like a new beginning. Everything is crisp, everything is new, and everything is possible. The limitations are up to me.

Why didn't I take the time to feel the freedom of a hike when I was alive? There are so many things I would have liked to have achieved, but they were not a priority. I expected to have a long, full life ahead of me.

Meera moves, unfolds her body from the position she has been sitting in for the last thirty minutes, and stretches toward the sky. She comes toward me with easy steps. The height does not seem to bother her.

"Are you ready?" Her silky voice evokes a deep reverberation inside me. My legs sway beneath me, and I struggle to stay upright. I send her a nod and leave my large backpack to one of the porters, who has come to my rescue.

"Well, then, there is no time to waste." She signals to our guide that we are ready.

Despite his short legs, he sets off at a rapid pace. After just a few meters, I start to gasp for breath; my old body was definitely in better shape.

Behind us, I can catch a glimpse of some of the kilometers traveled. Several of the mountain peaks are now below us. The air is clear, the birds are singing, and we are almost one with nature. We are here on nature's terms and grace. The plants begin to change—from being filled with rhododendron plants, there are now more low shrubs with curled leaves. There are larger areas of snow in the darkness under the bushes. From here, there is just one way, and that is up as far as the eye can see. I edge myself along a small ledge and set off to the next one. A few stones roll under my feet, and I do my best to keep my balance. Our guide turns around to make sure we keep up. My legs are already starting to burn, and we have only just started the day's hike. The few kilos I carry on my back feel like twenty bricks. Thoughts are filling my head. They get plenty of space here in the thin air where nothing disturbs them. Meera walks alone a bit further ahead, and I let myself fall back to the point where I can no longer see her. Then I lean against the mountainside and close my eyes while focusing on my heart. Right now, I'm closer to In-Between, and therefore, in theory, it should also be easier to get in touch. Could something be wrong there? Maybe it's just me who cannot figure out how to make contact?

"Have faith in yourself." It's the same voice I heard on the bench in the park when the butterfly came. It's not in my head; it's somehow all around me.

I open my eyes a bit, making a slit between my eyelids. The steep slope has an abrupt drop to a wilderness of trees and bushes right in front of me. The path is so narrow that it is not possible to get away from the edge. I take a small step to the side. My breathing is building up, and I am getting a little short of breath. I rest my hand on the cliff next to me. It is filled with cracks, where small crystals shine in the sunlight.

"We are all connected."

The voice is back. I can hear it just as clearly, but the white, phosphorescent light is not there.

I look up the mountain, which rises to the sky. I'm not sure if the mountain reaches the sky or the sky reaches down to the mountain. I see spots before my eyes, and a glimpse of another reality breaks into the present in a split second. It is the image of me hanging on the cross. The blood drips steadily from my wrists. It is as if I see the same experience but from a different perspective. This time, I am a spectator. I continue to look up the mountainside, and the two visions merge.

The air tingles in my lungs as I breathe. I move my fingers to assure myself that I can still feel my body and support myself with all my weight against the side of the mountain. The vision is still there as a veil over reality. The man on the cross next to me is unconscious. I want to move but give up and lean back against the mountainside. All I can see now is the image of me on the cross. I am pale, and my face is ravaged, but somehow, I look as if I'm at peace. It's evening, and several of the women are on their way up to us. The sound of my breath connects with both the present and the past.

The pain in my wrists returns weakly, and the fatigue spreads in my body. I look at the man on the cross next to me for the last time. The ropes around my feet are cut, and I fall into the women's arms.

Inside the cottage, there is a faint glow from the campfire. They place me on a bunk, and I begin to feel the heat from the room. Slowly, very slowly, I turn my head and look into the eyes of one of the women.

It's Meera.

The small stones begin to slip under my feet. Pain cuts through my body from my elbow as it hits the ground. I blink feverishly to see what is happening. The slope comes with explosive speed toward me. I grab hold of a large rock and kick desperately with my boots to regain my footing. The image of my inner eye is still there, and I can see the woman smiling at me. My feet hit a small rock and find a foothold. Slowly but surely, I use all my strength to crawl back up the slope.

"Angela!" Meera's voice disappears in the distance.

I turn onto my back, resting on my elbows and looking down into the abyss just below my feet. From the corner of my eye, I can sense her hiking boots running toward me. The pain overwhelms everything inside me. I'm lying completely still. Someone squeezes my arm, and I lift my head from the ground. Meera has got ahold of me.

"Come on; let me help you."

I roll over onto my side, ensuring that my feet are still placed on the small rock for support.

"What happened?"

Meera squats down in front of me. Our guide has thrown his backpack on the path and comes rushing toward us. I lean against the mountain and try to signal that everything is okay.

"I stumbled." My voice stammers, and I try to clear my throat.

"You're bleeding," Meera pulls a mat out of her backpack and spreads it out next to me. "Come here."

My elbow throbs and hurts insanely. I put one hand on the ground and push myself toward Meera. The pain rushes from my elbow through my arm. A burning heat follows.

"Let me take a look at that." She helps me take off my jacket and gently pulls up my sleeve. "You cut yourself, but it doesn't look serious."

The guide stands behind Meera and watches. He does not respond.

"Where were you?" Meera looks me straight in the eye, and I look down.

"I was in my own thoughts," I reply without hesitation.

"Interesting how we get closer to heaven." She smiles crookedly and winks at me.

The wind blows fog over us, and the abyss is transformed into a soft, white mass. Within seconds, I can only see a few meters around us; we are surrounded with poor visibility.

"Can you stand?" The guide steps forward. "We have to keep going."

I put my hand on the ground, and the guide helps me up effortlessly. "You're in the middle now." There is no reason to argue; he is in charge up here.

We walk non-stop for hours, and my legs feel like lead until our guide finally signals to stop. There is a cave with big flat rocks in front of us. I head directly toward them and collapse.

Meera joins me; she has a map in her hand. "I thought you might want to see where we are and where we are going."

"Only if there's not that far to go." I try to smile. There is a spasm of pain from my elbow, and my body contracts convulsively.

She sits down next to me and gives my hand a squeeze. "Don't worry; the path you have traveled in life will never be repeated."

"Which one of your past lives do you remember the best?" My feet cannot reach the ground and hang limply. Meera puts the map on the ground next to her.

"There are several fragments I can remember, but my experience is also that when I look for places that may relate to past lives, more pieces of the puzzle become visible." She speaks calmly and gives me a gentle push to make me move and make space for her on the rock chair.

Does she basically already know who I am? Has she known it all along?

"Why are you here, Angela?" She puts a hand gently on my thigh and looks straight ahead.

During the time we have traveled together, she has not once asked why I wanted to join. Now, there is an opening.

It is all or nothing.

24

THE WAY FORWARD

Thomas kneels next to the bed where Gabriel is resting. He looks pale, and the blanket covering his legs and stomach moves slowly up and down. The walls are bare, and a sparse light fills the room gently. There is a small table next to the bed; on it sit several small stones, all painted in colorful shades, and on a piece of paper is written a number of words: Love, Gratitude, and Compassion in red ink. Thomas places his hand softly on Gabriel's chest, and he opens his eyes a bit.

"How are you?"

Gabriel turns his head slightly to the side; his eyes are swollen. "It's quiet inside me. I'm tired, and it feels like something's pulling at me." His voice sounds rustier than usual.

His wrinkled forehead is strained, and his body looks fragile. Thomas feels a delicate energy flow from Gabriel's heart through his hand and up his arm.

"I do not recognize the pull you experience, but I can sense its power." He looks at Gabriel, who closes his eyes and slowly opens them again.

"There are twenty-six days until Angela returns. Can you hold on that long?" Thomas nearly whispers as he maintains his gaze on Gabriel. All thoughts in his head are gone; he only focuses on Gabriel.

Gabriel opens his mouth, but it is dry, and no words get out. He lifts his arm and reaches for a glass of water on a small table next to the bed.

"Here, let me help you." Thomas gets the glass and supports Gabriel's neck so he can drink.

He takes a sip. "I will do everything in my power to hold on, but you may have to prepare Angela for the fact that she could be coming back before the forty-two days have passed." His voice is subdued.

Thomas nods slowly as he tries to stifle his nervousness with a deep breath. "I better talk to the Master about re-establishing contact." He lets his gaze wander around the room. Next to the bed is a large round window where the clouds drift past, reminding him that everything carries on, no matter what happens. Opposite the bed is a chair, where a pile of books lies and collects dust. Thomas never read any of them, but Gabriel has always read a book a day. But not lately. Maybe he has been ill for longer than Thomas knows. He looks at Gabriel again. "It's not until we are truly challenged that we can see how far we have come in our personal development. And you have come far, my old friend. Hang in there; we are so close."

Gabriel closes his eyes, his breathing is almost invisible, and the bit of color he had in his face has completely disappeared. His head gives a slight jerk up and down. Thomas says nothing, feels the silence inside, and finds no words that are important to say. Gabriel's lips slide apart, and he tenses his face. He raises his hand, grabs Thomas's shoulder, and pulls him closer to his mouth.

"Look..." The word erases itself.

Thomas leans forward, but there is no sound.

"Ani..." He closes his mouth again and dozes off.

Thomas gets up and gives his hand a squeeze. "I'll be back. Hang in there."

THE MASTER SITS in his armchair. He is watching the news on the paper-thin screen floating slightly away from the wall. Pictures from a courtroom where a woman is on trial for killing her violent husband run over the screen. The prosecutor, a dark woman with frizzy hair and a tight black suit, makes a comment while the other lawyers protest. The sound is turned all the way down, but the images leave no doubt about the tension. Thomas moves a chair over next to him and sits down in silence. Outside the big windows are swans walking around freely and clouds drifting by. The Master turns off the news feed with a light hand gesture and turns to Thomas.

"The situation is unusual." He sits back in his chair and breathes calmly. His eyes have a glossy glow over them, which gives a rare depth.

Thomas sits perfectly still in the illuminating light in the room. Before he left Gabriel, he called Shiva, and she promised to stay with him. They can't risk him being alone anymore. If Angela finds the last two people for the Ring, they need Gabriel to come through too.

"Frank was one of those people we paid special attention to when he was here." The Master's long, light beard hangs down over the light brown robe, which falls loosely around his marked body. Next to him is a small table with five pens and a small pad. The pens are studded with small glittering stones.

Thomas is sitting with his hands folded in his lap. Slowly, the inner calm returns, and he lets the Master's intense clarity fill every little cell in his body. The Master leans slightly forward and looks Thomas straight in the eye.

"Gabriel's soul has begun to move toward the next stage, and it is uncertain how long he will stay in In-Between." He leans back in his chair again. The silence cuts into the walls and makes the room seem even brighter. If it weren't for the Master's calmness and strength like a rock, Thomas would not be sure if he could hold onto his faith. He knows that he has to lead the way for the Ring members now that Gabriel is weak. But he has always been terrified of making mistakes, and for that reason, he has never taken the lead before. In a split second, he feels the insecurity he carried with him as a child. His father didn't tolerate mistakes, and he wanted Thomas to follow in his footsteps and become a politician. And not just any politician, he wanted Thomas to do what he didn't manage himself, to become a governor. He folds up his sleeves with precision and narrows his eyes a little. Outside, a swan has sat down overlooking the small pond. It looks like it owns the place. Thomas pushes the chair back and walks quietly to the window with his hands resting in the middle of his chest.

The Master continues in a low voice, "If people hear about In-Between on Earth, we may risk that many who are not happy with their life will see it as a way out." He pauses and bends his head slightly. "If the Ring is not completed this time, humanity will not get the help it needs to reach the next level of consciousness. This will mean that the negative energy will have even more power, and those who want to strengthen their awareness will find it very difficult. It could be the downfall of mankind."

Thomas turns, so he is facing the Master and makes a sweeping gesture. "It has consequences...." He holds back.

The Master gets up and stands right in front of Thomas. Thomas tries to relax his body, but the calmness seems to disappear every time he gets a grip on it. The intensity from the Master's gaze comes toward him with enormous force. Thomas takes a deep breath and remains standing. The strength does not decrease; it is like a constant current.

"It may be that the time is not right after all, that the world is

THE RING

not ready." The Master's eyes are luminously clear and feel like a sword cutting through everything.

It is completely quiet. Thomas says nothing; he is focusing on his body and is trying to absorb the light and intensive power that hits him. He does not even blink. The Master raises his hand and places his index finger right between Thomas's eyebrows. A strong force begins to flow through him, so he is about to tilt backward.

"Time, give yourself a little more time and keep trusting what you see. From now on, I will leave all the decisions about Angela to you."

25

MEERA

Thomas pulls a chair over to the long table in front of the row of screens that extends across the wall in the control room. A box appears saying "Searching…" in the middle of the center screen. David is staring at the screen, and now and again, he mumbles a few words that Thomas can't hear. "Yes," he stands up in a rush, "come on." Without taking his eyes off the screen, he takes a sip of his energy drink and acknowledges it with a burp.

Thomas places his chair next to David and watches him. He is completely engrossed in the screen and sees only the codes he is writing. All Thomas can see is a big jumble of random numbers.

"I know that what I'm asking of you is next to impossible." Thomas puts a hand on his shoulder.

David is drumming on the edge of the table and turns his chair in a full circle. "Nothing is impossible. The advantage is that we managed to have contact with Angela before we lost the connection. Even though it was only brief, it's enough to help me to search for her."

Thomas leans back while watching David's gumption that fills him with joy. David approaches every task with great fervor and sees only opportunities. He hits the keys so fast his fingers occasionally stumble over each other.

"I can make a link, so it is possible to see where Angela is. But you cannot get in touch with her." He writes more codes and finishes with enter. "Unless you want to open the high-frequency connection from before."

"No, no, definitely not." Thomas leans forward and moves closer to the screen, totally concentrating.

It's just the two of them in the control room. Thomas came straight over here after visiting the Master. He hasn't decided yet whether he will let Angela know that Gabriel's days here could be numbered. This is just a careful move to see if it's possible to locate Angela and then decide what to do next.

David stares at the screen and is engrossed in codes and shifts between more than ten different windows on the screen. "If I pair this one with this one over here, and then just write the number here…" he mumbles to himself. Thomas moves back in the chair, sits still, and watches David. He is fascinated by the way he uses his talent—so devoted to solving the challenges and never giving up.

The light falls softly from the sky and spreads a pleasant warmth around the room. If only Angela had found one of the two, then it would be easier for him to tell her about Gabriel. He gets up and takes a glass from the small coffee table by the green chairs. He fills it with water and turns toward David, who tries to wring out the last drop of energy drink from the can, and then he throws it over his shoulder, so it lands in a bin full of empty cans, revealing the amount of his consumption. Thomas takes another glass, fills it with water, and places it next to David.

"Are you trying to poison me?" David shakes his head in despair.

"I just need to give Angela a short message; that's all. Can it be done without anyone being able to detect it?" Thomas takes a sip of water and moves a little closer.

"First, I have to strengthen the signal and find the frequency…." David presses the keyboard; long codes and commands fill the screen. He casts a sidelong glance at the water. "And then you have to get something other than that," he pushes the glass of water as far away from him as he can reach.

Thomas gets back up; his body feels light even though the restlessness tries to sneak under his skin when he is not completely present.

"Here you are. Is that better?" Thomas hands one of the yellow cans from the cupboard to David. It spurts as he opens it with one hand and takes a huge gulp. His other hand keeps writing. Suddenly, Angela appears. A sinking feeling rushes through Thomas, and he folds his hands in front of his chest. She is pale and looks very affected. Next to her sits a woman with long straight-cut hair. They look absorbed in conversation.

"Can you turn up the volume and give me all the information you can find on her?" He points at the woman on the screen next to Angela and turns to David, who is writing more codes and doesn't pay attention to Thomas.

Thomas waits for David to finish.

"Anything else, boss?" David stretches his arms forward and makes a cracking sound with his fingers. Then he moves around some windows on the screen. The screen to the right lights up, and a small window appears.

Name: Meera J. Sunderland

Age: 52

Single

Education: Doctor

Position: Chief physician at a private hospital

Thomas lets his eyes wander over the information. There must be a reason why Angela is talking is to her. David pulls a map to the screen and zooms.

"Where are they?" Thomas searches the map, and several flashing circles become smaller and smaller. There are no towns to be seen nearby, and the area looks very deserted. He drags the image onto the next screen, and with a light touch, he presses it.

The image zooms out. "Himalaya…" He looks over at Daniel, who is busy making different calculations and connecting them.

"Angela must be onto something; otherwise, she would not go to the Himalayas."

"What?" David looks up. "What are you talking about?"

"Who is Meera?" Thomas takes out his Skycon and presses it lightly.

David shakes his head in despair and returns to his codes.

A picture of Yoge appears on Thomas's Skycon.

"Wait a minute, Yoge." Thomas sits down and presses the Skycon, so the picture splits in two; Shiva also appears. Then, he places the image in front of him so that it floats above the table. Thomas covers his mouth with his hand and rests his elbows on the long, dark red table in front of the screens. "Have any of you experienced a connection to the Himalayas in a previous life or meditation?"

He looks at Yoge, who is standing in on one of the many hallways in In-Between; there is no one to be seen, only a row of doors and an orange stripe on the floor behind him. He shakes his head no.

"Why?"

A map appears on one of the large screens, indicating with a small green dot where Yoge is; a short distance from it is a red cross marking the Ring's control room. Shiva interrupts before Thomas has time to say anything.

"I have. I've been there in a past life. I have had several glimpses at times, but each time, they have been associated with an early death." She takes a sip from a cup. The room behind her is full of people. She is sitting in the café; on the screen, she is marked with a yellow dot.

Thomas breathes calmly. His thoughts want to take over, but he washes them away with calm breathing. "Does the name Meera mean anything to you?"

Shiva shakes her head. Her black hair is pulled back in a ponytail, making her deep motherly eyes surrounded by deep wrinkles stand out. "Can I see a picture of her?"

Thomas presses his Skycon a few times, and a picture of Meera emerges.

"I'm not sure." Shiva squints, and her forehead furrows. She gets up, walks out of the café, and stands a little further down the hall, where there is an undisturbed notch with a chair and a small table. "I sense some dark energy around her, but I'm not sure if it belongs to her."

"Theoretically," Yoge takes over, "we should not be able to recognize each other when we meet." He stops. "But I have made several different calculations that show that it is not completely possible to delete all information from previous lives from our memory, even though we have thought so for a long time." He creases his brow so that his eyebrows almost meet. "Well, one thing is theory…."

"Angela was here some time before Gabriel recognized her," Thomas says with a hesitant voice. If only he could get some clear answers that could help him decided what to do next. He knows that Shiva and Yoge will do everything they can to help him, but in the end, he is the one who has to make the decision about Angela.

Yoge grabs the pen from behind his ear and starts to write in the little notebook he always carries in his breast pocket. "It cannot be ruled out that there will be glimpses of the common journey of our souls because the energy is beginning to gather and thereby becoming more powerful." He looks up from the paper.

"I'm assuming Meera has something to do with Angela since you're showing us her picture," Shiva speaks with her soft, calm voice. She is sitting at a small round table in the notch in the hallway where the people walking by can't hear her. The light from the windows surrounds her like a warm blanket that she can wrap around her.

Thomas nods; he takes a deep breath and senses the love around Shiva like a transparent veil she always carries with her.

The silence is interrupted when David hits the table. "COME ON!" He looks up at Thomas, "Sorry, I was so close…." He points a little confused at the Skycon. "I didn't know…."

Thomas smiles at him and looks back at the picture from the Skycon that is floating in front of him.

"Just because we cannot remember her doesn't mean that she is not one of the members of the Ring." Yoge is staring directly into the Skycon, waiting for the reaction from the other two. "I have no calculations to support this, but I will look into it." He looks back at the notebook and flips it to an empty page.

Thomas looks at the picture of Meera. Her long gray hair is cut straight in a line parallel to her bangs, and her dark blue eyes are very charismatic. He senses a depth in her gaze. She radiates a well-balanced and wise look. He doesn't remember anything about the Himalayas, and he is certain that he has never seen her in In-Between. "I won't contact Angela until we have something concrete to tell her. There is no reason for her to feel more pressure than she does already."

Shiva leans forward, "I will try to focus on the Himalayas and see if I can remember some more. But only Angela can know whether she has found one of the people we are looking for."

"Well," Yoge speaks without looking up from the paper, "actually, Angela can only follow her intuition. We won't know if she is the right one until we test her here."

26

A MOMENT OF TRUTH

Heavy clouds surround the mountains below us; only a few peaks just manage to get through the clouds and break the frayed surface. It thins out with fewer bushes, and the mountainside becomes rawer. We slowly climb up several large rocks that have formed a staircase.

I was so close to telling Meera about In-Between, but the uncertainty held me back. Instead, it became a diversionary maneuver, so we got to talking about her instead. If I don't start to open my heart and share some personal things, I will never find out if she is one of the people I am looking for. I need to have a sit down with her again, where I have her by myself.

We walk along a narrow path that takes us around to the other side of the mountain, where some people come into view. From having a sense of being alone in the world, a small village suddenly appears in the distance. The houses lie side by side; they are painted in vibrant colors and are in amazingly good condition. There are no real windows; they are painted on the walls. From several of the houses, smoke comes up through a hole in the roof. The path winds, and we enter between the houses. An old, wrinkled lady raises her gaze as we pass by, goats roam free, and children in colorful red suits play with sticks and tires. As soon as they catch sight of us, they come running with shouts and smiles that are contagious.

I step up next to our guide; Meera walks on the other side of him, smiling all over her face. The children are dancing around us, laughing. She waves to them and says, "Namaste."

Thomas once told me that it means, "I greet the divine in you, which is also in me."

The children laugh and jump up and down in front of us while shouting something in a language I don't understand. But their joy speaks an international tongue. Our guide points to one of the houses a little further ahead. This is his village, and the house belongs to his family. It gives a tick in my stomach, and I can feel a humility to be allowed to experience their world. Here, in the middle of nowhere, sit about twenty houses in their very own universe.

"We will stay for the night and continue in the morning." Meera puts her arm under mine, and we follow the guide over a small, partly broken bridge that runs next to the houses and end up at a blue wooden door. Outside are triangular flags in all the world's colors on a line.

It's getting dark, and the clouds are building up around us. The view from here is stunning. The mountains are so close. I feel like pinching myself on the arm just to make sure it is real. A lump is growing in my throat, and I try to swallow, but it is hard. It is the last time I will ever experience something like this.

"Do you want to come along and watch the sun set?" Meera takes my hand, and I let go of the thought.

"I would love to."

We only have one day of hiking left. Tomorrow, we will reach our highest point, and after a short walk back down on the other side of the mountain, we will be picked up by a helicopter. If I'm going to make a move, I better do it soon. This time, I cannot fail. I close my eyes and take a deep breath. We walk next to each other in silence, looking out over the mountains and ledges. The landscape has become more rugged, and most of the ground is covered with snow. I pull the sleeves of my jacket down over my gloves so the cold air can't get in.

"Have you experienced in some of your glimpses from previous lives that you were part of something bigger than life?" I take a step to the side and break a branch of a random bush.

"Why do you ask? Have you?" Meera continues along the path.

I clench my fist tightly and kick a small rock as if it were to blame that she just sent the question back to me. "Yes, I have." I walk back on the path and throw the branch over the side.

There is no one else here; it's just Meera and me and the soaring mountainsides.

"I haven't. But I can't say that I don't believe there is a higher power or that I hope there is. But if I'm a part of a grand plan, I don't know." She shrugs and calmly walks up toward some big rocks formed as a chair.

The disappointment fills my body. My legs get heavy, and a feeling of despair spreads inside me. *Come on*; I'm trying to encourage myself as I kick at a slightly larger rock. It flies over the edge and disappears into the cloud that hangs below us. It may well be her anyway. I must not give up so easily. But the frustration evaporates the power inside me. I try to mobilize all my strength, but even though there may only be fifty meters up to the rocks, it seems impossible to reach them without getting exhausted. I gasp for breath and try to pull myself up with my arms where it is possible to get a fingerhold.

After half an hour of huffing and puffing, I can finally sit on the rock, and I let my body collapse. The sunset is not that nice tonight. The colors are vague. I jump down from the rock and go to the edge of the mountainside. One more step, and I'm home in In-Between.

"What's going on? You seem a bit tense." Meera steps forward and stands next to me. The clouds open beneath us, revealing an abyss of darkness. A small, completely blue butterfly perches on a

THE RING

rock in front of Meera's foot; it opens and closes its wings. She leans forward a little.

I don't say anything, thinking only of jumping. It's just one small step. I'm already dead, and I know the trip. I have nothing to lose. I have already lost everything. How hard can it be?

"What do you think will happen if we jump?" Meera smiles and looks at me.

I look puzzled at Meera and know exactly what will happen; it's not a matter of thinking or believing. I shrug reluctantly and look away.

"I sometimes get a picture of an older man. It happens when I'm at places where I have the opportunity to take my own life. It's the same man who appears every time. Somehow, it feels like he is looking after me. He has deep wrinkles across his forehead and a red mark on his skin over his right ear; he is not that tall and pulls a bit on the right leg. He always comes to me with outstretched arms."

I turn in a fast jerk toward Meera. "When was the last time you experienced this?"

"Right now. First, a white light came, and then I saw the picture of the man, but it was a little weaker than usual." Meera is looking straight ahead. We are standing right on the edge of the mountain.

I clasp my hands and narrow my eyes. It is Gabriel she is describing. It must be her. She is one of the two I'm looking for. This can't be a coincidence.

"Meera, there's something I have to tell you." I open my eyes wide, bite my lower lip, and gently slide it back and forth between my teeth.

Meera laughs. "Hey, what's with that serious look? You're scaring me even more than my estranged ex-husband" she mumbles, and I'm not sure if I'm supposed to hear it.

I take her hand and pull her away from the edge. "This is not the time to jump."

She pulls her hand toward her and steps a little to the side. "Now, you're really scaring me. I wasn't serious about jumping."

I reach for her hand again. "I'm sorry, that was not my intention. Do you want to sit for a moment?" I point to the rock shaped like a chair.

She crosses her arms. "I'm not sure what you want to tell me is particularly nice."

I sit down without saying anything and make room for Meera next to me. Out on the horizon, the last rays of the sun break through the clouds. Several large eagles are flying over us, and one of them comes closer now and again. It screams and dives down in front of us; somehow, it seems that it is keeping an eye on us. Meera sits down on the ledge, a safe distance from me.

"What I want to tell you, you must promise never to tell anyone else, no matter what happens."

She looks at me, narrows her eyes slightly, and nods once. "I promise." Her usually so silky voice becomes a bit determined.

My heart gallops away. I take a deep breath and begin to tell Meera about the plane crash and my own experience in In-Between —about the Ring and why I'm here. She looks at me, then turns her head and looks out over the mountains and back at me again as I speak.

The small blue butterfly takes off and flies past us before turning into a little dot and disappearing. The eagles do the same. Now, we are all alone here in the dark.

"What I'm saying is...." I take a break, "If you want, and believe that you are part of the Ring, then you must come with me within the next twenty-five days." My throat tightens around the words. I did not think it was possible to experience a silence like the one that is here now. I'm waiting and waiting. I have played all my cards and sit devoid of defense.

Meera leans forward a little on the rock. "What you are saying is that I should commit suicide. And another person, who you don't know where to find, should do the same?"

"...Yes." I keep looking at Meera.

"And there are no guarantees. I just have to take your word for it… You are out of your mind. You know, my ex-husband was a psychopath, and you are starting to remind me of him." She turns and looks me right in the eyes. "I need to be alone." She jumps down from the rock and begins to crawl back down toward the camp.

27
TRUST OR FEAR

The sun is rising behind the mountain, and the men collect the last things before moving on. I have slept with all my clothes on, just to try to stay warm. We are sleeping in tents, and the temperature was below minus ten last night. Meera had her back to me all night, and we didn't exchange a single word. I stand by myself with a nearly empty cup of hot tea. The heat of the tea slowly defrosts my body. I'm watching one of the carriers who is about twenty years old. He is so thin that I am afraid he will break every time he gets the pack on his shoulders. He needs to sit down to get it on his back, and then the others push him up on his feet.

It is completely quiet here; only the sound of the wind whistling in my ears breaks the noisy silence. The snow lies white and untouched next to the trail, which consists of a few footprints. Today, we have to hike to the top of the mountain, which is our final destination. I zip my jacket all the way up, pull my knitted hat well down over my ears, and cover my face with a golden-brown scarf.

I have decided to give Meera time and space. I don't know what I would have done if anyone had given me the choice when I sat on the plane—the choice between continuing living or going somewhere whose existence I had only a stranger's word for. I have made so many choices unconsciously in my life because I took that life for granted. If I really knew what each choice meant, there was a lot I would have done differently. It is too late now.

The chef has gone on ahead, and the porters are following in his footsteps. They quickly disappear behind the mountain, even though they carry all the luggage. While the silence may be intrusive, it does give me peace of mind right now. I had no choice; I had to be honest with Meera. *Trust.* I remember Thomas mentioning several times that trust is the hardest thing to learn in life—having confidence that we made the right decision.

Trust and confidence in what I perceive, confidence in myself, confidence in others, in love, and life.

The sun dazzles me, and I take my sunglasses from my pocket and polish them. My boots make the snow crunch with every step I take. I walk slowly and observe all my movements. Meera walks further ahead at a safe distance from me.

A buzz in my pocket followed by a vibration makes me stop. I tear off my gloves, unzip my jacket, and pull out the Skycon. It is flashing green. I press the small image of Thomas on the screen.

"Angela."

I gasp for air, push the sunglasses into my hair, and look around to make sure no one is looking.

"Angela…" The picture of him slowly fades through on the small screen.

"Yes." I squint and sink to my knees. "Do you realize how much I have missed you!" I whisper. The heat spreads from my chest all over my body. "Where have you been? Why have I not been able to get in touch?"

Thomas does not have time to say anything until I continue. He just smiles at me.

"I did not know what to do and…." I stop and look in the direction of Meera, who is still walking up ahead.

"It's great to hear your voice, Angela; I've been following you since yesterday."

My body starts to tremble. "Do you think Meera is the right one?"

"I think you have listened to your heart and followed it. I do not know if it is her." He smiles warmly at me, and his eyes beam.

"Angela, we do not have much time, and there is some important information I need to give you."

A guy walks past behind him, drinking from a yellow can. It's not someone I know.

"We had to close the connection because of Frank. He is using the frequencies to communicate with people in In-Between. We still do not know how he managed to return to Earth."

"But…"

"Although it is risky, I have chosen to open up to the frequencies briefly. We have to make it quick."

I straighten up; Thomas looks tired, his eyes are shinier, and the lines around them more distinctive. Perhaps it is the glow from the snow that reflects on the screen.

Thomas steps closer. "You have to go back to the city and make sure Frank doesn't tell others about In-Between. It is crucial that the Ring is gathered and that we have time to carry out our work before anyone on Earth finds out about In-Between." Thomas maintains eye contact without blinking. "Otherwise, we risk that too many people will choose to come here instead of accepting the challenge their soul has chosen for them on Earth. Suicide is not the solution. It never is. No souls are given greater tasks than they can manage. When people commit suicide, they interrupt the journey of their souls and will face even greater lessons later. There are no shortcuts in personal development."

I get on my feet and trample the snow around me, forming a small circle.

"There is one more thing." Thomas looks directly at me, "Gabriel's soul is pulling him toward the next level of consciousness; it could mean that he will leave In-Between before time. Soon."

THE RING

The air is icy cold. My breath is short, and I only just get enough air. "Does that mean…"

Thomas puts his finger to his mouth. I swallow my words.

"If it is in any way possible to bring back the two who are to complete the Ring before forty-two days have passed, it would be preferable."

"Well…" I step out of the circle I made in the snow.

"Angela, I know it's a difficult task. But you have already come a long way. Keep believing in yourself and the help you get."

I drop my gaze and try to avoid relating to what he is saying. It will only create unnecessary chaos inside me.

"I have to shut down the connection again. We can see and hear you, but we can't communicate with you." Thomas speaks clearly. "Only when you have made sure that Frank does not spread the word about In-Between can we reopen the connection."

I look up, and the feeling of being abandoned flows through my body. I stomp hard in the loose snow and make a clear imprint with my boot.

"I get it." My hand holds the Skycon so tightly that, if possible, I could squeeze the life out of it.

A gust of wind lifts some loose snow from the mountainside, and it falls lightly over me. The cold sensation from the snowflakes cuts against my skin, and it melts, but my doubts and insecurities do not.

"Take care of yourself, Angela. I'll try to be with you as much as I can, but occasionally, I need to check on Gabriel too. We look forward to your return." Thomas sends me a smile, and I smile back with pursed lips.

"But…" I reach out for Thomas. The image fades away, and the small screen goes dark. I stare at the Skycon and wish that I could make it come back to life. Meera hasn't noticed my absence and is now far ahead of me. I place the Skycon in my pocket, zip my jacket, and hurry after her the best I can. The sun's rays make the snow twinkle as I walk.

I wish I could take a time out.

28

ONE MORE CHALLENGE

The rotor starts, and a loud rumble overpowers everything, including my thoughts. I get a sinking feeling, and I'm pushed back into my seat. Meera sits next to me. She has not said a single word to me since I told her about In-Between. I have not tried to get her to talk. Instead, I decided to give her some space to think, and hopefully, she will let me know when she is ready to talk some more. The moment Thomas told me about In-Between, my whole world collapsed. But I was already there; Meera has a choice she needs to make. There is no way I can put myself in her shoes right now. I can only guess that there is chaos inside her, which is why she is shutting me out. The helicopter makes its way through the clouds. I stare out the window but can only see the floating white mass.

Meera turns her head and looks at me with a determined look. "And that's where you want me to go? I don't really see anything."

I shrug. "I have told you everything I know; the rest is up to you." I try to smile gently, and relief rushes through me, knowing I have told the truth without reservation.

"Why should I believe you?" Although there is not much space here, she manages to move further away from me. The sound of the engine drowns her words.

I don't know what to answer and look speechless at Meera. We are alone in the helicopter; the others hiked back to the village. If I try to convince, discuss, reason, or negotiate with her, I will lose the impact of what I told her. The choice is quite simple, either she believes me, or she doesn't.

"Do you realize what you're asking me to do?"

"I need you to trust me. I've told you everything I know; now, the rest is up to you." I sit still. She seems a little indifferent to what I say now. Meera has closed her heart and is in turmoil. If I only knew how to reach through her armor, through to her heart, but I don't. I try to find a comfortable position, but I'm sitting crouched up by the cold door and can hardly move. We fly along the mountaintops, where the snow is torn loose by the wind, and the villages are small dots far down in the valleys.

"Meera, can we not talk about it? I know it's hard." I try to turn toward her. She looks out the window and does not answer. I raise my voice a little and reach my hand toward her shoulder, but I pull it back before I have time to touch her. "What's going on inside you? Is there anything I can do to help?"

Meera continues to stare out the window. I look at her, waiting. She heard me. I know she did. The fine energy around her is gone and replaced by a shield of ice. Meera breathes quickly and turns quickly toward me. "There is a great fight inside me. I do not want to be near you." She turns back to looking out the window.

I close my eyes. There is nothing I can do. Time will hopefully make amends. But I don't have much time. Especially now when Gabriel might be moving on before time. Maybe I should give Meera a break and see if I can track down the last person. I remind myself of the story Thomas once told me about the old man and the horses. The old man said that you never know whether something is good or bad; only the future will tell. Never judge because we can't see the whole picture. There was one question that always helped him when he was in doubt. Asking himself, *what do I know right now?* I know that I'm here to find the missing two. That Frank has traveled here too, and that I believe Meera to be one of the two. That is all I know. The rest is speculation. I take a deep breath; if only I could connect more pieces of the puzzle that I have seen through my visions.

A bump makes me open my eyes; we have landed. The door opens next to me, and the sunlight blinds me. I get up and jump down onto the runway. Meera stays seated until I'm out. The helicopter has landed on a small landing site where several military aircraft are lined up.

"Can I call you?" I turn to Meera. Our eyes meet for the first time since I told her about In-Between.

"Why?"

"To answer any questions you may have… and to hear how you are."

She shrugs, takes her backpack, and starts walking toward a low building in front of us. "You'd preferer to see me dead, so why bother?"

"Maybe we could meet somewhere?" I walk right behind her like a child trying to get through to a busy parent. She speeds up and enters through the revolving door. Through the windows, I can see passengers waiting. They look like tourists and are probably going on a ride on a small plane to take pictures of Mount Everest. A tall guy with white hair stands out from the crowd. He stares intently at Meera, who stops, her body stiffens, and then she turns quickly toward the exit and disappears.

I stay outside.

29

TWO STEPS FORWARD AND ONE STEP BACK

My eyes are like sandpaper. I lift my hand and grope for my watch. It's still dark outside. The time is only twenty minutes past five. My body is tired, but my inner self is wide awake. It's chilly in my hotel room, and I pull one more blanket over me. I have stayed at this hotel for a little over a week now. The last few days I have spent searching for Frank to no avail and trying to make some sense out of the glimpses I got earlier. Neither has produced anything useful. I have not contacted Meera yet, but I will. There are sixteen days left of my mission. And since I haven't heard anything from Thomas, I believe that Gabriel is still hanging in there.

The room is not large. One window faces the street; it does not appear to have been cleaned for several years. My backpack is on the floor, and my clothes are in two piles, the clean and the dirty. The clean pile is vanishingly small. The urge to call Daniel has been there, but I have needed to be alone and take it all in. The shift from the vast expanses to the bustle of the city has drained me of energy. I have become more sensitive in many ways, and it feels as if the environment is hitting me, so I need to protect myself.

I'll give Meera three more days, then I'll call her. That gives me ten days to convince her that the Ring exists. I gasp for breath. If only Gabriel holds on for that long. And if only I also find the last person...

At that exact moment, I get pushed down against the mattress, and it gets completely dark. It feels like a heavy duvet has been placed on my body. Far in the distance, I can glimpse a flash of light, like a star twinkling in a dark sky.

"It's time." The voice is back with its usual calm and precision.

The weight decreases and I feel like I am being lifted into the air. I cannot feel my body nor see the room. It gets hot here, very hot. I look down. Under my feet are stacked pieces of wood. I can hear a crackle, but it's still dark around me. Out of the darkness emerges a slightly diffuse crowd, which howls and fights with their arms. I try to move, but my hands are tied together on my back around a pole. Right in front of me, a flame bursts forth, and it stings my feet. The cheering from the crowd gets louder. A rope tightens around my chest; my dress is torn, and someone from behind cuts off my long hair.

"They do not understand that all people are the same, that we have the same feelings and needs, no matter what color skin we have, we are the same on the inside. We need love and care, and we long for freedom and respect." The voice speaks calmly. "That your abilities are their shortcomings."

I want to move my feet but cannot. An indescribable pain cuts into my skin like a thousand shards of glass being pressed against my feet.

"That there is no good and evil or right and wrong. There is only a lack of consciousness."

I look at the crowd. A younger woman in tattered clothes and with tousled hair becomes visible. She reaches out her dirty hands toward me. The rest of the crowd is indistinct. I sense their angry energy and hear their yelling but cannot see them clearly.

"People who judge others try to be superior to others, and those who base their lives on power and external wealth are far from their hearts. They are betraying their souls."

I want to scream but cannot. The sound from the crowd subsides, and I can do nothing. They have taken power over me, but they cannot take my soul.

Just below stands a young man with a torch; his face is a big spasmodic laugh. He looks up at me and out at the jubilant crowd. He is reminiscent of the young man whom I saw losing his girlfriend in an earlier vision. Now he has blond hair and is somewhat younger. There is something about his eyes that is the same—they lie deep in his face, making his eyebrows seem very threatening.

The flames rise around me like a wall, and the heat is unbearable.

It goes dark again.

I pull the duvet aside and stagger out into the bathroom. The sight of myself in the scratched mirror sends chills down my spine. I cannot recognize myself. I know who I am on the inside, but not on the outside. I step closer to the mirror and study my eyes. The white ring around my pupils has become more apparent. The frayed edges are sharper. I close my eyes. Glimpses from the fire come back, the woman crying, and the young guy cheering. I turn on the cold water, form a bowl with my hands, and dip my face. It sends a shiver down my spine. I never believed in past lives. Now, I realize the significance of my soul's journey. I take a big mouthful of air. How have I ever been able to live without that knowledge? How could I have been so arrogant toward people that I perceived as superficial spiritual seekers? Now, I know I am the unconscious fool. All that I have blamed or loathed in others are aspects of myself that I do not want to acknowledge. I keep looking myself in the eye and experiencing a humility that I have never felt before, filling me. "Thank you," I whisper.

The shower creaks as I turn on the water, and the pipes start to rumble. The water comes out coughing and hitting my body at intervals. It's freezing cold, and I jump to the side. An explosive noise comes from the street. I step out of the shower and look through the small, elongated window, pulling the tattered white curtain with worn embroidery a little to the side. A team of workers and cars have lined up on the sidewalk and are starting to break it all up. There goes the nice warm shower. I return to the shower, which has recovered from its start-up difficulties. My whole body gasps as the cold water hits me, and I quickly run my hand over my soft skin. The soap smells intensely sweet, and I let it foam up. There is only one kind of soap, so it goes in my hair too. It will be an ultra-fast shower.

The sun is rising, and the light from the energy-saving light bulb is overpowered. There is no need to open the window to ventilate; the cracks around the frame are so large that there is natural ventilation here.

I dry myself quickly and throw the towel on the toilet seat. Then I pick up my clothes from the floor and stuff them all into my backpack. I have more clean clothes in my car, which is parked at a long-term parking space. That will be today's first stop.

The phone rings. Secret number.

"Hello..." My voice is a bit determined. I don't mind anyone calling, but it's just nice to know who it is.

A dark, round laugh comes out of the speaker. I look at the phone and get ready to disconnect.

"Sorry, but you just sounded so serious."

It's Daniel. I put the phone to my ear while poking on my boots. They leave a trace of gravel on the floor, which is the most tangible memory from my trip with Meera.

"I miss you, and since you haven't called me, I thought I better reach out. Do you want to meet?"

I drop down on the bed and lie on my back with my legs hanging over the edge. I feel honored that he misses me and warm at heart. "We can do that." It sounded very relaxed and not too eager.

"Great! What are you doing this afternoon?"

"Nothing yet." I pull a smile and look at my watch. I'll have to look for Frank too—it is crucial to find him before he tells anyone about In-Between.

"Well, then, meet me at Pier Five at the harbor at two p.m. I will be waiting for you, Princess."

"It's a deal." I'm about to hang up but remember to be a little polite. "By the way, is there anything I need to bring?"

"No, you just come as you are. I will take care of the rest. See you."

Daniel hangs up, and I look up at the empty ceiling, put my hand on my chest, and sigh.

30

A CONSPIRACY

"What are we going to do now?" Thomas looks at Yoge and Shiva, who are walking next to him. The wind blows cold against his face, and he tries to turn his back to it. Far down, he can see the sea as a large, black mass. They walk a fair distance from the main area, and they are all alone. Shiva walks with easy steps across the cloud, and Yoge looks a bit absent.

"I don't know what to do with Frank. Angela has not found him yet, and the days go by." He turns to Shiva, who stops walking. Yoge walks on and suddenly realizes that the others have stopped and turns back. He looks at his Skycon—they are out of range of the signal. His broad nose and narrow face look a bit tormented in the wind. "One thing is that Angela takes care of Frank, but we also need to find the person who helped Frank get back to Earth." Yoge turns to Thomas, "and there might be more than one."

Shiva takes a step toward Thomas so that they stand in a triangle. There is a delicate, bright glow around her, and her voice is soft. "Thomas, have you spoken to the Master about this?"

Thomas lowers his gaze, feels an unceasing sensation creeping through his body, and takes a deep breath. Even though they are together about the mission, he finds it difficult to stand firm in himself and not let the uncertainty take over. He doesn't want to make any mistakes; just the thought of it makes him crumble. He pulls down his coat and brushes away any creases. His eyes meet Shiva's gentle gaze. "The Master said it's up to me whether we should contact Angela."

"IT'S A DIFFICULT SITUATION...." She looks away, and the wind lifts her long black hair. "Just a minute," she looks up into the infinite sky. "I see an elderly, fair-haired gentleman with withdrawn eyes, dressed in black, going from door to door, preaching the word of God. He wants to save people from their pain and wipe out evil." She bends her head forward and folds her hands to her chest.

Thomas looks at Yoge. He is silent and has his eyes fixed on Shiva. Thomas can't work out what is happening inside him; he never says anything personal, and his facial expression doesn't reveal anything either. "Do you see anything else, Shiva?" Thomas looks back at her.

"Not right now; I am filled with the urge to be in silence. It is a challenge for me to speak." She looks down. "It is in the silence that I can see clearly." She puts her hand in her pocket and takes out a package of gum. "Anyone?"

Thomas knows the urge Shiva talks about. For years, he hunted it himself. But he didn't find it until he came to In-Between. The struggle between living up to his father's expectation and the fragile vulnerability he carried inside were like two sides of a coin. He extends a hand toward Shiva, and she accepts it, returns the package of gum to her pocket, and puts a piece in her mouth. Thomas knows that she only chews gum when she feels under pressure. He has known Shiva for a long time; she was the one who received him when he arrived in In-Between.

He continues in a slow voice, "I read Frank's profile. His father abused him from when he was five years old. For many years, he blamed his mother for not protecting him and the authorities and teachers for never finding out. His mother wanted a divorce, and his father had begun drinking. He beat up the mother so badly that she went into a coma and never came out. Frank never forgave her and believed that the coma was her way of escaping—that she betrayed him and left him behind with his father."

Yoge is about to walk on but stays still. The clouds have closed around them, and the ice-blue sky lies above them as a roof on the sky.

Thomas looks at Yoge, whose narrow face is tense. "From what Angela has said, it's my feeling that Frank's angry about not being offered to stay here at In-Between." Thomas pauses. "But it could also be that he has a motive he is not even aware of, one that originates from a previous life."

Yoge looks over at Shiva. "Can Frank have any connection to the man you described? Is there something we are not seeing?"

She stops chewing the gum. "I don't get more glimpses—right now, the connection is unclear to me." With a slight movement, she waves her hand in front of her and disappears through the cloud. The others follow, and on the other side, the cloud goes on for miles like a flat desert landscape.

"We have to assume that the person who helped Frank may share the same agenda." Yoge takes several measured steps and gets a little ahead of the others without noticing.

The wind carries his words back to Thomas and Shiva. They step up next to him. Thomas raises his voice a little to drown the wind. "It's not unthinkable." He holds up his hand to shade from the sun. "But it could also be someone who just wants to help and does not have the same motives as Frank. Maybe the person is not aware of Frank's real motives at all."

Suddenly, an abyss opens in front of them. The cloud has split in two. Thomas stops and signals for them to turn around.

"Every time we open the connection, we make In-Between more vulnerable and allow Frank to communicate with people here. But maybe we should still ask Angela if she can help us?" Yoge looks at the others.

The cloud they walk on dissolves itself behind them.

"Do we have a choice?" Thomas holds his hands up to his face and tries to rub his thoughts, doubts, and not least the uncertainty away.

"Yes," Yoge nods thoughtfully. "We can ask David; he knows many, particularly among those who are interested in the technical wonders of In-Between. Maybe he can figure out who is helping Frank."

Thomas slides his hands away from his face and nods to him. "I'll talk to him."

"We have to find this person. As long as we do not know who or how many are involved, we also don't know what consequences it may have for the Ring's work." Yoge runs his hand over his thin hair, grabs the pen placed behind his ear, and he starts to flip it between his fingers. "We also don't know if anyone other than Frank has been sent back."

31

BE CAREFUL WHAT YOU WISH FOR

I'm standing outside the cafe where I last spoke to Frank. The windows are dirty, and it's hard to see if he's sitting in there. It's still early, and I hoped that he would come here for breakfast. Quite a few people are walking the streets, all looking very focused with fixed glances. They do not see each other, only the holes in the crowd where they can move forward toward their planned destination. There is a strong wind, and I'm happy with my windproof jacket, which is long enough to cover my hips.

The thoughts in my head are tripping over each other. Should I look for Frank or trust that he will come to me? Maybe I should try to ask for help finding him. I look up at the sky and send a thought out into the universe. *Dear Existence, Universe, or God, whoever you are—I need help finding Frank.* I pull a smile and decide to get some fresh air in the park opposite the cafe.

Several flocks of pigeons are eating bread that the tourists have thrown for them. They look happy but eating bread crumbs is also the best thing in their lives. In front of me, an elderly couple walks arm in arm, and at regular intervals, a jogger comes by. If I could just get in touch with Thomas, he would probably be able to tell me where to find Frank. I walk toward the bench where I was sitting when the voice first came to me. Now, the voice is like an old friend who comes to visit whenever it wants. A young couple is entangled in each other on my bench. I am air to them, and I continue past them to the path that goes around the lake. I unzip my jacket a bit and look around. I'm amazed at how many people are here and not at work. It is the same if you go shopping in the morning. I'm always puzzled where they find the time. When I was alive, I worked all day. I look at my watch; it's been five minutes since I asked for help. How long can it take?

"EVA!" The sound of fast strides comes from behind. I turn around. It's hard not to smile.

"Hi, Frank, how nice to see you." I fidget a bit on the spot and fold my arms across my chest.

"Where have you been? I have not seen you for a long time," he says with his sleek voice and comes closer. Before I know it, he hugs me and lets his arms slide down my back.

I shrug lightly and keep smiling. "Are you busy? Maybe we could have a cup of tea?" I'm looking at my watch; it's only half-past nine.

"Well, Angela, that would be so nice, but I don't have time today. I have an important appointment at ten." His eyes look almost gray today. He keeps looking at me like a predator watching its prey before attacking. On his back, he has a red backpack, which has lost its shape.

I reach out and grab his arm. "I need to talk to you!"

He looks at my hand and smiles one of his smooth-tongued smiles. "Angela, unfortunately, I cannot help you. Another day—it's been too long since we talked." He removes my hand, takes a pack of cigarettes from the backpack's front pocket, and raises them toward me.

"No, thanks." I stand with my arms crossed, and my fists tighten as a feeling of resignation fills me. "But there is something important that I think you would like to know." I look down, take a small step back, and bow my head slightly forward.

Frank keeps a straight face. "So, tell me now." He gets a cigarette out of the pack and pats his pockets. "Do you have a lighter?"

I shake my head. "I didn't know you smoke."

"I don't, but today I got such an urge for a cigarette. You know, we better live life to the fullest while we are here."

Frank walks over to a young guy who comes toward us. He is wearing a gray suit with light stripes and a purple tie that is tied perfectly. He hands something to Frank. I cannot see what it is. Frank turns, walks back, and stands right in front of me.

"It's not common for people to remember something from In-Between when they come back here," I speak quickly, hoping he will stay, and he does, for now.

He opens his hand and strikes a match right in front of my face, holding it so close that I feel the heat from the tiny flame. Slowly, he turns it vertically so that it looks like a small torch and looks me straight in the eye. The scars on his face tighten, and his eyes get cold and a little distant. Then, he lights the cigarette and blows out the flame.

"There is a reason why people cannot remember anything and…" I say, hesitating more than I like to.

"What do you want to say, Eva?" His pretend-to-be-nice facade has disappeared, and he narrows his eyes.

I'm standing closer to Frank than I feel comfortable with. But my feet are nailed to the ground. "Frank, what are you going to do with the knowledge you have?" My gaze briefly meets Frank's.

He smiles complacently. "That I will tell you. I have a meeting with an editor at a lifestyle magazine in thirty minutes; she's really interested in my story. Think about how many people would have an easier life if they knew about In-Between." He pats his backpack. "I'm well prepared."

A large raindrop hits my face and rolls down my cheek. I stand completely still. Everything has come to a standstill inside me. Most of all, I want to hit Frank on the head and tie him to a tree.

THE RING

"I also think the world should know about In-Between." I am surprised by my words. What am I saying? Have I completely lost my mind? "But do you think it is possible to wait for, let's say, three months?"

Frank narrows his eyes even more and runs his hand back and forth over his chapped lips. "Only if you tell me why I should wait."

Several raindrops hit me, and a cold sensation spreads around us. Most people flee the park, and the rest seek shelter under the big trees. We stay.

I begin to shake my head, "I can't...."

"Well, that is a shame. See you another time, EVA." He turns on his heels and walks away from me.

I stand alone on the path. Even the pigeons have slipped. I clench my fist and slam into the air after him as I rage inside. I have to do something.

"FRANK!" I run after him. He turns around and forces a smile at me. "Yes, Eva."

"It does not release your pain to tell others about In-Between. You have the opportunity to do the right thing now." My heart gallops away, and I exhale.

"Who says I have pain, and what do you know about right and wrong?" His face is tense, and he stares at me with a smirk on his face—exactly the same look that the young guy with the torch had in the vision I got when I was burned on the bonfire. Has Frank persecuted me for several lives? I gasp for breath and pant. "What I wanted to say was, how can you know that people will believe you and not make fun of you?" I stand completely still and wait for his answer. My shoes are soaked, and the cold water is slowly seeping through my socks.

He steps closer to me, opens his mouth slightly so I can smell his rotten breath, and looks me right in the eyes. "People who have lost dear ones live in pain. They live in the dark, unaware of where their loved ones are." He slides his hand over his bald forehead and wipes the water off with his hand. "Other people live in pain, and they need to know that there is a way out. I do this to help the people who are in pain."

"But... how can suicide be a way out? Is that really what you want to tell people?"

I stand completely still and look at him, but I see beyond the man standing in front of me. I see a series of figures from different lives standing in a row behind him. I can see how one incident has led to the next and shaped Frank as he is today. A shiver of discomfort permeates through my body.

"What if there is a greater whole that will be destroyed if people know about In-Between? If there is a reason that they don't know." I look at him with an urge as my heart beats several fast beats. I have to be tactical now.

"You have such a naïve way of looking at life—as if the world is a perfect place. What you don't see is that personal freedom is important; no one should be in charge of you, and no one should be forced to be in a life with pain that they can't get rid of."

He gets distant in his eyes for a second, and then he smiles with a cavalier attitude. "Tell me what you know, Eva...." He drills his gaze into mine, and even though he is shorter than I am, he manages to look down on me.

"If I tell you what I know, you have to promise me not to tell anyone until I say so." I can barely breathe. His smile crackles, and anger emerges behind the smile. Suddenly, he looks very serious. He doesn't say anything but stands waiting.

I close my eyes, take a deep breath, and look at Frank again. "Okay, some new opportunities have been discovered. There is a way to communicate and influence human development, and they needed a test subject." I smile smugly at Frank and hope he buys it. "That is me—that is the reason I'm back."

Frank bursts into a loud laugh. "How inventive you are, Eva. I like you very much, but I do not buy it." He raises his arm and pats me on the shoulder. "You are the most loyal person I have ever met. You would never risk revealing In-Between." He smiles with his lips pressed together, and his eyes draw even further into his face. "I have to go. The world is waiting for me." He laughs out loud again.

"Frank, you're right, that's not the whole truth, but that's what I know. Maybe we could help each other find out the rest?"

He takes a step forward and stares me straight in the eye. His gaze is like knives, and I struggle not to look away. I don't say anything but use all my strength to stand firm.

"See you, Eva." He turns around and waves to me with his back facing me.

32

THE TWO WOLVES

"Even though it can be risky to establish contact, I have chosen to take the risk and have faith that no one will find out." Thomas sits back in the chair that hovers over the floor. Slowly, his face becomes more apparent. "Can you see me, Angela?"

I nod eagerly and am still overwhelmed. Suddenly, the Skycon started to flash, and before I knew it, Thomas's picture appeared in front of me. I'm sitting in my car with the seat folded all the way back, drowning in blame and despair. The rain is hammering against the roof and forming a wall around the car.

"Angela, I have followed the development with Frank. There's a story I want to tell you." He smiles at me. The room he is in is dark; only three low candles on a glass plate in front of Thomas break the darkness and give his face a warm glow.

My jacket is tossed on the passenger seat, the windows have steamed up, and my insides boil every time my thoughts return to Frank. I have failed. It is my fault that In-Between is becoming publicly known. My fault that many people will choose the easy solution and miss out on their life lesson. My hands clasp around the bottom of the steering wheel, and my clothes stick to my body. Water runs from my wet hair down onto my face.

"What is it you want to tell me? You saw what Frank is doing, didn't you?" I release the grip on the steering wheel and mechanically wipe my sleeve across the side window. The sight of Thomas fills the entire windshield, while I can still glimpse the crowded parking lot in the background.

Thomas clears his throat and begins to talk. "Once upon a time, there was an old native Indian who had lost his tribe and his land. The only one he had left of his family was a grandson."

At first glance, it does not sound like Thomas is affected by Frank's plans to expose In-Between. It's cold in here, so I turn on the engine.

"One day, the young boy asked his grandfather if he was not angry with the white man who had taken his land, killed his family, and ruined his life." Thomas pauses. The rain picks up, and the drops drum against the windshield, so I have to make an effort to hear Thomas's voice.

"The old man looked at the young boy and said, 'I feel like two wolves live inside me, and they both want rule over me.'" Thomas leans forward a bit, and his deep blue eyes become clearer. The glow from the candles flickers a little, following his breath. "'One wolf is angry, bitter, full of hatred and distrust. It wants revenge against the white man. The other is forgiving, compassionate, trusting, and full of love.'"

I frown. It's easy to relate to the wolf's anger; of course, it wants revenge. I cannot find trust inside myself right now.

"'The two wolves are constantly fighting inside me,' said the old man, taking the boy's hand and looking him in the eye." Thomas takes another break. I sit still and listen intently as the warm air spreads from my feet and begins to dry my clothes.

"The young boy looks at his grandfather and asks, 'Which wolf wins, Grandpa?'" Thomas looks directly at me.

It is tranquil here. I move my hands down on my thighs and rub them back and forth. Good question, I think. Thomas says nothing. He looks at me without blinking.

"The old man replied, 'The wolf I feed.'"

Just as suddenly as the rain picked up, it stops. The water runs off the windshield, and the sun breaks through a thin crack in the clouds. I take a deep breath; it almost pinches my heart, and I hold my hand to my chest. I open my mouth to say something, but no words come out.

"Angela, I could see in your eyes that it was important to get in touch. You did what you could in the situation. Now, you can decide which wolf you want to feed inside yourself." Thomas's words are hovering in the air.

My fingers start fiddling with the car keys, which are in the ignition and dangle loosely next to my leg. I still say nothing.

"We don't know what is happening, and therefore we must minimize the contact with you. We're trying to find the person who helped Frank get back to Earth. Do you know anyone up here who has the technical ability to do that?"

I shake my head. "The only person I can think of is a guy named Ian. He once helped me… He is nice, and I don't think he would do anything wrong."

Thomas nods. "I'll try to talk to him. He might not know what Frank is doing, nor is it certain he can help us. Let me know if you can think of others."

I search my memory of the times I have seen Frank in In-Between, but no one else comes to mind. The only one I know who also knows Frank is Lucy. A lady passes by outside the car. She is completely soaked and sends me a reproachful look as if it is my fault that it rained.

"Angela, we have to close the connection again. Is there anything you need before we do so?"

I shake my head. "No, but it would be nice if I could get ahold of you."

Thomas smiles; the candles on the table in front of him are

almost burned down. "I will do everything possible to help you, and hopefully, we can soon keep the connection turned on. But if you need help, let us know. We are checking in on you every day."

Relief runs through my body, and I do not feel so alone anymore.

"But it is important that it is only in an extreme emergency." Thomas looks a bit more serious than usual. Is there anything he is not telling me?

I push a smile through. "Thank you; it's great to know."

My hands slide across my face. The clock in the car ticks and catches my attention. It's almost two o'clock. It gives a jerk in me. I have an appointment with Daniel in three minutes. I reach out for the rearview mirror, try to get my hair to look a bit presentable, and rub on my teeth, so they look clean.

"Thomas, I have to go." I put the car in gear.

"Remember to pay attention to which wolf you are feeding." Thomas blows out the candles, and the room gets dark.

33

THE TEMPTATION

The pier is completely deserted. Numerous small boats rock in the water, while a flock of seagulls has a party with the leftovers from a fisherman. I stand on my toes, trying to get a glimpse of Daniel, but he is nowhere to be seen. At the end of the pier is a large yacht, which oozes luxury. It has three floors, mirrored windows, and an outdoor bar on the deck. That's just my style. A pair of hands grip my waist from behind, and I jolt a bit.

"There you are, Princess." Daniel laughs heartily.

I turn around with a small jump. He is dressed in a tight-fitting white sweater, and his sunglasses are in place in his dark hair. His skin is golden brown, and he looks like someone who has just spent two weeks in the sun.

"You look beautiful, stranger. It's been way too long since the last time. Come with me." He takes my hand and pulls me along. I nearly stumble and begin to laugh. In his other hand, he has a basket full of white wine, grapes, apples, and nuts. It looks like there is also chocolate in a nice box with a gold bow and a magazine. The seagulls take off as we walk out onto the small pier. The boards are worn, and the water splashes up onto the sides. I walk behind Daniel and try not to get wet.

"Where are we going?" I pull my arm a little toward me and invite him to slow down.

"I'm going to spoil you for the day, Princess."

"Okay… but where are we going?" I wrinkle my nose a bit.

Daniel starts whistling, looking straight ahead, and smiles all over his face. The clouds hang in large, heavy clumps above us. The sun lights them up from behind and makes their edges luminous. The air is humid, and I get a feeling that the sky can break out in a storm without warning. We head toward the big yacht, which makes all the other boats look like small dinghies. A dark-skinned man in a white uniform walks around the deck. I can easily see myself on the top floor in a deck chair with a drink in hand.

"It's right here." He jolts my arm. Behind the yacht is a small motorboat with tiny round windows along the side. It is wide at the front and has a railing all around.

"That looks really nice," I say, trying my best to hide my disappointment.

Daniel bends and gestures with his arm, "Welcome aboard, Princess." He smiles enigmatically as he hums.

I crawl down from the pier, and Daniel leads me up to the front of the boat.

"Have a seat." He wipes the seat next to him with a cloth. "If you're cold, there is a blanket here." He lays a blue blanket over the back of the seat.

When we leave the harbor area, he speeds up, and the sea opens up in front of us. The wind rips my hair, and the boat bumps every time a wave drops. To the right, a forest stretches along the coast; behind it is Luke's Kindergarten. Beyond the sea, a line on the horizon indicates that the world is not infinite. Daniel is standing up and steers, the wind tearing his spiked hair back. He stands still and looks straight ahead while wearing his dark sunglasses.

"I have always dreamed of going sailing." I get up and lean

forward over the windshield. The wind pushes me back, and I have difficulty squeezing the words out of my mouth. I cannot help but laugh. It looks so easy when Daniel is standing there.

I should feel happiness spreading in my body right now, but I feel nothing but hunger. All my life, I have been good at convincing myself that external things would make me happy. But it's superficial, like whipped cream on a layered cake. It tastes good but makes no difference in the long run. I have been chasing hollow happiness all my life, an illusion. Right now, I feel like I'm wasting my time. The boat gives some bumps when it lands between the waves. I hold on tight to the railing with one hand and look over at Daniel. It's clearly his way of relaxing. He's a sweet guy. My lack of happiness has nothing to do with him. It's all about me, whether I am true to myself and what matters to me.

"Now, we are almost there." Daniel's voice is drowning in my thoughts. He points toward a small opening in between the trees, where a white sandy beach lies desolate.

I sit down in the lee of the windshield. There is a small pier, and further up on the beach is a scorched campfire site. This, I would have given everything for when I was alive as Eva—a man who could save me from myself and soothe my inner by making the outer extremely fascinating—someone who could seduce me and take care of me. But that's not what I need now. I have chosen. I look at my watch; we have only sailed for half an hour, but it feels much longer. A yawn presses from within, and I try to hide it and rub my hands back and forth over my face.

Daniel slows down. "Are you hungry?"

I nod and can feel his happiness. Now, I must be careful not to get carried away by his agenda. He awakens my old self.

"It's going to be a picnic." He looks toward the beach, "I've never been good at bonfires; neither have I been a boy scout."

The boat slides almost silently toward the small pier.

"Angela, I have a confession to make." He sits down next to me.

I move around a bit on the seat and place my hands between my thighs.

"Don't worry," he laughs, "it's nothing dangerous."

I try to force a laugh, but it only turns into an awkward grunt.

The cell phone rings in Daniel's pocket. "Sorry, just a moment." He smiles so the dimple in his cheek becomes visible. "Frank, what can I do for you?" He walks down the side of the boat and starts to tie it to the bridge.

A shiver races through my body. I get up and want to get off the boat, away from Daniel, but there is nowhere to go. *FRANK*, not that Frank, it cannot be. *Relax*, I say to myself. Frank is a totally common name. It is not enough to calm down my amygdala; it has taken control of my fear and makes my hands sweat and my heart beat faster.

Daniel continues to talk on the phone. The wind blows his words away from me. I focus and try to listen, but it is too hard to make any sense of the conversation. Daniel hangs up and turns to me again. "It was just one of my mates. He needed a little help with the press." He walks toward me. I do not move. "He can wait," Daniel turns off the engine, and before I can say anything, he has planted his mouth on top of mine. My lips stiffen completely, and I close my eyes. Slowly, he moves his mouth and looks at me. "I want to go back with you," he says and casts a deliberate glance up at the clouds.

34

AMBUSHED

We sit on the beach—the beach that should have been the setting for a nice lunch. Now, it seems deserted and windswept. The big trees behind us stand side by side like a thick wall, and the open sea is in front. I nibble on a bit of bread and sip my wine. A sweetness fills my mouth and stands in direct contrast to the frustration I experience inside.

"I think I'm one of the people you're looking for." Daniel reaches for the cheese and breaks off a piece.

My body starts to tremble. "I don't know what you're talking about!" My inner warrior wakes up abruptly, and without me being able to react, she has taken control of me. It feels like a wall around me is rising, and no one can break through it.

"I've known Frank for many years." Daniel continues to eat and doesn't seem to be affected by my rejection. "I never believed that the place he was talking about existed, and not at all that there should be a Ring of people who are supposed to save the world." He puts down the cheese, takes a napkin, and wipes his mouth. "Right up until I met you."

I drill my hand into the sand. It bumps into a rock. I pick it up and throw it into the water. *Frank knows about the Ring!*

"There is a special scent around you. Frank is the same now. It must have something to do with the place up there, wherever it is." Daniel looks up at the clouds and smiles. Then he draws a circle in the sand with his finger.

My inner warrior is ready to crush him. I use all my self-control only to use words as my weapon. "Let's say, just for fun, that you're right. What makes you think that you should be part of what you're talking about?" My hands are planted firmly on my hips, and I do my best to control my voice so it doesn't tremble.

"When I got sick, I saw some clear, inner images of a man with half-length, dark blond hair and unusually clear blue eyes." Daniel extends the wine bottle toward me. I put my hand over my glass. "The person I saw called himself Thomas."

I shake my head. "Nice try. You're not going to fool me." I get up and walk to the water's edge, away from Daniel. The clear blue water galvanizes the sandy bottom as if trying to expose a more profound and, until now, hidden truth. My inner self is in revolt; there is something that does not fit. Daniel's picture of Thomas is so accurate. Frank must have told him about Thomas. I turn around and go back to Daniel.

"What else has Frank told you?" I'm trying not to sound too accusatory, but it's not working.

Daniel starts packing the food and brushes the crumbs off the blanket. He stretches his arms to the air and leans back. "Angela, has it not occurred to you that I actually like you?" He gets on his knees in front of me. "I don't want you to leave again. You can either stay with me," he smiles through his dark eyes, "or you can tell me how I can come with you."

I reach for my glass, and Daniel takes his. "Cheers for the future." He winks at me. I empty the glass into the sand and give it to him without saying a word. My inner struggle is overwhelming, but I have promised myself to explore all possibilities. There's something old that's waking up, and I've lost control. Is it because he's getting too close? Because I can't know if he speaks the truth. Or is it because I simply don't know what to do that I withdraw and become hard?

Daniel rummages in the basket and picks up a magazine. "I stumbled upon this the other day and thought it might be something for you." He hands the magazine to me.

I have to shake the armor off and get my inner warrior to loosen its grip on me. Otherwise, I'll scare Daniel away. I force a smile and look at the magazine. There are some different animals on the front cover.

"Here, it's for you." He sits still and smiles at me. The sound of the waves washing up on the beach makes me relax a bit, and I try to convince my inner warrior that I will manage without her help.

"Thank you, that's nice of you." I pick up the magazine and roll it without looking at it. The best move right now would be to spend more time with Daniel to figure out how it all fits together. But a big part of me just wants to get away as soon as possible.

"Can you take me back to the city?" I get up and walk toward the small pier where the boat is rocking softly in the water. A wave sprays up on the pier as I step onto it.

"Angela, I know something you don't," Daniel yells at me.

I stop.

"Frank goes back and forth to that place."

I turn around. Daniel is busy collecting the last things. I yell, "If you're lying, I will push you into the water!" That was meant to sound frightening, but by the look on Daniel's face, it wasn't. He walks toward me and steps onto the narrow pier. We stand facing each other. Daniel has his hands full. I only have the magazine.

"I'm not lying. Why would I lie?" Daniel is looking at me in despair.

"If you care about me, then help me," I say determinedly.

"Choose who you want to be loyal to, Frank or me?" I stare into Daniel's eyes that look nearly black.

"Frank is my friend; we've known each other all our lives." He steps past me and walks over to the boat. I follow right behind him like a little terrier.

"Is that your answer?"

The boat creaks as it rubs against the bridge. Only now, I see that the boat is called Annabel. My heart misses a beat, and I look at Daniel. I have only known one Annabel. Annabel opened the door to my femininity in In-Between, to a feminine universe that I had never before acknowledged or been in contact with. Love flows through me, and the grip of my inner warrior melts like a snowflake landing on a warm cheek.

Daniel places the food basket on the pier and lays the blanket on top. Then he jumps onto the boat, reaches for the basket, and then me. I crawl down, and we face each other.

"It is sometimes difficult to judge what is right and wrong when you know a person and have a history together." Daniel steps closer to me and reaches out for my hands. "I believe that people should help each other and do what is best for the world." He squeezes my hands. "You're right. It's Frank who told me you're looking for some people."

I breathe through my nose without moving a muscle in my face and stare at Daniel, attempting to look behind his facade. If Frank knows about the Ring, he also knows that I lied to him this morning in the park.

Daniel takes my hands and lifts them in front of his chest. "Whether you choose to stay here on Earth with me or go back to whatever it is, you have my support."

I stand completely still and look into his dark eyes. It feels like the thread in a spiderweb is broken, and I regain control over my feelings. The inner warrior has lost control over me.

"Thank you…" I smile at him, and my body begins to relax.

"I hope you believe me; I just want to be with you." He stays standing in front of me and looks at me with loving care.

"Do you know any more?"

"I know there are more people up there who help Frank; that's all." He steps a little closer, so I can smell his fresh aftershave. "Do I get to go with you then?"

I freeze, open my mouth to answer, but remain silent.

35

THE CONFRONTATION

It is early morning, and the traffic flows efficiently. I am determined to contact Meera. In my pocket, I have a piece of paper with her address. It is with the stone Luke gave me when I met him at the Kindergarten. I left it in the car while I was in the Himalayas; now, it has a fixed place in my pocket. I just left my hotel heading for her apartment. It is seven blocks from here. The road is full of cars with half-asleep men and women on their way to work. Many of them only do it to make money. If they had a free choice, they would do something different. But maybe they don't know what their real longing is, what the purpose of their life is. I laugh a little to myself. If someone had asked me six months ago, *Eva, what is the purpose of your life*? I would have thought it to be nonsense and not have known the answer. The only thing I cared about was finding interesting stories that I could sell and, in that way, make a living. On the street, a man is sweeping the pavement; another is getting his small store ready. The city is preparing for another day of wear and tear.

I got Meera's address from the white pages online. She was easy to find. There are not that many with her name who are doctors.

My steps are longer than usual and targeted. I left the car by the hotel and decided to get some fresh air. A quiet shiver under my skin reminds me of the seriousness of the task. Daniel agreed to call me if he heard any news from Frank. I made it clear to him that I could not stay. He seemed sincere, and I have decided to trust him. Luckily, I succeeded in persuading him to give me Frank's cell number. Unfortunately, he does not answer. I walk in my own thoughts and try to make sense of it all. When I try to connect the people I have met, either in the flashes or reality, a motley picture emerges of several souls whose paths have crossed before. Among them all, Meera is the only one who has seen glimpses of the past that she is aware of. But on the other hand, it does not have to be a criterion. I take a deep breath.

A few days have passed as I have been hanging out in cafes, hoping I would coincidently bump into new people, but I've been sitting by myself. Daniel has called me several times; he's begged me to meet, but I chose not to. He can make me forget my task. I dare not risk that. Not anymore. The same goes for Luke. The urge to drop by the Kindergarten has grown every day, but I have suppressed the desire the best I can. Today, there are only eleven days left before I have to return to In-Between.

I turn off the main street and walk up a small side street. There are cars parked with hardly any space between them on both sides of the road. The buildings are painted in a warm yellow color and have small carvings between each floor. I look at the numbers above the doors and find numbers one and three, but five is nowhere to be seen. Farther ahead, an elderly lady is walking a small poodle dog. A newspaper blows toward me, and I just manage to step to the side so it does not hit me. Here is number seven. The sign hangs obliquely over the door and is written on a black plate with gold, which is about to crumble. The wooden door with carvings seems to have welcomed many people over time.

I turn the handle; it's locked. There is an entry phone to my left. It's unlikely that Meera will let me in if I make myself known, and I will not risk being rejected. I look down the street. The lady with the dog has disappeared. It's quiet. Only the noise from the main road can be heard as a steady buzz.

I place my finger on the button for the first floor on the right. Jefferson lives there. Meera lives on the fifth floor on the left.

"HELLO!" An angry and firm voice spills out of the rusty speaker and makes it crackle.

"Newspapers," I say in a friendly voice, smiling to myself.

There is a sound of a furious hum, and the door is unlocked. I turn the handle and have to use all my strength to push the door open. The stairs are dirty and littered with bits of paper and take-away cups. This is not a place I would associate with Meera, not at all. The door slams behind me, and I start walking up the stairs. I can hear voices further up. Second floor to the right, center, and to the left, I continue up the stairs.

The ceiling is high and painted dark blue. It feels like it's falling on me. The walls were white once, but that must be a long time ago. Third floor—luckily, it was not here that the sound of voices came from. I move on and cannot help but read the names on the doors. Jensen, Hansen, and Miller. Fourth floor. I politely greet three elderly gentlemen who are standing talking on the landing. Now, I'm almost there. My steps are getting heavier, and my brain goes into neutral. I have no plan, but I definitely expect to succeed in persuading Meera to go back to In-Between with me. There is no name on her door. My finger presses lightly on the bell. No sound is to be heard. In front of the door is a reed mat, which is worn out in several places. I raise my hand and clench it but hesitate for a moment. Waiting. My heart is pounding. Then I knock on the door. It resounds throughout the staircase. Still, no sound is to be heard inside the apartment. Maybe she's not at home.

The conversation on the fourth floor stops, a door closes, and the sound of footsteps down the stairs disappears. The front door slams. I am alone. It's tempting to see if the door is open. What if she is home and didn't hear the knocks? Maybe she forgot to lock the door. I grab the handle and turn around to make sure no one is coming. Then, I let go again, take a deep breath, and step back. I exhale, and with a fast move, I go forward and turn the handle. The door opens.

A sweet, slightly rancid smell greets me. Without thinking about it, I enter the hallway and close the door behind me. The odor fills my lungs, and my stomach contracts. I only just manage to prevent my breakfast from making a reappearance in Meera's hallway by putting my hand to my mouth and swallowing hard. It's dark in here, and I slowly grope my way forward for a light switch.

"Hello, is anyone here?" I cautiously call out.

No reaction.

Further ahead, a door is ajar, and a streak of light falls on the opposite wall. I take a step but stumble and land on my knees. The pain spreads in my leg, and I put my hand on the floor to get back up.

"Hello... Meera...?"

Shoes and clothes are left lying around on the floor. It looks like she emptied her suitcase here, and I have to tread carefully to avoid another fall. The smell gets more intense, and I try to inhale as little air as possible. I have reached the door, which is a bit ajar. With a gentle movement, I push it open. A strong backlight pours through the window. I hold my hand up to shield the light. I grab the doorframe tight as my jaw drops.

There, right in front of me, is Meera.

An icy cold sensation rushes through my body. I take several steps back, groping out with my arms to grab ahold of something, anything. My body wriggles in spasm, and a sour mass forces itself up from my stomach and spills out onto the floor. My legs are like jelly, and I fall, but I just manage to lift my hand and grab the door handle before I hit the floor. I hold on convulsively and slowly pull myself back on my feet.

Meera hangs in front of me on a rope from the ceiling.

36

DESTINIES COMBINE

I sit on my knees on the floor and shake. The smell is piercing. Meera hangs on a rope from the ceiling in front of me. Her face and hands are completely gray, and her arms hang limply down beside her body. The light penetrates through the curtains and falls on her body from behind, but it cannot bring her to life. She has traveled on to In-Between.

I sit completely stagnant and stare at Meera. There is no life in her formerly so lively eyes, and the fine energy is gone. Her head hangs at an angle, and her mouth is slightly open. I straighten up a bit. My mind tells me to cut her down, but I don't dare to touch her. I try to close my eyes and focus on my heart, clear my head of thoughts, but it does not help. The image of Meera thunders onto my retina and prevents me from thinking clearly. Thomas, help me out here. It's definitely an emergency.

In a way, I should be relieved. Meera has moved on by herself, and there is one person less to care about. But I'm not relieved. My inner self trembles as if an avalanche has just hit me, tearing everything on its way. I open my eyes and look at Meera. My gaze becomes blurred, and my body begins to sway back and forth. I press my hands down between my thighs and tighten, just to get a little bit of control over myself. I'm in over my head, and there is nowhere to swim to and no lifelines to call.

The smell of death drills into my nose. The urge to vomit overwhelms me again. I'm empty inside, and all I feel is a sour sting in my mouth. I have to do something. I can't just sit here. My gaze wanders feverishly around the room, but all I see is Meera hanging from the ceiling. I free my hands from my thighs and get on my feet. With reluctant steps, I move toward her. It gets more real as I approach. I take my hand up to my mouth and hold my breath.

I don't know much about Meera, even though we were hiking together for over a week. Her front pockets look empty, and her shirt hangs loose. She is wearing her watch on her wrist and several rings on her fingers. If it were not for the grayish complexion, she would be just like the last time I saw her. I stare and move in jerks around her. The high ceilings have a large stucco flower in the middle with a hook where the rope is attached. On the floor is a chandelier, which most likely used to be on the hook. Next to it is an overturned ladder. I look around the living room. Some papers are lying on a small table. I walk with quick steps away from Meera and grab them. They fall to the floor while I flip through them. There are old pay slips and notes. Although I know exactly why she has left her life, I still feel insecurity in my stomach and an urge to find tangible evidence. I look around for something that can give a reason for her decision—a letter or a hint for me. But there is nothing but furniture, pictures, and Meera. Nothing indicates why she has decided to leave her mortal life and hopefully travel to In-Between.

I TEAR the front door open, run out onto the sidewalk, and take a giant gasp for breath. The fresh air is spiced up with petrol fumes, but I don't care. My body shakes, and I look up and down the street —it seems that I'm all alone.

I cleaned up most of the mess before leaving the apartment, but I did not dare move Meera. I don't know what to do. Right now, Frank is my only contact to In-Between. I shudder at the thought. Since we split up, I've checked newspapers and magazines every day, and to the best of my knowledge, there has not been an article about In-Between yet.

"Angela!" A woman comes running toward me. It's Lucy.

I try to raise my hand, but it does not respond.

"Hi, Angela, where have you been? Someone told me that you went with Meera to the Himalayas, is that right?" She comes close and puffs between the words.

My face gets stuck in a severe grimace. I move my gaze and place my clenched hands in my pockets.

"I'm just on my way up to Meera. How funny to meet you here." Lucy fidgets on the spot, and her arms are in constant motion.

A car drives past us, and a woman rings the bell on her bike as an elderly, stray Golden Retriever strolls out into the street. Lucy keeps smiling. She is wearing a green tracksuit, which highlights her pregnant body, and her golden-brown hair is piled up on her head.

"Lucy, do you know someone named Frank?" I look solemnly at her.

"Yeaaaah, you know, that is so funny that you ask. When I was at the café yesterday, I ran into someone named Frank—he seemed so familiar, a bit like you." She laughs and claps her hands together.

I do not laugh and still have the feeling that I cannot move my face freely. I want to shake my body, but it just freezes even more.

"Angela, are you okay? You're so pale?" Lucy suddenly looks serious. "You're not sick, are you?"

I manage to shake my head a bit. Lucy buys it and continues.

"That Frank guy I met, he said he had something he wanted to tell me, so we are meeting in an hour."

A postman is walking further down the street. I stiffen even more if possible. Did I close the door to Meera's apartment so the smell would not penetrate the stairwell? I look up at Meera's windows.

"Angela, you look dead serious. What is going on?" Lucy takes my arm and shakes it a little. I try to laugh but fail.

"You know what?" Lucy lights up, and her crooked teeth come into view.

I'm waiting.

"Frank also mentioned you. Maybe you want to come along? It would be nice to have company." She laughs. "And I also would feel a little more comfortable if you were there. He seemed a little, you know…." She pulls a face and casts up her eyes.

It undeniably reminds me of In-Between and the first time I met Frank. Back then, I was with Lucy too. Now, it's only me who knows Frank. Before I have time to think the thought through, the words fly out of my mouth. "Yes, why not?"

"Super, if you wait here, I'll quickly go and say hello to Meera. You can come along too?"

I reach for Lucy's arm but grab hold of her hand. "You can't go up there."

"Excuse me?" Lucy laughs and shrugs in astonishment. "What's going on, Angela?"

I don't say anything, and I cannot pretend I don't know because then Lucy will find Meera in a moment, and she will figure out that I have seen her already. A horror scenario from a bad crime story unfolds in my head in record time. Maybe she will think I murdered Meera, and maybe the police will pressure me to say what I know. The blood draws from my face, and I start shaking.

"What? Come on, tell me," Lucy squeezes my hand. "You're scaring me." She starts laughing nervously.

My mouth has dried out in no time, and it feels like the words are stuck.

"Meera…" I manage to say.

"Meera is dead," I whisper, and the words are struggling to get out of my mouth.

"WHAT?!" Lucy's laughter strains and she pulls her hand toward her.

"Meera has hung herself." I feel like an empty shell saying words.

Lucy shakes her head, and her laughter stops abruptly. "What are you saying? That is dark humor, Angela." She looks up at the windows of Meera's apartment and back at me. "Don't pull my leg; it's not something to joke about."

The front door to the stairwell opens, and a younger woman with a stroller comes out. Lucy takes a step to the side without looking at her. Her face has become empty of expression. She looks at me and only at me.

"You are serious."

37

LUCY'S CHOICE

"Hey, Lucy, great to see you; come on in." Frank stands smiling in the doorway. He reaches out to hug Lucy. "How nice to see you too, Angela. What a surprise." I get a pat on the shoulder.

Using all my self-control, I manage to pull a smile and nod politely. He moves just enough for me to step inside. We walk directly into a large room, an old factory hall. There are raw metal beams across the ceiling, where several big masonry lamps light up the space. The floor is made of concrete, and at the back, there are large windows from the floor to the ceiling. In front of them are two black sofas and a chair. They look tiny in the big room.

Lucy texted Frank, so he knew that I was coming too. I have to remind myself constantly that Lucy thinks that she has only just met Frank and is not aware that she knows him from In-Between unless he's already told her. Lucy chose not to go and see Meera; instead, she called the police. I persuaded her to leave me out of it and left before they arrived. We agreed to meet up before we came here. That was five minutes ago, so I don't know what happened to Meera or if Lucy stayed for long. I look at her. She seems as relaxed as possible. Her laughter is not as free as usual, and I sense that she is a little tense. I don't know if she has an idea what Frank wants, but something must have turned on her curiosity.

We walk through the large room, heading toward the sofa arrangement. On the walls hang huge paintings, each resembling a bucket of paint thrown on a canvas. One yellow, one green, and one blue. My gaze shifts from Lucy to Frank. His eyes seem, if possible, even more withdrawn in his worn-out face.

Lucy clears her throat and claps her hands together. "It's a little funny that you two also know each other." She looks from Frank over to me and back, and neither of us responds. "Have you known each other for long?"

Still, no response.

Frank walks to the sofa. "Here, have a seat." There's a teapot and three white cups on the glass table.

I move into the middle of the couch; Lucy sits down with a little distance from me.

"Tea?" Frank looks at me, and I nod. He pours all three cups and pulls an armchair over for himself.

"Well." Suddenly, he smiles excessively. "It's great that you're both here."

Liar. I lock my gaze on him.

"There's something I want to tell you, Lucy." He looks over at me to emphasize that I can do nothing to stop him.

Lucy adjusts the loose pillows on the couch a little and looks at Frank. "That sounds so exciting." She laughs a little falsely.

Frank stares at me. I have to use all my self-control not to be a part of his game. I fold my hands together and place them on my lap. Anger forms like a fireball and spreads in my body. It could explode at any moment.

"Frank, give us some good news. I need it." Lucy is a little restless on the couch and smiles expectantly.

I keep looking at Frank. He will not get my approval to tell Lucy something she should not know or need to know. "What's the point of what you want to say, Frank?" I bite my teeth hard together and press my tongue on the inside. The fireball inside me is at a breaking point.

"Angela, you know that very well." He looks at me a little indulgently and lifts his head so he can look down at me.

"Well, Lucy..." He pushes a cup of tea toward each of us. "I have some interesting news for you...." He gets up and walks with confident steps back and forth across the floor with his arms on his back and chin raised.

Lucy looks at me and holds out her hand repulsively toward Frank. "Wait!" She turns toward me, "Angela, do I want to hear this?"

I take a deep breath. "Lucy, it's up to you. But..." I pause. I can try to convince Lucy that she should not listen to Frank, but she must find out for herself if she wants to know what he is about to tell her. That's not my decision. "My best advice would be to follow your heart."

I can see Frank looking at me out of the corner of my eye, but I keep eye contact with Lucy. Something is happening inside her—I can feel it. She falls deeper into herself and keeps looking me in the eye. I have a feeling she can look through me and maybe connect with my soul—that she already subconsciously knows what Frank is going to say, but she can't put it into words. Somehow, the information has been stored deep inside her and is now on its way up to the surface—to her consciousness. She recognizes something in me. She is no longer just thinking. She has connected to her heart and feels what is right for her.

"Frank," her voice is hesitant. She looks at me and then back at Frank. "I do not quite understand. Something is going on here that I don't want to be a part of." Her usually happy and easy facial expressions are drawn together in a grave countenance.

Frank walks over to Lucy and sits down next to her on the armrest of the couch. "Lucy, it's for your own good. There's *nothing* to be afraid of." He puts a hand on her shoulder. "Angela makes it sound so serious… so dangerous….” He smiles and laughs a little superiorly. "It's typical Angela. She can be such a drama queen." He sends me a phony smile to justify himself. "Trust me; I've known her longer than you have."

Lucy says nothing, gets a little distant in her eyes and moves back on the couch. She grabs a pillow and hugs it. "Angela, I once had a girlfriend I could laugh with. When I look deep into your eyes, you remind me of her."

I sit and wait for a reaction in my body, but nothing happens. Frank doesn't say anything either. We're both looking at Lucy.

"After I woke up from the coma, I have had some authentic dreams, and in the dreams, I have seen things I don't understand. I have seen my old friends and other people, but I have chosen my life with Tim and do not want it to be any different. I just want to be happy." She strokes her stomach with her hand.

My heart is pounding away.

"I don't want my dreams to come true or in any way affect my life. I shouldn't have come. It's a mistake." Lucy shifts her gaze to Frank. "I don't want to know what you know." She shrugs and moves away from Frank, closer to me.

Frank keeps smiling his superior smile as if it got stuck to his face. "Lucy, there is nothing to be afraid of. I just want to help you and make a difference for your child."

The strength of the fireball has diminished a bit inside me, and I lean forward, taking a sip of my tea.

"No, thanks, Frank, I have to go now." Lucy turns to me. "We may see each other again?" She reaches out and hugs me, and I reciprocate it and enjoy feeling her warmth.

Frank gets up and stands right in front of me. "Angela, you may as well stay. I also have something I want to tell you."

38

THE CHOICE IS YOURS

The front door slams and I'm alone with Frank. He walks over to the kitchen and takes a bowl of chocolates from one of the cupboards. There's a lighter on the table; he picks it up and begins to turn it on and off. The sound is rhythmic and sends a shiver through me. I get up and go to the fireplace at the back of the room, where one picture after another of Frank is lined up on the mantelpiece. Frank and a famous sportsman, Frank and an actor, Frank and... I squint. Frank and Daniel with their arms across each other's shoulders and their feet resting on a football in front of them. They do not appear to be more than eighteen years old.

"Here," Frank places the bowl of filled chocolates in colorful paper wrappers on the table. He pulls up his trousers a bit and sits down in the armchair opposite the sofa. He turns the lighter on and off once more and then lays it down on the chair's wide armrest. I go and sit on the couch at a safe distance from him.

"I also have some chips if you would like that?" Frank moves the bowl of chocolate toward me.

I lean back on the couch without saying anything. I do not feel like filling myself with sugar right now. I intertwine my fingers in my lap, and without thinking about it, my lower lip glides between my teeth several times. "What is it you want to talk to me about?" I narrow my eyes a bit.

He takes a piece of chocolate from the bowl, pulls at the ends of the shiny red paper so that it unfolds, and slowly leads the chocolate up to his mouth. "It's great that you could stay for a while." He tilts his fingertips toward each other.

I await his proposal and look slightly uninterested around the room. Over in the corner is an aquarium with crabs; there are no fish in it. On the wall above it hangs a bulletin board with obituaries.

"I spoke to a journalist the other day." Frank smiles confidently and throws the crumpled chocolate paper on the table, so it rolls toward me.

I fix my gaze on him.

"I told her about In-Between." He looks me straight in the eye, and I could kill him. But that wouldn't do any good. If only I could lock him up in a place full of so much light that he would not be able to sleep and be forced to look at himself.

"I haven't told the journalist everything, just a pitch. I said she could get the whole story tomorrow." He moves in the chair and tries to find a comfortable position, but he doesn't seem to succeed.

I bite my teeth together. "And?" Every little muscle in my body is tense.

Frank shrugs. "Well…" he smiles and reaches for another piece of chocolate from the bowl. It is also carefully unwrapped. He is not telling the whole truth; I can sense it. There's something about the way he says it.

"How much are they paying for the story?" I straighten up and feel for the first time that I can look down on him.

Frank smiles so that the small scars on his face tighten, "Eva, you have an outstanding imagination, but I would advise you to take me seriously." He leans forward, and his face becomes solemn. "We can make a deal, the two of us." His lips are compressed. I take a sip of my tea; it is still a bit too hot to drink.

"If I have to drop the story, you have to give me a position in the group you are gathering. The Ring, I believe it's called."

I lean back on the sofa in a controlled manner and only just avoid spilling the tea on the white pillow next to me. "Why do you think …?"

"Eva, I'm not stupid," he keeps smiling, but his body language tightens up, and he raises his voice. "I have some very reliable sources." A third piece of chocolate slips into his mouth and is rinsed down with a sip of tea.

I stare at him. It is as if his face crackles and a glimpse of the young man who lost his girlfriend comes into view. Frank puts his cup on the table and waits for my reaction. I fumble with my hands and decide to take a piece of chocolate just to buy a bit of time. A new glimpse makes me jerk back in the chair. I see an elderly man walking from door to door, preaching the word of God. My breathing stops, and every little muscle in my body gets tense. Both the man who lost his girlfriend and the man who goes from door to door has withdrawn eyes, just like Frank.

"Well, Eva, what is it going to be? It can't be that difficult." He leans toward me and narrows his eyes. They are icy cold without any empathy. But the glimpses tell another story about Frank. In past lives, he wanted to help others find peace of mind if they lost someone close to them. Now, he wants to convince people that In-Between exists. I blink feverishly and start unwrapping the chocolate. Another glimpse appears inside me. I see the young man with the torch next to the bonfire where I was burned. He smiles superiorly at me, wearing garb with a white cross on his chest.

I cough a bit to get back to reality. "Let's pretend such a group exists…." I fail to look Frank in the eyes. "Then why do you want to join it?" The chocolate falls out of my hands and rolls across the floor. I stay seated, and Frank does the same.

THE RING

"Thomas made a mistake when he failed to recommend to the Master that I should stay. I belong in that group."

I can feel his intrusive gaze embrace me, but I look down at the floor. His words linger in the air.

"It may be that Thomas has failed, but what do you think the so-called group is about?" I look up, and now I make eye contact with Frank.

"That's what you have to tell me." He keeps looking at me, and I have to use all my willpower to stay seated. If it weren't for the mission, I would run out of here and never come back. His penetrating look is causing everything to freeze to ice. He knows that I already lied to him once, but it doesn't seem like he knows that the members of the Ring are not random. There is no point in telling the truth. He will not believe me anyway. I have to listen to my intuition. I close my eyes briefly and focus on my heart. I take a few deep breaths. What do I do? What is right? I open my eyes again and look at Frank. He sits reclining in the chair with his legs crossed and his fingertips resting against each other in front of him.

"Why don't you just tell your story to the press? It is fascinating." I force a smile. I have to push him to see how far he will go.

Frank says nothing. He pours another cup of tea and fills up the cup with sugar, so it nearly spills on the table. "Either I reveal In-Between, or I get a seat in the group."

My mouth is dry, and the tea doesn't help. "Do you have a glass of water?"

Frank walks to the kitchen, finds a beer glass, fills it with cold water, and puts it on the table, so it slops over the rim and leaves a small puddle around it.

"When do you need my answer?" I say with a determined tone of voice.

"Now." Frank doesn't blink and just keeps smiling his sleek smile.

I get up and walk over to the window. It is a long way down from the fourth floor. *Thomas, what should I do? Help me here.* No answer. Then, I turn around. Frank has found a car magazine that he flips through while crunching a sugar cube.

"Well, Eva, what is it going to be?" He repeats and puts the magazine down without looking at me.

There is an echoing silence inside me. My normally so active inner judge keeps quiet.

"Frank." I even have a hard time saying his name. At that exact moment, something happens inside me. The emptiness and the thoughts change, a lightness arises, and white light fills me. Everything suddenly becomes clear to me. I don't know if In-Between is supposed to remain a secret, and it is not up to me. The light separates my body and my mind from my thoughts. The thoughts are no longer affected by my personality or by my emotions.

"I cannot help you, Frank. If you want to reveal In-Between, then it's your choice. To me, it has been a place that has allowed me to learn about myself." I get moved by my own words and let my arms fall along my body. The light inside me is replaced by sudden pain, but it's not my pain. I look at Frank, and a sting is etching its way from my stomach to my throat. I wait for a thought of regret, doubt, or at least that I hit myself on the head and feel guilt. But nothing happens. I stand firm. It's Frank's pain that I perceive, but I also sense his longing for love.

He gets up, walks over, and stands right in front of me. His hands are clenched, and his complexion has changed from gray to red in record time.

"You will regret this, Eva."

39

IT IS NEVER TOO LATE

I see spots before my eyes, and light comes toward me. I have parked the car on the path leading into the forest. The place is not so far from the city, just a little up the mountain. When I went sailing with Daniel, we passed it. Next to the car is a small, abandoned hut. The windows are broken, and the roof is leaking in several places. Luckily, there is no one here but me.

The car is hot, and I'm a little dizzy. I must have dozed off for a moment. The sun is shining right into my eyes. For a moment, I just thought it was another vision. I grab my Skycon. I can't believe that the connection that should help me has not been a help at all. It doesn't matter if it's on or off. Frank is going to reveal In-Between no matter what I do. I press my finger on the side of the Skycon, and it starts to flash yellow. The display remains black. I stare at it. If only I could call Thomas. I close my eyes and am not sure how long I sit here. It could be less than a second or more than minutes. But suddenly, the Skycon vibrates in my hand, and I get so scared that I drop it on the floor. It buzzes and buzzes as I grope for it between my feet. Finally, I get hold of it and sit up straight. I press the button as fast as I can, and there in front of me, a picture of Thomas appears.

"Angela, are you busy?"

"Thomas." I smile, and my body becomes warm. Suddenly, tears well up inside me, and I break down over the steering wheel. I shake, and tears drip down onto my pants in a gentle stream as I think about Meera, Frank, and all the decisions. I have tried to get in touch with Thomas several times but have not succeeded, and now he is here. I sob loudly. Thomas calls my name, but I hide my face and pull my hair. "I can't do this any longer…." My eyes sting, and my gaze is blurred. I hit the steering wheel with my hand and look up. "It's all one big mess inside me. I don't know what is right and wrong anymore."

Thomas is in the control room, sitting in one of the mint green chairs, looking calmly at me. The image floats transparently in front of me. I slide back into the seat, take a napkin, and blow my nose. Thomas is quiet. The sun shines from the skylight and falls on his face, making his blue eyes shine.

"You can return to In-between whenever you want. If it doesn't feel right anymore, you don't need to stay." He pauses to see my reaction, and when I don't say anything, he continues. "A task must never become more important than yourself. You need to be selfish, use everything around you as your playground, and everyone you meet on your way as extras in your development. Remember that others use you too." He stops and looks at me. I listen but stare out at the tall trees, which only have to concentrate on growing.

"I thought there were enough selfish people in the world already."

Thomas laughs heartily, and his eyes twinkle. "This is about taking responsibility for yourself and seeing opportunities in everything you experience." He sits still and rests his hands on the armrest. His blue tunic hangs loosely down from his broad shoulders, and I can also see the bear he wears around his neck.

"It's never too late to regret. It's better to stop now than continuing doing something you don't feel like doing." Thomas gets up and walks to the red table in front of all the screens. It looks like he's alone in the control room.

"I'm glad you said that," I whisper. My breathing is calming down again. I reach for a napkin and wipe my eyes. All around the car, the forest floor is filled with small purple flowers. And to the left is a path that leads to a bench with a view of the whole city.

"As you take your time and consider whether you want to continue or return here, I can tell you that we've been keeping an eye on Frank. That is why I opened the connection to you. Also, I had a strong feeling that you were calling out for me, is that right?"

I nod without saying anything and turn my head toward Thomas. I'm not used to others caring about me as much as Thomas does.

"Frank has not made any deals with any journalists." Thomas's voice is calm but determined. His hair hangs loosely, and his eyes twinkle in the glow of the sun.

"What?!" I move forward and hit the car horn, so I jump half a meter at the sound.

"He was trying to bluff you. As I see it, he is divided. He wants to make others aware of In-Between, but when he heard about the Ring, he was so fascinated by the idea of being part of something bigger that he tried to negotiate with you." Thomas looks at me. "He longs for attention and recognition, whatever that means."

I let myself drop back into the seat and run my hand through my hair numerous times. The sun's rays make their way down through the treetops and light up small spots on the forest floor.

"That means we can open the connection permanently," Thomas leans forward, and the beautiful features of his face become clearer.

I gasp for breath. There is almost no air in here; promptly, I grab the window handle and roll it down. It scratches a bit, and a wave of fresh air flows into the car.

"But Thomas, Frank goes back and forth, and Daniel has told me that there are more people helping him in In-Between."

Thomas frowns. "That's not good, and it does not make the task easier." He looks thoughtful and knits his eyebrows.

"We also don't know what Frank's next move is, and we cannot trust him." My words almost stumble over each other.

"Angela, right now you have to focus on completing the Ring, then we will take care of Frank later." He looks at me seriously and gets a little distant in his gaze. I have never seen Thomas with a faraway look in his eyes like this before. Is there something he is not telling me?

"There is one more thing," I hold back, my heart races away. "Have you been receiving people the last few days?" I look earnestly at Thomas.

Thomas shakes his head slowly. "I have been with Gabriel. His condition has worsened, and right now, I'm not sure if he will stay here until you return. David has been keeping an eye on Frank. I hope you haven't needed me."

I struggle to hold back tears and shake my head mechanically. "There is a woman named Meera. She arrived yesterday, I hope." I speak fast, and my voice is about to break. "She is…" I gasp. "She is one of the two. I mean, I think she might be the sixth member of the Ring."

Thomas smiles, and love flows from him. I open the car door, and slightly intoxicated by his love and the thought that I might have found one of the two, I step out. The picture follows about a meter in front of me, so I can still see both Thomas and the trees in the background. The fresh air tickles my skin, the forest floor crunches under my feet, and a small frog jumps for life.

"It's not certain that it's her," I quickly say and hold my breath. I just put my biggest fear into words.

Thomas sits still and looks at me. "Angela, I will find her and ask if she wants to be tested, just like we tested you. How much does she know?"

"A lot," I look down at the ground and walk along the small path to the opening.

"She has long, gray straight-cut hair, a bit like Cleopatra, completely dark blue eyes, and around her neck, she wears a silver piece of jewelry on a leather cord. It is quite special, oval and pointed at both ends. She has a nice, slightly silky voice."

"How tall is she?"

"I would think she is about five foot five."

"Thin or?"

"She has a female shape." It's really hard to describe another human being accurately, but I think I succeeded quite well.

"That's great. We will take it from here. If you want to continue, you can concentrate on finding the last one. We won't know if Meera is the right one until we have tested her," Thomas pauses. "But I trust your instinct." He smiles warmly at me. I push a few branches aside. The city appears to the left of me, and far ahead, I can glimpse the sea. The sun hangs behind the pink clouds and draws bright streaks down from the sky. I stop and breathe all the way down into my stomach.

"Thomas." There is a bench on the right, and I sit down. It is split at the sides, and a board is broken off. "If it's not Meera, then what do we do?"

"Let's deal with one thing at a time." He sits quietly. "There is no need to worry about something you do not know. Relate to what you know." He smiles at me, and again I remember the story of the old man with the horse who kept insisting on relating only to what he knew, even though the people of the village were continually trying to draw conclusions. It is such a liberation. My body relaxes a bit, and I lean forward and support my elbows on my legs. With a slight movement, I move Thomas's image a bit to the side so I can look out over the city.

"I want to stay and try to find the last one." I pull my feet up under me. "I just needed to get some air. The doubt is gone now." I put my arms around my legs and pull them toward my chest.

"It's your choice, Angela. We have no expectations." He sits silently in the chair. The room around him seems quiet. "As I said, Gabriel is not well, but I hope he perseveres."

I look away and try to hide my face.

"Angela…"

I bite my teeth together and clench my jaws, so it hurts.

"Yes."

"Do what you can and remember that if it is meant to be, then we will succeed."

I say nothing, sit still, and look at Thomas. How can he be so sure? Why did Meera not stay here so she could help me find the last member of the ring? Then I would have had someone to talk to. While it's nice to speak to Thomas, it's not the same as having someone by your side.

"Try to get a good night's sleep and get up early. The morning is often a great time to receive good ideas." Thomas smiles at me.

If only I could get a hug right now; I need it.

"Let me just search for Meera before we say goodbye." Thomas presses the keyboard. I let my gaze wander over the city. Maybe the last one is somewhere down there; I just don't know where. The clouds change color to deep orange. The sky looks like a dramatic painting in rebellion against all that is predictable. I close my eyes, and calmness settles internally. I try to stop my thoughts and enjoy the breaks that occur when I succeed.

"Angela."

"Yes." I open my eyes and look at Thomas. He has two deep clefts between his eyebrows and folds up his sleeve with precision.

"I just looked Meera up in the system…."

I sit still and feel my body calm down completely. "And?"

"I can't find any information on her."

40

NO COINCIDENCE

The doors to the supermarket slide open as I step closer. It's precisely nine o'clock, and I'm back in town. I have no idea what I will do or where the day will lead me, so I have decided to be open to all possibilities. Inside, to the left of the door, there is a basket full of reduced items. There is a racetrack with two loops, dolls adorned with colorful pearls, and plastic knights on horses. Next to it are buckets with flower bouquets, which have certainly seen better days. There is already a tangle of people who set off with their shopping trolleys without heeding anyone but themselves. They move mechanically like programmed robots. In their world, they are the most important thing, and everything revolves around them. I take a trolley from the trolley bay and notice a bulletin board with several small notes on it. Although I do not need anything, I feel an inclination to go and take a closer look. Car for sale, boat for sale, pram for sale. Cleaning, babysitter, casual work. I look around. No one notices that I'm standing here looking at the ads. I have to meet new people somehow, and one option is to find a job or do some volunteering. I let my hand glide through my hair, which sticks out a little randomly. Babysitter sounds easier than cleaning and casual work at a restaurant, which properly means emptying the rubbish bins and cleaning the dishes. I may be lucky that it's a nice family. It's worth a try. I only have a few days left before I return to In-Between, but somehow, I feel drawn to the babysitter job and find myself grabbing a slip with a phone number.

I get my shopping done in a hurry and get into the car with a bread bun and chocolate milk in hand. My cell is almost out of battery, but hopefully, there is enough power to make one call. I dial the number from the slip. I have no idea how long the notice has been on the board, and maybe they have already found someone—the phone rings and rings.

"Hello." A shrill female voice cuts through to me.

It gives a jolt in me, and I emerge, "Yes, uh…."

There is silence at the other end.

So, I continue, "I'm calling regarding your ad for a babysitter."

"One moment, I'll just get my husband." The phone slams down on a table, and I can hear her shouting in the background.

I keep the cell a little distance from my ear, take a bite of my bun, and wait. I'm parked outside the supermarket and can't help but look at all the different people who go in and out. It's fascinating how different people are on the outside, but deep down, it's the same thing we all long and struggle for, love.

"Hello, Andreas speaking, who is this?"

I'm about to choke on the chocolate milk and start to cough. I can neither move nor get a single word out of my mouth. The phone begins to beep low battery.

"Who is it?" His voice is a little harsh.

I manage to swallow the bread, which has swollen in my mouth.

There is a chaos of people with stuffed bags outside the car windows, and tears start to build up in my eyes, making it hard to see anything. "Yes," I clear my throat, "Sorry, I'm calling about your childcare ad." I swallow.

"Finally, yes, thank you. I need someone to look after my son in the afternoons. You know, pick him up and be with him a few hours after Kindergarten. Can you do that?"

I put the bun on the passenger seat and sit up straight. "Yes." My hands get cold and clammy. *I can't say yes to taking care of Luke!* He will figure out who I am. I have to hang up right now.

"Great, can you come over today so we can meet each other and have a talk?"

It's Saturday today, and the Kindergarten is closed. Outside my car, people are pushing each other, and a man shouts angrily that there are no more shopping trolleys. It's nothing compared to the chaos that reigns inside me.

"Today? Yes." I pinch myself with my nails and bite my teeth together.

"Super, how about, say, eleven o'clock? We live at 72 Elm Street. Do you know where it is?"

I open the glove compartment and get out the sat-nav from the darkness. It looks like it belongs to another century. "I'll find it." My voice starts to tremble a bit, and I better hang up as soon as possible.

"Great, see you then. Oh, by the way. I completely forgot to ask your name, and how old are you?"

"I'm thirty-five, and my name is… Angela. I have taken care of children before."

"Sounds good, see you then."

"See you." I turn off the cell and stare at the crowd blankly moving in front of the car. I can't feel my heart beating, and I can't hear any sounds. It's like being in a time bubble that will burst in a minute, and I will realize that I have just agreed to the dumbest thing EVER. Someone honks, and I blink a few times. Now I just have to kill time until eleven o'clock. It's hard to think of anything else right now.

"TURN RIGHT." The sat-nav's voice is mechanical. Not the most inspiring company, but luckily, it does not contradict me. I'm in a residential area a little outside the city, not too far from Luke's Kindergarten. The houses lie side by side, all with low hedges in front and driveways toward the street. They are identical, two-story and white with a red roof. The only thing separating them is the house numbers on the small, black mailboxes by the road.

There are ten minutes until I have to be there, and I do not want to be too early, so I drive very slowly. One thought shouts at me after another—it's like having a political debate in my head. I turn on the radio, and the tones of "I'm Alive" with Celine Dion drown out my thoughts.

"You have arrived at your destination," the navigation lady says in her always polite tone of voice.

I slowly drive past number 72, which has a small flower bed filled with small bushes along the edge of the house. Could it be Longlegs who has a green thumb? The engine sighs as I turn it off, and I pat the steering wheel lightly. The sun is high in the blue sky, and the birds are singing lively from the trees along the quiet residential road. I slam the car door and look up at the house. There is a swing set and a football goal in the front yard. The house is a little too square for my liking, but the large windows facing the road look nice. I take a deep breath so that my lungs expand. My jacket and handbag are on the front seat, and I reach for them before slowly walking toward the small gate. This may be the last time I see Luke and the closest I will ever come to him. The small gate squeaks a bit as I push it open. I have to admit that the garden looks nice. Andreas has never been a "house and garden" kind of person. He always wanted to live right in the city in an apartment when we were together. I walk up three steps and stand in the front yard. There is grass on both sides and small red and yellow flowers next to the path leading up to the front door.

"Catch me, Dad," is Luke's voice. He must be on the other side of the house. I start walking backward, down the steps toward the gate, and I grab the handle. Stop. I breathe deeply and look up at the sky. This is my last chance to be with Luke. My heart is pounding, and I am trying to disconnect all rational thinking. Then, I quickly go back up the stairs and along the path to the house.

"Daddyyyyy, come on."

My legs continue in the direction of the front door. The house looks expensive. Andreas Thomsen, Emma Diaz, and Luke. The brass nameplate is next to the door. My arm feels heavy. I stare at the doorbell and then press my finger against it. All I can see is the heavy wooden door in front of me.

"I'll get it." It's Luke's voice followed by the sound of small steps coming closer. I take a step back. There is a bit of fumbling with the lock, and then the door opens.

Luke is standing right in front of me.

41
DISGUISED

"Here is a list of everyone who has arrived in the last two weeks. Each profile number has a picture and description of a soul." David looks at Thomas with apologetic eyes and hands him a very thin screen with a built-in computer with several thousand profile numbers.

"Thank you," Thomas smiles. "Then there is only one thing to do now."

Thomas sits down with the screen in the mint green sofa in the Ring's control room, where the diffuse walls float effortlessly around them. David takes a seat next to him in one of the chairs. A tray with glasses, a jug of water, and a fresh bouquet of orange flowers is on the table. There is another thin tablet on the table. It's turned off.

"Shouldn't we keep an eye on Angela?" David looks toward the screens, which float slightly in front of the red wall. They are filled with images from Earth. The ocean, the forest, the desert, and the mountains. He gets up and walks around the room. His pants are too big, and they can only just stay up around his hips when he moves.

Thomas looks up at David. "I have chosen to give her a break." He flips through the first profile.

"How can Angela be sure Meera is the right person?" David stops.

"She cannot." Thomas's finger presses lightly on the screen, and the next profile becomes visible. The room is filled with a soft light, which falls through the large windows from above. He sits still and absorbs the calmness from the room.

"When is Angela coming back?" David's voice is a bit hesitant.

Thomas flips through the subsequent few profiles. "In six days."

David mumbles a few words, walks to the cupboard with drinks, takes one of the black and yellow cans, and opens it with a snap. He takes a few gulps. "Is there anything we can do?"

Thomas looks at him and shakes his head slightly. "This is the ultimate test of trust." He leans forward and takes the tablet on the table. With a touch of his finger, he pulls half of the numbers from his tablet onto the other and hands it to David. "The best we can do now is try to find Meera based on Angela's description."

David looks into the air. The silver chain around his neck hangs heavily down over his chest, partly covered by the curled-up shirt. Thomas moves a bit to the side and makes room for David, who takes the tablet. There are women, children, and men of all ages from all over the world. He creates three groups, the ones he can exclude, the unlikely, and the very possible. There are quickly several pages in the group with those that can be excluded.

Thomas pauses and looks at David. "We will find her." His voice is soft, and he breathes slowly in and out, so he doesn't sound hesitant.

David flips through a few pages and stops at a blonde in her twenties.

A low hissing sound makes Thomas lift his gaze from the screen. The door to the hallway slides open, and before he can blink, Yoge stands right in front of him. His hair is in disarray, and he wipes sweat from his forehead while puffing loudly.

"I think I've seen her!" His head tilts slightly from side to side, and he sits down on the edge of the couch next to Thomas to catch his breath. "I was standing in line in the café, and she was right in front of me. She has dyed her hair black, but the rest of Angela's description fits." Yoge exhales, pours water into a glass, and drinks it in one mouthful.

"Honestly, why does anyone dye their hair up here?" David twists his face. "Isn't the whole point here to be truer to yourself?"

"Some people think it's enough to change their appearance." Thomas sets down the thin tablet on the table in front of him.

"It could also be that she is trying to hide. She doesn't know if we have registered her arrival or not." Yoge continues to wipe his hand over his forehead to get rid of the pearls of sweat.

"That is true." Thomas looks up, the windows in the ceiling open easily, and a cool breeze spreads in the room. He gets up and puts a hand on Yoge's shoulder, "Where is she now?"

"Shiva is keeping an eye on her. I called her before I ran over here." Yoge gets up and walks toward the door, which slides open slowly. Then he turns briefly. "There is no time to waste; we have to find out if it is her."

Yoge disappears out the door, and Thomas quickly turns to David, who is completely engrossed in the next profile, yet another blonde. Then he sets off after Yoge.

ALL THE TABLES in the café are busy. Most of the people are eating while others just sit and talk. Thomas scans the room as he enters. Light streams from the large arched windows by the end wall, where people sit close together on the sofas. He catches sight of Shiva; she is seated to the left of the entrance, drinking a cappuccino. She looks casual in her light white blouse, with embroidery on the front, and her dark canvas pants. Her thick black hair falls loosely around her face in different lengths.

"Hi there," Shiva gets up and opens her arms toward Thomas;

THE RING

the intense heat from her slender body fills him up. "She's sitting right over there." Shiva nods discreetly toward one of the round tables in the middle of the café.

Thomas shifts his gaze and catches sight of the woman. She has pitch black, straight long hair cut like Cleopatra, just like Angela described her. The woman has the big round table to herself, and she is staring into her bowl of soup without eating.

Yoge is still panting and grabs a chair. "I stood right behind her in the line and could see that her hair was dyed. There is a light gray stripe on her scalp and some gray strands that have not been dyed. It looks like she was in a hurry." He rubs his broad nose with the back of his hand.

Thomas stares at the woman as he pulls out a chair and sits down. The sound of small talk from the cafe lies like a constant buzz around them. There is a lot of activity behind the bar, with several young people laughing out loud while serving those who are waiting. He looks at Yoge and then over at Shiva. Then, he breaks the silence. "One of us has to get in touch with her."

"The café is pretty crowded today." Shiva keeps her voice down. "So, it would not seem suspicious if I sat down at her table." She pulls her sleeve up a bit and grabs a piece of gum from her pocket.

"You have to proceed cautiously; she must not know that we are focusing on her. First, we have to try to figure out why she doesn't want to be recognized."

"Yoge is right. We can't risk scaring her off." Thomas places his hand on Shiva's. She looks at him, and he realizes that she is the one comforting him and not the other way around.

She gets up, takes her food tray, and walks steadily toward Meera's table. Thomas senses his breathing tighten a little. He swallows a lump in his throat, sits back in the chair, and folds his hands on the table in front of him. Yoge tries to turn his body and discreetly keep an eye on Shiva. She has reached the table. It is impossible to hear what is being said, but Shiva points to the table and looks around the café. Meera shrugs a little.

A young guy walks around, wiping tables clean. He stops in Thomas and Yoga's field of vision. They move a little to each side so they can see what is happening. Meera pushes her chair back, takes her tray, and walks away without even looking at Shiva. Within a few seconds, she has made her way past the people queuing up at the bar and disappeared out of the cafe.

"I will follow her; she has not seen me yet." Thomas pushes the chair back in a quick motion, and he feels Yoge's grip on his arm.

Thomas signals an okay to Yoge and sets off toward the café's exit.

42
THE DOOR TO ANOTHER LIFE

"Hi, my name is Angela." My voice is about to crack. Luke is standing in front of me in the doorway. Most of all, I want to take him in my arms, hug him profoundly and never let go, but I lock my hands on my back and fold them firmly together.

"Hi… Daaaaad, it's the woman from my Kindergarten." Luke turns and runs down the hall. He is wearing a green and white checkered shirt over a white long-sleeved shirt and cowboy pants and looks smart and grown-up. There is no longer anything babyish about him. When I don't see him for a long time, I sometimes forget how big he has become. The same happened when I went on trips abroad for a couple of weeks. He had always grown when I came home. Lately, it has been hard to tell from images only. The sight of Andreas further down the hall tears me out of my thoughts and back to reality.

"Hi, I'm Andreas," he steps closer and reaches out his hand. Luke hides behind him. "Have I met you before?" I don't have time to reply before Luke pulls at Andreas's arm. "Luke, what is it?" Luke keeps pulling his arm until Andreas bends down. He tries to whisper, but it is so loud that I can't help but hear every single word.

"Daad, can't you see it's the woman we met at Kindergarten?"

Andreas looks back up at me. "Uhm, sorry, come in. Do you work at the Kindergarten? We are very pleased with the place. We just moved here a few weeks ago, you know. Maybe that is why I didn't recognize you." Andreas moves back and signals to me that I can come in. He has bare feet, and the day-old stubble dominates his face.

"Luke." It's Longlegs' shrill voice that cuts through the hallway. He lets go of Andreas's arm and runs to her. I take a step forward, and Andreas moves further back so I can get inside.

"Yes, yes, again, come in." He takes my jacket. "Please, come this way." He walks down the narrow hallway where the walls are full of large paintings in gold frames; along the wall, there's a row of glass display cases with small sculptures. Jackets hang on a twisted brass hanger on the wall, and shoes are a little randomly scattered all over the floor.

"Sorry about the mess. Our cleaning lady let us down this morning," Andreas pulls a face and shrugs.

I step over a pair of wellingtons and into the hallway. Shivers run down my back. Every little muscle in my body is tense, and I squeeze my bag under my arm.

"I'm happy you could make it. In fact, we need someone to look after Luke tonight, so I was hoping you might... I know it's a bit short notice." Andreas looks me in the eye, and I immediately look down. He better not recognize me. Imagine if you could recognize a soul through their eyes. But unlike Lucy, he hasn't been to In-Between, and there are no pieces of his memory that haven't been erased.

There is a staircase to the second floor from the hallway where I can glimpse a door that is ajar and toys that spread over the doorstep.

The house smells of home-baking. Could it be that Longlegs is the housewife type? I follow Andreas down the hallway into a large bright kitchen with a dining area in the left corner where Luke has settled down. All the kitchen elements are shiny and look brand new. The drawers are wide and the fridge huge. Longlegs is standing in the kitchen, ready to take freshly baked bread rolls out of the oven.

"Sorry, I'll be there in a minute." She casts a glimpse at us as we enter. "Holy shit! It's you. The woman with the past lives." She opens the oven, and the heat flows up her face. "Auch, stupid oven." She throws the plate of buns on the kitchen table, which is made of dark granite.

Andreas walks over to her. "Do you need help?" He was also very helpful and polite when I first met him.

He is kept at a distance with an angry I-can-handle-myself gaze. She turns on the cold water and says, "No, you take care of Angela."

She remembers my name; I really have to control myself now. I'm standing at the dining table where Luke is sitting. On the wall behind him hangs a picture that I bought with Andreas. It depicts a monastery in Tibet where some elephants are walking next to an elderly lady. Her face is wrinkled, and, on her arm, she wears several thin bracelets in various materials. Luke is busy drawing; all the crayons have been taken out of the box and are scattered all over the table. My stomach sinks—next to the door we came from hangs a picture of me.

"This is my ex-wife; she is unfortunately not among us anymore." Andreas follows the direction of my gaze and then looks over at Luke, who draws further.

"It's Luke's mother," says Longlegs with a rather harsh voice.

"It's important to Luke that she's here too." He strokes Luke's blond hair that has grown down over his eyes.

Longlegs pretends to concentrate on her buns, but it is obvious that she follows every move I make. It warms my heart that she has agreed to have a picture of me on display. Not everybody would be willing to have an ex on the wall.

"Here comes fresh buns and juice." Longlegs walks toward me

with a tray full of plates, jam, cheese, and steaming buns. "By the way, wasn't it you who went traveling with Meera?"

"Yes, it was a great trip." It's not certain she's heard what happened to Meera, so I don't say anything. She places the steaming buns on the table, pushes Luke's crayons aside, and puts the jug of juice on the table.

"Oh, it must have been terribly hard to hike in all those mountains. Was there a proper place to sleep? Could you take a bath?"

I pull a chair out in front of Luke and sit down. "It was fine," I smile at her. "The primitive conditions were part of the experience."

She disappears back into the kitchen and picks up cups, butter, and knives. "Don't make an effort to help," she looks at Andreas, who has sat down next to Luke.

I reach out and point to the paper. "What are you drawing?"

Luke looks at me and smiles. "Can't you see it?" There are some long yellow streaks on the paper. He holds the top of the pencil and presses it down so hard against the paper that it is difficult to move it.

"Is it the sun?" I smile and feel the warm sensation of love spread through my body.

"Yes!" Luke's face lights up. "You can have it when I'm finished." He looks me straight in the eye. "Do you still have the rock I gave you?"

"Right here," I take it from my pocket, where I always carry it and struggle not to start crying.

"Cool." Luke looks pleased that I value his gift.

"Well, why don't you tell us a little about yourself, so we can get an idea of who you are. It's important to us if you are going to look after Luke." Andreas smiles at me and reaches out for a hot bun.

"For sure." I clear my throat. "I am a Kindergarten teacher and have just returned from a seven-week journey abroad." The words come to my great surprise quite convincingly out of my mouth. "I like children," I continue while Longlegs hands me the basket of buns. Luke struggles with a lump of butter, which he insists on smearing on his bun himself. Andreas sits still and listens; he looks tired, and the lines under his eyes have become more distinct.

"If there is anything, in particular, you want to know, please don't hesitate to ask me. I know how important it is to feel secure when it comes to the wellbeing of your children and their safety." I reach for the butter and put a thin layer on my bun; it melts as I spread it. Andreas looks at Longlegs; she says nothing. It seems like it's his decision.

"I don't have any other questions; what matters to me is my gut feeling, and it's good." He smiles at me and puts a thick layer of Nutella on his bun.

My mouth has dried out completely, and I try to smile, but I fail. Instead, I take a sip of the juice that Longlegs has poured for me.

"So, the next question is, can you look after Luke tonight?" Andreas takes a bite of his bun, and a little Nutella gets caught in his stubble.

"Definitely." I look at Luke and am overwhelmed by the joy that instantly flips into anxiety.

"How about that, Luke? Is that cool with you?" Longlegs' voice is piercing, and she says the words with no emotions attached. "Do you want Angela to take care of you tonight so we can go out? It is important to your dad and me."

Luke looks at me. He keeps eye contact and then looks down at the lump of butter he has smeared on the bun, the table, and his shirt. "Yes."

"Well, but then there is only one question left." Andreas smiles and licks the remnants of the chocolate off his fingers.

I sit completely still and stop chewing.

"Can you come back at six o'clock tonight?"

43

MIRACLES

"Angela, we found Meera." Thomas's voice travels like a shock through my body. His voice is so clear inside my head that he could just as well be standing next to me. I just stepped out of the shower. My hand grabs hold of the edge of the sink, and I manage to keep my balance. I have a worn towel wrapped around my body. The Skycon started to flash while I was in the shower, and I hurried out, which means that I am standing in a puddle of water and my hair is dripping on the floor. I'm at my regular hotel in town. Sleeping in the same bed for several nights in a row gives me peace and a feeling of being at home.

"Angela," Thomas's voice sounds severe, and I look at him.

The image of Thomas hovers in front of the mirror, and I can glimpse myself through his image. He's sitting by himself in the control room.

"I have spoken to Meera, and she confirms what you have said." Thomas smiles infectiously. "Now, you only need to find the last one."

"Have you tested her already?" I turn around and step into the room where my clothes are scattered across the floor. The picture of

Thomas floats with me. I have a hard time hiding my excitement and am about to fall on the bed, but I see that Thomas is shaking his head.

"I trust your feeling, but she still needs to be tested."

I bend down for some dirty clothes on the floor and throw them in the bag next to the bed. "When will you test her?"

"She's going with Yoge this afternoon," Thomas looks at me with his clear gaze. "Are you getting uncertain?"

I look away, remove a pair of dirty socks from the worn-out armchair in the corner, and sit down. The cover scratches my legs. "Yes, I sincerely wish she is the one."

"I know, but remember that whether it is her or not, you have followed your heart, and that is the most important thing. You can do no more."

"But..."

Thomas puts a finger to his mouth. "There is no 'but.' Try to observe what it will do to you if it is not her."

"I will be extremely disappointed...."

He looks at me. "Be aware that finding the last two members of the Ring doesn't become a goal or an ambition that makes you forget yourself. When we have goals, we look to the future and can forget to listen to what is happening at the moment because we will do everything to achieve our goals." Thomas doesn't seem to be influenced by my insecurity.

"But everybody has goals today." I am shaking my head.

"Imagine you want to swim across a river, and the goal is to cross the river. As you get out into the river, the current is much stronger than you had anticipated. What do you do?"

Without thinking, it flies out of my mouth: "I put more effort in and keep going."

"Exactly." Thomas stops. He looks at me. The floating picture is hanging right in front of me. "It is important to be able to distinguish between goals and the longing of the soul. A goal will often only satisfy the mind for a short time, where a longing will help to get closer to yourself, your potential." He pauses to give me time to take it in. "If you are aware, then your surroundings will guide you, and if you float along and drop your target, you will be carried with the current down the river. But then you are left to the uncertain where anything can happen."

"Okay, let's say I float along." I cross my arms and lean back in the armchair.

Thomas continues with his always calm and trusting voice. "Suddenly, you hear a roar. Further on, the river becomes a waterfall. What do you do now?"

I laugh, a little strained. "Grab a branch that hangs from the shore."

"So, once again, you try to gain control instead of going with the flow."

"Well, there must be a balance between leaning on trust and being a bit too naive...." I look at Thomas and wait for his answer.

"We cannot know where the universe is leading us if we insist on controlling life and taking over ourselves. Only when we let go and go with the flow can the universe step in."

"But we have to have some influence. I mean, I cannot just sit here and wait for the last person to appear by himself."

Thomas leans back in the chair. The room is all dark around him, and only the flashes of light from the screens in front of him make it possible to see him. "You can leave be, and you can control. The trick is to find a balance in the middle where you take responsibility while letting the universe guide you. But you must always put yourself beyond your personality and your goals and ambitions. Otherwise, you become blind." He places his palms in front of his chest. "Easy is right."

I don't say anything but let the words sink in. *Easy is right.*

"Remember, it is not a matter of either standing idly by or taking control. When you listen to the opportunities and are aware if you start to fight to reach your goal, then you will know when things are easy and when they are not. It is a very fine balance, and it takes a great deal of courage and trust too. And maybe it is the best thing to reach for a branch...."

The light changes; the sun breaks through and forms a vibrant red pattern on the wall behind Thomas. The sky seen from the window in my hotel room is cloudy and dull.

"Most people get caught up in the fight to reach their goal, and they miss the opportunities on the way. Who knows if we are meant to reach the goal or another even better opportunity? Maybe you haven't seen the greater picture?"

I can hear someone humming and behind Thomas is a young guy drinking from a yellow can while being completely absorbed in a screen that he holds in front of him.

"Angela..." Thomas looks thoughtful.

"Yes," I walk to the bathroom and put toothpaste on my toothbrush.

He lets his chair tilt forward and gets up. "Do you have any idea who the last one is?" His words echo in my head. *The last one!* I have no idea, but I can't bring myself to say that. On reflection, I might as well be honest. Why lie? He sees through me anyway.

Thomas walks slowly to the guy immersed in his small, handheld screen, whispering something to him. He looks up and whispers something back.

"Angela, David has kept an eye on Frank. He has kept calm, but we cannot expect him to continue like that." Thomas reaches for a glass of water and takes a sip. "Even though David is monitoring Frank, we still have not found out who is helping him."

I spit out the toothpaste and rinse my mouth with cold water.

"Have you thought of anyone else who may be connected to Frank?"

I shake my head. "Have you talked to Ian, as I suggested?"

"Yes, Ian knows who Frank is, but he is not helping him."

"We will keep searching here. Right now, you don't need to worry about Frank. Stay focused on finding the last one."

I haven't thought much about Frank since I was at his place. So many other things have grabbed my attention. Thomas breaks my train of thought.

"I have one last hint for you."

It better be something that makes sense. I need that.

"If you think you know, you do not know. If you do not know, your soul will guide you."

I sigh and look up at the ceiling, where the paint is peeling off in several places. One thing I do know is that if I find the last member of the Ring, I must kill the person. I bite my teeth together, so my jaws get tense. It is not a thought I like to think through to the end.

"You cannot imagine what the right thing to do is. Your ego will try to confuse you and pull you into your emotions. See if you can separate things so that you step out of your thoughts and feelings and see it all from a neutral place."

I do not say anything because what should I say? I can't see the finish line; I do not know in what direction it is. It all seems hopeless right now. I'm already dead; I've made my choice.

"Thirty-six days have passed." Thomas pauses.

I am perfectly well aware of that. He does not have to rub it in….

"I'm not sure Gabriel will last another six days."

I step closer to the picture. "What…" One more step, then I go right through it.

Thomas continues before I have time to say more. "He thinks he will probably be able to hold on till tomorrow, but not any longer."

I rest my hand on the windowsill. "There must be something we can do. Something." My voice is shaking, and I have a hard time swallowing. I hear Thomas's words, but I do not take them in.

I drag myself back to the room and sit down on the edge of the bed.

"You must prepare to return by tomorrow."

"But, well, I don't know…." I grab the duvet and clasp it. I can barely breathe.

"Remember that there is a meaning with everything." Thomas

THE RING

sits quietly and looks at me. "And easy is right… We can't change the way life unfolds, but we can make the best of it."

"What would you do if you were me?"

He smiles sincerely but says nothing, and that is an answer in itself.

I close my eyes and focus on my heart. The only thing that feels right now is to stick to my appointment with Andreas. If I have to go with the flow and do what comes easy, then this is it. *Easy is right.* I fall back on the bed, and my heart starts beating excessively. Why fight it or try to invent something else?

"And Angela?" Thomas interrupts my flow of thoughts. "When you arrive with the last member of the Ring, we will have tested Meera. But it is only when we are all gathered in the Ring that we can know for sure."

"Yes…" I hesitate and notice that my arms are full of goosebumps.

"Thomas," my voice is low, "how can we know if we are the right seven?"

"If we are the true seven members of the Ring, a white light will descend upon us as we sit together on the chairs in the octagonal room." The light changes behind him, a single ray of sunlight settles gently from behind and leaves a soft light on his back.

I reach for the duvet and wrap it around me. My hair is still wet, but at least it has stopped dripping.

"Thomas, I've been thinking of something. Meera could have been anyone and anywhere. The Earth is enormous. Isn't it a little too random if I find both the missing people from the Ring right here?" I stop and pull my legs up under me. "Do you think I should travel farther away?"

Thomas keeps silent. I can hear the sound of other guests passing by with their rolling suitcases out in the corridor.

"I don't think it's that strange nor coincidental." Thomas breathes casually. "If we are as close to gathering the Ring as we think, then our souls will be closely connected and most likely have found places near each other to incarnate." He leans back in the chair.

I pat the quilt a bit, and it forms a hilly landscape around me. There are several people I have met where I have felt that I knew them already. Some have also come close in a short time, even closer than my own family. But I have never given it a thought before now. Annabel was one of them. Although we only knew each other for a short time, Annabel became closer to me than any other human being. There was no need for many words between us; it was as if we knew each other already.

Thomas steps closer so I can only see his face. "Well, no, I do not think it's strange, but nothing is certain, and whether you have to travel farther away, I don't know."

44

GO WITH THE FLOW

This is my last night on Earth, and I have to look after Luke at six o'clock. That is all I know, and I'm doing my best to stick to it and not let my mind wander off in assumptions and interpretation.

Right now, I'm trying to make all my clothes fit into various sacks, bags, and the backpack. I'm at the hotel, and it's time to erase the traces of me here on Earth. There is still an hour before I have to be at Andreas's place. Time is dragging along even though I have tried to occupy myself all day, asking myself, what would I do if I knew I had to let go of this life? Is there anything left on my bucket list? The answer is yes, but nothing more important than spending time with Luke. And of course, it would be nice to find the last person in the Ring. So, I walked the streets, had some lunch at a café, and then went to the movies. None of it has brought me any closer to the last person. A part of me already feels that I have lost, and to be honest, has given up a bit. I tried, but maybe I should have tried a bit harder. The duvets and pillows lie in a pile on the bed, and the Skycon, cell phone, and car keys are on the little bedside table. I go to the bathroom and throw my toothbrush, toothpaste, and creams in the toiletry bag. This represents my life on earth.

If Thomas is correct, the last person in the Ring could be in my circle of friends. Daniel is one of them. We have talked several times, but I have insisted that we not meet despite his persistent efforts. I'm fascinated by his life, and he's charming, but to be completely honest, my gut tells me it's not him. He's just in love. I giggle. It could be Longlegs, too; the giggle turns into loud laughter and makes my stomach shake. That would show that the universe has great humor. I smile, yes, but it could also be Jane, the prosecutor that picked me up just after I arrived here. Her controlled attitude toward life would definitely be challenged in In-Between. Imagine if I had been that close from the start without knowing it.

I notice the magazine Daniel gave me; it's on the floor and has just surfaced. I never bothered to read it. It was buried under a pile of clothes and only came into view because the pile moved into my bag. On the front, there are hundreds of animals. It is only now that I read the headline, *The Magic of Animals*. I flip through it so fast that one of the pages gets ripped to pieces. "Animals have for thousands of years, blah, blah... The Incas, Indians, and Hindus have used sacred and spiritual animals... See an overview on the next page." I flip the page without reading the rest, and my gaze runs down the list of the various animals. It says that the elephant can communicate telepathically and is a protector. The horse stands for rebirth and past life, and the owl is the symbol of wisdom. It can see what others overlook, and the eagle shows the way and teaches us to face our greatest fears.

I close the magazine and stare into space. The chairs in the octagonal room had carved animals on their backrests. But I can only remember the eagle on my chair. I notice the time; it's twenty minutes to six. If I don't leave now, I'll be late. I get up, grab the bag, and swing my backpack onto my back. The Skycon, cell, and car keys are in my pocket, where the little red stone I got from Luke is too.

THE RING

The door slams behind me, and I stand outside in the long narrow corridor where daylight never reaches, and the carpet is worn off in several places. The stairs down to the reception are old and creaking under my feet.

"Good evening, madame," a chubby man with small, square glasses, which barely cling to the tip of his nose, greets me as I pass the reception. He's counting coins. On the counter is a piece of paper with a lot of crosses on it.

"Good evening. I would like to check out."

He looks up and can just see over the counter. "It has been wonderful to have you here, madame." He smiles all over his face.

"It been nice to stay here; thank you." I pay and leave. My car is parked just down the street, and it doesn't take me long to get there. The streets are quiet. I guess most people are about to sit down with their families and have dinner. For many people, this is just another Saturday; for me, it could be the most valuable one.

It's five minutes to six. I pull up in front of Andreas's house and park the car. The streetlights are switched on, the road is deserted, and spotlights light up the trees outside the house. I rest my hands on the steering wheel and lean my head forward, letting the seconds go by while I observe my breathing. Then I get ahold of the car door and push it open. It squeaks. The chance of finding the last member of the Ring dwindles hour by hour, but time with Luke is well spent. I will have the opportunity to say a proper goodbye to him, look him in the eye, and smell him once last time. This time, I will not take it for granted. I will be present every second with him. I step out of the car and walk toward the house. Through the window, I can see Andreas standing in the living room. He is talking to Luke, who is sitting in front of the television. Longlegs comes by in a flash. She looks busy. I clasp the car key in my hand and walk through the garden gate and along the narrow path leading up to the house. Before I get all the way there, the door opens.

"Oh, thank God you're here, Angela. We're running a little late." Longlegs is standing in front of me, wearing a tiny top that cannot hide her marked collarbones and a dark blue skirt, which is tightly tied with a silk ribbon around the waist.

I throw a glance at my watch. I'm two minutes early. Longlegs gets an indulgent smile.

"Just go in. Andreas is in there, and he can tell you all the practicalities."

I walk past her, take my shoes off, and hang my jacket on the only available coat hook. Jackets hang in several layers on top of each other on all the other hooks. I have my bag over my arm and put the phone and car key in it. The Skycon is already there. The way into the living room seems long. I walk slowly; somehow, it feels like walking through a gateway to my old life.

"Hiiii, Angela." Luke's happy voice greets me as I enter the living room. He is sitting on the large leather sofa that Andreas and I bought when we moved in together. It's placed a little randomly in the middle of the room, in front of the television. The TV is showing a movie with a giant green troll talking to a donkey. Luke is already wearing his pajamas. They are blue and white checkered with a little horse on the chest, no plastic print—that would please my mother, I think to myself.

"Hi, Luke," I walk toward him with open arms, and tears well up. My whole body vibrates.

"Well, you're here," Andreas is right behind me.

I turn quickly and put my arms on my back. Andreas is tying his tie and struggling with the knot.

"There is food in the fridge, and Luke has to be in bed at eight. He knows where the toothbrush is." Andreas looks at me, and I look back without saying anything. "Okay, I better get going." He glances at Longlegs, who is standing in the garden looking quite impatient. "If you need us, you can call this number," he hands me a small, crumpled note. "Otherwise, we will be back at ten o'clock and no later than eleven; is that okay?"

"It's fine." If only he knew that I have taken care of Luke way more than he has.

THE RING

Andreas fixes the tie knot one last time, walks over to Luke, and kisses him on the forehead. "Take care, buddy; see you in the morning."

Luke gets up on the couch and hugs Andreas. "Why can't Mom be here to take care of me?"

I stand completely stiff behind the sofa and look at them.

"Luke, I know it's hard, but you know why she can't." Andreas hugs Luke even harder and looks up to stop tears from running down his cheeks. "And we have spoken about this. You will be fine; it's only for a few hours."

My heart aches, and it is about to break into a million pieces. I want to run out of here and scream as loud as I can at God and the universe, or whoever it is that has put me in this inhuman situation. But I stay put. Luke lets go of Andreas and sits back in front of the television. He has hidden his emotions inside himself, and his little face gets a slightly hard expression.

"Bye, Luke, see you later. I love you." Andreas waves from the door. Luke does not move.

I walk Andreas to the door. The light is on in the small glass showcases with iron figures, which stand in different positions. One is searching, one reads, and one cries. That could be me, Andreas, and Luke.

"Just give him some time; he'll be okay. It's just a little difficult right now. It's the first time we've gone out since… I wasn't going to go… I'm happy we found you." Andreas turns to me. "He's a good boy." Then, he walks through the front door. Longlegs is no longer to be seen out in the garden.

"It's all right." I rest my hand on the doorframe. "I will look after him."

"Call if there is the slightest…." Andreas stops and looks me in the eyes.

"Come on, Andreas." It's Longlegs' shrill voice. She is sitting in the car with the window rolled down.

"I have to go...." He takes one more step to the car, but it is like he is pulled back to the house.

"Enjoy."

Finally, Andreas manages to make it down the small path and out through the gate. Longlegs is sitting at the wheel, and he only just slams the car door before she hit the gas and the car takes off.

The kitchen seems a bit characterless; there are no colors, and everything is white. Even the candles on the large, oval dining table are white. There is a wide double glass door facing the garden, which is lit up with a scattering of small solar-powered lamps. I find a bowl, open the fridge, and get eggs, milk, and carrots. Then I just need some flour, sugar, and vanilla sugar. Everything is neatly organized in the big wide drawers, making it easy to find what I need without snooping too much. I have invented my very own pancake recipe, and I know that Luke's favorite dish is my pancakes. He is still in the living room watching TV. I go and stand at the door. For a minute, I just look at him before I say, "Luke, would you like to join me in the kitchen? We'll be eating soon."

He turns to me. "What's for dinner?"

"Pancakes." I can't help but smile and feel love rush through my whole body like the biggest waterfall has just been turned on.

"That's my favorite." He looks at me with his blue eyes that are nearly covered by the long bangs.

"Well, that's lucky."

He turns off the television and comes a little hesitantly toward me. It is almost impossible for me not to grab him as he comes closer and give him the biggest hug ever, but I control myself. I walk back into the kitchen and start mixing it all up. He stays in the doorway and looks at me.

"Would you like to help?" I smile at him. He nods, pulls a chair next to me, and starts stirring the bowl to mix flour, milk, and eggs. It was moments like these I never appreciated when I was alive. I always had a thousand other things I needed to do at the same time, or I was somewhere else in my mind—never present, enjoying the moment. I grate the carrots and pour a little more flour into the bowl while Luke vigorously stirs, so the flour flies out onto the table and up into his face. He tries to blow it away, and when that doesn't work, he uses his arm and makes some white streaks across his forehead and on his cheeks. He starts to chuckle, so pure and innocent, right from his stomach. I just stand and watch him.

"Are you not going to do anything?" Luke stops stirring.

"Of course, now we have to get the dough on the frying pan." I open the cupboard next to the oven, find a frying pan, turn on the hob, and pour a thin layer of dough onto the pan.

"Come, let's set the table." I look at Luke, who jumps down from his chair.

"Can't you just do it? I'm going to the bathroom." He looks at me with pleading eyes.

Without thinking about it, I stroke his hair. "Of course."

Luke disappears out the door in a hurry. Meanwhile, I find plates and glasses, turn the pancake over and place sugar, Nutella, and jam on the table. A sweet scent spreads in the kitchen, and the pile of pancakes grows steadily. I light the candles on the table and dim the light in the ceiling. Luke is back and jumps back up on his chair, and I sit down across from him.

"I'm ready." He reaches out for the dish full of pancakes. They're steaming, and the sweet smell is intense. He throws one over on the plate. "Let's see who can eat the most?"

"Yes, let's do that." I take a pancake with my fingertips. It's hard not to laugh, and I feel euphoric happiness in every tiny cell of my body. It hurts in my jaws. That is how much I'm smiling.

"So, you're five years old, Luke, and go to Kindergarten?"

Luke nods eagerly. "Yes, I'm five years and two months old." He is eating the pancake with his fingers, and melted Nutella runs down his hands.

I reach for the jam and spread it on the pancake in a thin layer. Right now, I wish I could make time stand still. Luke grabs another pancake, his second. He rolls it and gathers the two ends so none of the sugar is wasted. After taking another bite, he looks at me. "They taste like my mother's pancakes."

"Oh, really?" flies out of my mouth, sounding just as surprised as it should.

"She makes the best pancakes." He takes another bite before saying, "Do you believe in angels?"

"Yes, I do," I hesitate. I have to be careful now. We cannot talk about me. But before I get to change the subject, he continues.

"My guardian angel has said that you go to heaven when you die." He takes the last bite of the pancake. "I want to die because then I can be with my mom."

My insides are torn in millions of pieces like a glass dropped on the floor. I gasp for air, but it feels like my lungs have collapsed. I can't move, and I can't find any words that will make sense.

The doorbell rings.

"I'll get it." Luke jumps down from his chair and rushes out into the hallway.

I hold my hands to my face; everything goes dark. I feel like someone put a knife in my stomach and is cutting me right open. What have I done? How could I choose myself over Luke? He is five years old and wants to die.

"Hiiiiiiiii, Grandma!"

45

THE MIRROR OF THE SOUL

I stand completely frozen in the kitchen, staring at the picture of myself on the wall. My mother here? Why? And why now?

"Hello," she yells in a cheerful voice as she enters the kitchen and walks toward me with an outstretched arm. She is wearing a thin, orange windbreaker that hangs loosely and hides her shape. She has thick wool socks on her feet, and there is a hole in the big toe on the right foot. Luke holds her arm tightly.

"Grandma, you need to see my new room." He tries to pull her back out into the hallway.

She looks at Luke. "I certainly want to, but I just have to say hello to the lady who is looking after you."

The pancakes are still on the table. They are no longer steaming hot, and I have covered them to keep them warm. There is a half-rolled pancake with small bite marks on Luke's plate. I reach out and meet my mother's soft and warm hand. I want to say something, but my lips are glued together. I press the backside of my teeth with my tongue and try to move it, but nothing happens. My mom just stands there, looking relaxed. It's a disaster if she recognizes me. I feel like I'm in the middle of a game, and I have just been made.

"Ehh," I clear my throat. "Hi... My name is Angela... I'm the babysitter."

My mother stands there with her hand in mine. Most of all, I want to pull her close, collapse in her arms, and reassure her that I'm fine. I want to tell her all that has happened and how much I love her. How happy I am that she is my mother, for all that she has given me, and that I am sorry that I did not believe in her spiritual experiences. But I just stand here with my hand in hers.

She shakes my hand a few times, and our hands slide apart. I walk over to the dining table and move the sugar, jam, and Nutella from one place to another.

Luke is still holding onto her other arm, waiting for her to be ready to go to his room.

"I'm sorry, I didn't mean to come unannounced, but I was in the area." She has heavy bags under her eyes, and her silver hair lies flat on her head. She strokes Luke's bangs away from his eyes, and he wraps his arms around her belly.

It doesn't make sense. This is in no way in the realm of anything related to my mother's life. Maybe Andreas has called her and asked her to drop by—maybe he doesn't trust me after all.

"I will not stay for long." She looks at Luke, "but long enough to see your room." She laughs with contagious laughter.

"You can stay as long as you like...." I walk over to the kitchen table. "Would you like a cup of coffee?" I open and close several of the cupboard doors without finding coffee cups. Then I realize they are already arranged on the table next to a huge coffeemaker.

"Yes, thank you; that sounds lovely."

"Grandma, come on, let's go." Luke pulls her arm, and she looks at me; I acknowledge with a smile.

"I'll bring you the coffee, no problem."

Luke eagerly pulls on her arm, and they disappear up the stairs. I'm left alone in the kitchen with the coffee and pancakes.

Is it a coincidence that my mother is here? I catch a glimpse of my reflection in the window and take a step back. Thomas said that the souls of the Ring could incarnate close to each other. It gives a jolt through my body. I pour the coffee and go upstairs to Luke and my mom. Now, I better be astute.

Luke's room is full of toys: a desk with a game console, LEGOs, a pile of teddy bears, various plastic animals, and lots of knights. There are enough toys for an entire Kindergarten. The walls are decorated with posters of a LEGO warrior. By the window is a bookcase, which is also filled with toys. Some of them I have bought for Luke. Next to his bed is a picture of me in a golden frame.

"That is a really cool room you have, Luke." My mother claps her hands together. She looks tired but has got back the spark in her eyes. She takes off her jacket and places it over Luke's chair by the table; the chair's backrest is shaped like a teddy bear head with a mouth, ear, and nose on it. She is wearing a light, knitted sweater and a shawl over her shoulders.

"Here, Grandma, look, it's the angel you gave me." Luke looks up from one of the drawers and hands a small frame to my mother. The angel is painted with gold on a small canvas. It has a fine, white light around its entire body and holds something that looks like a magic wand in its hand. "It should be right here next to Mom." Luke places it on the table next to the picture of me.

I stand in the doorway and look at them. My mother turns to me. "Yes, well, Luke's mother, my daughter, is no longer with us here on Earth." She takes a napkin from her pocket and blows her nose.

"I know." I hand the coffee to her. My legs start to shake under me. I look from my mother over at Luke and back at my mother. *If you think you know, then you do not know. If you do not know, your soul will guide you on its way.* I shake my head and cough a bit. "Well, Luke, should we go down and eat the last pancakes before they get too cold?"

"Yeah, but Grandma, look at this bird. It can just fly here and bite the horse." He holds a plastic eagle in his hand, leading it over to a white horse standing on the bookshelf. The eagle dives down, grabs the horse, and lifts it. He throws them on the floor and looks back into the drawer, and I stand completely still and watch. From the drawer, he pulls out a box. "Grandma, will you play this game with me?"

My mother squats next to him. "Yes, it looks exciting. Maybe we can eat the pancakes up here while we play?" She turns questioningly toward me.

"Why not?" I send a smile back to her.

"Jubiii," Luke raises his arms and throws himself on the blue carpet where a road network is printed. He pulls the lid off the box and pours all the contents onto the floor before either of us can stop him.

I return to the kitchen. The most important thing right now is to keep my mom at an appropriate distance so she doesn't get suspicious. I put the dish of pancakes into the microwave. There is a tray on the kitchen table with some small jars. I move them and place jam, sugar, Nutella, plates, cutlery, cups, and the kettle on the tray. The microwave pings and the pancakes are steaming hot again.

I can hear my mother and Luke laughing. I walk with silent steps back up the stairs.

"Here's dinner." I step into the room, push the plastic animals over to the side a bit, and move a glass with colorful rock crystals on Luke's desk, leaving just enough space for the tray.

Luke sits with dice in his hand. "The one who rolls the highest can begin. What color are you, Grandma?"

She reaches out for the purple pieces and places them in a small house on the board. "Luke, we just have to agree on the rules."

I sit down next to them; my mom moves a little toward Luke to make room for me. I smile politely. Luke takes the dice and starts shaking it between his hands.

"Yes, well, everyone has four pieces, and we have to make it all the way around." He rolls the dice and runs his finger while concentrating across a small path on the game board. "You are safe when you make it to the middle." He points at a white circle on the board and lights up in a smile. "If I catch you, you have to start all over." He rubs his small hands eagerly against each other. "And the one who gets all four pieces to the middle first has won."

My mom takes the red pieces and places them in the little house on the board in front of me. "You can be red. And remember, to get your piece out of the house, you need a six." She smiles at me and has already put her winning face on. My mum just loves playing games, and she hates to lose.

I reach for the dish of pancakes and place it on the floor. The scent rises from them and spreads out into the room.

"They look delicious." She reaches out, "I can always eat a pancake." They are still warm, and she blows on it a bit before taking a bite. Then she looks me right in the eyes and maintains eye contact without blinking.

The fork drops out of my hand and falls to the floor—the sound cuts through the room. My mother does not move her gaze; she sits entirely still and says nothing.

Everything turns numb inside me, not a word, just the connection with my mother's eyes.

"I've only known one person in my whole life who makes pancakes like this…." She finishes chewing while still staring at me.

I know what she wants to say, so there is no reason for her to say it. Either I have to come up with a really good explanation, or I have to tell the truth. I'm not saying anything—that's my answer for now.

"Are you ready? I'll start," Luke rolls the dice. It lands on five. "Oh, no, I cannot get a piece out of the house." He doesn't sense what is going on and places the dice in front of my mother.

She is still not moving her gaze. Her gaze is penetrating me, and it feels like she sees right through me. It is indeed a trait I have inherited from my mother, and now I get to feel it myself.

"Luke, you can throw the dice three times to try to get out," I reach across the board and return the dice to him while still looking my mother in the eye.

He takes it, blows on it, and throws it up in the air. It hits the board, rolls across the floor, and stops.

"YEEEah, a six!" He jumps up and dances around.

"Now, it's your turn." I hand the dice to my mother. She reaches out and takes it, rolls the dice, and it comes to a standstill. Six, she moves her purple piece out onto the board.

I roll the dice three times. No sixes.

"That is interesting. Someone I knew was always lucky—maybe luck eventually runs out...." She says no more, and Luke is busy keeping track of his pieces.

It takes several turns before I manage to get a piece out on the board. Luke smiles and laughs. He has several pieces on the board and sits triumphantly on his knees with his arms out to the side. We move forward in shifts, and my mom is constantly right on my heels.

"If I roll a three, you're going back to where you started," she laughs and looks at me. Then she picks up the dice and holds it in her hand while looking me in the eyes. With a calm motion, she opens her hand and lets the dice fall toward the board. It hits the plate and jumps a few times. Several other pieces move, and the dice's sound hitting the board rings out until it hits the plate again and lies still. I stare at my mother. Luke holds his hands to his mouth.

Three.

"Jubiiiiii..." Luke claps his hands and laughs out loud.

46

WHO ARE YOU?

My mom is tucking in Luke. I can hear them talking upstairs. He will not let her go and keeps finding more books she has to read. I'm sitting downstairs on my old couch. It's getting dark outside, and the streetlights are on. The sound of slow, heavy footsteps comes closer, and I look up. My mother steps into the living room. She comes toward me and sits down on the chair opposite me.

I cannot fool her; a mother knows her child. No matter how you try to hide something from your parents, they will eventually find out. I have made coffee and reach for the pot and pour a cup for my mother. She likes it strong. The scent spreads in the living room, and she pulls a suspicious smile and looks me straight in the eye.

"Who are you?" Her voice is very determined.

It is quiet here, very quiet.

"My daughter left here a short while ago, but something tells me she's back."

I don't blink and don't move a muscle in my body. I'm like a robot waiting for someone else to program my next move. At the same time, it feels like an explosion sets my entire collection of fear, guilt, and anger on fire. My hands are icy cold and clammy. There is no way I can tell her anything. And I can't go back to In-Between tomorrow! I push the cup of coffee over toward her.

"Don't you want some coffee?" I only get small shallow breaths of air and feel like I'm breathing through a straw. The television is turned on and shows pictures of several police cars and an ambulance parked outside a courthouse. The sound has been turned down completely.

"I will stay here until you tell me who you are." My mother's eyes stubbornly rest on me. She sits facing me as she fiddles with a napkin in her lap.

"I..." I look down at the table. "I'm not sure who you think I am." Our eyes meet.

She does not move a muscle in her face.

"I can understand that you miss your daughter." I take a break. "But I'm not her." I pinch my nail into my other finger and hope she buys it.

The light from a car passing by on the street forms a soft shadow on the wall, like a ghost sweeping by.

She breaks the silence. "I don't know what is going on, but you are not who you say you are." Her voice is sharp and cuts through my lies.

I feel like the king in a chess game. I have lost my defense and have run out of moves. Most of all, I want to tell my mom the whole story. I'm sure it will make it easier for her to accept that I'm dead. Maybe it will ease some of her pain to know that I'm in the most beautiful place and that I'm with her. It will make it easier for me too.

She reaches for her orange windbreaker and fishes out an older cell phone from her pocket. "If you do not tell me who you are, I will call Andreas."

I know my mother well enough to know that these are not empty words. I stare at her and gasp for breath. Out of the corner of my eye, I can see the TV news presenter with a serious look on her face. A headline appears on the screen, *Prosecutor Stabbed in front of Courthouse*, and a picture of a dark woman with curly hair appears. My jaw drops down, and I blink a few times as I reach for the remote and turn up the volume. "...was stabbed at 15:09 this afternoon and taken to the intensive care unit at the hospital. She hovers between life and death."

I am paralyzed. It's Jane who has been stabbed. The words from the television fade into the background. I look at my mother. She is waiting for my next play, but I do not know what to say or do. If Jane is the last person in the Ring, she will die, and the universe itself will have taken action. But she's not dead yet. Are they trying to send me a message? Was I supposed to watch TV? I need help, and maybe it's sitting right in front of me. After all, she has more experience with the spiritual stuff than I have. My journey has only just begun. I have to give it a try; I have no choice. Tiny chunks of air seep in through my lips, and dizziness takes power in my body. My mother holds out her cell phone and looks at me. I bite my lower lip, and my heart gallops away.

"If I tell you something now, you have to promise me that you will never repeat it to anyone. Not Luke or anyone else?"

She straightens up and leans forward. "I do not have to promise you anything. If there's something you want to tell me, you say it; it's up to you."

I take off my black knitted cardigan and put it behind me.

"Your daughter is dead."

The room is more quiet than quiet. Not a sound or movement. Even the old grandfather clock that I inherited from my father's father has come to a stop.

"But you are right. You know me." I can't look her in the eyes and let my head fall forward. It feels like I'm sinking in a thousand shards of glass, my lips are trembling, and I try to hide my face in my hands. I have promised not to tell anyone about In-Between. I close my eyes and try to swallow repeatedly. Then I lift my head very slowly. We make eye contact again, and I start talking about the accident, In-Between, about how we sent her light, and that I have been keeping an eye on Luke and Andreas. I tell her about the Ring, about the glimpses I have received, about Jane and Meera, who has been taken to In-Between. Tears roll down my mother's face. Her eyes are like mirrors, and her expression is petrified. She takes it all in without saying a word.

"Grandma," Luke is calling from his room upstairs.

She opens her mouth and is about to say something but holds back and wipes her eyes with a napkin. Then she strokes my cheek with her warm hand and gets up slowly. She leans on the couch for a moment and then walks toward the door. I exhale. Now it is out, and I can't take it back.

I put a teabag in a cup and pour hot water. The time on my watch says it's nine minutes past nine, and there is still nearly an hour until Andreas and Longlegs could be back.

The sound of heavy footsteps on the stairs makes me straighten up. My mother stands in the doorway, holding on to the frame. I get up and walk over to her. Her shawl drops from her shoulders to the floor, and she does not respond.

She keeps looking at me. "I have had this feeling you were still among us, all the time. But no one has believed me." Her right hand shakes. She speaks in a low voice and looks me in the eye. "When I meditate, I see images that are reminiscent of what you are saying, and it is only now that they make sense."

I reach out and take her hand in mine. She lifts my hand and turns it around, investigating it.

"I recognize the soul behind your eyes," she smiles, "and your pancakes, but not your disguise." She releases my hand and strokes my hair.

I step one step closer to her so that our bodies are almost touching each other. Her brown eyes are filled with tiny black dots. When I first discovered them as a child, I asked her if it was a mistake. There is a fine light ring around the black pupil. My heart skips a beat—I never noticed that before. She opens her arms to me;

THE RING

I take hold of her, and our bodies meet. I can feel her warmth, her breath, and smell her. Her perfume smells of roses. It is the same perfume she has always used. A tear rolls down my cheek and is followed by more. We stand entirely still without saying anything. I'm in a different body, but I can feel my mother, and she can feel me.

After some time, I slowly loosen the grip around her and step back a little. "There is more...."

She frowns, widens her eyes, and stares at me. Her eyes have become bloodshot, and while maintaining eye contact, she picks up her shawl and puts it around her shoulders.

"I have to go back to In-Between tomorrow, at the latest." It is unbearable to look her in the eyes, so instead, I look up at the ceiling.

She puts her arms around me again and hugs me so tight that all the air is squeezed out of me.

I continue in a low voice. "For the Ring to be completed, I must find the last missing person."

She leans forward and whispers in my ear, "I know who the last one is...."

I let myself fall into her embrace.

"So do I."

47

THE DECISION

It's past ten o'clock, and Andreas and Longlegs could be home at any time. My mom went to the bathroom to wash her face in cold water. I stand by the window and look out onto the deserted street. I have the Skycon in my hand and flip it between my fingers. If it had worked the whole time, I wouldn't have gotten all those glimpses from past lives or contact with the voice. I might not have had the same understanding of the journey of the soul. It all starts to make sense. It would probably have been easier in many ways if it had worked, but I can feel that it's my ego that would prefer it, not my heart. It would rather walk the path of love.

Yet this is the worst-case scenario that doesn't bring any kind of justice. I remind myself of Thomas's words about putting myself beyond my emotions and thoughts. What if something that seems unforgivable right now turns out to be inevitable, or maybe it is a piece in a bigger game—something that will affect my next life. I exhale. Energy rises from my loins and runs up my spine. It passes my neck and makes its way up to the top of my head. It feels like it's burning its way out through the top of my head. It brings clarity with it, and I let my shoulders drop a bit.

"How much time do we have left?" My mother has walked right up behind me without me noticing.

"Andreas and Emma could be here any time now." I place my hand on the icy cold window and try not to think.

My mother puts her arm around my waist and hugs me. "I'll get Luke, and then we better get going." She looks at me. "Have you thought about how you want to leave?"

I shake my head and remove my hand from the window. It leaves an imprint on the glass. "I did not expect to find the last one, so..." I shrug, and an emerging panic tries to take control over me, but I avoid giving it attention.

My mother steps closer and lowers her voice. "I have some very powerful sleeping pills that I was prescribed by the doctor when you were in a coma," she gets them from her bag.

I breathe slowly and feel like someone just dropped a kettlebell on my chest. *Tell me. This isn't real. Please, Thomas, call me and let me know that Jane is the one or you have found the last one yourself. Tell me I am wrong.* I turn around, and we stand facing each other.

"There are more than half left." She shakes her hand so that the bottle rattles and blinks mechanically with her eyes.

The large grandfather clock suddenly moves the minute hand, and the bell begins to toll. There is still no one to be seen on the street; it could be a matter of minutes before Andreas and Longlegs get home.

I bite my lower lip, so it starts to sting. "Let's do this. I can't see any other options." Together, we walk to the kitchen as two allies on our way to complete a mission. I find two water bottles in the fridge and empty some water out of them. My mother pours the pills out on the table and starts crushing them. We do not look at each other and are both silent.

What if it's not right? What if it's just me who is determined to bring someone back? What if I'm wrong and am letting my ambition, feelings, and needs come before the task? Is this true? Have I managed to put myself beyond my thoughts and feelings? I sigh and rub my hand across my face.

"How much do we need for them to work?" I put the water bottles on the table, and they are three-quarters full of water.

My mother shrugs; she has only taken the pills to soothe her pain. She collects the crushed powder on a spoon, sprinkles it into the bottles, screws on the lids, and shakes them well. "I would think that sleep occurs quickly and gets deeper and deeper." She opens the fridge, takes out a bottle of red cordial, and mixes it in the water. "It should cover up the ugly taste." Her lips are pressed together, and her gaze distant.

The small hand on the old clock ticks loudly, reminding me that precious seconds are passing.

"We have to go now...." I take the bottles. The water is pink and filled with small white grains.

The sound of a car out on the street increases. I place the bottles on the table, run into the living room, and over to the window. The light approaches, the engine noise becomes louder, and the car slows down and drives past. It's the neighbor coming home. My mother stands petrified in the kitchen.

"Come on," I call out. "Put on your jacket. I'll get Luke."

There is no more time to think. I must take action. If not, I will start to doubt myself, and it's too late for that. I sneak into Luke's room. The light by his bed is still on, and he is lying on his back with his mouth slightly open. I reach for a piece of paper and a pencil on the table. I have to use all my power to keep the pencil still as I write, "I'm sorry." A tear twists free from the corner of my eye and wipes my name halfway out. I fold the paper and place it next to the picture of me. Half of Luke's duvet is on the floor. I pick it up and wrap it around him. He smells so sweet. With a firm grip around his neck and legs, I lift him. I have been dreaming of holding him close for weeks. I stand still, take it in, and let the scent and the feeling fill my whole body. I feel it in every little cell. Right now, here, with Luke.

My mother stands out in the hallway with her orange windbreaker on as I come down the stairs. The light is off as we don't want to wake Luke. He breathes heavily. The stairs creak, and I stop. Luke doesn't respond. My mom opens the front door and takes a peek at the street. Then she opens the door wide and exits. Her shoulders hang down heavily, and she walks a little wobbly down the path.

I grab my bag and coat and quietly close the front door behind me. Small solar lamps light up the path down to the road, and I can see my mother's car parked right behind mine. She drives a little red Ford. I pull the duvet even tighter around Luke and stroke his soft hair with my hand.

The neighbor's dog barks three times when it catches sight of us, then lumbers away again. I look at my mother; she seems fragile. There is no time to waste.

"We can't leave either of the cars here. Shall we meet at the hut in the forest? Do you know which one I'm thinking about?" My voice gets a little harsh; I didn't mean it to. We walk to my mother's car, and she opens the back door.

"What is the address?" She shivers. I hope she doesn't change her mind.

"It is located on the forest path, right at the end." I'm sure there will be no one at this time of night. I have never seen anyone out there. "Luke had better go with you, just in case he wakes up. He will feel safer."

Together, we get him in the car seat and wrap the duvet tightly around him. A couple of headlights appear at the end of the road. We look at each other. It better not be Andreas. Quickly, I look at my watch; it's half-past ten. The light dazzles me, and I hold my breath. It will be hard to explain why we're out on the street, and Luke is sitting in his grandmother's car when he should be in his bed.

The car drives past.

"Let's go," I close the door softly. "Are you going to follow me?"

My mother goes to the front door of the car, looks at me, nods defeatedly, and gets in.

48

MY RESPONSIBILITY

The light from my mother's car is right behind me. The road out to the forest feels as long as if we were driving through a desert without water. I'm trying not to think, but it's impossible. On the one hand, it seems so obvious and straightforward, but on the other hand, there is chaos and rebellion inside me. As I embraced my mother, I experienced a certainty from a place so deep inside me that it was not up for discussion. It was only afterward that the doubt came thundering back.

We are on the outskirts of town, and the road is wide and dark. It winds its way up the mountainside along the forest. A little farther ahead is the road that leads into the woods and to the forest path.

I stare out into the darkness. I cannot take another person's life, not even for a good cause. I'm on the horns of a terrible dilemma. Meera made the choice herself. I have not dared to think the mission through to the end, and deep down, I have hoped that I would not get into this situation. But now I'm in it, and it's me who has to make the decision. I have to take responsibility.

I put on my turn signal and drive into the forest. To the right is the forest path and at the end is the slightly dilapidated forest hut.

Only the light from the cars' headlights breaks the darkness. I look in the rearview mirror and gasp. Where did my mother go? The light from her car headlights is gone. They were behind me just before; did she take a wrong turn or change her mind?

I drive into the small parking lot next to the cabin and turn off the engine. It is completely quiet and a bit cooler here. I still cannot see my mother's car, and I gently open the car door. Imagine if she has driven to the police station instead, and they're on their way out here to arrest me.

Stop, stop, I shout inside my head. Of course, she's coming. That is the thought I want to give my attention and not least my confidence.

I walk up to the cabin and look through the broken windows. It is dark, and it smells damp. The paint on the exterior woodwork is tired. An owl hoots from a tree, and I look up. The stars hang low, and the moon shines brightly above my head. It's so quiet here, and I'm all alone.

The sound of a car in the distance becomes clearer. It is slowly approaching. I walk to the road and keep an eye out. It better be my mother's car. *It is.* The light inside the car is on, and she's talking to Luke, who's awake.

She parks next to my car and turns off the engine. Everything goes quiet again. My steps on the ground are noisy. I open the car door on the side where Luke is sitting.

"Hi, Luke," my voice is shaking a bit. He does not know me that well.

My mother nods to me and whispers, "I didn't say anything to him, but we just had to stop for a pee by the roadside."

"Have you ever been up here before?" I squat down next to him. He looks at me, rubs his eyes, and shakes his head.

"I want to go home to my bed. I'm tired." His hair sticks out to the sides, and he pulls the duvet up over his nose.

My mother takes over. "Luke, we can sit together. There is a great view from over there." She steps out and staggers over to me, loosens his seat belt, and lifts him. We go to the bench, and the most stunning view of the city lies in front of us—the light in different colors and the silence. Luke snuggles up to her and falls asleep in her arms. I stroke his hair. He's so amazing.

My mother looks at me, and I at her.

"How could you not choose him?"

"I don't think I can explain it. It is a deep longing that has nothing to do with Luke or others. It has only something to do with myself." Right now, I can't feel that longing. My inner co-commentator runs at high speed and does not leave me many seconds of peace to reconnect with myself. My mother says nothing, and I can't justify my choice or convince her. She can ask, and I will answer, but my choice cannot be discussed.

"You are close to the longing that all people run away from." My mother's voice is collected, and I can feel that she accepts my choice. She smiles at me. "I respect you for having the courage to follow your heart and dare to go your own way. It is always easier to walk down others' paths."

I listen to my mother's words and take them in. I know she's spent a lot of her life looking inward. There are many ways to do it and several paths leading into the same place inside us.

It's quiet here. Only the sounds from the wind in the trees and birds talking in their sleep are heard. Luke is breathing heavily, and there is an occasional rattling noise from the forest floor, where small purple flowers sway softly. The city street lights below us testify that another day has come to an end. Slowly, the moon glides down across the sky like a white glowing sphere with a delicate, soft white ring around it.

We both know what's going to happen now. In a way, I would just like to stay here with Luke and my mom. It's moments like this I've never been present in. I have always been elsewhere in my thoughts. Small, unimportant things have torn me away from the moment. That's why I've always longed for more—more love, more recognition, and more security. The gaps in me were never filled. I prioritized the safe rather than going my own way. At this moment, I am being filled up. I take my mother's hand and squeeze it.

"Were you able to see us all the time you were in a coma?" She turns her head and looks at me. Her eyes are still bloodshot, and the skin around her eyes is puffed.

I nod and look down. "I have been looking at you every day—I have followed you for hours." I smile. It must be strange to be told.

The sound of the wind in the trees increases. Luke moves a little, and it seems like he is dreaming.

"As much as I would love to stay, time is running out." I get up. "Do you have the bottles in your car?"

My mother nods a little. I walk with slow steps toward her car. I can see the bottles on the back seat and open the door, so the light comes on. I have no idea how much is needed or how it works. There are also two thick yellow blankets on the back seat. I reach in, take them, close the door, and walk back to my mom and Luke.

My mother has collapsed forward and hugs Luke close. He sleeps heavily again and snores a little bit as he breathes in.

"Here..." I hand the bottle to her.

The wind hits my skin, and the cold creeps up from my feet. The temperature drops rapidly. It's almost eleven o'clock. I try to breathe calmly and look for the next word. But I do not know what to say. There are a hundred things I would like to tell my mother, but I do not know where to begin.

"Thank you so much for all that you have given me and taught me. I'm glad you were my mother." I lean forward and put my arms around her and Luke. I hug both of them, feeling my mother's cheek against mine and Luke's hair against my other cheek. We sit still with our eyes closed. It feels like white light is being turned on around us, but I tell myself that it's probably just the moon.

I press my hand against my mother's back. There is no need to wait any longer. Slowly, I release Luke and my mother. She moves to the edge of the bench. I gasp for breath. It was hard to make the decision to stay in In-Between, and I was in doubt for a long time.

But suddenly, it was obvious. There is nothing obvious right now. I hold the bottle in front of me and look at the milky red water.

"I hope to see you again." My mother looks at me with a genuine stare.

"So do I."

49

IT IS NOW OR NEVER

I have spread the yellow blankets out on the ground, picked some of the purple flowers from the forest floor, and laid them in a circle on the blankets. They lie on the grass next to the bench, where my mother sits still with Luke in her arms and watches me. The bottles are standing next to her. The white powder has settled to the bottom of them. I look at my mother, and our gaze meets as she hands Luke over to me. He sleeps on, and I put the duvet tight around him.

"He is an old soul." My mother strokes her hand lightly over Luke's hair. "I hope you make it." She looks at me with a look that pierces all the way through to the center of my heart. Hesitantly, I step into the ring of purple flowers and sit down on my knees. Nausea creeps in, and I get a bad taste in my mouth. I need more time. Everything in me is in revolt. No matter how I turn it around, this is entirely unreasonable. How could my mother agree to it? How can *I* even think the thought? I snap for breath, and the cold hits my body. I shake inside and close my eyes.

Help... If only there were someone or something who would help me now. Help me, please! I shout inside myself. But nothing happens. I hug Luke close to me, feel the warmth of his body and his gentle heartbeat. How can I even consider cutting the roots of a small tree and be the one to blame that it never was allowed to grow big and strong? I can't do this. I can't take him with me, no matter how much I want to.

But I can't leave him here either because then the Ring will not be closed.

"No thought can justify your action."

It's the voice. Suddenly a glow lights up inside me, and a wave of heat washes through my body.

"If you could look into the future and see the connection between souls and events, then you would understand." The bright white light is everywhere—like it's trying to light up in the dark so I can see better.

"But…" even inside myself, it is hard to get the words out. "I have no right to take another person's life and especially not… my own child's."

"Your mind will always try to justify your actions, whether they lead to something constructive or destructive." It goes silent, and a figure steps out of the light. It's an older woman with a wrinkled face. Her hair is dark and braided in two strong braids that hang on each side of her face. Around her pupils shines a clear white ring. This is the woman I've seen the outline of before, and the voice I have heard belongs to her.

"We don't own other people. As a mother, you are responsible for bringing life into the world. You are responsible for giving the child love, care, and helping it develop the qualities and abilities that can support it on the journey through life."

I sit completely still and listen. My body no longer shakes, but I sense a quiet shiver underneath my skin. It's freezing cold here.

"After all that you've been through so far, do you still think life is coincidental?" The woman speaks with great calm, and her voice has a deep tone of credibility.

"It has been about me and my development… this is different...." My voice is breaking. The woman sits down cross-legged in front of me. She says no more, just looks at me. Her gaze is infinite, like a well filled with wisdom.

"But what about Luke's father and the rest of the family?" I squeeze the words out and can hardly bear to think the thought to the end. Imagine if I had lost Luke while I was alive. My heart beats so fast that I fear it's breaking down. Where is my compassion? Am I so focused on the goal that I forgot to be true to myself?

"What about them?" Her voice is calm in stark contrast to my condition.

"I'll inflict enormous pain on them, and they will never understand it." I hug Luke even closer to me if possible. He stretches and mumbles some incomprehensible words in his sleep.

"Open your heart and listen to your soul. How much evidence do you need before you surrender?"

I can't help but smile. The woman is right. First, there was the plane crash, which caused me to learn more about myself and find my way back to the Ring. Then all the people I have met while I have been here. They kept popping up at exactly the time I needed them. I take a deep breath. Can it really be true? Is there a larger whole, a meaning to it all that I have not yet noticed? Am I really part of something bigger and not just an insignificant piece on my selfish journey?

"What is your conclusion?" The woman sends a warm smile to me. The wrinkles on her face fold together, and she radiates a love I have never experienced before.

"This is the most terrible thing. I can't imagine anything worse." I bite into my lower lip to remove focus from the pain that etches under my skin.

"There must be another way?"

"Listen to your heart and remember that the universe takes care of us all." The woman looks at me with an intense gaze, the light around her becomes even brighter, and she slowly disappears. I exhale and wait a moment to breathe in again.

THE RING

This is the ultimate test of following my heart and sticking to what I know deep down is right, no matter what the stickler inside my head is trying to tell me. It is the choice between being a part of something bigger or continuing to be selfish. The time has come for me to surrender totally and fervently to serve the universe, whatever that entails. Slowly, I open my eyes and look up. Small, delicate, transparent clouds drift in front of the moon, surrounded by twinkling stars.

My mother sits silent and collapsed with closed eyes. My hand shakes. I have to do it. There is no way around it. I'm about to step over a fine line where there is no turning back. I close my eyes. Suppose I put myself beyond my right and wrong thoughts and skip to find justice in my actions—let go of my doubts, my anxieties, and my hopes. Then I can hear in a split second that my soul speaks to me and gives me certainty about the last two people in the Ring. But that does not make the situation any easier. The thoughts and feelings come back at me at a hundred kilometers per hour. It feels like a knife is being stabbed into my heart, the pain is drilling into my chest, and my nausea increases.

I keep looking at Luke. He breathes calmly. The bottle rests heavily in my hand. My mother has opened her eyes and looks at me with a blank stare. I unscrew the lid of the bottle and hold it to Luke's mouth. My whole body is tense. All sounds around me disappear. Luke opens his eyes and looks straight into mine. There, in the left eye, I lean even closer to him. There is a very fine white circle around the pupil. He holds my gaze and then closes his eyes again. My insides get ripped into a thousand pieces, the pain permeates my body, and I squeeze hard around the bottle. With a heartbreaking scream, I toss the bottle over the cliff. The pink water hangs like droplets in the air before disappearing into the darkness.

Luke sleeps calmly on, and I hug him so close to me that he twists a little. How could I even think of it? It can't be God's will that I should take the life from my son. I feel the warmth of my mother's hand on my back, and the cold inside me subsides. The crying pushes forward, and I try to suffocate it by swallowing. I fail. It grows with an explosive force, and it wants to come out, to be set free. The tears start to run free, and I collapse, sobbing over Luke's little body. My mother gets up and sits quietly behind me. I can hear her soft breath. I put my mouth to Luke's ear and whisper softly, "I'm so sorry, Luke, forgive me…." The words are drowning in my tears flowing down my cheeks.

The wind howls in the treetops, and an owl screams a lonely sound.

I close my eyes and try to make contact with my heart. It gets hot, and a quiet shiver seeps into my body. Then I get the Skycon out of my pocket and press the small picture of Thomas on the screen.

"Hi, Angela," Thomas's picture fades up in front of me.

"Thomas, I can't…."

There is complete silence around him, and I can only see a white wall in the background. Thomas says nothing, waiting in silence for me to continue.

"I know who the last one in the Ring is, but I cannot…." My voice breaks and the words disappear. I tense all over my face and try to encapsulate all my emotions so they can't be seen. Thomas sits quietly. He's inside a smaller room, but I can't see where it is.

"Angela, I am sorry; it could be too late."

I shake my head. "What do you mean, too late?"

Thomas takes a deep breath. "Gabriel has gone into a deep sleep, and I can't get in touch with him."

"But…" My hand is sweaty and shaking. I wipe it off on my pants. "But I was just about to…."

Silence again. The darkness from the forest moves closer to us.

"Angela, who do you think is the last in the Ring?" Thomas leans forward toward me. His eyes are a bit swollen, and the fine lines around them are more marked than I have seen before.

"…It's Luke. I think he's the last one. You said it yourself. It can be family. Our souls can incarnate close to each other."

Thomas does not say anything; he sits still and listens. His eyes are calm, and his face is relaxed. He looks away for a moment and then disappears out of the picture. He can't let me down now.

"Thomas."

The floating image is just white. I sit quietly on the rug with Luke in my arms and my mother by my side. Slowly, I move my one hand and let it slide up and down her back.

"Sorry, I'm here…" Thomas appears again. "I still can't get in touch with Gabriel, but as long as he breathes, there is hope. Angela, you have listened to your heart, and that is the most important thing."

Heart. Brain. Right now, it's all one big jumble inside me.

"Angela, are you coming back tonight?"

"Yes…" my voice is a bit hesitant. There's no reason I should stay here until tomorrow.

My mother sits still and looks at Luke and me. She doesn't seem surprised or impressed by the Skycon.

"Angela, I will get ready for you."

"But wait, there's more." I get a faraway look in my eyes, and the picture of Thomas is blurred. I sit and stare blankly into the air. The words line up inside me, waiting to be set free, but I hold onto them.

Angela…"

I can hear Thomas's voice calling to me in the distance, and I blink hard and whisper, "I'm not so sure that Meera is the right one anymore." I hold my breath and wait for Thomas to respond. But he does not say anything.

"Did you hear me? There is a woman who helped me when I first arrived here. Her name is Jane, and it could also be her and not Meera; I may have been wrong…."

"We do not know whether you were wrong or not. But it can be that Jane is the last one."

My heart skips a beat. Then maybe it was my ego that wanted

Luke to come with me. A shiver runs through my body at the thought of how close I was to taking him to In-Between.

"We can talk more about it when I see you...." Thomas sends me a smile. I have a hard time smiling back, so it only becomes an automatic nod.

"Angela, if you start to get ready for transmission, I will go to the receiving room. Is that fine with you?"

"Yes," I manage to say, even though it's hard. I have failed big time.

"Maybe I should just drink the rest of this." My mom shakes the other bottle with the dissolved sleeping pills. Her voice is a bit defeated.

"No!" I look firmly at her. "You have a life here. Luke needs you."

She shrugs resignedly. The spark in her eyes is gone again.

"You cannot tell anyone about In-Between, or that we have met, never. Do you hear me?" I look solemnly at my mother. "I will try to contact you when I get there."

We sit quietly and let time go by. No words are needed. She knows that I have to go, and I know that I have to leave. I'm just here on a brief visit, but it was worth it. Even though I didn't succeed, I got to say a proper farewell to my mother and, in a way, also to Luke.

"Angela." Thomas appears on the little screen, and I pull the image back up in front of us. The image soars clearly and transparently in the dark.

"Yes," my voice is soft, and I close my eyes briefly.

"Are you ready to come back?" Thomas is in the reception room; I can see the big screens behind him.

I nod and stroke Luke's hair and run my hand down his cheek. "Goodbye, my sweetheart," I lean forward and kiss him on the forehead. My mother sits directly opposite me, and I place my hand on top of hers and look her in the eyes. "Thank you for everything. I

THE RING

love you." I lean forward toward her; she puts her arms around me and holds me close.

"I love you too," she tightens her grip around me.

"See you," I whisper into her ear.

She smiles. "Take good care of yourself."

"You, too. And I do not want to see you up there for a long time." I smile at her and put my hands on her cheeks—they are warm and soft. Then I let go and hand Luke over to her. She tucks him in as I lay down on my back on the yellow blanket.

"I'm ready, Thomas." I look at my mother and feel a pang in my heart. There is nothing I can do; I have to go back. But I wish I could stay—that everything was like three months ago, just for a brief moment so I could take it in and appreciate it, enjoy it all. A small moment can fill an entire life with joy.

The carpet is soft, but the surface is hard. The water bottle is standing next to me. My mother bends over me and strokes her hand lightly over my forehead. The cold creeps up from the ground, but at the same time, heat spreads from my toes up through my body. The treetops rattle a bit, and a large bird chirps and flutters its wings.

I look into my mother's eyes and smile at her; she smiles back. Flashes from my childhood, youth, and adult life flash by in short glimpses. A lifeline of experiences and an ending way too soon—not one I had known or seen coming.

Slowly, I unscrew the lid of the bottle and let the cold water fill my mouth. Swallowing. The taste is sweet, but the small, crushed pill pieces scratch my throat a little as I swallow them. I hand the empty bottle to my mother and lay down my head. She holds my hands, which rest on my chest. Slowly, very slowly, tiredness begins to appear. Right now, I need a miracle if my journey is not to be in vain—if the Ring is to be assembled. Thoughts slip away, and I forget to breathe. Everything turns white. I can no longer feel the carpet or my mother's hand. I'm hovering. The light is dazzling, and

I can't move or feel my body. There is no time. No direction. No emotions.

50

IN-BETWEEN

The white light lifts away like a mist that dissolves, and I slowly open my eyes. My body is limp and sore from the feet and up. The light in the room dazzles me, and I want to move my hand up to shade my eyes, but it does not listen. Thomas sits with his eyes closed by my side. He is wearing a long, off-white, Indian-looking tunic that hangs loosely around his chest and down over his legs. I smile down to my stomach without moving a muscle in my face. He is resting a hand on my arm. I'm home again.

I can see the moon and the stars through the big window above me. They are somewhat closer now.

I turn my head in small jerks and move my arm a bit. Thomas slowly opens his eyes.

"Hi, Eva, welcome back," he smiles so his eyes light up, and his whole face is one big smile.

"Hey," I look him in the eye and reach for his hand. He leans forward, and our hands meet.

"Have I failed?" My voice is hesitant, and the words wipe away each other. I try to sit up, but my head is spinning. Everything is swimming before my eyes, and I have to support my elbows on the light, mat-like bed that is set into the floor.

Nothing has changed since I arrived last time, the white walls and the bright, slightly floating floor and the intense white clear light and the feeling of being surrounded by love. It is just Thomas and me here.

"It depends on how you look at it." Thomas is sitting still next to me. Most of all, I want to throw myself into his arms and tell him about everything I have experienced. About the decision and how horrible I felt. About finding Meera, about Frank, Daniel, and Lucy. I want to tell him everything, but I don't say anything. I just look at him.

"It is so good to have you back. You followed your heart, and that is the most important thing."

Maybe he is right; maybe he is not. I'm not sure. "Thomas, am I Angela or Eva now?"

He laughs and leans back. "It's just a wrapping. You're the one you've always been."

I look down at myself. The pants are too long; they extend over my shoes. If only I could catch a glimpse of myself somewhere; I look around for something to see my reflection.

"But, I mean, am I in the old body or another?"

"You are in your old disguise. It is up to you what you want us to call you."

"Eva, I want to be called Eva again." I touch my face—pointed nose and marked cheekbones. I pull out a strand of hair; it's going a bit gray.

"What do we do now? The Ring is not assembled. It has all been in vain...." I put my hands down and try to get up. But I forgot how hard the transfer is, and I have to stay on my knees. My fingers press against the floor, and I make another attempt to get to my feet. This time, I succeed and sway from side to side. Thomas puts his arm around me. It does not seem that he is affected by the situation.

"There is still time. We do not have to gather until tomorrow."

I shake my head in despair. "Have you tested Meera? And what about Jane, have you found her?" I sigh and let my eyes wander around the room. It is so tranquil here, with no traffic, no people, and no stress—just Thomas and me and the bare floating white walls. The floor is bright, with a transparent mass that lies softly over it. Everything is the same here as when I left.

"Meera was tested today." He pauses and looks at me. "It was Yoge who tested her. She was with him in the reception area exactly the way you were." Thomas smiles at me and starts walking toward the door.

"And?" My voice is eager, and I try to stop him.

"I have not heard anything yet."

Even though I feel convinced that she is the right one, I can still sense the doubt creeping up on me. The door slides open, and we walk out into the empty hallway. There are several doors in the hallway, but no people are to be seen.

I step carefully. My joints are sore. And with every move I make, I'm reminded of places in my body that I didn't know existed.

"And Jane, what about Jane?"

Thomas turns toward me and puts a hand gently on my cheek. "I don't know. But I know we can test her if we find her. Let's see. There is still time."

I look down. If only I could borrow some of the compelling, unwavering confidence that Thomas has. If only I could believe he's right. I sincerely wish that the Ring assembles and that I have not failed—that my choices are not in vain. I swallow and look down. Thomas is right, there is still time, and it may well be Jane. This is the wolf inside me I choose to feed.

"I would like to go to the control room." I hold my breath and look intently at Thomas.

He reaches out for me and takes me in his arms. I feel his warmth, can hear his heart beating, and stand completely still. He puts his head against my hair. Now, we are more equal. I also know about his life on Earth; it makes him, in many ways, more human. We stand completely still. I relax and inhale his love. It's over; I have done everything in my power, and there is nothing more I can do.

"Thomas," I whisper. "Thank you for helping me. I was so happy that we could communicate even though the Skycon didn't work."

He breathes softly. "Angela, that was your spiritual power coming through; I didn't do anything." He slowly releases his grip on me and looks me in the eye. "You have done a great job."

"But..." I hold my words back.

We walk down the aisle; it feels like ages since I last walked here. The bright energy is so clear.

"We are meeting in the Ring at half-past seven tomorrow morning. The Master is with Gabriel and will spend the night healing and recharging his system. Hopefully, that can keep him from moving on. He is still unconscious."

"Thomas, why do we have to meet when we don't know if we are the right seven members?"

"We will meet no matter what happens." His facial expression becomes serious. "We still do not know who helped Frank. David has kept an eye on him; he has been calm until now, but something tells me that it will change when he discovers that you have left again."

I have happily forgotten Frank and stop abruptly and look startled at Thomas.

He smiles at me with surplus energy that I do not know where he finds. "Even though the Ring may not be completed tomorrow, he can still harm our work. I have left the matter to the Master." He shrugs; I can see that he struggles not to make me nervous.

"Come, let me walk you to the control room." He squeezes my hand.

I look at my watch; it's half-past eleven. I'm exhausted but need to check on my mom and Luke before I go to bed.

"Eva, I know there are many loose ends right now. I hope you

THE RING

have confidence that you have made the right choices and that everything is as it should be." Thomas puts his arm around my shoulder, and I let my head fall on it.

"I'm not sure. I don't know if I have done the right thing." I slide my hands down into my pockets. A shiver strikes through my body. My Skycon. I widen my eyes and turn to Thomas in a quick motion.

"I forgot my Skycon." I hit my pockets feverishly. "It is on the floor in the forest."

51
DESTINY

The door to the large, common control room opens, and I enter. I can't help but smile. I'm back in the office. In front of me are the transparent, blue-green floor, the stairs, and the small platforms with screens that float down from the ceiling. The large screens on the end wall are turned off. I walk down the stairs to my screen. It feels like I have not been away at all. Thomas has found me a spare Skycon, which is in my pocket.

"Heeeeey, Eva." It's Allan from Alabama, my old workstation neighbor. He jumps up from his chair and comes over to me, as always wearing his Alabama sweater and cap down on his forehead. Some things do not change.

"I thought you had taken off. Cool that you're still here. Where have you been?"

I smile and hug him. Under no circumstances can I tell him what happened. "I've been in a process." It sounded a bit self-righteous. Hopefully, he buys it.

"Well, sure, exciting." He nods eagerly and gives his cap a little push up his forehead. "I've been allowed to stay here a little longer." He smiles and shrugs a bit, "It's unbearable to let go of my life and my girls. I didn't have any insurance, and my wife is unemployed. I don't know how she will manage with four girls. It must be hard for you too with your son. Luke, was it?" He makes a slightly crooked grimace with his mouth.

I smile back. "When the time is right, you will be able to say goodbye and let go." I feel a warmth flow through me. Did I really say that? I keep smiling.

A younger girl and an older man are sitting on the landing too. They are busy with a workstation each. Behind them is a man in his forties. They are at the opposite end of the room. They must be new because I do not recognize them. I can't see Heidi from Sweden, who also used to sit here. Maybe she made her decision.

"I just have a little I need to check up on," I point to my screen and pull out a chair, and it cradles me easily while hanging in the air.

Allan stands a little awkwardly and steps on his toes. "Yes, yes, of course, I will not hold you back." His dark brown eyes radiate so much sadness. He reaches out and hugs me. "So nice to see you again, Eva."

The chair shapes itself to my body, and I tap lightly on the screen. A search box appears, and I type my mother's name and press enter. A flashing dot indicates that the computer is searching.

The girl on the landing breaks down in tears, and without hesitating, the older man gets up and comforts her. The guy sitting in the corner is singing with his earphones on. It's squeaky fake, so he must have turned the volume on the headphones up high so as not to hear it himself. The dot on the screen flashes tirelessly. It does not usually take very long. I look over at Allan. He is sitting in his spot, enjoying the sight of his four girls playing in the garden.

A picture of my mother appears on the screen. She is driving through the forest. Luke is sitting in his car seat in the back seat behind the passenger seat. He is awake.

"Grandma, I'm thirsty." Luke pulls up the duvet and yawns.

It is dark, and the light on the main road is sparse. My mom turns out onto the main road, and her car quickly picks up speed. She reaches out and rummages in the glove compartment. I smile. My mother always has something to drink in the car. Just in case the car should break down, or she got stuck in a long queue.

The crying from the girl up on the landing is getting more intense. The older man helps her to her feet. I look back at the screen and try to shut out everything else.

"No, get back on the road, watch out for…." I shout at the screen and get up resolutely while hammering on the side of the screen.

My mother is heading straight for a large tree next to the road. She has not seen the road turn.

"Here it is," she looks at Luke, shaking an apple juice. "I knew I had one," she smiles triumphantly all over her face.

There is a loud bang, and everything becomes quiet. I sit down, staring blankly at the screen. Luke's head hangs limply down against his shoulder, and my mother lies under the once white airbag. There is blood all over it.

"Do something; help them!" I scream at the screen as I clasp my arms around me and rock back and forth. It cannot be true! My legs give way, and an explosive pain rushes through me as my knees hammer against the floor. I cling convulsively to the screen. "Do something, someone!" The crying floods my voice, and something dies inside me. I stiffen and say nothing, only feeling the heat from the tears rolling down my cheeks. Time has come to a standstill. I release the screen and let myself fall forward while staring blankly at it. How long I'm sitting here, I have no idea. My body is crumpled like a piece of paper.

Numbness. Silence. No mind, nothing. I begin to hit my head against the screen and am happy to feel the pain. At least I feel something.

My hand is heavy. I slowly lift it and tap the screen. The computer is searching. It only takes a moment. Then a direct image emerges from Andreas's house. He sits on the couch inside the living

THE RING

room and talks to Longlegs. His eyes are red, his face pale, and he makes a sweeping gesture with his arms. Longlegs says nothing. She reaches for his hand and listens. Opposite them sits an officer. I do not need to see anymore and turn it off.

Suddenly, a powerful force rises in my body. I look around and run out of the control room, down the long bright corridors. The walls become a tunnel that I run through, and I can sense light at the end. I run as fast as I can. My feet barely touch the floor. My breathing picks up, and my heart beats faster. I stop and pull the Skycon out of my pocket. I press Thomas's name and wait. Nothing is happening. It is empty here. I fidget on the spot, staring at the small screen on the Skycon. *Come on, Thomas. Pick up.*

A small image appears. "Eva…"

"Thomas, where are you?" I shout.

"Eva, I was just about to call you. I'm sitting here with someone I think you know."

The crying overwhelms me, and I bite myself on the lip and try to hold back the tears.

"Where are you?" Thomas's smile turns on the heat in my body.

"I'm in the reception hall… where are you?" I look up and down the aisle in short jerks.

"In number five, come on in, the door is open…."

I break into a run. Number three is right next to me. Number five must be the next door. I tear the door open. There, in the middle of the room, Thomas is sitting with his back toward me. In front of him, I catch a glimpse of a pair of small feet. I want to run over there, but I can't. I feel torn. Something is pushing me back and paralyzing my body while something else is pulling me. Slowly, I am filled with joy. Luke is here. I carefully walk closer. He lies just as still with his eyes closed on the mat-like bed on the floor. One step closer. I kneel next to Luke. Thomas puts an arm around my shoulders.

"It is not certain he will wake up until tomorrow."

I nod and try to control my breathing. "But there is something I do not understand…."

Thomas extends his hand and caresses Luke's hair. He is so beautiful as he lies there. His small mouth is slightly open, and his hands are resting on his stomach.

"If Luke was supposed to be up here no matter what, why should I…?" I hold back. It is almost unbearable to think that I was close to taking the life of my own son.

Thomas takes a deep breath and tightens the grip on my shoulder. "There are many aspects that come into play." He looks at me, and the circle around his pupils is bright white.

"You found out that Luke is the last person in the Ring, but you did not know if you were supposed to take him with you. You chose to listen to your heart."

I sit still and take in his words. My inner co-commentator has thankfully fallen asleep. I place a hand on Luke's chest and feel him breathing quietly.

"If Luke had come up here without you connecting him with the Ring, I'm not sure we would have found him in time."

"But we still don't know if it's him…."

Thomas nods slowly. "That's right, and we can't test him until we meet in the Ring tomorrow morning."

The light from the moon falls on Luke's face and casts a white glow around him.

"But what about Jane?" My voice trembles.

"Let me talk to the Master. Now, it's up to him who will meet in the Ring tomorrow. But no matter what, you can take Luke with you."

The relief spreads in me, and I collapse. I have done what I could, and it is no longer my responsibility. And I don't want to be apart from Luke again.

"There is a greater connection between people and events than we can ever understand or explain. We can't force things to happen until the time is right. And basically, we also do not know what is meant to be. The true art is to find the confidence that what is meant to happen will probably happen, no matter what we do. And yet still take responsibility and make our support available to the universe."

I let Thomas's words sink in. They land somewhere good inside me and bring a calmness with them.

"Shall we carry Luke over to his room?" Thomas releases the grip on my shoulder.

"Yes..." I take a deep breath; it is almost incomprehensible.

He leans forward and lifts Luke. There is something about their charisma that is similar.

"Shiva is making up Luke's room. It is the room next to yours, and we have established a door between the two rooms."

"That was fast." I smile and take Luke's little hand in mine. It is a bit cold.

Thomas smiles at me and starts walking. "Time belongs to the world of the mind; the heart does not know time. Up here, everything happens a little faster...."

I grab his arm. "What about my mother? She was the one driving the car."

Thomas looks at me. "I don't know. I have only registered Luke's arrival."

52

A GLIMPSE OF TRUTH

Thomas places his finger on a small red circle, and the door to the Ring's hallway slides open. All seven doors are located on the left side. We walk calmly up the hallway and past the floating screens next to each door. I slide my hand across my screen as we walk past. "Welcome, Eva, No messages."

"Do you think Luke will be able to understand where he is and what has happened?" I look at Thomas with an inquiring look.

He smiles as he always does when I'm in doubt, keeping calm. "Even though he is a little boy, he is an old soul. Don't underestimate him."

The door to Luke's room slides open, and Shiva comes toward us with open arms. Her long dark hair is set back in a ponytail, and around her neck, she wears a pink scarf that makes her dark hair seem even darker. I enter the room. There is a lit candle on a small table next to the bed.

"Welcome back, Eva." Shiva lets her hand slide lightly over my shoulder with care and warmth. It feels like I'm getting five pounds lighter—like I'm being held in the safety of Mother Earth's energy.

"Thanks…"

THE RING

She looks at Luke and takes his little hand in hers. We go to his bed, and Thomas gently lays him down. I pull the duvet up over him and sit on the edge of the bed; my gaze is fixed on him and nothing else.

"If you want to sleep in here, we can extend the bed." A fine love is flowing from Shiva, soft like a morning breeze. Her energy reminds me a bit of the energy that the woman in my vision radiated, only not as powerful. Shiva presses a small button on the wall, and the bed expands. "You just get your own duvet and pillow." Her eyelids look heavy, and she hides a yawn with her hand.

"Let me get it for you." Thomas disappears into the room next door. On the wall above the bed hangs a poster with two angels playing. By the window is a chair with a stack of Donald Duck comic books. The room is as big as mine, but it seems cozier.

I gently move Luke slightly toward the wall so that there is space next to him. His duvet moves quietly up and down, and his mouth is slightly open.

Shiva squats down next to me, hugs me, and strokes my cheek. "You've done really well. Is there anything you need?" A few strands of hair fall free around her face.

"I just need to sleep." My voice is low, "and then I need to know what happened to my mother."

She smiles at me. Thomas is back, and he hands me a duvet and pillow. "I can go and check on your mother. Right now, you cannot do anything to change the situation. Try to get some sleep so that you are fresh when Luke wakes up, and we are to meet in the Ring."

I press my lip together and nod. "I'll try." I can still feel all the adrenaline rushing through my body. Like when you have been to a great concert full of energy, come home, and sit by yourself. I always need to sit on the couch for half an hour for my body to calm down before I can go to bed.

Shiva gets up and walks toward the door. "See you at half-past seven in the octagonal room; I'm assuming you'll bring Luke with you."

"Absolutely."

Thomas follows Shiva, they leave, and the door slides closed behind them.

Luke is fast asleep; he still doesn't know what has happened and where he is. I sit completely quiet beside him and look at him. If I had a place inside me where I could store his energy, it would be filling up right now. I reach out, and I feel his silky hair. The sound of his quiet breathing is so breathtaking. My head nods forward, and I pull the duvet aside and lie down next to him. Before I close my eyes, I set the Skycon to ring at half-past six. Then I let myself fall back into bed and close my eyes.

AN IMAGE of an eagle soaring high up emerges along with the feeling of being free. Lightness turns into a hounding pain, and I can once again see myself hanging on the cross and the crowd below. *Michael, Michael,* a voice says. The image changes. Now, I'm standing on a dirt road. There are fields full of golden grains on both sides of me, as far as the eye can see. I am swaying from side to side. Out in the distance, a vast crowd appears, led by a man on a black horse. The sky is in turmoil, and several mountains look like small shadows on the horizon. A large cloud of dust is approaching. I stand completely still. The people are far away but moving furiously quickly toward me. I stand in the middle of the road, which continues straight ahead of me and leads toward them. I'm in a male body, dressed in a black outfit. I have a long sword with brown leather tied around the shaft, hanging by my left side in a black holster. There's a shorter sword next to it.

The crowd comes closer. Heat vibrates in front of me and blurs the men's faces. I breathe, drill my boots down into the gravel, and let my arms hang loosely by my side. *This is it.* I hear a voice say inside me. Now, you must die. I clench my hands and look straight ahead. Out of the crowd come angry men in dark clothes. They shout and gesticulate with their arms as they run toward me. I stay standing still.

The horseman on the black horse wears armor with a cross on his chest. He swings his sword; it flashes in the sun and dazzles me briefly. The rider's head is shaved, a long scar runs down one cheek from his eyebrow. The crowd behind him rises in front of me like a wall of anger. I'm not scared. The horse snorts and stomps the ground. It comes to a halt right in front of me. I stand completely still. My feet are placed firmly on the road, and I look at the horseman who has his sword raised above his head. Various symbols have been etched into the blade. Anger flashes from his eyes. He raises his other arm, and the crowd falls silent.

Slowly, I put my hand on the hilt of my sword and draw it while looking the rider in the eye. He tightens the grip on his sword. The horse neighs and stomps with its front legs. I hold my sword in outstretched arms in front of me, then I turn the tip downward and put it in the ground. I kneel and take a deep breath.

The horseman swings his sword and stops the movement just above my head. I remain completely still, fold my hands in front of my chest, and maintain eye contact. Then he slashes his sword against my head. A white flash of light explodes, and the image changes. I can see myself lying on the ground in the male body with my head split in two—the crowd cheers.

"You had to die for speaking the truth. A person who speaks the truth can be a threat to an entire society." The voice is calm and relatively clear inside my head.

I wake with a start at the sound of the Skycon alarm. Where am I? I rub my eyes and look around the room. Light is breaking through on the horizon. My body is boiling, and I feel queasy. Luke sleeps heavily next to me. I stroke his hair and bend over to enjoy his sweet scent. Sweat is running from my chest, and I throw off the duvet. If I'm quick, I can have a shower before he wakes up.

53

TWO WORLDS COME TOGETHER

"Mom. Is that you, Mom?" Luke sits up in bed and rubs his eyes. I stand in the doorway to the bathroom with a towel wrapped around me. He throws the duvet to the side and lands on the floor with his small bare feet. I bend down and extend my arms. In no time, he throws himself into my arms and hugs me tight.

"Yes, Luke, it's me."

I have been dreaming about this moment for weeks, even months. I keep holding onto him and have to be careful not to squeeze him too tightly.

The sun is rising above the clouds and is beginning to share its heat generously.

Luke is pressing his little head under my chin, and it does not seem as if he is going to let go of me for the time being. I can smell him, feel his warmth, and hear him breathing. It's incredible, the best feeling ever. Slowly, he releases his grip, puts his little hand on my cheek, and looks me in the eyes.

"Mom, where have you been?"

I smile at him, tears welling up in my eyes.

THE RING

"Did it help that I tickled you?" He has a hard time standing still.

"Luke, I have not awakened. You have come to me. We are in heaven."

He turns his mouth down and wrinkles his nose. "Where is Dad? Daaaad?" He looks around the room.

"Dad is not here. It's just the two of us." I place my hand on his cheek and try to make eye contact.

"I miss Dad." He lets himself fall against my body.

I say nothing, just stand still with my arms around him. The clouds are moving past the window. It is still early, and there is still time.

"Come here; let me show you where we are." I gently let go of him and take his hand. "Over here..." We go to the window where the clouds are passing by as the most natural thing in the world.

"It looks cool. Can we fly, Mom?"

I can't help but laugh, squat behind him, and hold him tight.

"Well, yes and no. We are up in the clouds, Luke."

"Can I go and see Dad now? He must see that I can fly." Luke places both hands on the window and presses his nose flat against the glass. A flock of birds comes flying past the windows. They fly in an apex, with the middle bird in front and the others in a straight line out to the sides, like an arrow.

"Luke, there are so many things I need to tell you, but we are meeting some people in a short while. After we see them, I can tell you much more." Luke is still wearing the blue and white checkered nightwear, and his hair is spreading randomly to the sides.

"I'm hungry. Do they have muesli with caramel here?"

"Definitely." I reach for a pile of clothes on the chair. "Here, let me help you; then, we'll go and have some breakfast."

We get dressed really quickly and don't have much time to look in the mirror. I take Luke by the hand, and we walk down the hallways in In-Between. His eyes are wide open, and his mouth hangs slightly loose. He is deeply concentrating, trying to balance on the yellow line. Several people pass us on the way to the café: a young girl in an all-red sweatsuit, a man with a long beard, and a lady with a cane.

"Mom, it's like being in a movie on TV. This is cool." He walks into the wall and disappears completely. When he appears again, he is one big laugh. I have not seen anyone disappear into the wall before; I frown, but I have not seen anyone try either. My stomach is full of bubbles of joy. I'm relieved he's not asking any more questions. Right now, he seems content with what he knows—that I'm here.

It's quiet in the cafe. Most of In-Between is still asleep. Only the early risers have gradually begun to appear. My favorite table at the far end of the cafe is vacant. The candles on the tables are lit, and there are slim glass vases with red flowers on all the tables, leaves spraying out on all sides.

"Come on, Luke," I squeeze his hand, "let's order some food."

He accompanies me, and we approach the bar. Everything is just like it was when I left it six weeks ago, the light on the walls, the tables along the curved walls, and the oval bar. I have to admit, I feel at home here. Luke runs to one of the high stools and tries hard to climb it. A woman with long black hair is in the process of ordering—she stands with her back to us. I give Luke a push, so he gets up on the chair, and he looks triumphantly out over the cafe. There is a menu card on the glossy disk. I reach for it and flip through it: Corn Flakes, fresh fruit, and porridge.

"I can't find the muesli, Luke. We better ask."

The bartender places a glass of orange juice in front of the woman. She turns to me as Luke accidentally touches her back.

"Meera?" I frown and get a little closer.

"Yes, do I know you?" She leans back twists her head so that her hair falls on her back.

I laugh, "It's me, Angela."

"Angela!" She holds her hand over her mouth and closes her eyes. "So, you made it. Did you bring the last one?"

Luke pulls on my blouse. "Mom, why did you say your name is Angela?"

I shift my gaze to Luke.

"No way, that can't be true!" Meera's gaze drills into mine.

I take a deep breath before answering, "I don't know yet, but...."

Suddenly, a large crowd of people enters the cafe, as if they have synchronized their alarm clocks. Several of them line up around the bar. I catch the bartender's attention and order.

"It's a cool restaurant, this one, Mom." Luke grabs my hand and jumps down from the chair.

I look up at the clock on the wall above the entrance. We still have forty-five minutes until the meeting in the octagonal room, and there is enough time for us to sit down and enjoy our breakfast.

"Would you like to sit with us?" I look at Meera and cannot work out why her hair is black and not gray.

She grabs her tray with juice, omelet, and toast. "Why not?"

I head over to my favorite table, which is thankfully still vacant. Now, I finally have a home-court advantage. Luke throws himself up on the couch, rests his knees against the seat, and looks out over the backrest at the clouds. I sit down next to him, and Meera pulls out a chair and sits across from us. Luke is already engrossed in counting the clouds drifting past beneath us.

"What's with the black hair, and why did you leave so suddenly?" I lean over the table. To be honest, I'm angry at Meera. It was a horrible experience seeing her hanging dead from the ceiling, and I shudder at the thought. A young guy dressed in black comes over and places a tray of muesli, fruit salad, and freshly squeezed orange juice on the table. I pour milk on the muesli and put it in front of Luke. He is absorbed by the view of the sky and landscape below.

"Look, Mom, that cloud looks like a dragon."

I look, put my hand on his one foot, and turn my gaze over to Meera.

"I'm sorry you had to find me like that; it was not my decision to leave…." She holds back.

I'm not sure if I believe her; I saw her hanging there. What she did was devastating. I'm so happy that she has no kids. "What do you mean? And why could Thomas and Yoge not find you?"

She pushes her glass toward the middle of the table and leans back. "Because I didn't want to be found. I mean, not by you. I didn't want to be found by my ex." She lowers her gaze. "He did find me, though. When we got out of the plane in the Himalayas, he was there waiting for me. I tried to disappear; I changed my hair color and took a detour home. But he managed to track me down…."

I take a few mouthfuls of my fruit salad but have no appetite.

"But I thought he was long gone…." I look over at Luke, who is absorbed by the great abyss beneath us. He is not listening to Meera.

She shrugs. "So did I."

I look at her, reach for her hand, and gently squeeze it. We sit there for a few minutes before I turn to Luke, who is still staring out the huge windows. "Luke, you better start eating your muesli. We'll have to leave soon."

"But…" I hesitate for a moment. "I thought you did it yourself…."

She looks down at the table. "I fought the best I could, but he was stronger and still so furious that I left him. The darkness in him took over."

There are only twenty minutes left until we have to meet up in the octagonal room. I take one deep breath and another. "We have to go, but we'll see each other again, right? I still have so many questions."

"Let's do that." She pauses and looks out the window. "It's not easy for me." I put my hand on hers. She looks at her watch. "I also have an appointment; I don't know how long it will take."

I look her in the eye. It's probably Yoge she's going to meet. It does not seem as if she even knows the outcome of the test yet.

"Come on, Luke, there are some people we need to meet. Are you ready?"

Luke takes one last spoonful of muesli; milk is running down his chin. "Sure," the words squirt out along with a bit of muesli. He lays the spoon on the table and jumps down from the couch. "Who comes first?" He looks at me and starts running, and I go after him.

54
THE RING

We stand in the elevator that will take us to the octagonal room. Luke balances on top of my feet. Next to the door are two circles, one to get there and one to get back. The walls are white and diffuse, and the ceiling is one large window. Luke looks around with big eyes while making various humming noises. We're running a little late, and the others are probably already waiting.

"That's the one you have to press, Luke." I point at the top button.

He raises his hand and gently puts his finger on the circle. It gives a very small jerk, and the pressure increases in my ears. Luke laughs. "Mom, it tickles in my stomach." I lovingly run my hand through his hair. He leans against me, and I put my arms around his tiny shoulders. My heart skips a beat and continues at a high pace. It's incomprehensible that I'm standing here with Luke.

The door slides open and the candles and the octagonal space appear. The room is empty, or at least, I cannot see any of the others. There are a few steps down to the round space where the chairs stand in a circle. The red banners with simple symbols formed by thin lines hang loosely from the ceiling, and the candles in the tall, large candlesticks are lit. The stone floor is mirror-gloss and reflects the light. It is hot in here, and I pull up my sleeves. I have never experienced a room with so much energy, and I feel lifted as I step inside.

Luke is right next to me. I reach out, and he takes my hand. It feels like stepping through a gate and into another universe.

"This is so cool." His eyes light up, and he jumps up and down while holding onto my hand. "I want to show this place to Dad."

The pyramid in the ceiling cuts through the sky and gives a marvelous light. Luke releases my hand and runs down the steps to the chairs. Slowly, I walk toward my chair. It stands with its back to me, side by side with the others. My hand slides down the wood carving. The eagle with outstretched wings and hooked beak emerges clearly on the back of the chair. Luke has disappeared behind the other chairs, but I can hear him. He brings lightness with him. It's nice because it's anything but calm inside me.

There is a low hiss, and the elevator door slides open. I turn around. It's Shiva. She almost floats into the room wearing a long white dress. Her hair hangs loosely around her face. She lights up in a smile as she catches sight of Luke hanging over the back of the chair with a carved elephant. I try to breathe calmly, but my body is tense, and I fidget a bit. Shiva comes over and stands next to me without saying anything. Luke is totally in the moment, trying out all the chairs, and seems to be having a good time. I want to ask if she has heard from Yoge but don't get a chance because, at that exact moment, the door slides open again. Thomas steps in with Gabriel, who is sitting in something resembling a wheelchair. It is round in shape, hovers slightly above the floor, and looks comfortable. Gabriel's head hangs a bit, but his eyes are open. He is pale and thin, very thin. My heart skips a beat at the sight of him. I breathe a sigh of relief. As long as he perseveres, there is still hope. At once, Luke comes running to me, and I lift him.

"Hi, Luke," Gabriel extends his hand. It shakes a little.

"Hi…" Luke hides his face in my hair.

I take Gabriel's hand and squeeze it. It is soft and warm.

"This is Thomas," I point to Thomas, and Luke looks out through two strands of hair. "And Shiva."

She steps forward and gives his thigh a loving squeeze.

"Hi," Luke's voice is a bit shy.

"I love you, Luke," I whisper in his ear, and he tightens his grip around me even more, if possible.

Thomas walks to the chair with a carved owl on the backrest and gently helps Gabriel into it. The chair to the left of Gabriel's has a carved elephant. It's Yoge's chair. Next comes a chair with a horse—I don't know who it belongs to. And after that is my chair with the eagle. To my right is Thomas's chair; it has a carved bear. Next to Thomas is Shiva's chair, with a snake. The last chair between Shiva and Gabriel has a butterfly on the backrest.

The sound of the door sliding open again makes me turn my head. Yoge steps in, and behind him, Meera appears. The banners move a little bit, and the candles flutter. My legs start to shake. She *is* the right one. Now, it's just a question of whether Jane will be here too. Meera hasn't seen me. She stares blankly into the air and walks toward the chairs with Yoge. Thomas signals that we should sit.

"Luke," I whisper, "we have to be here for a little while, but afterward, we will have all the time together we need." The light descends like a drizzle into the room from the giant pyramid in the ceiling. "You can sit with me." The chairs suddenly look so big and awe-inspiring with their high backs and intricate cutouts.

Thomas holds his hand on the chair next to mine. "Luke, you don't have to sit with your mother; you can sit here." He bends down to Luke and pats lightly on the chair with a horse carved into the wood.

"It's so cool. It's the best one," Luke releases my hand, jumps up on the chair, and sits down with crossed legs and a straight back.

"Is Jane not coming?" I look at Thomas, and he just smiles back at me.

Luke better be the right one. I can't stand the thought of anything else. I sit down on my chair and look over at Meera. We make eye contact. She is sitting on the chair with the butterfly. Her eyes are calm, and now she knows that I was telling the truth. It must be a relief for her too. It is to me.

Thomas waits until everyone is seated before stepping to his chair and sitting down. He nods slightly and looks around, making eye contact with every one of us. The light dims in the room, and it gets even warmer. He leans forward a bit and reaches out to the side. My hand meets his, and I reach for Luke's hand. Within a few seconds, we are all holding hands and have completed the circle.

"As you know, Gabriel is debilitated, so I will lead our meeting today." Thomas swallows and blinks a few times. He looks at Gabriel, who is breathing very slowly. Gabriel turns his head a bit, and I make eye contact with him. He nods to me, and the relief spreads in my body.

"Welcome back, Eva. You have made an invaluable effort to assemble the Ring." Thomas pauses, and I look at him. "And welcome to you, Meera, and you, Luke. Because Gabriel is debilitated and time is short, we have not had the opportunity to make sure that everyone who is here today also belongs to the Ring."

I look around. It's magical to sit here without the two empty chairs. Imagine if I found the right ones and the members of the Ring are finally gathered. Luke can't reach the floor, and his legs dangle back and forth. Now and again, he looks over at me to make sure I'm still here.

"How long are we going to sit here, Mom?"

I lean over to him and whisper, "Just a little while—I don't think it will take that long."

He lets go of my hand and leans forward in the chair so that the tips of his toes can just reach the floor.

Thomas continues. "As you know, we cannot gain the insight that the Earth needs until the right seven members are gathered. Therefore, it is time to find out if the Ring is complete again."

I close my eyes and see a glimpse of the Ring when we were last gathered many thousands of years ago. That was when we were sitting by a campfire up on a mountain. I fail to register if Luke and Meera are there. The picture disappears, and I open my eyes. Gabriel sits limply on the chair, his eyes closing at regular intervals. Thomas looks around; nobody says anything.

"I would ask you to hold each other's hands and close your eyes."

"Do I have to close my eyes?" Luke wrinkles his nose. "I'm not tired, Mom."

I move my chair a little closer to Luke, but not so that I can't still reach Thomas.

"Yes, close your eyes." I smile at him and hold on tight to his hand.

Meera has closed her eyes, so have Yoge, Shiva, Gabriel, and Thomas. Luke squeezes his eyelids excessively. Now, I need to close mine too. The moment of truth has come, and now, I will know if it was all worthwhile.

Thomas sits absolutely still in his chair with his back straight. Silence falls over the room. Only a faint crackle from the candles and my breath can be heard. I let my eyes slide closed. It goes dark. The time has come. I hold on tight to both Luke's and Thomas's hands. Now, something better happen. I wait. And wait. The only thing I can feel is the warmth from Thomas's hand and Luke starting to swing his arm back and forth. Suddenly, heat strikes my body, and the light around me becomes brighter. I'm pushed back into the chair, and the heat burns through my skin. I try to move on the chair, but nothing happens. My insides are boiling, and it is getting completely dark. I'm sitting still. The darkness envelops me like infinite space.

THE RING

Far above me, I sense a white light. It slowly descends and pollinates my soul. The light is everywhere—refined small grains that lie gently around me. Inside the light, a golden ring appears. It floats just above us and shines with an inner force.

Suddenly, I see the octagonal space in front of me and all the members of the Ring. Behind Thomas's chair stands an Indian chief. Slowly, the woman carrying the two small children emerges and becomes visible. She stands behind the chief. The children she carries rise. One child becomes the woman in the crowd who cried by the fire. She walks over and stands behind Luke's chair. The other child stands behind my chair. An elderly man in dirty clothes that I have not seen before stands behind Yoge's chair.

The light keeps falling on me. Inside the Ring, there are several smaller rings intertwined. They hover all around me and draw fine lines from one time period to another—from one soul to another. We are all connected.

Out of the light steps the most beautiful woman in a golden gown with jewelry in turquoise and gold around her neck. She stands behind Meera. Behind her stands the woman who was by my side when I was taken down from the cross. The light becomes even brighter if possible, and a dark woman, who wears a snake around her neck and holds a stick of gold in her hand, appears. The woman smiles at me and bends slightly forward. She stands behind Shiva's chair, and I can see people lining up behind Gabriel's chair too. None of them have I seen before.

The light burns the people away, but the Ring still hangs over us. Suddenly, it is as if it falls and creates an invisible bond between us. It is completely quiet in here. The energy runs from my hand through my heart and out through the other hand, and all I can see is light.

Thomas slowly releases my hand, but I can feel that the Ring remains intact. I open my eyes and look over at Luke.

"Mom, did you see that?!"

I kiss his hand, and a tear runs down my cheek. It is allowed to run free. There is complete silence inside my head, and deep gratitude fills me. I feel heat down my back, and I gently turn around. The Master is standing right behind my chair. I did not hear him come in at all. By the door stands the two women who are always with him. He wears a long black gown, his white beard fills most of his face, and on his head, he wears a small, knitted hat studded with glittering stones.

"Your work can begin."

I look at Thomas, and he looks at the Master.

"The energy you have opened up must be brought back to Earth to set in motion the new development. You all hold a central role." The Master enters the middle of the circle. "You will be re-energized in order to handle the task." He sends a glance over to Gabriel, who nods once.

"But first, you must all go through an intense transformation process to be ready to return to Earth for the last time."

The light in the room is brighter than ever before. Everyone sits completely still and listens, even Luke.

"It will require courage, confidence, and inner strength. Even though you are all part of the Ring, it does not mean that our efforts will succeed." The Master lets his hand glide through his long beard.

I make eye contact with the Master, but his gaze flashes toward me with such force that I am forced to look down at the floor.

"Time is inadequate. As you know, fear, anger, and anxiety spread faster than love. You must be ready in ninety days. After that, the energy will begin to wane, and it is unknown whether the Ring will ever be able to gather with the same strength again." He steps forward and turns, so he is standing right in front of me. "Eva."

I hold my breath.

"I will ask you to come to my room in twenty minutes. There is an urgent task that you have to solve." His gaze cuts right through me, "The outcome of the task will be crucial for the Ring's ability to succeed or not."

I look around, "Why me?"

Want do know what happens next?
Get Book 3 in the IN-BETWEEN Series,
THE HOPE here:

readerlinks.com/l/2170867

ABOUT THE AUTHOR

Sagar Constantin is a bestselling Scandinavian author with more than seven books. She writes stories that are both captivating but also highly inspirational.

The In-Between series came to Sagar on her way home from a business trip to India, and she instantly knew that this was a story that she had to share with the world.

She has a great ability to make psychological issues easy to understand and comprehend, and through her reading, it is possible to grow inside and at the same time be highly entertained.

Sagar is also an international speaker and lecturer for businesses. Every year, she trains thousands of people in subjects like personal development, change management, EQ, and High-performance teams.

When she is not writing and teaching, she loves to spend time with her family and enjoys nature walks. Sagar lives in Denmark but travels the world with her work.

To be the first to hear about new releases and bargains—from Sagar Constantin—sign up below.

(I promise not to share your email with anyone else, and I won't clutter your inbox.)

TO SIGN UP TO RECEIVE THE NEWSLETTER GO HERE:
https://books.sagarconstantin.com/news

FOLLOW SAGAR CONSTANTIN ON BOOKBUB HERE: https://www.bookbub.com/authors/sagar-constantin

Follow Sagar on BookBub

Connect with Sagar online:

https://www.facebook.com/SagarConstantinAuthor
https://www.instagram.com/sagar.constantin.author/
https://twitter.com/ConstantinSagar
https://www.goodreads.com/sagarconstantin
https://www.linkedin.com/in/sagarconstantin/

Website: https://livingbetween.com
Mail to: info@sagarconstantin.com

Ingram Content Group UK Ltd.
Milton Keynes UK
UKHW041226010523
420847UK00007B/5